THE CRYSTAL GUARDIAN

Melan

The Guardian Series
Book One

Cover Design by Sara Sandor (S Sandor Photography)

Dedication

This book is written for all of those children born with special needs. You brighten my life and remind me to enjoy the simple things that happen daily.

In Memory of:
Jayne Dinsmore

CHAPTER 1

Seth tossed and turned, kicking off his blanket. His breathing slowed and he found himself in the bright sunlight high in the blue sky. He stretched his dark green wings, causing faerie dust to fall onto the edge of the golden chariot where he was now perched. Seth blinked twice before his almond shaped eyes adjusted to the brightness piercing through his thick glasses. He leaned over and looked far below him, where treetops lay thick together, a river wound along the landscape, and a lake sparkled in the centre of the trees.

"You might fall off if you lean any further over the edge of my chariot," said a voice that startled Seth. Seth grabbed at the edge and then turned to face the striking god draped in white. The god held golden reigns in each hand and had a smile that was as blinding as the sun.

"Apollo," exclaimed Seth, "what am I doing here with you? I was in bed only a moment ago."

"You might sill be in bed, Seth. How can you be sure that you are here with me?" the sun god asked.

Seth shook his head and his wings. "You always do this, Apollo, talk in riddles that are difficult to follow."

"Do I really?" Apollo lifted his reigns and the chariot sped forth across the sky.

Seth sighed, "Yes, you really do, Apollo."

"It adds to my charm, Seth," he insisted. "I am pleased that you decided to join me on this fine day."

"Day? I went to bed during the night," replied Seth.

Apollo lifted his reigns and turned to the left, as the sun stretched across the sky. "We are following the sun, dear Seth, therefore it must be day."

Seth shook his head and spread out his wings. "Did I sleep long enough for it to be day? Have I overslept and no one awoke me this morning?"

"It's day for me, not for you," corrected Apollo. "I thought that this would be a perfect time to meet up, rather than at night, like it is for you."

"It is night, then," said Seth as he pulled at his hair.

"Maybe," agreed Apollo, "although I did not bring you here to chit-chat. I have a much more pressing issue to discuss."

Seth looked into the sun god's bright blue eyes. "What issue is that, Apollo?

Apollo turned the direction of the chariot again. "Something is coming to Faerie. I need you to take note of any changes that may occur. Be vigilant in paying attention to your senses."

"Oh, how exciting. We haven't had anything new in Faerie since I can remember," exclaimed the faerie.

"This is not something to be excited about," declared Apollo with exasperation. "I would not be warning you about something wonderful! Do you think that I have the time or the desire to waste my day on trivial matters? I have better and more interesting things to do than to call you here for something good to come."

Seth looked away from the sun god. "I've only known of good things in Faerie. How can there be something that's not wonderful?"

"There are many dark things in most worlds, Seth. You have been fortunate to experience only light in your realm. There is a darkness coming. I need you to be aware of it, so that you can recognize it before it arrives," Apollo said.

"If I haven't experienced anything but light, then how am I going to recognize the dark?" asked Seth.

Apollo slowed the chariot. "It will be a shift in the energy, a shift that makes you uncomfortable, like when you feel sick."

"What am I to do once I feel this sickness?"

"Find me when you notice it. I am aware that it is coming, but I do not yet know when the darkness will be here. You will be able to sense its arrival before me. Once you-" Apollo quickly turned his striking face away from Seth. "Do you hear that? It must be her. Oh, the sweet sound of her voice makes my heart sing. Can you hear her, Seth?"

Seth looked around. "Hear who?"

Apollo smiled widely. "Daphne. I can hear her whispering to me on the wind. She has been hidden well since her escape as a laurel tree, but now I can hear her." He grasped the golden reigns and turned the chariot around. With one swift movement, Apollo caused the chariot to hurry forth.

Seth fell backwards at the unexpected speed. He grabbed for the chariot but missed as he began to tumble in the sky. Seth spread out his wings to break his fall. His hand grabbed at the air, yet he found a blanket instead. He pulled at it, covering his face in bed.

CHAPTER 2

The ancient gnome enjoyed working with the Guardians. They always made him laugh. They kept him feeling young. Other faerie folk often wished to work with this special group of faeries, but alas, it was one of Alexander's life missions to help these superheroes focus on their talents. Of all the magickal folk in the realm, Alexander had been the one chosen to teach the superheroes. Certainly, Alexander was old, but he was young at heart and wanted what was best for the Guardians.

Today he was particularly excited to meet with the small group of heroes. They were anxious to learn a new skill that might assist with refining one of their gifts, for each superhero had many gifts of faerie. They were to meet in the meadow in early afternoon. This was the time of day when most faeries were playing, as their daily work was often completed.

Alexander opened a small cupboard near his desk. He pulled out a worn leather rucksack. He shook off the dust and placed it on top of his desk. Rummaging around in another drawer, Alexander pulled out a bottle of ink, some parchment, and a writing feather. He placed these in the rucksack. He then moved along a bookshelf, carefully looking at the titles. When he found the desired book, Alexander removed it from the shelf and gently opened the cover. The pages were yellowed; some were torn. When he found the page he had been seeking, Alexander spread it upon the desk.

Lists of ingredients, with vivid pictures of each, were scribed on the pages. Many of the pictures accompanying the ingredients were hand drawn by a faerie long forgotten. Alexander, though, remembered her from his youth so long ago. She had taught him much about plant magick. Alexander noted the ingredients; he slowly walked across the room to his cabinet full of potion bottles. He selected several bottles and then placed them in the rucksack.

When he was satisfied, Alexander lifted the rucksack onto his left shoulder. He then took a hand-made mug from the desk, walked towards the arched doorway, and began whistling as he left the library.

* * *

The butterflies clung to the balls of light; they were immersed in its energy, lines, and beams. The butterflies twittered and caught the light. Even the birds, who never paid any attention, noticed. The deer was pleased with the antics. He always wanted such silliness in the meadow. The balls of light glistened in the sunlight. As they moved ever so softly towards the grass, one bounced off a tree while the others giggled. Oh what fun! Silly nonsense. Alexander couldn't help but shake his head as he watched from the trail. He could not see why they kept going back to the original form of play when they could do so much more.

Alexander brushed against the yellow rosebush and entered the meadow. The deer looked from the balls of light to him, then bowed his head in respect. One ball of light landed in front of Alexander. The light expanded and formed into a young faerie. His wings were dark green, the colour of a fir tree. His short stature was soft. A smile played upon his lips, brightening his round face. As his thick glasses slid down his wide, flat nose, green, almond shaped eyes blinked at the gnome in front of him. Seth clasped his stubby hands together in excitement.

"I've been waiting all day for this, Alexander," Seth spoke around his thick tongue.

"Ah, Seth. You are always the first to stop playing and get down to learning." Alexander smiled warmly.

The other balls of light began to land close to Seth and Alexander. One by one they formed into young faeries. Each faerie was unique in some way, harvesting a power of super strength and ability. There were nine of them in total, including Seth. Their wings were a sight to behold. Each was a beautiful colour that radiated in the sunshine, shimmering as the light touched them. The blues and pinks immersed with one another while the yellows and oranges remained bright within nature. Each colour sparkled, drawing the distinction of this special group from other faeries.

Mercury twirled around, dancing gracefully towards Alexander, moving around him as though she were performing a ceremony. Her blond hair was long and straight, flowing in the breeze. It glistened in the light. Her willowy figure was strong. Mercury's wings beat in pleasure, complementing her dance. She touched the grass with her bare feet, leaving not a print. The birds twittered in appreciation of her movements. A butterfly came to rest upon her right shoulder, breathing in her energy of warmth.

Alexander laid his rucksack on a stump. He watched Mercury as she echoed nature around her. Her dancing encompassed fluidity, gracefulness, and poise. Mercury ran and skipped to the sound of the leaves moving. Animals crept out of the trees to watch her. Before long, a crowd had gathered, silent, intent, and basking in her radiance. She did not notice the eyes upon her. To end her dance, Mercury moved into a skip that brought her facing Alexander.

Javier, Sabrina, Georgia, and Ryan stood where they had formed into faeries. Jayne and Geoff stepped forward, moving to the right of Alexander. Shoshana stood to the left of Alexander. Each faerie bowed in respect. Smiles played upon their faces, as they anticipated the afternoon's adventures. The deer watched with curiosity, while the birds continued to chirp in pleasure. A few butterflies alighted upon the flowers nearby, while two rested upon Jayne's shoulders.

"Welcome, my Guardians," Alexander spoke. "I am pleased to see that you are all ready to begin. I have a special lesson for you today." He opened his rucksack and pulled out the bottles. "We will be working with potions of the greatest importance."

Seth stepped towards the bottles, his fingers reaching for one. The bottle was clear, while the liquid within almost glittered soft green. He held it up to his face, peering through his glasses in an attempt to decipher the contents. When he could not identify the individual elements, Seth shook the bottle, hoping that each ingredient would reveal itself. Alexander chuckled.

"You will learn to separate the contents today. They will not simply identify themselves to you. These potions contain ancient properties, which do not align with the workings of modern power. Once we have separated the contents, our next step will be to identify the elements of each."

Sabrina lifted herself off the ground. Her wings fluttered as she flew towards the rucksack. She held out her hand for one of the bottles. Alexander selected one with a purple essence. She thanked him without words, turned around, and stood again in her spot.

Each faerie came forward for a selection. No bottle was similar, so each faerie would identify a different potion from the others. The deer watched the proceedings quietly. Slowly, he lowered himself to the ground for comfort; he would remain for the lesson in hopes of catching glimpses of the superhero accomplishments. Spending the afternoon this way was always promising and delightful.

* * *

Javier whistled while he flew to the top branch of a willow tree. He could hear the birds chirping up high, building nests for their families. He weaved between the branches, nodding his large head to the creatures living in the tree. When he reached the topmost branch, Javier placed the bottle in a notch. He sat beside it and crossed his legs. When he was comfortable, Javier closed his eyes and listened to his surroundings.

There was a scurry of squirrels collecting nuts below him, a swoosh of a bird, the movement of wings as they touched the air, each of his comrades' wings brushing at different intervals, the breathing of the deer who lay in the meadow, the soft crunch of Alexander's feet stepping on the ground, the buzz of bees two hundred yards away. Slowly, Javier could hear his own breathing, his own heart beating, and his own thoughts extending outward.

Javier searched with his mind, focusing on what could not be seen. He reached out, touching, feeling, and asking for assistance. A thread wisped near; close enough to touch. He reached further, enticing the thread into his own thoughts. It coiled, stretched, turned from white to pale pink, and back to white. Carefully, Javier touched the thread, wrapping it around his own thoughts.

Assist me, please. I require your strength, your knowledge, and your wisdom in this task. I do not ask for my own sake, but for the good of all. I am here to learn, to separate the contents and to identify the elements of this potion. I cannot do this alone. I humbly ask for your assistance in this task. I give thanks for your strength, your knowledge, and your wisdom.

Javier embraced the knowledge as it flooded his mind. It warmed him to his very core, to where his magickal superpowers rested. His body tingled to the very tips of his thickened toes. A surge of strength coursed through him.

Wisdom became clear. Javier reached for the bottle. He unstopped it. The liquid within began to swirl. Its iridescent form lifted from the bottle, stretching into the sunlit air. Javier watched the potion as it changed into several rainbow colours…blue, violet, and indigo. Each colour spun in the sun, twirled around, then dipped back into the bottle, keeping separate one from the other.

Javier placed the stopper upon the bottle. He kissed the air, giving thanks for all that he had learned. Javier stretched, flying into the air. Taking his time, Javier flitted from treetop to bush to flower before landing beside Alexander in the meadow. A newly opened calla lily caught his attention and he drew a heady breath, listening to a bee sucking nectar within the flower. When Alexander turned to smile at him, Javier presented his potion.

"For you, dear Alexander. I do believe that the ingredients of this particular potion contain opal dust, lapis lazuli, and scarab beetle. This lovely potion has the magick to reveal that which cannot be seen." He bowed low in respect.

Alexander took the potion from Javier. He examined the bottle, his smile widening in pleasure. Alexander placed the potion on the stump near his rucksack. "I am much pleased, Javier. I did not expect such quickness and such success. You are wise to have attempted a form of magick separate from your given gift." He paused. "Come, we shall sit near the deer and drink some nectar in celebration, while we await the success of your comrades."

* * *

Seth crawled under a dark hydrangea bush. The leaves were dark green and the flowers a lush purple. The earth was cool and damp against his skin. Earthworms squirmed across the ground, eating as they burrowed within the coolness. Seth breathed deeply, inhaling the smell of earth and new growth. He moved further into the bush, allowing the darkness to surround him.

Seth found a clearing near the roots of the hydrangea and settled himself into the crook, placing the bottle of potion in his lap. His wings rested flat against the roots, his back erect. Seth crossed his ankles, feeling comfortable away from the sun. He picked up the bottle and viewed the three iridescent colours within. He knew that the others would not be able to see the three colours unless they were separated, but Seth always saw colours in their separate forms. Of course, these colours were mixing together and did need to be officially separated.

So, the question was how to separate the colours from each other. Seth moved the bottle around in his hands, noting how the colours mixed. He could clearly identify the elements just by the movement of the colours; orange for gold, black for silver, and green for copper. It became clear that this particular potion was meant to purify water, thus making it safe to drink. The potion would remove any impurities or salts from water, allowing it to be as fresh as water from a mountain spring.

I need to connect the elements in this potion to those elements around me. So how do I do that? They would have been connected before they were separated. Now they are connected again, but need to again be separated within the bottle. Oh, it is like a never-ending circle.

Carefully, Seth removed the stopper from the bottle. He peered inside, looking at the swirl of colours. Seth looked about, searching for a simple way of officially separating the elements. He knew what they were and he knew what they could do together, so perhaps all he needed was to ask.

Seth took a deep breath, "Elements of gold, silver, and copper, I ask that you be released from each other." Within moments, the elements swirled about in the bottle, creating the look of swamp water. The smell of a spring and the sound of rushing water echoed beneath the hydrangea. Seth closed his eyes. It was as though he were on top of a mountain. He breathed in the coolness; he tasted the cold, refreshing water on his tongue. When the sensation passed, Seth opened his eyes. The elements were separated; they layered the bottle like sand on a desert hill.

Seth closed the bottle before he used his wings to lift himself from the ground. He flew up the branches to the top of the hydrangea. When he reached the light, Seth beat his wings and turned in the direction of Alexander. He noted that Javier, Georgia, and the deer were within the gnome's proximity. Seth flew in that direction, eager to show his accomplishment.

* * *

Shoshana tipped the bottle upside down and back upright, continuing in this way for a few moments. She watched as the liquid coated the inside of the vial, sliding up and down as she moved the bottle. "Whatever do you contain?" she asked the contents. "How do you feel inside this bottle? Do you want out? Do you want to hide forever inside? Are all of your ingredients happy together?"

She flew over to a group of tall stemmed mushrooms, hidden behind an old log at the edge of the clearing. Shoshana held tight to the potion and lowered herself onto one of the mushrooms so that she stood on the mushroom cap, yet remained hidden behind the log. She held the vial above her head and examined the liquid as a ray of sunshine filtered through it. Colours appeared and spun within the liquid, jumping at the confines of the glass. While still watching carefully, Shoshana pulled the bottle down and moved it into the shade of the log. A spark of light erupted like a firework and fizzled into nothing, as though it had never occurred. She blinked at the potion and smiled to herself.

"Dark and light hide between the two;
One survives while the other is absent.
Yet without each other, neither can exist.
Together you form that which cannot be seen.
Separate you rest
Waiting to make a revelation of all that is and all that was

With the pull of the moon and the warmth of the sun,
You come together for a purpose.
If the moon were to push and the sun were to pull,
What inside you would break apart?
Unfurl each component as though it must be so,
Sharing your essence and releasing your name."

Shoshana watched as the potion swirled and broke apart into beads of separate liquid, bumping one colour against another. She hugged the vial to her chest before flying to Alexander, who was bent over scratching at his left foot. "Words formed just so can separate the ingredients to reveal their individuality," she told him as she handed over the potion. "They feel like bat breath, witch hazel, and lizard tongue."

"Words are our emotions formed in the air. One must listen to the truth of the words when looking for the emotion," acknowledged Alexander.

* * *

Geoff sat perched high in one of the trees at the edge of the meadow. From here, he could see the deer and Alexander. He did not bother to hunt for the other Guardians with his eyes, even though he knew Jayne was somewhere close to him. He swung his legs back and forth in the air as they dangled over the small branch upon which he sat.

He listened to the birds chirping and the crickets singing. A green caterpillar slithered along the branch towards him. Without thinking, Geoff turned inwards and transformed into a caterpillar identical to the one on the branch. He used his powerful muscles and legs to crawl across the branch until he was face to face with the true insect. "What is it that makes you realise when you need to create a chrysalis and become a butterfly?" he demanded of the insect.

A smile spread across the caterpillar's face. "I will feel the need to change. It is a yell inside my body. Change is part of nature and I am just one of the many examples of such change. What makes you morph from faerie into something else?"

"Sometimes I just want to have fun," admitted Geoff. "Other times I want to learn and I find that becoming something else allows me to learn quickly. It's a great distraction from my joint pain as well." Without further discussion, Geoff shimmered and became his usual self. He picked up the vial that rested in a knot on the branch and examined it in his swollen hands. "Can you transform into individual ingredients?"

The vial remained as it had when Alexander had given it to him. The contents were dark, yet as he stared at them, they seemed to become a deep blue with intermittent slivers of red. Geoff clutched the vial tighter in his hand and pressed it against his forehead. He liked the red slivers in the vial, yet he had no idea how he was going to separate the contents into their original form. Funny, really, that he was able to change form and yet he had no idea how to change the form of someone or something else.

He kept the vial against his forehead while he contemplated the situation. *To transform the ingredients from the whole to the individual is essentially the task. So what if I changed each part into something other than an ingredient? Could that separate it?* Geoff grinned before he uncapped the lid of the vial. He touched the liquid with his left index finger and pulled from his core. *Become a lizard.* The liquid solidified; slowly, it moved from a solid mass of deep blue with one line of red to a gecko blinking up at Geoff from inside the vial. His tail wrapped around his body. His four feet stretched as he began to walk up the inside of the vial until his head popped out. He looked around and blinked at Geoff.

Geoff held out his finger for the lizard to crawl upon. He was a cute lizard, but Geoff knew he would not be cute for long. *Each ingredient needs to become a separate part of your body. Let us begin with your tail. The last ingredient that was added to this potion shall represent your tail. Your tail will become a maple leaf.* The gecko's tail swished back and forth once, at which point it became a green maple leaf, as though it was mid spring. Geoff laughed out loud and swung his legs in time to his laughter.

What shall I change next? How about your feet? Or would you like to be changed all at once? The gecko just blinked up at Geoff. He did not appear concerned about the change in his tail. *Your feet…let's make your two front feet and legs into the first ingredient that was added. They will turn into seaweed as a representation of the ingredient.* The gecko fell forward onto his belly without the support of proper feet and legs. *Let the remaining ingredients show themselves on the remainder of your body as colours.* His body swirled into pink while his head became indigo. No other changes occurred on the gecko. *You contain four ingredients, which are ginkgo biloba, chaparral leaves, peppermint, and suma.* He picked up the strange gecko and placed him back into the vial. *All of you remain separate yet now change into your original liquid forms.* Geoff watched as the gecko liquefied into the potion ingredients.

Geoff replaced the stopper on the vial. He raised himself into a standing position before flying down to where Alexander stood with the others who had completed their task. He handed the vial over to Alexander and sat himself down on the grass with his legs crossed.

* * *

One by one, each Guardian joined the gathering in the meadow, handing the individual potions to Alexander. Seth leaned against the deer for comfort while everyone awaited further instruction. Jayne and Geoff sat near the stump, holding hands and talking quietly. Mercury was entertaining Javier and Ryan with balls of fire she would blow on so that they danced into flames on her hands. Seth sighed with contentment and interlocked his stubby fingers. Shoshana giggled when Georgia snuck up behind Mercury and started to freeze her flames. Sabrina was the last to join the group.

Alexander lined up the potion vials on the top of the stump. He gestured for everyone to gather around. "You have all done very well with this task. I had not expected such success on a first attempt."

"We are the most amazing Guardians you have trained, Alexander," yelled Geoff. "Our superpowers must be the strongest ones you have come across."

"I have to agree," chimed in Ryan.

Alexander picked up the vial farthest to the left. Ignoring the disruption, he continued, "Separating the ingredients in each potion was only the first step. To identify each ingredient within a potion is essential. If you can decipher what is in a potion, then you can remove at least one of the ingredients, which would render the potion useless."

CHAPTER 3

Alexander's books rested upon the shelves, tattered and worn, his prized possessions. He had spent many a year collecting each and every word, and while others wrote most, some were his. He had learned long ago that knowledge was best preserved in the word rather than in the mind. Minds were tricky things. They could not reliably hold the truth. Nor could they reliably decipher fact from fiction. But books...ah books...they stood the test of time. They never wavered in their memories. A written word remained for all of eternity. One could add to it, but no one could erase the meaning of what was written. When he felt particularly troubled, Alexander would run his fingers over each spine. Sometimes it took hours to touch each book in this way.

When he first began collecting his books, Alexander would turn each page as though it were fragile. His fingers would stray over the words, while he breathed in the scent of the new pages. He rarely bent the bindings, hoping each book would remain new forever. Of course, time aged the parchment. Over the centuries, he had taken time to re-scribe some of the books as the ink faded. He had become the keeper of knowledge; he prided himself on ensuring that the written word would survive even when the book disintegrated into dust. Each book now carried additional knowledge from previous readings in the form of dog-earing, scribbled notes along the margins, and other annotations, including drawings of plants, creatures, and ideas.

His collection was unique. It varied from the tongue of elves to the language of faeries to the lore of trolls and gnomes. Some of the books were ancient, many of them written in Elf Gaelic and other elder languages, all of which he could read. Since his early youth, he had been fascinated with languages, driven to learn them all. It had, of course, become easier to absorb the various languages since his meeting with Ice Moon two millennia before, when she provided him with Alexandrite magick. As dialects evolved over time, he became fluent in those as well, making certain to teach Troll Lore and Elf Gaelic to his Guardian Faeries, as part of their daily lessons.

Of course, as the centuries progressed, he had incorporated modern nuances, and yet had never forgotten the lost tongues themselves. The language he learned as a child, for example, was no longer in use. It had faded away along with many beings he had loved. He tried not to think of them too often, especially when it came to the loss of his wife, but some days he truly missed Beth. It had taken a very long time for him to release her from his soul. If it had not been for an ancient faerie with a gift from the gods, he most likely would have died from a broken heart.

He ran his fingers along a particularly old book, reflecting on how much he truly enjoyed life nowadays. His time was all spent with books, potions, magick, and Guardian Faeries, all of which made him smile daily. He was revered not only because of the work he did, but also for his contribution to this and other worlds. Were it not for Guardians, he knew beyond a doubt, that he would be drifting aimlessly.

With a sigh, he moved his fingers again along a few of the books. When Beth had died, along with their child, his soul had been shattered. He had wandered aimlessly over the lands, barely eating and never bathing. When Ice Moon had found him and took his pain for a brief moment, he had known that life would get better, that he would carry on and make a difference. Of course, it had been a moment that flashed so quickly he was barely able to grab onto it. It wasn't until she had taken care of him and welcomed him into her home that the reality of a change started to sink into his body and seep into his soul.

His reattachment to this dimension was long and arduous, yet satisfyingly cleansing. The process seemed to bathe his soul, to renew his body, and provide continual sustenance. From that moment on, Alexander felt he was a part of something bigger than the universe, bigger than all of the gods and beings inhabiting planets everywhere. It was humbling, really. He was simply a speck in a larger scheme of something destined to occur. He felt honoured and had always respected every form of life since.

Alexander pulled out a book from one of the larger shelves and carried it gently over to a small table made from the stump of an oak tree. The leather cover cracked as he opened to a page near the back of the book. Ancient letters of a lost language covered the parchment in glistening ink, changing colours as he touched each word with the tip of his middle finger. "Ice Moon, you were an amazing teacher of magick and all things important," he whispered into the room. "I teach my faeries in your honour, not because it is my destiny."

He read from the page: *When the moon is full and the angels sing, ask for forgiveness and be sure to forgive those who cause the conflict. You are never alone, not truly. Your journey is long, yet it is so necessary. As you teach each new group of superhero faerie, be aware that this may be the group chosen to fight the long awaited threat. Also, be content with each faerie's abilities when the threat has not come. Many generations of these faeries in training will live before the chosen group is brought to this realm. Do not think that your destiny lies in these first generations. You are in training just as much as these special faeries are. Once your destiny is fulfilled, another journey will await you.*

"How long has it been, dear Ice Moon, since you were here with me? I have lost count of the years. I tried for so long to keep track of the years and the generations of special faeries that passed through my life, but after the first millennia, I realised that keeping track was irrelevant to the needs of my charges. Sometimes, I go to where you treated me so that I can feel closer to you. Although, I must admit that it has been several years since I was last there," Alexander said aloud.

He turned through several of the pages, noticing the words and the penmanship. Detailed drawings illuminated each page, either as a description for the written word or to complement the word. Several magickal creatures had written down their spells and potions and added them to this book for Alexander. Over time, he had become confident enough to add his own knowledge. Once in a while, a being would still provide a precious piece of parchment to this thick tome of magickal history.

He turned a few more pages before his eyes fell upon the last entry, made by a dwarf the previous year at training camp: *How to prevent immediate death when subject is fatally wounded.* Many of the instructions included verbal spells mixed with three different potions. As wonderful as Alexander thought this entry would be in a difficult situation, he was well aware that the potions would need to be made ahead of time, which would force the user to anticipate the need for them. Plus, the words would need to be formed in one's memory, rather than relying on the book. Of course, Alexander had managed to memorize most of the pages in this book over the millennia.

Alexander flipped through a few more pages before he closed the book reluctantly and returned it to the shelf. He walked slowly across the room to a small fire burning in the corner. He rubbed his hands together before holding them above the flames for a touch of warmth. The wrinkles in his fingers folded over each other, causing his leathery skin to appear old in the light of the fire. If he was honest with himself, Alexander would agree that compared even to magickal standards, he was ancient. However, he did not feel physically old. He took his time with everything he chose to do, so that he could make the most of every moment. Maybe others thought the he was slow due to his age, whatever age he actually was, but he knew his movements had nothing to do with physical time.

Alexander moved from the fire over to his desk. He sat down carefully on the stool. He reached for his cup of green leaf tea and took a sip of the cold drink. Early mornings were always pleasant. He liked to spend time in this room, gathering his thoughts and planning out the day.

A tap at the window brought him out of his reverie. With his head pressed against the small panes, Seth stared intently at Alexander. His flat, large nose disappeared into his face. Seth smiled and waved when Alexander acknowledged him.

Seth pulled his face away from the window and disappeared from sight. Within a moment he opened the door to the small hovel home and half-walked, half-flew across the room. His large ears flapped in the breeze he created with his movements. Alexander poured another cup of tea from the pot beside the fire. He handed it to Seth, before the Guardian Faerie forced himself to sit in one of the chairs.

"What brings you here so early, Seth?" Alexander asked quietly, in an attempt to calm the energy Seth had brought with him.

Seth took a quick sip of the tea to appease his host. "I had another vision last night," he began. "I couldn't really identify when it will occur, but you were in it. I needed to tell you as soon as I awoke from the vision, even though I tried really hard to go back to sleep."

Alexander eyed Seth with interest and concern. "Well, Seth, if it bothered you that much, then I am glad you chose to join me for early morning tea." He gestured for Seth to begin his tale.

The faerie readjusted himself on the chair, spreading out his wings to help fill the space he occupied. "I was in a rather large room full of mushroom chairs and a wooden table. It was high up inside a tree. I knew this, because I could see the lake from a window. There were a few faeries sitting around the table and they wore some sort of costume. At first I thought it was a private party, as there were drinks and food and everyone was chatting. Three other faeries tended to the plants along the wall. They must've been in charge of the food and drink, because they were not dressed in costume. One of the faeries told everyone that they needed to come to an agreement before you arrived. She called you by your name, at which point everyone stopped talking and focused on her."

Seth took a sip of his tea while Alexander eyed him silently. "She asked if everyone would like to vote on how they should proceed. Once they all agreed to vote, she then asked them if they were willing to take on the knowledge of the Guardians and assist you in selecting who would be trained. Every single faerie at the table voted to help her. It gave me chills down my spine." He shivered at the memory. "They all seemed to want to be helpful, but it didn't feel good to me. She was about to tell them something else when you entered the room. At that point, I awoke from the vision."

Alexander took a long drink of his tea, while contemplating this revelation. "So this group of faeries want to help with my responsibilities? They would like to make things easier for me when it comes to selecting and training you and your peers?" He drummed his leathery fingers against the cup. "Your description of this group is accurate. I do not think that you have anything to worry about, Seth, yet

I thank you for bringing this to my attention. Know that you have done the right thing and that I will take on the responsibility of what happens from now."

Seth smiled widely. His wings drooped for a second and then fluttered in pleasure. "I knew it was good to come here right away, before our afternoon lesson."

"Always follow your instincts, Seth," stated Alexander. "There is great power within your body and your soul. When you listen to both of them, you will be more powerful than the one who chooses to ignore such things." He got up slowly from his chair. "Now, if you will excuse me, I have some work to do before I prepare for this afternoon's lesson."

Seth spread his wings and flew across the room. "I'll see you later today," he said on his way out the door.

CHAPTER 4

Mercury hurled the flame across the meadow. Before it could reach the group of trees, Georgia froze it in midair and Ryan flicked his wrist to bring it back to the centre of the clearing and kept it hovering above the grass. Geoff quickly ran over to the frozen flame, examined it, and turned himself into a duplicate of the new object. Ryan lowered his hand and allowed the frozen flame to drop to the ground. Shoshana rushed forward and picked up the identical frozen flames and brought them back over to the group.

"Which one is Geoff, Shoshana?" asked Alexander calmly. He remained seated on the rock, beside which lay the deer who always seemed to be waiting for the group to arrive for their daily lessons.

Shoshana closed her eyes and focused on each flame that lay in her palms. She lifted her right hand and then her left. "The weight is the same," she mentioned. "Geoff is the right flame," she declared. Shoshana placed both flames onto the grass and stepped back. The right flame rocked and slowly grew, and then suddenly transformed into Geoff. Everyone in the meadow clapped.

"That was well done," stated Sabrina.

Mercury stepped over to the frozen flame and picked it up. "Georgia," she said, "could you release my flame from your freeze?"

"Certainly, Mercury," replied Georgia. She waved her fingers and the flame began to dance upon Mercury's hand. She tossed it into the air and caught it with her left thumb.

"Oh, wow," exclaimed Seth. "You can sure do some fancy things with flames."

Alexander stood up from the rock. "Now I would like Ryan to transport Seth and Sabrina to somewhere in the woods around this clearing. Sabrina will cloak all three with her invisibility. Once that is done, Javier is to locate them with his acute hearing. Jayne, I would like you to sing a song that will distract Javier's ears and will create a bit of grass growth for our deer here."

Jayne flew over to the deer and sat down beside him. She reached out and touched his nose. "Would everyone who's staying here like to sit with us while I sing?"

"I certainly will," said Geoff. He walked over and sat beside Jayne. She smiled at him and glanced away to watch the others. Georgia found a spot near Alexander and Mercury stood beside the deer.

Javier stood still and closed his eyes. "I won't look until Alexander gives me the okay to do so," he stated.

Ryan took one of Seth's hands and one of Sabrina's hands. He whispered to them, "Hold tight. This won't take long and it won't hurt a bit. You might find that you're separate from everything but your own thoughts. This is to be expected."

There was a crack and the three faeries disappeared from view. Jayne began to sing.

"She clung desperately to her home
Frightened to go on,
Alone.
Everything was so familiar

No.
Unfamiliar.
Her friends had come to die
Soon,
She would join them."

Alexander interrupted Jayne to say, "Javier, you can now look."

Javier opened his eyes and examined the meadow before him. He cocked his large head to the side and twitched his ears. Slowly, he moved in a circle to allow his ears to pick up any sounds.

"Yet she knew nothing of what lay ahead
If she would feel the warm sun,
Not the cold.
The seasons had changed
She knew,
And winter was creeping into autumn.
The snow would serve as a blanket
Covering the world in white,
Leaving her alone."

Javier stopped moving in a circle. He opened his wings and began to walk south across the meadow.

"How sad that she must die
Now that she was old,
Withering into nothing.
Some would remember her existence
Yet not as an individual,
As a part of others.
Bending over her threshold
Barely keeping alive,
She could feel herself falling."

Javier kept his eyes open, so that he would not trip on any stray twigs or rocks dispersed across the meadow. He attempted to tune out Jayne, but her voice was extremely enticing; it penetrated into his soul. Javier took a deep breath and refocused his thoughts to all the sounds that touched upon his ears. A lark was singing to the east and two chipmunks were arguing to the west. It was the breathing that drew him south. Javier continued to move towards the breathing he could hear amongst a group of birch trees.

"A gust of wind
Cold,
Crept into her wrinkles.
Carrying her away
She wept away her time,
Hoping for a new life.
The wind stopped
Dropping her,
Nowhere.
She could feel the bottom
Getting closer,
Until she touched."

Javier entered the thicket of birch trees. He walked slowly, keeping his wings close to his body. He took two steps to the left and then three steps forward. He reached out his hands and touched something solid, yet unseen to his naked eyes. The air shimmered, revealing Sabrina, Seth, and Ryan. They were crouched on the ground holding hands and smiling up at Javier.

"The last breeze had come
And gone,
Leaving her alone.
A sharp cold appeared
Allowing the snow to fall,
Softly."

"Let's go join the others," suggested Seth. The four faeries came out of the confines of the birch trees and into the open meadow. They flew over to the group that had been listening to Jayne sing about the last leaf of autumn.

Alexander took off his hat and gave a short bow to Javier. "Very well done, young Guardian." He turned to Jayne and said, "Your voice, as always, is rich and enticing, Jayne.

This deer will enjoy the grass that you have grown for him." He gestured to the long blades now surrounding the deer, who did not yet appear at all interested in the grass.

The faeries gathered around Alexander. It had been an enjoyable afternoon. The lesson had been simple, which allowed each Guardian Faerie to practice their superpowers. Seth dug his toes into the grass and pushed his thick glasses up the ridge of his nose.

"It is obvious that all of you are taking these lessons seriously and you are quite focused during our time together," said Alexander with pride. "You are all supportive of one another, which is important when you are part of a team. Although we tend to meet every afternoon, I must cancel our lesson for tomorrow. Another obligation has arisen, which I must deal with immediately. So rather than practicing what you have learned recently, I suggest that you take the day and find something fun to do. We will meet here again the following day, at our usual time," concluded Alexander.

The faeries turned into balls of soft white light. They bounced against the ground and each other. One white ball touched the deer before floating into the air. Laughter echoed in the meadow as the faeries spread apart and left the clearing.

CHAPTER 5

Billy the troll rummaged through his kitchen drawers; the clattering of utensils blocked the sounds from outside. He pulled hard on one particular drawer beside the sink. It stuck, grinding as he pulled harder, and then gave way to his strength as it flew across the room. Billy stumbled backwards, grabbed for the nearest kitchen chair, and fell hard to the ground. The landing sloshed the water in which Hermy, his pet frog, was bathing.

"Ooooh! Hurt. Hurt. Hurt." Billy pulled his hand away from the chair, placed it in his mouth and proceeded to suck the oozing blood clean. The throbbing pain in his bum prevented him from standing up. He turned his head to examine his small kitchen. Drawers were sticking out haphazardly. Kitchen items were strewn about the room. Dirty dishes filled the sink. One of the curtains hung by a thread from the rod. A half eaten piece of toast and raspberry jam remained on the table.

Billy groaned. Pulling his hand out of his mouth, he said, "Hermy, I have a sliver in my hand. I need a needle." He ignored the pain in his bum. Getting up slowly and unsteadily, Billy shuffled over to the couch. He bent beside it, lifting a box from the floor. He opened the lid and searched within. Small droplets of blood dripped on the threads, buttons, scissors, and other sewing items as he hunted for a needle. "Ah ha!" He pulled out a long, thin needle from the bottom of the box. With great care, he began to poke into his skin, prodding at the sliver embedded there.

"It's coming, Hermy. There it is." He dropped the needle back into the box, closed the lid, returned it to the floor, and held up the sliver. He shuffled over to the sink and flicked the sliver amongst the dishes.

"Well, I still need my kitchen things." Billy continued pulling out wooden spoons, forks, and serving dishes. He placed each selected item in the centre of the table. A ball of string was the last to meet the pile. When he was satisfied with his work, Billy pulled his hat off the coat rack and slipped into his shoes. He took one of the rucksacks from the rack and filled it with the items from the table.

He heaved the rucksack over his shoulder, opened the door, and walked out into the sunshine waiting for him. He breathed in the fresh scent of morning. The flowers at his door bent to greet him. He leaned over to touch a few of them with his unhurt hand. He straightened, reshuffled the rucksack, and proceeded down the dirt path away from his small home.

Billy began to whistle. His step lightened. He had forgotten all about the incident in the kitchen. He smiled wider the further down the path he walked. Butterflies flitted in and out of the flowers, collecting nectar on their morning feed. Hummingbirds zoomed amongst the trees. Billy noted the early morning risers, pleased to be one among them. Morning dew dripped from a leaf, brushing against his shoulder.

A rustling under a lilac bush caught his attention. He stopped. The rustling continued. A grunt and oomph came from the plant, or rather from someone under the plant. Billy took a closer look. His rucksack slid over his shoulder, hitting him in the head, and causing him to fall forward. The rustling stopped. Billy peered under the bush without moving. His arm remained tangled in the rucksack.

"Goo' mornin'," Billy cheered. He attempted to wave, yet only his fingers were free to move.

Holding an armful of sticks stood Javier, staring squarely at Billy. Surprise filtered across his face. Javier nodded his head. "Top of the morning to you, Billy. What brings you under here this morning?" He shifted the sticks in his arms.

"Oh, jus' on my way ta th' lake for some fun. Aren' ya up rather early, Javier?" Billy struggled to sit up, the rucksack impeding his movement.

Javier shrugged his shoulders. He looked around for further creatures he might know. "Uh, maybe a touch early. Things to do, you know."

Billy nodded his head, smacking his chin against the ground. "Yep. I know o' things ta do." It suddenly occurred to him that Javier was in the middle of a task. He looked at the sticks. "Whatcha doin' with those there, Javier?"

Javier glanced at the bundle in his arms, then back at Billy. "Oh, these? I was just.... Well, that's to say, I was..." his voice faltered. Billy struggled unsuccessfully to sit upright. "Billy, do you want some help?"

Billy sighed, "Yes, please, Javier. I can' move. I's this rucksack. I's too heavy ta get off my arm."

Javier dropped the sticks to the ground. He bounded over to the rucksack. He pulled at the straps, loosening them from the knots they created around Billy's arm. He soon had Billy free of the rucksack, and the two of them proceeded to dust leaves and dirt from Billy.

"So what'd ya say you's doin'?" Billy questioned.

Javier shifted his eyes. "I didn't say."

"Some big secre'?" Billy persisted.

"No, not a secret. It just might seem juvenile." He kicked the dirt with his bare foot.

Billy nodded in understanding, and then shook his head. "Wha' is juvenile?"

Javier laughed. "Childish."

"Wha's so childish 'bout sticks?" Billy waved at the bundle on the ground.

Javier looked at the dirt under his toenails. "It's not the sticks so much as what I plan to do with them."

"'Kay. Ya gonna burn 'em? For like a fire?" He scratched his head, shifting his hat to the side in the process.

"No," Javier shook his head. "I'm going to build a raft."

"A raf'?"

"Yes, for using on the lake. I could float on it. I could paddle it." Javier's voice began to rise in excitement. "I could watch the stars from it or even have a magickal lesson while lying on the lake."

"Lesson? I's gonna be tha' big? So's all ya superheroes can ride i' a' once?" Billy's eyes began to twinkle. "Maybe i'll be big 'nough for me ta ride?" He pressed his hands together.

Javier looked from Billy to the pile of sticks at their feet. He rubbed under his chin, thinking while he spoke, "I'd love to make it big enough for you, Billy, but I don't think there are enough sticks here."

"Oh," Billy's face fell, crestfallen. He picked up his rucksack. "Tha's okay. Don' really need a ride on th' lake. 'Sides, I was jus' gonna' swim in i' an' play on th' beach." He began to back out of the bush.

Javier reached out for Billy. He touched the troll's buckle on his boot. "Wait, Billy," he pleaded. The troll stopped. "Maybe we can find more sticks." He looked around. "I mean, really, I only just started collecting these this morning. There must be more all over the forest."

"Really? Ya mean i'?" Billy's face lit up.

"Yes, I mean it," exclaimed Javier. "We can collect more sticks together. We could even work together and build the raft, if you want."

Billy bobbed his head vigorously. "I have string here in my rucksack. We can use i' ta tie th' sticks together." He fumbled in his pack, digging for the string. He pulled out a grater and tossed it to the ground. A small cup flew towards Javier, barely missing his leg.

He jumped towards Billy. "Not yet, Billy," he said as he grabbed the troll's arm. "We need more sticks before we tie them all together."

Billy stopped tossing items out of his rucksack. He looked down at the faerie. "Righ', Javier. Righ'. We needs sticks." He looked at the small pile strewn on the ground. "Lots more sticks." He returned the items to the pack and added the sticks.

They stepped out from under the bush. Javier looked around in search of more strong sticks. Billy walked behind Javier, nearly bumping into him. Javier ignored the lack of personal space. "I find great sticks just off the path. Most of them on the path are split or broken from feet and paws."

"Ya wan' me ta look under th' trees?"

"That would be a good idea, Billy. You look over there and I'll search near here." He pointed behind them as an indication for Billy.

Billy turned in the new direction. He stepped off the path and into a group of birch trees. He crouched low to the ground, sliding on his belly as he searched for sticks. The ground was hard. Several rocks poked into his stomach. He brushed against the bottom side of a tree branch and a caterpillar dropped from a leaf and landed in his hair. Billy reached further forward, touching a few sticks. When he grabbed them, two of them broke in half. He tossed those aside and placed the good ones in his rucksack.

Billy backed up on his belly. A ladybug looked up at him from her resting place on a stump. "Goo' day," he mumbled as he tipped his hat in greeting. He caught his hat as it began to slip off his head. Billy straightened up, dusted off his shirt, and began to search across the path. He selected a few sticks as he wandered down the path. He waved hello to creatures who crossed his way, to those who popped their heads out of homes, and to those whom he noticed out of the corner of his eye.

It was not long before Billy had a rucksack full of sticks. He swung the pack onto his shoulder before retracing his steps down the path. The dirt covering his hands and face felt thick on his skin. He brushed at his chin, smudging more dirt into his pores. Satisfied with his stick hunt, Billy whistled a tune. Two bluebirds called out in greeting. He waved at them, winked, and carried on. On a purple mushroom near where he had begun his search sat Javier and Georgia.

Georgia shook her head, "No, it wasn't like that, Javier. I really think everything was innocent."

"How could you tell?" He peered at her face, searching for an answer.

"Because she said so. Isn't that enough?" Georgia looked away from his stare.

Javier shrugged his shoulders. Without looking up, he said, "Did you find some good sticks, Billy?"

Billy shook the rucksack, "Yep. Filled 'er up." He placed the pack onto the ground. "How ya doin', Georgia? Ya gonna' join us for a paddle on th' lake?"

She smiled up at the troll. "I'd love to join you, Billy, but I have other plans for the day." She rose from the mushroom, which shrank slightly in size, "I was actually on my way to visit with Seth before we join the others later, when I came across Javier. It was quite a surprise to see him at such an early hour." She looked at Javier sideways. "He wouldn't tell me why he's out so early. You said something about a paddle, Billy?"

"Yep, a paddle on th' lake. We gonna' -," Billy paused as he noticed Javier jumping up and down behind Georgia, waving his arms and wings frantically. He added, "We gonna do somethin' tha' is secre'. So's I can' tell ya more 'n tha."

Javier dropped his head into his open hands. Georgia looked from one to the other. "Well, really, I should be going. You two have fun paddling at the lake with your big secret."

"Wha' do ya know 'bout our secre'?"

Javier placed his hand on Billy's arm. "Nothing, Billy. She knows nothing. Just quit talking and let her go." He spun around and waved, "See you, Georgia."

She waved back as she flew down the path. Javier watched her until she was out of sight. He then hurried behind a jagged rock. "Over here, Billy. I have the sticks hidden under some leaves. I couldn't very well let Georgia see them. She asks too many questions as it is." He brushed away the leaves, revealing a pile of pristine sticks. "I was beginning to think she'd never leave."

Javier handed each stick to Billy, who placed them into his rucksack. "I think we have enough, Billy. Let's go before anyone else finds us."

They hurried along the path, veering off at a fork. When they reached the lake full of bubbling blue and white water, Billy and Javier emptied the rucksack. Javier separated the sticks from the kitchen utensils. He examined the peeler and set it aside. Billy pulled the string out of the pack. Several utensils were entangled with the string. The clanging distracted Javier.

"Do you want me to untangle the string for you, Billy?" Javier put down the sticks in his hand.

"No, I can do i', Javier. I' won' take but a minute." He laid out the utensils and string as far as they would go. With his injured hand, Billy began to unknot sections of the string, pulling them apart from the utensils. In a few minutes, the string was free. Granules of sand shimmered in his sliver wound, where the string had rubbed it open.

With great satisfaction, Billy dragged the untangled string over to Javier. "All done, Javier. Ya wanna string th' sticks, or ya wan' me ta do i'?" He rubbed his nose with the back of his bloody hand, streaking red across his face.

Javier stood up, shook his wings, and took a look at the troll standing eagerly in front of him. "How about if you lay out the sticks, hold them together, and I'll tie them up?"

Billy nodded his head in eager excitement. "'Kay, I'll get them together. I can do tha'." He began to gather up the sticks, laying them in a straight line side-by-side. He started to whistle a tune.

Javier worked beside Billy, looping string around a stick, knotting it, and re-looping it against the next stick. As they worked together in unison, Javier picked up the tune to Billy's whistle. When the raft was complete, Javier and Billy examined their work. For the most part, the raft was not too crooked. Each knot was small and meticulous. The sticks were laid in a parallel line, except for three in the middle.

Javier rubbed his hands together. "Let's get this raft on the water, Billy." He picked up the two longest sticks, which he had set aside before they began building the raft. "We can use these as paddles. If we stay close to the shore, these should reach the bottom and allow us to push ourselves around the lake."

Billy lifted the raft and placed it in the water. He and Javier climbed aboard. It tilted to the left, the right, then sank a touch into the bubbling water before it resurfaced again. Billy grinned widely. He stepped into the centre of the raft. "This is gonna be so much fun, Javier. We're floatin' on th' water!" He laughed with joy and rubbed his hands together.

"Yes we are, Billy," Javier replied. He gave one stick to Billy then pushed the other one through the water. He felt the lake bottom through the resistance on the stick. He used his strength to press down on the stick and shove against the lake floor. The raft slowly inched away from the shore, causing the water to bubble up even more than when the surface was untouched. Javier pushed again. "Billy," he said, "can you help me push us away from the shore?"

Billy appeared beside Javier. The raft tilted into the shore from the shift in weight. Billy sank his stick into the lake bottom. He shoved with all his might. The raft shifted away from the shore, causing Billy to lose his balance at the sudden movement. He held onto the stick as he began to fall backwards. Javier quickly grabbed hold of Billy's arm, yet Javier was too small to keep Billy on his feet. As Billy lay on the raft, Javier was flung over the troll and into the lake. Billy heard the splash as he stared into the clear sky. He attempted to sit up, although the raft continued to move precariously on the active water. He rolled over onto his belly. From this position, Billy was able to spot Javier treading water about two feet from the raft.

"Sorry, Javier. Ya wanna reach fer my hand? I can pull ya onto th' raf'." Billy stretched his sore hand as far as he could reach.

Javier shook his head, his soaking hair spraying droplets in a fray across the lake and onto Billy. His lips turned up in a huge smile. "Thanks for the offer, Billy. I'll just wait out here until you are back on your feet. Then I'll join you on the raft."

Billy nodded his head, "'Kay. Give me a minute." He pushed against the raft, lifting himself onto his knees. Billy was then able to use the stick to help himself into a standing position. The raft rocked, yet he was able to maintain some balance with the assistance of the stick. "I think i's safe now, Javier. Ya can come back 'board."

Javier shook his wings and arose out of the lake. His clothes dripped and clung to his body as he flew to the raft. Once he was standing on the edge, he shook himself. "I think, my friend, that you ought to stay in the centre of the raft. I seem to have lost my stick when I went for that unexpected swim. Why don't you give me your stick and I'll push us along?"

Billy reluctantly handed over the stick. "I could paddle, Javier."

"I know, Billy. But this was my idea, so why don't you just enjoy the ride?" Javier began to push the raft along the shore. "Besides, you helped so much in building the raft. We wouldn't be on the lake right now if it weren't for your skills at carrying all those sticks."

Billy smiled. He puffed out his chest and nodded his head, "Yeah, I'm good a' knots. Yep, good at 'em. 'Kay, I'll le' ya push us 'round."

The raft moved across the water as Javier pushed with the stick. Reeds were scattered along the shoreline, bending towards the friends in greeting. The bulrushes changed from deep brown to mocha to a sparkling mauve that spread down their stocks. Twice Javier had to disentangle his stick from a few of the reeds. Billy remained in the centre of the raft watching the scenery and enjoying the lapping of bubbling water against the bottom of the raft. The sun felt warm against his skin. He looked over at Javier.

"Ya startin' ta dry, Javier. Them's muscles o' yours is strong too. I can see 'em ripplin' when ya push th' stick in th' water."

"Thanks, Billy. These muscles are all natural. No super hard labour for these." He flexed an arm.

"Don' ya work ou' with Alexander and th' other superheroes each day?" Billy enquired. "Ain' tha' labour?"

Javier shrugged his shoulders. "Maybe, although that can't really be considered hard labour. It all sort of comes natural to me." He winked at Billy, "No need to put in more effort than required, eh?"

Billy nodded his head in understanding. He scratched his chin in thought. Two butterflies tagged each other in the air then came to rest on Billy's shoulder. Chatter drifted from the trees. A group of faeries emerged on the other side of the lake. They placed a picnic basket and a blanket on the sand. Two young trolls took up a spot not far from Billy and Javier. As they paddled further along the shore, more and more magickal creatures descended upon the lake.

Javier stopped the raft near a group of dancing hydrangeas. He pulled the stick out of the water and placed it on the raft. "Well, Billy, I had a great time with you this morning. Thank you so much for all your help."

"I'm still havin' fun. Can' we keep goin'?" he pleaded.

Javier shook his head, "It's nearing noon, Billy. I need to get home for lunch before meeting up with Georgia, Seth, and the others."

"Ah, right. You have trainin'." Billy looked at the butterflies before he stepped forward. The raft tilted towards the shore. His arms flailed as he kept his balance while climbing onto the beach. Billy shifted his rucksack so as to balance its weight upon both of his shoulders. Once ready, he turned and waved at Javier. "Thanks 'gain for th' paddle, Javier. Enjoy yer af'ernoon trainin'."

Javier jumped off the raft and began to pull it ashore. "Well, training has been cancelled for this afternoon, but us Guardians are getting together anyway." He looked up at Billy and added, "Would you like to keep the raft for this afternoon, Billy? Maybe do some more paddling on your own?" He brushed the sand off his hands.

Billy looked longingly at the raft then back at Javier. "Uh, maybe 'nother day, Javier, when we can play together." He paused, "Where ya gonna keep th' raf' for safe keepin'?"

Javier stared into Billy's brown eyes, "Would you like to keep our raft safe, Billy? Take it home and look after it until we can get out on the water again?"

Billy lit up, "Really? Ya wan' me ta keep i' safe?" He reached for the raft.

Javier gave Billy the paddling stick. "I wouldn't trust it to anyone else. I know you'll do a great job, Billy." He lifted his wings and began to fly towards the trees.

Billy gripped the stick in his injured hand, while he lifted the raft with his other hand. He began to whistle, while he stepped off the beach and onto a dirt path winding through the trees. It connected at a fork to the path he had taken earlier with Javier. The butterflies left his shoulder to find nectar in a honeysuckle, as Billy took a right on the path towards home.

CHAPTER 6

The green grass moved as though it was slithering across the ground. Trees, thick as mountains, lifted their roots, scratching at their base, flaking bark onto the ground. One particular spruce tree stretched and yawned. He reached above his top, touching the clouds. As a bird flew into his leaves, the tree shook his whole self, dropping nests, nuts, and wildlife. A chipmunk began to chatter as he clung to a branch, swinging precariously in the air.

Sabrina began to laugh, rocking on her feet amongst the slithering grass. Shadow swung her tail back and forth. Thump...thump...thump. She nuzzled against Sabrina's neck, purring to the rhythm of her heartbeat. The ground rumbled in pleasure. Sabrina reached for the dragon and ran her hand back and forth along Shadow's nose.

"Sh. Sh," she crooned in Shadow's ear. "We musn't be more disturbing than we have been already. I think that we've caused enough trouble for one day." Shadow bowed her head, nuzzling closer to Sabrina. Her tail ceased to thump.

Sabrina pushed herself up from the ground, pulling her hands away from Shadow. A soft "umph" escaped Shadow.

THE CRYSTAL GUARDIAN | 45

She shook herself, allowing her wings to extend. Shadow moved her feet upon the ground, feeling the earth settle into place where it had been before Sabrina caused the ground to roll.

"Perhaps we should have some harmless fun. What do you say, Shadow?"

Shadow nodded her head, eager to pursue more excitement in the lazy afternoon. Sabrina laughed. They began to walk amongst the trees, Sabrina limping and Shadow keeping close behind. They touched the leaves and grass with every step. A group of birds were hovering under a juniper bush, still ruffled from the active trees. One of them began to peck at the ground. His beak dug into the earth, searching for food to sustain his angry appetite. A dragonfly fluttered near Sabrina as it searched for the perfect leaf upon which to perch.

"You know, Shadow, there are so many ways in which to have a great deal of fun. We could go down to the lake and skim across the surface, or we could fly high into the clouds." She shook her head, "No, that wouldn't be good. The rains would be chilly and I'd rather stay dry." Shadow remained silent, licking the bark of a tree; then moving forward to keep up with Sabrina. "We could gather soap and create bubbles. Maybe there're some bees who would like to fly within the rainbows of colour." She stopped suddenly, causing Shadow to bump Sabrina with her nose. Sabrina giggled. "I know! We should plan a fiesta! We would need food, drink, music, lights, and our special faerie lights for the occasion! Oh, and guests of course." She turned her head to look at her faithful companion. "What do you think?"

Shadow nodded her head and fluttered her wings. Thump…thump…thump. She began to rise into the air, excitement coursing through her veins. Sabrina lifted her feet, floating above the ground. She flew towards the tree, giving it a hug rather than ascending to the branch. Her bare toes grazed the roots jutting from the earth. Sabrina tilted her head upward, looking for the sun between the leaves. She shifted around on the branch, slipping as her shorter leg did not make contact with the bark, causing her to miss her footing. Shadow caught her by a wing, holding the faerie in her mouth.

Without letting go, Shadow left the branch, soaring into the air. She flew to the treetop and beyond. Sunshine fell upon the two of them, warming Shadow's scales and skin. Sabrina twisted in Shadow's mouth, looking her in the eye. "Can I fly on my own now? Or do you need to keep me in your mouth?"

Shadow released the faerie. She dove below Sabrina, looping the air in hopes of creating a wind. Sabrina fluttered above the creature created breeze, watching dust particles attract to the movement. She shimmered from her core, encouraging her invisibility cloaking particles to shift away from the two, bringing them visible to the skies, clouds, and birds.

Sabrina grinned at her companion. "I think that you've decided our afternoon fate, my true friend. A flight in the sun amongst those who share our desire." Flames burst from Shadow. They circled around the dragon, licking at the air. They danced, forming shadows, which moved as she beat her wings. Two eagles changed course, barely missing the flames. Sabrina lowered herself into the circle of flames. She shook her wings. Faerie dust floated down, turning the flames a bright pink, then blue, then purple, before they turned back to reddish-orange. Shadow blew smoke onto the circle of fire, extinguishing it from sight.

Shadow flew up to be with Sabrina. Sabrina touched the dragon's nose, smiling at the purr of pleasure rippling through her companion. Sabrina climbed atop Shadow, leaned forward and whispered in her ear. "Let's go find some of the others. Sometimes it's just nice to share enjoyment of a beautiful day with friends."

Shadow circled around, tilting to the left as she caught the wind. Ever so gracefully, she dipped towards the trees, brushing against their tops. The soft caress of their leaves tickled her belly, which rumbled through to Sabrina. Shadow breathed smoke, inhaling the scent from the lush forest. Sabrina let her arms reach above her head, touching the air of freedom. Her own wings kept her grounded to Shadow, not that falling was a fear or even a consideration.

The duo neared an opening, where the trees parted along a riverbank. The rushing water roared in their ears. It was crystal clear and inviting. As though their thoughts were synced, Shadow dove into the water, sped along the sandy bottom, and then veered upwards to the waiting air. Sabrina took a deep gulp of air. She laughed. Shadow rumbled in pleasure. The wet dripped from their bodies and Sabrina's clothes, spraying droplets upon the flowers laying along the bank.

They neared a wide opening in the river, where the lake bubbled blue and white. Several clusters of magickal creatures surrounded the lake; others frolicked in and above the water. Shadow and Sabrina flew around the lake, looking for certain creatures who would recognize their need for adventure. A small cluster of faeries sat upon the grass, just out of reach of the beach. Shadow dipped lower, coming to land beside the group. Sabrina jumped off her cohort. She waved her hands in excited greeting. She limped forward on the grass rather than continuing to use wings for the moment.

Georgia was the first to get up in greeting. She threw herself at Sabrina, enveloping her in a tight embrace. "Oh, where have you been? I looked for you this morning, but your mother told me you had left before sunrise. We," she gestured to the small group, "decided today would be perfect for swimming."

Sabrina looked at the others as Georgia let her go. She put her hand on her left hip. "Swimming, eh? It looks to me like the only ones wet here are Shadow and me."

"Oh, don't be silly, Sabrina. When do we actually swim?" questioned Mercury. She bounced up from the ground, radiating heat from her body.

"Everyone knows you hate water, Mercury," interjected Seth. He remained seated on the grass, his back against the tree.

She spun around, "I don't hate water, Seth!" Her hands clenched into fists. She shook her long blond hair. "I just prefer to remain dry, where there is always warmth."

A gush of water rushed from the grass, splashing over Mercury. A piercing squeal escaped her mouth. She sputtered, coughing as though she had been drowning. She shook her wings, leaving yellow glitter on the ground. "Now I'm all wet! It'll take forever to get dry!"

Javier shook his head. He waited for the others to say something. When they only stared at Mercury, Javier calmly and quietly stated, "Are you sure that you are wet, Mercury?" She glared at him, dumfounded at such a question. She looked at her hands, lifted them, touched her hair, and then smoothed down her dress.

The water surrounding Mercury pooled together. It rose, reforming into Geoff. Not a drop was left on the ground. Mercury slanted her eyes, flipped her hands in the air, and began to dance around the group. "Insulted! That's what I am! Absolutely insulted!" The others began to giggle. As she continued to rant, Mercury danced faster and faster. "There was no need for that! The universe is not laughing with any of you. In fact, I am certain it is actually scolding each of you!"

"Careful Mercury, or you might burn a hole in the ground," cautioned Seth.

Mercury stopped. She looked him in the eyes, and then carried on with her maddening dance. "If it burns, so be it. Georgia can always freeze it."

Geoff laughed, deep and strong. He moved away from Mercury and sat down on the grass beside Jayne. She took his hand and smiled up at him.

"Mercury," Jayne sang softly, "it was all in good fun. Come, sit again with us."

The faerie continued to dance around them all, yet her feet faltered, causing her to slow her pace. Jayne began to hum, softly, gently, and ever so subtly. Near them, gnomes, faeries, birds, and other living beings gathered, as though in a trance.

Jayne continued her tune, increasing the tone.

"Upon the beauty of the land
There was but one who knew from far and few
All that there was and all that there would be
So come my friends and join me

He knelt upon the earth that gave
All to those who whispered its name
Thanks for blessings of plenty
Fire, water, earth and air

No one questioned what he knew
For he taught them true
So all would not be forgotten
Yet shared in so many ways

It was of him they often spoke
Whispering amongst themselves
Pleased to be of the chosen few
Whom all would revere each day

Learned were the few he chose
To help in the saving of them all
So that one day each would know
The purpose of their gifts

Come to me all my friends
Give thanks and praise to one we admire
One whose selfless acts are many
Asking nothing in return

For he is our true keeper still

Happy to be amongst us few
Joining in our search for balance
Of fire, water, earth, and air."

Jayne softly hummed the closing of her song. Mercury had stopped dancing, rooted in place. Her anger was gone. Her features had softened, reflecting the glow of warm sunshine. Blades of grass grew tall around Jayne. She played with the blades, feeling the smooth of one side contrast to the sharp roughness of the other. A small pixie began to clap. It was a low echo. Another clap began, then a cheer. The applause became louder as someone whistled. Jayne looked up from the ground; her eyes met Geoff's. His smile was infectious and warm. She smiled back. Her cheeks flamed red as she viewed the scene around her. So many beings sat along the beach. Only those left floating on twigs and leaves remained in the lake. It was as though Georgia had frozen time.

Slowly those along the lake began to move. Some gathered up their belongings, others splashed into the water, while still others resumed their conversations. Seth stood up. His wings fluttered gently in the breeze as he approached Mercury. She glanced at him, a glint of pleasure twinkling. He took her hand, drawing her over to the tree. She allowed him to guide her. They settled amongst the group, Geoff on her right.

Sabrina leaned against Shadow, whose tail was still in the grass. The faerie's breathing was in tune with the dragon. Their hearts beat as one, soothed from the song depicting their teacher. As much as she was looking for companions to join an adventure, Sabrina now felt reluctant to break apart the party. It seemed silly to seek out flight when rest was obviously needed amongst her Guardian companions. A day off, that's what Alexander had wanted for them. Maybe, just maybe, this would be an okay way to spend the remainder of her day...drinking in the beauty of the lake with those who understood nature.

Javier stretched in the grass. His legs straightened as he lay there, soaking in the warmth, breathing in the sweet smell of grass, hot sand, and cool water. "You know," he said, "I think this could almost be a perfect day."

Shoshana focused on Javier's face. "What do you mean by 'almost perfect'? What could be better than this?" She paused, "Well, except of course for a great game of grass hockey to tire us out at the end of today."

"Ah, Shoshana," sighed Javier, "you think too much of movement. We might have a day off, but Alexander doesn't. He had an extremely important meeting to attend today."

"Really? How do you know, Javier?" Georgia sat up straighter.

"I heard about it." He tapped his right ear. "Can't get much past these babies, I tell ya."

Ryan gazed at Javier. "What'd you hear?"

Javier laughed, "I just told ya. That Alexander had a very important meeting today."

Ryan swatted at Javier. "What was the meeting, oh big ears?"

"Yes, do tell," encouraged Georgia.

The Guardians moved closer to Javier, who remained stretched along the grass. He closed his eyes and smiled up at the sky. Seth licked his lips, his thick tongue sliding slowly across his bottom lip. "Well," began Javier, "I was minding my own business after breakfast, when two council members happened to fly by where I was sitting under a shrub."

"Why were you under a shrub, Javier?" enquired Ryan.

"How is that relevant?" snapped Mercury.

Ryan jumped as though he had been slapped. "It matters. If he hadn't been under the shrub, he wouldn't have heard anything, right?" He looked to the others for support.

Seth shook his head. Georgia looked at the ground. Jayne moved away from her spot. She put her arm around Ryan and knelt beside him. "Go on, Javier. We are listening."

"Ah, listening. That is what I was doing early this morning." Shoshana shot him a look. He paid no heed. "Yes, early after breakfast, as I was saying, I was resting under a shrub. Two council members were flying by and chattering about Alexander." All ears turned to the sound of Javier's voice. "It was almost as though they were speaking in code. There was a council meeting at late morning today, with Alexander being a special guest. They didn't seem too enthused about the whole idea. One even mentioned things could become intense if there was dissention amongst the council. Really, I can't imagine what the meeting would be about."

"Alexander doesn't usually meet with the council, does he?" enquired Shoshana.

"No, I'm certain that he's above the council." Jayne bit her lower lip, unsure of what to think.

"No one is above the council, Jayne," said Mercury.

Seth twisted his hands. "Isn't Alexander older than the council, though?"

Geoff laughed, "I think that Alexander is as old as time. He has been around since always, hasn't he?"

Sabrina nodded, "Oh, I'm sure he has been around since before all the worlds were in balance. Really, wouldn't the council be asking Alexander for help? Maybe that's what the meeting was all about. Maybe they need his knowledge about something."

Ryan bounced his head up and down. "Yes, they'd need his help. Why else would they meet with him?"

The others looked around, nodding in agreement. "Of course they want Alexander's help," stated Javier. "I hadn't really given it much thought when I overheard the conversation. Of course they want his help."

CHAPTER 7

The council wore robes of deep blue over their casual clothing. Each member of the council had been elected into office 100 years ago. Their term would continue for another fifty years. Alexander had worn his best hat of daisy, which had come as a gift from the Guardians. He had chosen this particular hat so that he could be close to them. After all, he was here on their behalf, even if they were unaware of the situation.

Looking around at the round room, Alexander noted a large table of elder wood at the front, which was surrounded by large mushroom seats. On one side of the room was an assortment of wooden chairs, strewn about as though at a casual lounging area. On the other side of the room, a large window had been carved out of Oak Tree. It looked upon the lake where faerie folk, pixies, and other creatures were frolicking on the water. Many live plants were set within the walls of the room, giving the look of a garden. Three faeries tended to the flowers, making them bloom and give off a sweet fragrance.

A faerie with pink wings and dark brown hair flew from the council table. When she was in front of Alexander, she placed her feet on the ground. "Welcome, Alexander. Please, would you join us at the table?" She smiled at him before walking back to the table.

"Thank you, Mary," he replied as he followed her. His feet made no sound; he took his time walking, ensuring that he not show any eagerness to bring these proceedings to a close before they even began. There were two chairs available; he chose the one closest to the window. If he moved his head a tad to the right, he could see those having fun outside. This would give him a focus when he wanted to appear disinterested.

Papers shuffled to his right. Logan, a faerie of obvious importance within the council, held a quill in one hand and a bottle of ink in the other. He cleared his throat, put down the ink, and took a sip of water from the wooden cup in front of him.

A shrewd female with a pointed chin pierced her gaze into Alexander. She smiled slightly, as though it took great effort. "We are quite glad that you agreed to meet with us today, Alexander." She awaited his reply. When he remained silent, she drummed her fingers on the table. When it became apparent that Alexander had no intention of responding, she continued, "Well, as you may be wondering, we have invited you here to discuss our concerns regarding the Guardians." Lillian paused for further effect.

The others nodded their assent. They all moved their gazes towards Lillian, hanging on her every word. Lillian leaned forward. "As you can imagine, we are quite concerned that perhaps there are not enough Guardians. We are concerned that perhaps their gifts and talents may be forgotten or led astray."

Alexander stared at Lillian blankly, expectantly. He knew what it was that she sought; however, he had no intention of assisting her in the witch-hunt. Lillian took a sip of water before continuing, "We realise that you have been the teacher of our superhero faeries, honing their talents for centuries."

"Millennia," Alexander offered.

She nodded. "Yes, millennia. Well, we believe that it is time you took a break from this expectation. Perhaps you ought to share your knowledge with us, so that we may assist in furthering the gifts of our special faeries. We believe that sharing your knowledge will ensure the continuation of these teachings, assure our faerie folk that the knowledge will continue."

The council nodded, pleased with her speech. Alexander looked out the window, pretending to consider her words of wisdom. Quietly, he stated, "I can assure you that the knowledge will not be lost. When it is time, I will bequeath my knowledge to an apprentice of high quality."

The council did not look pleased. Lillian smiled fake reassurance. "Oh, we do not doubt you, Alexander. On the contrary, we only want to ensure that you have assistance now. We would not want for you to feel overwhelmed with your task."

There was a shuffling of more papers. Someone coughed. Alexander met Lillian's gaze. "Thank you for your concern. It is well noted and much appreciated. However, I do not find my position to be overwhelming, but rather I find it to be invigorating. It keeps me young." He placed his hands on the table and smiled endearingly at the council.

One young faerie smiled back. He seemed to be uncomfortable, as though he were pressured to be there. Well, young was an overstatement; he must be close to three hundred years of age. Relatively speaking, compared to the rest of the council, however, Travis was young. His smile was genuine. He shifted in his seat, attempting to get a closer look at Alexander. It was obvious that Travis admired Alexander, that he was not at all pleased about this council meeting.

Travis cleared his throat before speaking, "Perhaps you could tell us what it is you need from us, so that we may help you with your task, Alexander?" He chose his words carefully, certain to not show favouritism nor to anger the council. "We have convened here for the benefit of our special faeries. No one knows them better than you, Alexander. We completely understand that the development of these Guardians have been under your guidance since we can remember. However, there has been some concern raised in Faerie as to why so few of these special faeries are chosen to use their superpowers. There are many faeries with mental and physical specialties who are not chosen to become a part of the Guardian group." He looked around the room. "We thought that perhaps the reasoning for this is that as one being, you could not train them all. Therefore, we are offering our services in assisting to train all of these special faeries, thus increasing the group of superheroes."

"Well put, Travis." Lillian smiled genuinely at him. She then turned to face Alexander. "Now that you understand our position on this matter, I am certain you will provide us with the knowledge we require."

"While I may understand what you have said, Travis, I must decline the offer. You see, there are many reasons for only choosing a select few special faeries. The reasoning for this is ancient. Although the knowledge was bequeathed to me, I am not at liberty to share it with anyone other than she or he to whom Archangel Michael selects."

The council broke into discussion. There was anger in their tones and it was difficult to follow any one conversation. Lillian pounded a gavel on the table. "Council, please! We must have some semblance of orderly discussion." Her face turned scarlet as she turned to Alexander.

He merely looked away giving the impression that he had not noticed her glare. He pretended to remove a spec of dirt from his shirt. Alexander listened to the individual conversations, noting the opinions of each.

"No, Logan, we must adhere to the wishes of Archangel Michael."

"Are you against the idea of having more superheroes, Mary? Do you not see that it is important we cultivate more of their kind? There are so many special faeries who are not trained but who ought to be. What about them?" He swung his hands, causing the bottle of ink to spill over his papers.

"Of course we want to have more Guardians in our world. I am not disagreeing with you; I am just questioning our position of how to do this. We need more knowledge of how the process works. We cannot go about this training blindly," Mary insisted.

"Then how do you propose we do this without Alexander's assistance?"

"I don't propose such a thing. We need to figure out how to encourage Alexander and how to assist him in this task." Her voice was firm.

"He obviously does not want to share anything with us. What do we do? String him up on a tree?" Logan chuckled at this thought. "Oh, the trouble that would cause...."

"You are being ridiculous, Logan. There must be a way to convince Alexander." She glanced at the man in question. She examined him, contemplating ideas on how to reach the gnome's mind.

A willowy faerie discussed the situation with two other faeries, who all seemed to have differing opinions. She stood when she spoke, attempting to emphasise her point. "This is getting us nowhere. A complete waste of time I tell you. Did I not say in our meeting the other week that this would not work?"

"Lucy, again you are missing the point completely. It is not about making progress in one attempt. This is about protocol. In order to reach our desired outcome, we must follow protocol."

"Oh please, James. You and your protocol have done nothing but create more meetings. The only way to get anything done is to start at the top and the bottom. Leave out the middleman." She sat back down to make her point.

Daphne looked from one to the other. Timidly, she spoke, "Are we even certain that this is best for our special faeries? I have a niece who was not chosen to be a superhero. She is very happy with her life. She works as a party planner and loves it. Would forcing her to be a Guardian change that?"

"You are missing the point completely, Daphne," scoffed James. "Guardians are for the good of Faerie and our world. One cannot be distinguished from the other."

Daphne looked up from the table. Dawning appeared on her face. "You mean to say, what we are hoping to do here will ignore personal choices? Our superheroes are not created for our personal motives. These faeries have feelings, hearts, and desires. When you ignore all of that, you no longer treat them as living beings. Is our purpose as a whole not to create balance in nature? How would using these individuals for council gain keep balance?" She shook her head. "No. If this is the motive here, I cannot be a party to it. I will not be a pawn for personal gain."

Lucy looked alarmed. She glanced from Daphne to James. Dissension among council members would not result in success. "That is not what James is saying at all, Daphne. All special faeries want to become superheroes. How often as children did we wish to be special so that we could become superheroes?" She looked around the table. "No, we are not taking away personal choice, but rather we are ensuring it occurs."

James nodded. "Yes, we are ensuring that these faeries have the opportunity to reach their potential. When they are denied the final training and dismissed from the opportunity to become Guardians, we are doing them a disservice. All faeries are born as individuals. We need to nurture their individual growth. How many of these special faeries are devastated when denied the status of superhero?" He looked hard at Daphne. "If your niece had been given the status of Guardian, do you not think she would be even more elated in her life? Certainly we are not denying the fact that all special faeries find their way and create a life of happiness. What we are fighting for here is the opportunity for them to reach their full potential."

Daphne was not convinced. Something about this bothered her. Perhaps what the council was trying to do would result in an imbalance. Imbalance was worse than being denied personal choice. Many dimensions, realms, and worlds depended upon the balance faeries created in this world. If that were to be removed, well, there was no telling what damage could result. A private discussion with her niece might put her nerves at ease.

Alexander smiled to himself. It would appear there were at least two council members who knew the importance of ancient tradition. Mary would be sadly mistaken if she thought she could converse with and convince Archangel Michael of her wishes. Archangel Michael had great compassion for all living things, yet he also knew what was best for all creatures great and small. Not to say that he made choices for anyone. No, he merely allowed growth and assisted in the best possible way. He knew consequences of actions long before the choice to make those actions occurred.

Alexander was pulled out of his thoughts at the sound of Lillian's shrill voice and the loud banging of the gavel. It appeared she had lost patience. "Enough! Let us come to order now! We have much to discuss as a whole, and many plans to make." As all eyes rested upon her, she smoothed her hair and fluttered her wings as a way of gaining personal control.

"Obviously, Alexander requires time to think over our proposal." She smoothed out her skirt and folded her hands. "Now, Alexander, we do wish you well today. Once you have thought over the discussion here, I am certain that you will come to agree with us on this matter. Therefore, we thank you for your time. We will get in touch with you in the near future to discuss ways in which we can assist in the sharing of knowledge and training of more superheroes." She waved her hand. One of the faeries attending the flowers flew to her side. "Marco will see you out." With that, she turned away from Alexander and addressed the council. "We will reconvene after lunch."

Alexander stood and placed his hat back on his head. With a bow to the general group, he walked slowly towards the doors. Travis flew beside him, eager to speak with the ancient gnome. When they had descended the inside stairwell and stood outside the council tree, Travis offered his hand in a friendly gesture.

Alexander accepted. "Thank you, Travis. I appreciate an ally in there. You may be the youngest on that council, but you are certainly the wisest."

"My great uncle is a Guardian. I grew up knowing the importance of his work. I once asked him why I couldn't be a superhero. He told me that not all faeries are created equal to the tasks we are given. We each have a purpose; it is not necessarily to create balance in all worlds."

"You are fortunate to have a great uncle who knew how to teach you about his work. I do believe this will make you an asset to the council. It is faeries like you who will benefit our world and those beyond." Alexander tipped his hat to the faerie. "Please, do come over one day for a visit. I would be honoured to spend time with you."

Travis beamed. "I would be more than pleased to do so, Alexander." He bowed in parting.

Alexander walked slowly away from the young faerie. He moved in the direction of the bramble bushes. It would be faeries like Travis who would be able to keep a reign on the faerie council. A meeting like the one today gave Alexander great cause for concern. It had always been understood that his position in Faerie was not questioned. Although Alexander was not necessarily privy to all that Archangel

Michael understood and required, he was answerable to the higher being. It would not do to be caught between Archangel Michael and the faerie council. For, of course, Alexander would uphold all that Archangel Michael asked; this could make for a very difficult life in Faerie. Alexander sighed. Something would need to be done soon to protect his charges and all that the Guardians represented.

CHAPTER 8

The stars twinkled in the clear night sky. Alexander closed the door to his home, making sure that it would not open if a wind gusted. He placed his hat on his head, and walked down the grassy path. He could hear the sound of crickets and tree frogs singing in the air. A warm breeze tickled his skin. The smell of crocuses touched his nose. It appeared to be a perfect evening for a party at Oak Tree.

His footsteps were soft on the grass, barely marking each blade, while the moonlight gave enough light for him to notice several critters scurry in front of him. Two pixies hovered near the bramble bushes, arguing about something. The sound of laughter and the clink of cups reached his ears. Alexander stopped at the lilac bush and peeked through to watch the festivities. Bright faerie lights hung about Oak Tree, glowing in the dark. Faerie folk were scattered about in groups, chatting and drinking nectar. Two individuals were climbing Oak Tree. Billy the troll chatted with Shoshana and Sabrina as they sat upon a large mushroom.

Sitting on a low branch of Oak Tree were Jayne and Geoff. Geoff was blending into the tree as he changed shapes at Jayne's suggestions. A caterpillar, a snail, a twig, a leaf, and back to himself. Jayne's wings fluttered at his movements. He grinned when she laughed. *Ah, young love,* thought Alexander.

Starlight flowers grew in clumps near the base of the tree. They came out of the ground in groups of four, grew tall, opened to the breeze, and then turned into stars that lifted into the sky. Colours of purple, deep blue, and pale pink emanated from the blooms. Jayne was always happiest when she produced these flowers for all to see. It was her quiet way of bringing her soul outside of her body.

Fireflies flitted about the starlights, chasing each other as they sought the sweet, rare nectar. It tasted like virgin honey, filling their bellies as their bums lit the night. The nectar was dizzying, causing each firefly to bump into the other. Sparks of light flew from them, cascading upon the stars as they arose into the air. A glow formed around the fireflies and starlight flowers. The moon expanded the glow, encompassing the surrounding grass and tree. Mushrooms popped up from the ground, giving a resting place for those who sought one.

As a group of butterflies danced, the small touch of a rainbow appeared. It followed the stars into the sky, bending at the peak of the tree, then arcing down to touch the pool of water near Billy's home. Alexander watched the creation and the reaction of those in the vicinity. Several faeries stopped their engaging conversations and gasped in awe. A leprechaun stumbled out of his hovel, carrying a pot of gold. He placed it beneath the rainbow in respect of the creation. Raindrops formed on the rainbow beams, sliding down to touch the roots of each starlight flower.

Geoff leaned over the branch of the tree. He shook his wings, scattering faerie dust upon the beauty below. Child faeries came running, holding up their hands to catch the dust, giggling. As musical faeries played natural instruments, the children danced, their wings moving in time with the music. A crowd gathered, joining the children in dance. Two circles formed, one inside the other. Each circle moved counter to the other.

Lights glittered amongst the faeries, accentuating their wings in the moonlight. Colours of soft green, silver, gold, vibrant purple, and other colours of the rainbow glowed within the circle as faerie wings fluttered. Celtic music played, creating a beat to the dance. Birds flew from the trees, carrying twigs and bits of string. They soared above the dance, dipping amongst the onlookers. Quietly, more nature spirits and forest animals joined the festivities.

Alexander stepped out from the lilac bush. A feeling of peace and excitement coursed through him, as it often did when in the presence of his charges, his super-powered Guardians. He could tell that only four of the superheroes were currently at the festivities. By the end of the evening, all of them would be here enjoying the weekly social. All of Faerie insisted that the Guardians be at these gatherings. It was not so much for the superhero enjoyment as it was for the enjoyment of the other nature spirits. When the Guardians were around, positive energies seemed to form.

"Ah, Alexander! Alexander!" Billy stumbled forward, tripping on his own two feet. Alexander caught him before he fell to the ground. Billy stood up and dusted himself off. "Oh, thank ya. I didn' see tha' rock on th' ground."

Alexander smiled. "How are you this evening, Billy?" He did not point out that there was no rock, as that would be tactless.

"Oh, real well, Alexander. Th' festivities are goin' well. Did ya see tha' rainbow? I' was so beautiful. Th' colours were magnificent. Th' bes' part was havin' i' close ta my home." He looked off, "I sure hope i' stays there for a while."

"One never knows how long such beauty may last, Billy. We can only enjoy it while it exists."

Billy nodded, as though he understood. The two of them walked around the gathering together, waving at those who waved to them. When they came to a group of five brownies, Alexander and Billy sat down to join them. One of the males scooped liquid into cups and passed them to the new arrivals. He wore a black vest of felt, which was open at his chest. Alexander and Billy thanked him as they took the drinks.

"We are looking forward to the Equinox this year. It is our understanding that you and your charges will be staying here to celebrate this year, Alexander."

Alexander sipped his drink, and then held it in his hands. "From where did you hear that, Morton?"

"One of the council members mentioned it in passing two days ago." Two of the other brownies nodded vigorously.

"Yes, we were there when Lillian told Morton." Sasha looked to Andre when she responded.

"It was quite a surprise, really," stated Andre. "I don't remember a time when the superheroes ever celebrated an Equinox or a Solstice here in Faerie." He glanced at the dancing faeries. "Quite exciting, really."

Billy looked between the brownies and Alexander. He seemed perplexed. "Why did ya not tell me, Alexander?" His tone was full of hurt.

Alexander sighed. "I did not mention this because it is not true. Tradition denotes that we celebrate as we have always done. Only those who are part of the celebration may attend. Archangel Michael has requested this since the beginning of time; there has been no change in his request, therefore the council has no say in this matter."

Billy looked from Alexander to the rest of the party. "Why would Lillian say i' was changed if i' has not been?"

Alexander shrugged his shoulders. "I cannot speak for Lillian or the other council members. I can, however, assure you that tradition will be upheld."

The others looked somewhat uncomfortable. Alexander's declaration indicated that there was something wrong with information from the council. Dissension in the ranks would not be a good thing. Morton cleared his throat.

Sasha stood up with the pitcher of nectar in her hand. "Would anyone like a refill?" Everyone nodded, thankful for the change in subject.

The music changed to an old melody. The faerie circle broke apart, dancers scattering into separate movements. Their wings glittered in the moonlight, changing colours with the sounds of music. A tree frog croaked, enhancing the song. A group of four pixies joined the fray. They twittered against the music, their voices scratchy and irritating.

Javier appeared from between two rose bushes. Behind him were Seth, Mercury, and Ryan. Each faerie wore an outfit befitting of a celebration. Mercury glowed in yellow, her wings sparkling in the moonlight. Ryan was dressed in purple, with flowers woven between the hairs on his head. Seth was clothed in forest green. Javier was donned in a simple navy outfit. Each of their wings reflected the moon, shedding sparkling light around the forest floor.

Seth shook his wings in time to the music, spreading dust further about the forest floor. He smiled broadly, his face becoming more round than usual. "There are so many creatures here," he exclaimed. "I haven't seen this varied a group in a long time. When was the last time so many creatures came to the end of week celebration?" he asked Javier.

Javier scrunched up his nose as he thought. "It must've been for Winter Solstice."

"Oh, I always like Winter Solstice," said Seth. "The twinkling lights of white and the trees all decorated with food."

Mercury began to twirl in a large circle around the Guardians. "The bonfire is my favourite part of Winter Solstice," she exclaimed. "I especially love it when the flames grow one upon the other, encompassing the logs and becoming a life of their own."

"I think the hot drinks are the best," added Ryan. "I like them that way. It feels like a cozy bed on a cold night."

"Speaking of hot drinks," interrupted Javier, "I think we should go find one. I could use a warm nectar, one the bees have created this morning."

"How do you know the bees created a nectar this morning?" asked Ryan.

"I could hear them buzzing in their hives after Mom made breakfast. They made quite a noise all morning," answered Javier.

"If the nectar isn't the right temperature, I can heat it up for you," Mercury assured Javier. "Although," she said, "I think that I want to join in the dancing before I join you for a drink." She left the three of them and mingled amongst the dancers. Her wings shed sparkles onto the ground as she danced gracefully and with creativity to the music.

"She has a natural way of dancing," commented Seth. He sighed, "I wish I could move like that, but my feet just don't know which way is left and which way is right."

"Then maybe you should just use your wings when you dance," suggested Javier.

"Or don't worry so much about how you look when dancing. Just let the music move your body rather than having your body move to the music," stated Ryan.

"Isn't that the same thing?" queried Javier.

"No," insisted Ryan. "When you move your body to the music, you have control. When the music moves your body, the music has control."

"I don't see the difference," said Javier. He moved further into the gathering. "Let's join Geoff and Jayne over on that tree branch."

Seth looked up into the tree, where Jayne and Geoff sat, their legs swinging over the branch. "They must've been entertaining that group of faerie children. There are at least twelve of them clustered under that tree. They seem to be picking something out of the ground."

Ryan pushed past Seth. He lifted his hand and held up his palm. One of the starlight flowers uprooted and came soaring across the space between them. It landed on Ryan's hand with the petals opening wider. "Jayne has been making flowers," he commented. "She must really be enjoying herself."

Seth reached out and touched the flower. His small fingers slid across the soft petals. He leaned over and sniffed at their scent. "Pretty," he gushed. He followed Javier to the base of the tree, where the children clustered. "Didn't you want something warm to drink, Javier?"

Javier shrugged his shoulders. "I can wait a few minutes." He pushed through the children, careful not to step on the flowers or the fingers pawing at the ground. He raised his chin to look up at Geoff and Jayne. "Do you two have room for the rest of us up there?" he called out.

Jayne leaned over the branch and let go of Geoff's hand. Her eyes twinkled as she smiled warmly in greeting. "Come on up. There is always room for more."

Javier spread his wings and flew to the branch, sitting himself beside Geoff and dangled his bumpy feet. "How long have the two of you been here?"

"For a while," answered Geoff. "We came early, as we figured it'd be busy tonight."

"We noticed the amount of magickal creatures congregating here tonight," admitted Javier. "Is there a particular reason for the mass numbers of them?"

Seth and Ryan sat beside Jayne. "It hasn't been this busy since Winter Solstice," stated Seth.

"My mother heard that several creatures were specifically invited to be here tonight," replied Geoff. "Apparently, the council wanted a good turnout. Mom didn't say why."

"Sometimes it's nice to have everyone join in the festivities," mentioned Jayne. "It's like a homecoming, when everyone gathers and enjoys themselves. I think it was thoughtful of the council to personally ask community members to come and join in the fun."

"Maybe Alexander suggested that the council encourage everyone to come this evening," said Seth. "He was invited to join them for a meeting the other day."

"He never did say what they discussed," added Ryan. "So it would make sense that it had something to do with tonight."

"I did see Alexander and Billy over with a group of brownies," said Geoff. "They looked like they were all having a deep conversation and drinking nectar."

"Was it warm?" asked Javier, his attention refocusing on his earlier desires.

"Was what warm?" asked Geoff.

"The nectar. I could really go for a drink of warm nectar," replied Javier.

"Oh, I have no idea. Jayne and I hadn't even sought out drink or food. We thought that we'd wait for more of you to arrive before we left the comforts of this branch."

"Then I say we should go in hunt of food and drink," insisted Javier. He rose to his feet and flew away from the branch. The others followed close behind. As the five of them fluttered about above the festivities, their wings glittered and faerie dust fell in their wake. Jayne created and dropped handfuls of starlight flowers as the group sought out the food and beverage table.

Javier heard the tinkling of cups and made a dive for the refreshment table. He hovered above the table while he took a cup from beside the bowl of warming nectar. With one hand he dunked the cup into the warm liquid and filled it to the rim. Javier took a long drink of the sweet honey before he flew over to an empty mushroom upon which he perched himself. Jayne perused the tables until she selected a fresh lemon and leaf broth nestled in a wooden bowl.

When the five Guardians were content with their food and beverage selection, they sat upon a group of mushrooms amongst a variety of guests. Two pixies were playing toss across the group. They each threw a cricket, which spread its wings and flew as far as possible. The pixie whose cricket went the furthest gained points. A young brownie came over to the group. "Can I join you?" she asked tentatively.

"Certainly," declared Javier. He got up from his mushroom and gestured for her to sit down. "Aren't you related to Morton?"

"Yes, he's my father. How did you know?" she asked eagerly.

Javier smiled widely and his eyes twinkled. "You have the same walk as he does. It's very distinct and dignified."

She blushed. "I'm Arabella, the middle of his three daughters. Usually everyone notices my younger sister."

"Isn't your younger sister the one who writes poetry?" inquired Mercury, as she joined the group. "I once caught her writing, but she hid it before I could take a peek at the words." She created a flame on her pinkie finger. It turned from red to orange to yellow and then took on all three colours at various points in the flame.

Arabella nodded her head. "Yes, she writes wonderful poetry. She would eventually like to read it aloud to an audience, but right now she's still afraid that her work isn't yet good enough for others to hear."

"Maybe sometime she can read a poem to me," suggested Jayne. "I create songs all the time. They just flow from inside me and come out with music already attached to the words."

"Well, to be honest, I don't really know anything about words and poetry. My mind thinks more in terms of angles and numbers. I could tell you exactly what to put in a recipe and how much of everything, but I'd have no idea how to make it sound good," Arabella admitted.

"Everyone has a talent," said Ryan. "It's always best to appreciate what someone else can do well and to be content with your own talent. We," he gestured to the other Guardians, "spend a great deal of time honing our own skills. It's how we get better at what we do. Look at Mercury, for instance. She can make that flame dance on whichever finger she chooses and she can change it's colours."

Mercury demonstrated her talent for the brownie. The small flame jumped from her pinkie finger over to her thumb, where it became a blue fire with streaks of yellow licking at the sides. "I can do many other things with fire as well," she mentioned. With the touch of her index finger from her other hand to the tip of the flame, the fire turned to smoke and rose into the air where it disappeared.

"Are you here alone tonight?" asked Ryan. He searched the crowd behind them and over towards the table of food.

Arabella shook her head. "Oh, no. I came with my father, but he's busy chatting with his friends and Alexander. He was quite excited today when he heard that all of you Guardians would be staying in Faerie during the Equinox this spring. So, of course, he didn't want to miss attending this evening, especially since the council specifically invited him to attend. My father told me that the council would like to have more involvement from different magickal creatures in events taking place in Faerie. It builds more community."

Javier nearly dropped his cup of warm nectar. "Since when are we staying in Faerie? We never stay in Faerie for the Equinox. In fact, since Alexander has been the sage of all Guardians, he has taken his charges away for the Equinox. Your father must've misunderstood the information that he was given. We've already begun making our plans for the event."

"Yes, we will definitely be going away for our usual retreat," agreed Geoff.

"No changes will occur around that," stated Ryan.

Arabella shrugged her shoulders. "Then whoever told that to my father must have her facts wrong. It's amazing how fast incorrect information can travel."

Mercury got up from her mushroom. "Would anyone like to dance? The music is changing again and my feet cannot stay still for another minute."

Javier bounced up and put his cup on the forest floor. He took one of Mercury's hands and began to twirl her around the seated group. Her blond hair flew around her face and shoulders. Her wings sparkled red and threw faerie dust into the air as the two danced together. Geoff pulled Jayne off of her mushroom and took her in his arms. They began to waltz across the thick grass. Seth clapped his hands in time to the music while Ryan watched other creatures join his friends on the makeshift dance floor.

CHAPTER 9

Seth turned in his sleep. The simple sheet tangled around his short legs and he moved his wings slowly. The tree frog croaked outside his bedroom window. While a warm breeze fluttered the curtain as it moved into the dark room, moonlight shone through the curtain and onto Seth as he began to dream. He found himself atop a mountainside, where the landscape was bleak. Darkness surrounded the day, preventing sun and light from touching the world.

He knew that it was summer, but it felt like the start of winter, when the ground was frozen, yet the snow had not yet fallen. The trees had been stripped of life. No creatures, great or small, adorned the area. He felt emptiness, loneliness, and a great sadness. He turned from the landscape to look behind him on the mountainside. Apollo, the sun god, sat upon a rock with his face in his hands, shaking with sobs. Seth slowly walked over to the god and sat down beside him.

"Why do you cry so?" Seth asked with curiosity.

Apollo lifted his head and looked into Seth's caring face. "Can you not tell? All I have done for this and other worlds is gone. Helios no longer shines and daylight has gone with him. Without Helios, I cannot help the vegetation grow. The creatures have died off. I cannot escape this darkness."

Seth glanced from Apollo to the landscape again. Something about the area was familiar. He bit at his cheek in an attempt to remember, or to at least understand. "Where are we?"

Apollo laughed sardonically, "Where are we? Why, this is Faerie. Can you not recognize your home? Your world of magick and great balance?"

Seth felt his heart drop into his stomach. This was Faerie? He searched the horizon for a familiar place, a familiar monument to indicate where in Faerie he might be at this moment. The mountains were cracked from the top to the bottom. He searched for the lake and the river. Finally, he could see a gouge in the world floor, which once contained water. The feeling of loss returned to him. He grasped at it, attempting to understand and hold onto it before it too disappeared. "Magick," he whispered. "I feel the loss of magick."

"Yes," cried Apollo, "the magick is gone with everything else!" He rose to his feet and stumbled to the edge of the mountainside. "All magick is gone from here. It was ripped out with everything else in this world that creates balance. Despair. Your kind did not stop it. You did not protect this world or all the others with your special gifts. Now all is lost." He fell to his knees and cried out over the land, "Helios! I need Helios!"

Seth listened for any sound of life aside from Apollo and himself. Deadness. Despair and sadness seeped into his soul. Through the darkness surrounding them, Seth noticed the lack of moonlight. He looked up to the sky, searching for the clouds covering Luna. No clouds appeared to his vision. He gasped and sucked in the night air as he realised there was no Luna and the stars had disappeared in the clear sky. "We are in a dark hole! Everything has been sucked into darkness! How is this possible? Apollo, what has happened here? How is it that the magick is gone? How is it that the sun, moon, and stars are all gone? What do you mean my kind did not protect this world?" He hurried over to the sun god and pulled at his arms, attempting to lift him to his feet. Apollo resisted, becoming limp. He sprawled on the ground moaning. "Get up, Apollo!"

The sun god drew up his forlorn face. "Seth, it is daytime. This is not night. There is no reason to rise, as Helios no longer rises. I always rise and set with Helios. My magick and power has failed. I cannot reach the light in this deep darkness."

"Daytime? Night time? It doesn't make a difference of which one it's supposed to be," insisted Seth. "What matters is that we figure this out. What matters is that we find Helios, Luna, and the stars." He breathed heavily, gasping for the air that surrounded him still. "We need to find the others. We need to fix this. Do you know what happened? Do you know why my kind did not protect the world? Why we could not keep balance?"

Apollo pulled his arms out of Seth's grasp. "What is the point? We cannot fix this. Magick of the ultimate power is required to put the world back and there is no more magick here," he said. "We cannot access great power without a touch of magick."

"No," Seth insisted. "No. No. No!" He stood tall, searching the empty sky and the barren world. "Do not allow everything to be lost, Apollo. As a Guardian, I can change this. All of my kind can change this. We can bring light back into this darkness. Jayne can sing for the vegetation. She can re-grow the land."

"She is not here," stated Apollo.

"Where is she then? Where is everyone?" Seth questioned.

"Gone," Apollo whispered. "They are all gone. Only you and I remain."

Seth shook his head, trying to remember. There had been a celebration, a night of fun, of music, of singing, and of food. They had all been in attendance. Alexander had been there, sitting with Billy and other magickal creatures. What could possibly have happened between then and now? His head began to throb, pounding against his left temple. Something was missing. Seth pressed his hand against his temple. "Think!" he yelled. He began to pace back and forth along the edge of the mountainside.

"Focus on the celebration," he murmured. Who was there? All of the Guardians, the council members, and various magickal folk had attended. His family had been there. Much of the community had been there. Faerie lights had been strung amongst the trees, glittering in the evening. A beautiful night it had been; stars were abundant in the sky. Luna had been shining. So what happened between then and now?

His pacing was becoming emphatic. His feet echoed on the hard ground, reaching into the darkness in hopes of meeting other sounds, when it was clear that there were none. Seth pressed at his temple again. The throbbing increased. He attempted to reach further into the depths of his mind. The moonlight. He could see the moonlight in his mind. Where was it? When was it? "Luna, you were there that night. So where are you now?" He opened his eyes wider in the darkness.

Apollo remained laying on the ground, now curled into a fetal position. Seth stopped pacing and lowered himself to the ground beside Apollo. "When did Luna leave? She was here during the celebration."

Apollo did not respond. He closed his eyes against the dark day. Seth placed his hand on Apollo's shoulder. "Tell me what you know, Apollo. I remember the night of the celebration, but after that all is blank. I can't find the connection between then and now." The sun god shook under Seth's touch. "Please, Apollo, help me to figure this out."

"The celebration was hindered with malice, with the darkness that was seeping into Faerie. The tides had already begun to change. Yet our saviour did not notice the change. He was not aware of the importance, of how much that day was to end the balance. So much has happened since that night. It seems like such a long time ago that you were all celebrating together," Apollo responded with sadness.

Seth looked deep into Apollo's blue eyes. They did not shine like Helios, like they did during their last encounter. "It was only just last night that we celebrated, I think," Seth assured him.

Apollo shook his head, "No, it was much longer than that. It has been close to a year since the night of the celebration of which you speak."

Seth pulled back in shock. "A year? That is not possible. I have no memory of the past seasons. Forgive me for saying so, but you must be wrong."

"Ah, Seth, if only you knew all that I know. It has been a long time since Helios shone, since Luna appeared, and since life inhabited this world." He uncurled his body and sat on the dirt. "But then, you are not really here in my time, are you?"

"I'm not here in your time? What do you mean?"

Apollo searched Seth's features. "Think, Seth. Why is it that you have no memory between the night of the celebration and now?"

Seth shook his head. "I don't know. I can't retrieve any memories."

"That is because they have not yet occurred. You must still make those memories." Apollo wrapped his arms around his body.

"Where am I then?" queried Seth. He glanced around again, searching for an answer. His mind was confused. The pain behind his temple was impossible to ignore.

"You are in Faerie, Seth. But you are in my time, as I said. I called for you and you came ahead to me. I need for you to understand that this is your world."

"My world has magick. There is no magick here," he whispered. His mouth had gone dry. He licked at his lips, searching for moisture.

Apollo nodded his head. "Yes, the magick is gone. The darkness has swallowed it up and spit it out to somewhere far from here. I must find a way to bring it back. Magick feeds this world of yours. Without magick, the darkness lives."

"So without magick, darkness reigns. There was life here when there was magick. We had Helios, the stars, and Luna when we had magick," stated Seth. He ticked these off on his fingers. "Somehow, the magick left and darkness arrived."

"Yes," agreed Apollo.

Seth took a deep breath. "You said the darkness was seeping into my world on the night of the celebration. How was it seeping in? Maybe I can stop it from coming and taking the magick."

Apollo shook his head and croaked, "No, it is too late. Look around you, Seth. All is lost. How can this change now?"

Seth folded his wings flat against his back. "But…this is your time, not my time. You say that you brought me here. So there must be something I can do to change this outcome. Tell me how it changed at the celebration. I don't remember any darkness at the celebration. In fact," he assured himself, "there was much beauty when Jayne created the starlight flowers. The stars were shining brightly that night. They twinkled in the sky. Where was the darkness, Apollo?"

"It was there, with all of you. It was brewing within Faerie. Alexander knew about it, but he could not see it. He could not feel it. He dismissed it. Alexander was too focused on your training. He forgot about why he was training your kind." Apollo took a shuddering breath.

Seth knelt down and looked Apollo directly in the eyes. "Alexander missed the darkness? So he might know what the darkness is? Send me home, and I will find the cause of this darkness. I will make certain that Alexander notices the darkness and helps us to fight it."

"You are already home," answered Apollo.

Seth sat up in bed. His heart was pounding and his wings were fluttering in a panic. The breeze pushed the curtain aside and allowed the light of Luna to shine on his bed. He rubbed his eyes and climbed out of bed. Seth hurried over to the window. He looked up into the night sky to find all of the stars securely in their place, bouncing their light off of Luna. He breathed a sigh of relief. "It has not yet happened."

CHAPTER 10

Ryan got up from the breakfast table and cleared his dishes into the sink. His younger brother, Andre, stirred the food around his plate. "You really should eat your breakfast, Andre," Ryan mentioned. He watched his brother scowl in his direction. He stopped pushing the beans and began to pile them on top of each other so that they looked like a pile of black pebbles. Ryan left the dishes in the sink and went to sit beside his brother. "Why are you not eating?"

Andre shrugged his shoulders. "I don't like cold food."

Ryan touched one of the black beans. "It wasn't cold when they were placed on your plate."

"I'm not hungry," sighed Andre. "I want to go play."

Ryan nodded his head in understanding. "Yeah, I too want to play."

Andre looked at his brother. "Really?"

"Yes, I like to play lots," responded Ryan. "Let's go play now," he suggested as the thought entered his mind.

"Don't you have to go learn something today?" enquired Andre.

Ryan glanced around the kitchen. "Maybe later. Let's go play outside in the garden now. Maybe we can throw a ball around."

Andre got up from the table quickly. "I'll go get the ball and meet you in the garden," he gushed. He ran out of the kitchen with his wings lifting him slightly off the floor.

Ryan stepped into the sunshine and down the kitchen steps. Morning crickets were singing in the flower garden. Sparrows scattered along the grass, pecking at bugs attempting to hide. Ryan crossed the lawn and stood under a maple tree. He leaned his back against the bark and crossed his arms. He scuffed his bare foot on a root reaching out of the earth. The roughness of the bark on the bottom of his foot felt comforting, as though he was a part of the tree. Ryan pushed against the bark harder, breaking off the flaky skin of his heel. It was not until his brother stood in front of him with a ball and a look of shock that he noticed the blood seeping from his foot.

"Why are you bleeding, Ryan?" asked Andre quietly.

"I'm not bleeding," Ryan insisted. He looked at the blood covering the root of the tree. His foot was smeared in blood, dirt, and grass.

"Then where is the blood from?" questioned his brother.

"I don't know," said Ryan. He pushed off from the tree and grabbed the ball from Andre. "Let's play ball. You go near the begonia's and I'll throw to you."

Andre ran over to the edge of the flower garden and held his hands together as though catching water from a stream. He crouched low to the ground and waited for Ryan to throw the ball. Ryan tossed the ball up and down in his hand. He watched it spin in the air before landing in his palm. "Are you ready?" he called.

Andre nodded his head furtively, "Ready!" He wiggled his bum and reached for the ball. Ryan swung his arm behind him, and threw the ball as he took a step forward. Andre closed his eyes and reached for it. A soft thud indicated that the ball had flown passed him and into the flower garden. Andre opened his eyes and looked behind him to where the ball rested. The yellow begonia was flattened under the ball.

Ryan danced on the heels of his feet, while he waited for his brother to gather the ball and toss it back to him. Bits of grass stuck to the bottom of his bloody foot. He rubbed it against his other calf as he spun in a circle. His purple wings opened up and stretched. He tilted his face to the sun and called out to his brother, "Andre! Watch me!" He lifted into the air and spun around quickly. He smiled pleasantly as he heard his brother clapping.

"Good dancing, Ryan!" Andre yelled. Andre tossed the ball to Ryan, being sure to aim high into the air. Ryan did not notice the ball until it nicked his right wing.

"Ouch!" he screamed. "Why'd you do that?" He dropped to the ground and picked up the ball. He threw it hard towards their home in the birch tree where it bounced off the tree and rolled to a stop at the bottom of the kitchen stairs.

Andre ran towards his big brother. "I wanted you to catch the ball! We were playing ball!" He stumbled as he reached his brother.

Ryan glared at Andre. "Couldn't you see that I was dancing?"

"But we were playing ball," whimpered Andre.

"Well, we aren't playing ball now," Ryan stated. He shook his wings in an attempt to shed the sting from the ball.

"Then what do you want to do?" quipped Andre. He began to bounce on his legs, jumping around Ryan.

"We could go find some other faeries to play with," suggested Ryan. "Maybe they'll have some ideas."

Andre responded, "I'll tell Mom." He rushed away to the kitchen door etched inside the tree. He took the steps two at a time and left the door wide open.

Ryan rubbed his foot in the grass, attempting to brush off the bits of dirt and drying blood. He bent over and sniffed at a begonia. A small beetle scuttled at the base of the flower stock. Ryan touched the hard beetle shell with his index finger. The beetle scurried away and burrowed into the dirt. Ryan stood up straight and stepped backwards away from the flower garden. He tripped and stumbled as he crashed into something behind him.

"Uff," said the obstacle. Ryan found himself lying atop of Seth, whose thick glasses had become lopsided. Ryan rolled off of his colleague and pushed himself up from the ground. He offered his hand to Seth and helped the faerie back onto his feet.

"Hello Seth. How was it that you were under me when I fell?" asked Ryan.

Seth readjusted his glasses and brushed the dirt from his clothing. "I wasn't under you to begin with. You fell on me! I was waiting for you to turn around before I called 'hello'. I didn't want to startle you."

Ryan tilted his head to the left and examined his friend. "Yes, you were under me. I didn't see you behind me."

Seth shook his head. "Of course you didn't see me behind you. How could you see me from behind when you have eyes in the front of your head?"

"I have eyes on my face, not on the front of my head," Ryan insisted. He stretched out his leg and lifted himself off the ground with his wings.

"Anyway," Seth went on, "I've come to see if you want to fly together to our mid-morning lesson." He rubbed his right knee.

"What lesson?" enquired Ryan. "I don't remember a lesson for this morning."

"I figured you wouldn't remember the lesson," insisted Seth, "so I came to get you. Remember what Alexander said? We were to meet mid-morning today rather than after the noon meal. He said there was something special he wanted to show us."

"When did you hear of this?" Ryan persisted. "There was no conversation about this. I'd have remembered."

"Yeah, sure you would've," mumbled Seth.

The kitchen door swung wide open and Andre came flying out into the yard. "Mom says we can go wherever we want. We're to be back for noon meal." His cheeks were flushed in anticipation. He stopped in mid-air when he noticed Seth. "Hey Seth! Are you joining Ryan and I on a play date?"

Seth stepped forward and touched Andre's hand. "No, we have a lesson this morning with Alexander. We have to go and meet up with the other Guardians." He squeezed Andre's hand as the young faerie's lower lip began to quiver.

"Ryan didn't say anything about a lesson this morning. Why isn't it after our noon meal?" he sobbed.

"We have a very special lesson this morning. Alexander told us that it would take longer than our usual lesson time," responded Seth. "So we won't be back for the noon meal. But maybe we can play tomorrow morning," rushed Seth.

Andre slowly expanded his wings and lowered himself to the ground. "Tomorrow for sure?" he asked hopefully.

Seth nodded his head, "Definitely tomorrow. I promise."

Ryan gave his brother a quick hug. "Will you tell mom that I'm gone for an early lesson and won't be home until near night meal?"

Andre squeezed Ryan tightly. "Yeah, I'll tell her."

Ryan let Andre go and turned to face Seth. "Shall we fly? It'll be quicker."

"Oh yes. Besides, I'm looking for something that I might only see from above the flowers and bushes," responded Seth.

The two lifted off from the ground and caught a small gust of wind. "What are you looking for?" asked Ryan.

Seth shrugged. "I'm not sure, but I'll know what it is once I see it."

"How can you know what it is if you haven't seen it?"

"I think I will feel it inside. It will be familiar to me," stated Seth. "I've been looking for it all morning. I think it was at the celebration last night, but I wasn't aware of it then."

"So you are aware of it now?"

"Yes, I know it now," Seth assured him. "It's like how you didn't notice me behind you in the garden, but once you fell on me, you knew I was there."

"Okay. I understand that," said Ryan. "You fell on what you are looking for, but you can't see it."

"Sort of," responded Seth. "I felt it last night, but didn't know about it at the celebration. Now, I will be able to spot it because I've felt it and seen it."

Ryan contemplated these words as they continued to fly towards the lesson location. "Can I help you find it? Could you describe it to me so that I might be able to spot it?"

Seth paused in flight. He scratched his head. "I suppose that might work," he agreed. "I know that what I'm looking for is dark. It surrounds everything in darkness. So it feels desolate."

"Dark? Like when the lights go out?"

Seth shook his head. "No, it's more than that. It's like being inside a black hole. So inside yourself, it feels the same as a black hole."

Ryan tilted his head and looked quizzically at Seth before he spoke, "You can feel a black hole? Is that like having a hole from the front of your stomach to your back?"

Seth laughed. "No! It's just a feeling."

"Then how can you see a feeling?"

"You can see it because it is all darkness," responded Seth.

Ryan bit his lip. "You can see the darkness, but it isn't like when the lights are turned off. I don't understand."

Seth sighed, "Maybe you have to experience it to understand. When I see it, I'll point it out to you." He moved his wings and began to fly again.

CHAPTER 11

Alexander rummaged through his rucksack, which rested on a flat rock. Two glass vials clicked together as he pushed them aside. His fingers grasped a solid, rectangular box of Alexandrite. He pulled this out and placed it beside his rucksack. As the sunlight touched the crystal, its appearance of red-violet transformed into the green of life. Alexander ran his fingers over the surface; he could feel the etchings of knowledge that encompassed the crystal. His smile began inside and spread to his entire body.

At the sound of laughter, Alexander turned to greet Jayne and Geoff. The two of them descended upon a large mushroom while holding hands. Geoff brushed a wisp of hair out of Jayne's face. She stepped down off the mushroom and walked over to Alexander. "Oh, Alexander, I'm so excited to be here today. I can feel the healing in this area," she exclaimed. Jayne wrapped her short arms around Alexander and gave him a big hug.

"Jayne, I knew that you would be the first to feel the healing magick here. Because of that, I knew that our lesson today must take place this morning. I feel that we will soon

need the healing of this land. The magick is changing,"
insisted Alexander.

"How's it changing?" inquired Geoff as he walked
slowly towards the two. His bare feet and swollen joins were
silent on the soft grass.

Alexander looked up to the sky, as though searching
for the right words. "I cannot quite tell how it is changing,
Geoff, but I feel the change. It is a shift so small that it could
almost be missed. I have been a part of this world for
millennia, yet this is the first time I cannot place words on the
change in magick."

"Is there something we can do to help?" asked Geoff.

"Yes, there must be something we can do to identify
the change," encouraged Jayne. She fluttered her wings.

"That is my hope as well," responded Alexander.
"Today, I am teaching all of you a lesson that is extremely
secret. I have not shared the importance and location of this
specific land with any other super-powered faerie." He
watched as Sabrina and Shoshana entered the clearing. "Yet I
know that the time to share this land is now. It is essential that
I do so today, which is why I made sure you had the proper
instructions on how to find this particular purple bush."

"Hello!" called Shoshana as she and Sabrina came over
to the small group. They each had a small rucksack dangling
from one shoulder. "We brought water and berries for
everyone, as we weren't certain how long we'd be here
today."

"Also, since we've never been to this particular spot,
we thought that a snack of some sort would be welcome,"
added Sabrina.

"Oh," responded Geoff, "snacks are always welcome!"

Jayne laughed. She turned her head to the sky just as
Javier and Mercury appeared over the treetops. Not far behind
the two were Georgia and Mercury. Once they landed, they all
surrounded Alexander, as though protecting him in a circle.
"My mother complained this morning about how early I was

leaving for class," said Sabrina. "She was hoping that I'd help her with some chores. However, I told her that this comes first. So she sent along some snacks and water, as she insisted that if we were meeting this early, then we must have a long day ahead of us."

"That was extremely thoughtful of your mother," replied Alexander. "Remind me to thank her when next I see her." He turned to the group and rubbed his hands together. "As much as I would like to get started, I will, of course, await the arrival of Seth and Ryan before I continue."

"Oh, this sounds exciting!" exclaimed Mercury. She began to dance around, letting her arms move in the air. A spark of fire flashed on her right palm before turning to smoke.

"Good thing you don't have any sticks near Mercury, eh Javier?" teased Georgia.

Javier blanched. "What do you know about sticks?"

Georgia shrugged her shoulders and twitched her wings. "I know enough about sticks. They go great with fire, but sometimes they go just as well with water." She winked at Javier. He stepped back and turned away from her.

"Billy must have told her," he mumbled. "How else would she know?"

Georgia placed her hand on Javier's shoulder and whispered in his ear, "Someone saw the two of you floating around the lake. Although, from what I heard, it seems there was more swimming than floating," she paused and then added, "It sounds like a great deal of fun."

Javier twitched his wings at the memory. "Yeah, it was a lot of fun," he agreed as he turned back to her. He tilted his head to the side. "Maybe you'd like to come for a float on the raft next time?"

Georgia's eyes lit up. "Oh, I would love to! If Billy is in charge, then I could always freeze everything so we don't spend most of our time in the water."

Javier and Georgia laughed. Javier heard the voices of Ryan and Seth before they could be seen over the treetops. He looked up to the sky and waved at them in welcome. "Now we can get started on this secretive lesson," he stated. "I must admit that I'm quite curious."

Alexander turned from the group and picked up the Alexandrite box. He held it tightly, tilting it in the sunlight. The brilliant greens sparkled and changed as he turned the box around in his hands. The faeries watched silently, mesmerized with its beauty. "Today, I will teach you of where all magick was born. I will teach you of the beginning of time, the importance of your third eye, your heart, and your base chakras. I will teach you of regenerative power, rebirth, and the changing of ones world. This box is known as Alexandrite. It is the astrological sign of Scorpio. It facilitates in the connectedness of all nature, both within and around us. What you learn today must not be shared. Only the gods, the angels, and those who have come before us know of this sacred crystal."

Seth sucked in the air around him. "The birth of magick," he breathed.

Javier twitched his ears as he absorbed what Alexander had just shared and the whisper of Seth. He stepped forward to view the Alexandrite box closer and reached out his fingers towards the box. At Alexander's nod of approval, Javier touched the box in Alexander's hands. Instant warmth spread from his fingertips to the lumpy soles of his feet. He fluttered his wings in eagerness, which lifted him off the ground. Visions of the past filtered through his mind. "Wow," he whispered as he removed his fingers from the top of the box. He took a moment to recompose himself and float back down to the ground. He stared intently into Alexander's eyes. "How do you hold the box as though it doesn't contain all of that?"

Alexander smiled at Javier, as a father would at his knowledgeable child. "I have a special gift which prevents me from being affected by the birth of magick."

"Why don't I have that gift?" inquired Javier.

"You are made of magick, therefore you must be affected by magick at all times. Without magick, you would be unable to access your special gifts. Each of you," Alexander turned to address the group before him, "has a special gift. Without magick, your gifts would be mute. They would not work."

Seth stepped forward. He searched Alexander's face before asking, "Then how do we keep the magick alive? How do we prevent it from disappearing and entering the darkness?"

Alexander paused in an attempt to discern the trouble flooding Seth's features. "I will teach you today how to keep that magick alive, for once it is gone, there is no way to retrieve it back into our world. It is our world that keeps balance between all worlds. If our magick is gone, then also all other worlds are gone into darkness. It is our job," he expanded his arms to include everyone there, "to keep the magick from dying."

Several gasps escaped the mouths of the superhero group. Seth sucked in his breath, feeling despair take over his soul. He fought against it, eager to keep focus on the learning at hand. It was up to him to prevent magick from disappearing, because if he could not stop the darkness seeping, then he would not be able to bring the magick back and save all that was lost in Apollo's time. He had thought that there was a way to fix the darkness, but now he understood that the only way to fix the darkness was to stop the darkness from growing and taking over the world.

"I'm ready to learn all that you have to teach about the birth of magick," declared Seth. He stepped forward to stand beside Alexander. "I am certain that we are all ready to learn today. I feel the importance of this lesson, as I'm sure you all must feel it too."

Shoshana stepped forward and took Seth's left hand. She placed it over her heart chakra. "I feel the despair within you," she whispered to him. "I'll do all that I can to help you eradicate this despair. I don't know why it appears so suddenly in you, but I assure you that I will do whatever you think will help to end it."

Alexander held tightly to the Alexandrite. He picked up his rucksack with his free hand and slung it over his shoulder. "My wondrous pupils, please, follow me." He touched a deep purple bush with his hand. The mound opened in the ground to reveal an ancient, dirt stairwell. Alexander descended into the cavern. As each faerie followed him, a soft hymn swelled in the stairwell as though in welcome. Behind Javier the entrance closed, enveloping the entire group in a soft glow that wrapped itself along each step.

CHAPTER 12

Shoshana took the last step of the stairwell carefully. She could feel the magick, the life, and the knowledge before she came full force into the crystal cavern. She allowed the love to fill her very soul, to encompass her feelings and her thoughts. The warmth of it spread throughout her being, touching each cell and breaking forth to multiply. She lifted her head and spread her wings as far as they would reach. Shoshana smiled and began to laugh at the joy flooding through her.

She felt the wonder in the minds of the others. There were gasps of surprise and shock as each faerie entered the cavern. Shoshana noted the same physical reactions throughout the group. Although, she also noticed the deep sadness and fear bound inside of Seth. She moved over to him and touched his short arm with her left hand. "There is nothing to fear here," she whispered to him. "I can feel only complete love and peace in this place. Nothing to fear. Why do you hold such fear and sadness in your heart?"

Seth looked deep into her eyes before answering. His tongue was thick with clouded words unsaid. "Without magick, there is nothing; all is darkness." He bowed his head. A tear trickled down his round cheek.

Shoshana enveloped Seth in a deep hug. "Fear not, my Seth, for the most powerful magick surrounds us. Darkness cannot descend upon this sacred ground. Magick."

Javier joined the two. "I can hear the voices of those who've been here before," he said to Seth and Shoshana. "They're pleased that we have come. It's as though they are relieved, as though they've been waiting since the beginning of time."

"You don't understand," stated Seth. "There's a darkness seeping into our world. It's a darkness that destroys magick, and us with it."

Shoshana shook her head, "No, Seth, that is not possible. We belong in a world which keeps balance between all that is, all that was, and all that will be. Our magick and our special powers allow us to fight darkness. As long as we work together, nothing can destroy our legacy."

"Shoshana's correct," agreed Javier. "The voices here are rejoicing, they are not fearful or sad. The beings attached to these voices would know if something were infringing on our legacy."

Seth searched their faces. He brushed away a tear with his right hand. "I have seen the darkness," he croaked. "It is all encompassing. There is no magick within this darkness." He paused before whispering, "And there is no us."

Shoshana felt Seth's soul plummet inside his body. She reached for him again, pulling him toward her, toward her light. "We're here right now," she told him. "We are all here in this most magickal of places. Perhaps we can ask for guidance in fighting this darkness you've seen. If we ask, maybe Javier will receive an answer in the voices."

"Yes," Javier nodded, "I can hear them assuring me that they have answers. We only need to ask the right questions."

"Would you all gather around the pool?" Alexander spoke. He held the Alexandrite box in his dark hands. His feet were bare, as he had taken off his shoes and placed them beside his rucksack. Alexander stood not far from the magnificent pool that surrounded the most amazing crystal the faeries had ever laid eyes upon. Swirls of pale blue and light pink moved about in the water. The soft hymn that could be heard in the stairwell pulsed forth from the crystal. Although the Alexandrite appeared green above ground, it had now become a deep red-violet. Rays of the red-violet reached out from the box and touched the large clear quartz crystal in the middle of the pool.

The faeries created a semi-circle around Alexander, facing the pool and crystal. "As I mentioned above ground, you are here to learn of where all magick was born. It is this cavern which holds all the secrets to our world, and to those worlds we protect from our position here. This box I hold was carved from the bowels of this Mother Crystal. Although she is made of clear quartz, her roots are of Alexandrite. She is made of record keeper crystals and trans-channelling crystals. Mother Crystal stores all wisdom and she is able to channel this wisdom from the gods and goddesses to us. We are able to send questions through her to the angels and to the gods and goddesses. It was Mother Crystal who told of my arrival many millennia ago. She was able to heal my broken soul so that I would in turn bring all of you to her on this day."

Alexander took a step back. The pool lapped at his bare feet. "This pool, which surrounds Mother Crystal, is what some might call The Fountain of Youth." He placed the Alexandrite box into the water. "Many worlds have beings who believe that The Fountain of Youth will make one physically young and immortal. Those beings are incorrect in their belief. This magickal water does not make one young again, nor does it keep one young. It does, however, provide an immortality of sorts."

Mercury broke the semi-circle to step towards the pool. She lifted her hands, palms up. A spark turned into a flame on her right palm. She held out this flame and placed it in the pool where it floated upon the water, circling Mother Crystal. "I offer my gift to you in thanks for all that I can do with it." Mercury took a few steps back from the pool and rejoined the faeries.

Jayne squeezed Mercury's hand. She let go and took Geoff's hand as she led him to the pool. "I give thanks for my gift of healing," she said. Jayne touched the pool with her fingers. Forget-me-not blossoms sprung from her fingertips. They rained down into the pool, coming to the surface as they joined the flame around Mother Crystal.

Geoff crouched low to the ground. His feet and hands shrank and turned green. Webbed feet sprouted as he metamorphosed into an amphibian. He flicked out his long tongue and hopped into the translucent pool. He swam beneath the surface, lapping around Mother Crystal. Her hymn changed from soft to a deep throb. As Geoff resurfaced near the edge of the pool, he shifted to his faerie features and walked out of the pool. Water dripped from his clothes and wings. He rejoined the semi-circle, emanating a peaceful quiet.

Alexander bowed to the group of faeries. "I am certain that Mother Crystal is pleased with your offerings," he acknowledged.

Shoshana nodded in agreement, "I can feel a new pleasure within this cavern. I can't decipher from where it originates, but I can assure you that it exists."

Javier spoke quietly, "There are many beings who surround us here. They're all pleased with our offerings. There seems to be much chatter about our arrival being long expected."

"Yes," agreed Alexander. "Many moons ago, the archangels came to this cavern on a regular basis. They conversed with a seer, one who nurtured the superhero faeries. She went by the name of Ice Moon. She was one with earth, fire, water, air, and spirit. She foretold of a great threat to come, which your kind is required to fight. She read the prophecy that declared me as the saviour who would train all the Guardians and prepare you for this threat." He viewed the group before him, knowing that they still had much to learn and very little time left in which to learn it.

"You know of the threat?" Seth asked tentatively.

Alexander stepped towards Seth. "Yes, I know of the threat. I know that it is already seeping into our world, but I have not yet located the source."

"It's darkness," stated Seth. "I've seen the darkness. It destroys the balance between worlds."

Jayne shivered at these words. Mercury paced back and forth. Ryan twitched, causing a pebble to roll across the cavern floor and bounce against the wall. Georgia lifted her hands and froze the water lapping in the pool. Sabrina flitted in and out of visibility. Shoshana moved closer to Seth and took his hand in hers.

"Then I suggest we get started with our lesson," said Alexander. "The only way to fight the darkness is to learn and train so that we can conquer it before it destroys our world."

"Yes, let's learn to fight this darkness," agreed Ryan.

"As I was saying, Ice Moon prophesied of my arrival and of the ultimate threat that all of you here will have to fight. I have been training and teaching superhero faeries for millennia. You are the first group whom I feel will need to know about Mother Crystal and this cavern. I also feel the ultimate threat seeping into Faerie. Now, let me tell you about Mother Crystal." Alexander gestured for the faeries to sit at the waters edge.

"Mother Crystal is connected to all worlds and non-worlds. She was formed long before our world came to be. She is the source of all magick. Mother Crystal built our world around herself, so to speak. This is why our world is filled with magick and magickal folk. Other worlds have a touch of Mother Crystal, as of course she is connected to them as well.

In those worlds, however, magick is often hidden from most of the creatures. Our kind can be born into those worlds, but we are often only seen by the eyes of believers."

Sabrina asked, "Who would not believe in us?"

The others turned to her, nodding their heads with the same question unspoken on their lips. "I am afraid that there are many creatures who have difficulty believing in our magickal kind. However, that is not important in this lesson," answered Alexander. "What matters is that we live in Faerie with Mother Crystal. It is with her help that we are able to balance all worlds and all of nature. When we are in great need, the gods and angels will contact us through Mother Crystal. Because Ice Moon has long been gone, the connections between gods and us have been limited. I believe that now is the time for us to reconnect with them in this cavern."

"What if they are disappointed in us?" inquired Seth. "What if we haven't done as they hoped? Will they still be willing to converse with us?"

"Converse," uttered Shoshana.

"They will always be willing to converse with us, Seth, even if they are not pleased," assured Alexander. "We are important in the whole scheme of things. We will certainly make mistakes in our lives, yet that will not displease the gods. We learn from our mistakes. We teach these lessons to each other in hopes of preventing the same mistakes from happening over and over. If we inadvertently anger the gods, then of course they will find a way to let us know so that we may rectify the mistake."

"What if we can't fix our mistake? What if it's too big to fix?" quivered Seth. He squeezed Shoshana's hand.

Alexander sighed. He rubbed his chin and looked down at his feet. "Then, Seth, I can only hope that the gods and Mother Crystal will guide us in such a way as to mend said mistake."

"How do we access Mother Crystal?" asked Jayne. "That is why we are here, isn't it?" She stepped forward to better view the Alexandrite and Mother Crystal.

"Yes, Jayne, we are here to converse with Mother Crystal, to access her magick through our own gifts, and to converse with the gods," stated Alexander. "Javier has a special gift which allows him to hear the gods and Mother Crystal without touching her. The rest of us must place our hands directly on her to converse with her and the gods. Shoshana is able to feel the emotions of Mother Crystal and therefore the emotions of the gods through her. I have placed the Alexandrite in the water so that it will provide a more solid connection for us all. Because I am not Faerie, I require the use of the Alexandrite box to converse with Mother Crystal. It was forged for such a purpose, as the prophecy indicated that I would not be Faerie."

Georgia tilted her head toward the Alexandrite box and its connection to the crystal. "Is there any special way in which we're to touch the crystal? Do we need to say any type of spell? Or do we just swim to her and touch her with our fingers? Or do we place our entire palm on her?"

"It will most likely be different for each of you," responded Alexander. "I encourage each of you to search within yourselves for what you think will best fit your individual preferences. It may take a bit of experimenting. Rest assured, we will remain here until each of you has successfully contacted Mother Crystal."

CHAPTER 13

Sabrina broke from the group and limped over to the edge of the pool. "I'm willing to attempt a connection first," she said with eagerness. She did not wait for an answer, but plummeted into the pool of pinks, blues, and purples. She surfaced with a flourish and shook her wet blond hair. Sabrina shimmered in the pool and disappeared to the naked eye. She felt the invisibility cloak her body and soul. With a swift kick of her good leg, Sabrina began to swim toward Mother Crystal.

She dove down again to examine the crystal from the bottom of the pool. Edges peaked out at different angles below the surface. Sabrina touched the crystal tentatively, with great respect. Mother Crystal felt smooth and at one with the water. She was wet, yet not slippery. Sabrina ran her fingers along the crystal as she swam back to the surface. She breathed deeply of the air, searching for a particular scent that might give her a hint of how to communicate.

As though in answer to her unasked question, Sabrina felt her invisibility cloak short-circuiting. She could see her hands touching Mother Crystal, and then disappear from her vision. Cold touched the tips of her fingers as they enveloped her invisibility yet again. A warm, mothering voice whispered in her ears, "What can I do for you, my child? You must have questions that I can answer for you."

Sabrina quickly retracted her hand. She gasped for the air in a short start. Slowly, Sabrina placed her fingers upon Mother Crystal again. "I'm unsure of what I must ask," she responded out loud. "I didn't know of you before today, therefore I have no idea of what I need from you or what you need from me."

"I have known of your arrival since before time began," Mother Crystal said. "You have great gifts. Be certain to use these gifts for good, even when the choice appears difficult. Your powers are always magnified when with others of your kind."

"Yes, I do find when around my colleagues that I can turn faster and for longer periods of time," Sabrina stated. "I've been working on enveloping more than two others into my invisibility field. Instinct tells me that this is necessary. I haven't shared this with Alexander or the other faeries. I've been working on this in secret, in hopes that it'll work. I'd hate to share this idea and then find out it's impossible."

"Always follow your instincts, Sabrina. They often know what your head does not. You will be able to envelope others in your field, but really you should share this idea with Alexander. He has much magic and knowledge that can benefit this exercise. Ask him for private lessons if you do not yet feel comfortable sharing with your colleagues. Your power of invisibility is necessary for the darkness which looms ahead."

Sabrina ran the palm of her hand along Mother Crystal. The colours changed as she touched the smooth crystal. "Seth mentioned the darkness. He's afraid today. I keep thinking of the expression 'jump out of ones skin' when I look at him." She paused, then added, "Is there something I can do for Seth to ease his fear?"

"Just listen to him. He is not yet sure about the darkness. His fear stems from the unknown. Once the darkness becomes tangible, he will be able to fight and his fear will turn to strength. Go now, my child. Learn about your invisibility cloaking with Alexander. Expand your powers so that you can access them at full strength when the time comes."

Sabrina touched her lips to the crystal and pushed away into the pool. She moved her wings and shook her invisibility as she reached the edge of the pool. A smile spread across her face. Her eyes twinkled with satisfaction and excitement. "She spoke with me," declared Sabrina. "She truly spoke with me." Sabrina lifted herself out of the water. Her clothes dripped on the cavern floor and water trickled from her blond streaks. "She knew me, as though we'd always been a part of each other."

"How does she sound?" inquired Ryan. He shuffled forward, eager to hear about the experience. "Is she kind? Is she angry?"

"She is certainly kind," assured Sabrina. "Her voice is soft. It felt like she was crooning a baby. You know how a mother has such a caring, soft voice for a baby? That's how she sounds."

Shoshana stepped forward. She placed her hand on Sabrina's shoulder. "You have an inner peace now. Somehow your soul is singing about a piece that is now complete. Before you entered the pool your soul didn't even know that it was missing something. Now, your soul sings, like when Jayne sings vegetation to life." She glanced back at Jayne and smiled.

Shoshana turned from the group and fluttered to the pool edge, her wings carrying her until she released them and allowed herself to drop into the swirling pool of pinks and blues. She used her wings to keep her head and shoulders above the water. She took her time, gently swimming over to the beautiful crystal waiting for her in the middle of the pool.

Shoshana touched the side of the clear crystal quartz and hauled herself out of the water, so that she was able to sit upon one of the edges with a nook in it.

"You are more beautiful than anything I've ever seen," Shoshana told Mother Crystal. "I know that you're warm and loving. I can feel the peace emanating from within you. Is there anything that I can do to honour you?"

"Never forget who you are and where you have come from," Mother Crystal replied. "You have a gift that could cause you to get lost in the feelings of others. Be sure to ground yourself before you take on the emotions of others. Keep yourself separate and make certain to feed your own soul before you feed others emotionally."

"Sometimes I need to get lost in the emotions of others," admitted Shoshana. "It gives me a relief from my own troubles, when I find myself overwhelmed."

"Child, you become overwhelmed when you cannot separate your own feelings from the feelings of others. Focusing on their emotions is what actually causes you to become flustered and unsure of what is happening around you. It is extremely important for your own well being that you place yourself first and everyone else second. It is the only way in which you can be truly helpful," Mother Crystal concluded.

Shoshana sighed. "I'll do my best to follow your advice. It will not be easy for me, as I've always been in-tune with the feelings of everyone else. I don't really know who I am without connecting to those around me."

"Then it is time to find out who you are as an individual, my dear Shoshana. You will like what you find in yourself. Spend some time alone and get to know the inner you," she suggested.

Shoshana stood. She blew a kiss to Mother Crystal and flew away from the pulsing quartz. She nestled herself between Javier and Ryan, where she attempted to tune out their feelings of excitement and anxiety about connecting with such a magickal being who gave birth to all the magick in this realm. Shoshana wrapped her arms around her body and held tight to the comprehension that she was an individual.

"I'd like to go next," Ryan announced to the group. He lifted his arm and vanished from sight. The group barely had time to blink before Ryan reappeared atop Mother Crystal. He ran his fingers over the edges of her tip. She was smooth to touch, and she emitted warmth that spread through Ryan. He examined her closely, watching the colours inside her change ever so slightly.

"So you are the birth of all magick," he said to her. "I like magick, so thank you for giving it to me. I like being a special faerie, too. Sometimes it's difficult to do things that come easier to my family, but in the end, I wouldn't want to be anyone else. Besides, I have the power to move from one space to another just with thinking of it. It comes in really handy, like when I'm too tired at the end of a lesson to walk or fly home."

"Ryan," addressed Mother Crystal, "you are more than special to me. You have the gift to think things through and to enjoy every minute of every day. When you refuse to do something, no one is able to persuade you to do what you do not want to do. Your family means a great deal to you. Keep them close to your heart at all times. Put them before your responsibilities as a Guardian. For when you are old and are examining the parts of your life that mean the most to you, you will be forever grateful that you always included your family first."

Ryan glanced down at his fingers, which he was twisting together. "Yeah, I love my family. We always do fun activities together, and we help each other with chores. My mother and father are very kind."

"You have inherited their kindness, Ryan. When things seem frustrating or there appears to be no end to a task that is difficult, think of the kindness and the patience your parents have instilled in you. Use that also as strength. You are loved very much," she concluded.

"Thank you," whispered Ryan. He took a deep breath and vanished from the perch upon which he had been standing. Ryan stood beside Mercury before she had even registered that he was no longer with Mother Crystal.

Mercury jumped in alarm and tossed out two flames from her fingers, which she quickly stepped on before they took on a life of their own. "Are you feeling a little jumpy, Mercury?" teased Shoshana.

Mercury frowned at Shoshana. "Very funny. I was so mesmerized by the beauty of this cavern, that I was startled when Ryan was suddenly beside me. I wasn't paying attention to my immediate surroundings."

Jayne giggled. "I'll say. I haven't seen you spark like that since the time we were all hiding in the bushes watching you dance to the music in your head."

Javier began to laugh, although he attempted to stifle it with his hand over his mouth. "Sorry," he said between laughter.

"The best part of that dance was when Georgia kept freezing Mercury in mid-skip and she would let the flames keep moving so that Mercury was completely confused with the distance of her flames," giggled Seth.

"Oh yes, that was too funny," chastised Mercury. She flicked her fingers before closing them into fists that she kept at her sides.

Jayne beat her wings to lift herself into the air. "I think that it's my turn, if no one objects." She glanced at everyone milling about and took flight across the expanse between where she began and where Mother Crystal awaited her arrival. Jayne hovered just above the pool, beside the crystal. She opened her hand to create a starlight flower. It bloomed rather quickly, causing Jayne to gasp in wonder. The petals moved like wings and clung to Mother Crystal.

"You create the most beautiful flowers, Jayne," Mother Crystal said to her. "I am certain that you are able to make various flowers for different occasions, but I know that these particular flowers grow when you are most happy and content. There will come a time when more than just flowers will be required of you. You have the ability to heal others physically, but remember that you cannot remove emotional scars from those you love."

"Oh, I'm learning that," admitted Jayne. "There've been times when I've noticed someone is sad and I've touched them with the intention of taking away their sadness. It seemed to me that when I did that, I felt a touch of their pain."

"That is the consequence of attempting to do what is not meant to be done. Living beings must feel inner pain to grow and become strong in themselves. Without trauma and emotional struggles, the living become stagnant."

Jayne held out her hand and waved her fingers. The starlight flower shimmered, turned into a star, and shot forward and into the pool below. As though fireworks were exploding, the star erupted from all points and shot silver through the pool before settling back to the pinks. Jayne gazed one last time at Mother Crystal, waved a kiss at her, and flew back to Geoff, who watched her from the edge of the pool. Geoff reached out his hand, which Jayne put in her own.

Mercury skipped over to the pool. She opened the palm of her hand and formed a flame of orange, blue, yellow, and red. She placed this flame onto the surface of the pool and flicked her wrist. The flame danced across the water and circled around Mother Crystal. The flame submerged and turned to smoke, which corked up between the cavern walls to the world outside.

Mercury stepped into the pool. She splashed the water with her feet and spun around with her arms wide open. She lifted her legs and danced about, allowing the water to spray droplets upon her clothing. Mercury opened her wings and took to the air, flying close to Mother Crystal. She found the same ledge upon which Ryan had perched. She stood with the soles of her feet on that perch. "I have a fire that burns within me. It licks at my soul and must come out in the form of flames," she told the crystal. "I'm a free spirit. I like to dance and jump and fly wherever I might find myself."

"You have a warm heart, Mercury. This is what burns inside you. Your gift of fire is truly a reflection of your soul. You have great wisdom and you are able to sort it out in your thoughts. Others may find you to be flighty or unfocused, but when you move, you are actually cataloguing these ideas that come all at once."

"Sometimes I don't understand why others can't open their minds to everything in this universe. Why is it that they can't see all the possibilities as I do?" she asked with concern.

"Mercury, others have their own priorities and lessons to learn. Do not be concerned about how others think and what others do. Use what you know to build the strength that is so solid within your soul. Know that you are unique and well loved. Do not be concerned about how that appears when you are amongst those in your community. In time, you will be understood by many more than those who understand you now."

Mercury grasped a chunk of her hair and pulled at it, making a low screaming noise as she did. "Well, others may not understand me completely yet, but what they think is truly not my concern. I'll carry on being me, which will eventually be all that everyone needs." With that, Mercury took flight until she reached the first step on the stairwell. She sat down and placed her chin in her hands.

Seth repositioned his thick glasses upon his flat nose before he shuffled over to Mercury and placed a hand on her shoulder. Before anyone decided it was their turn, Seth flew over to Mother Crystal. He placed his feet in the pool and found a footing under the surface. He tentatively reached out and touched the beautiful crystal. She was warm to the touch, which spread to his feet and the water in which he stood.

"You have a very loyal friend who believes in you. When you think that you are all alone and no one will listen, this friend will follow you and be your companion when all seems lost. This friend knows who you truly are and he is proud to call you friend. It is with the assistance of this friend that you will be able to accomplish your destined task in this realm, Seth. Every day is a blessing," Mother Crystal said with great love in her voice.

"There's a darkness that is seeping into this world," stated Seth. "I fear that magick is going to die. I know that you're somehow connected to all the magick in this realm. So how is it that magick can disappear if you are here?"

Mother Crystal emitted more love and peace that enveloped Seth. "Magick can never truly die if you remember it and share that memory with those who follow," she declared.

Seth sighed. "I don't know how to fight against this darkness when I'm not sure how to voice it properly to the others."

"You will know what to do when the time comes, Seth. Believe in that."

Seth placed his hand over his heart. "I greatly appreciate the love and peace you have bestowed upon me at this time. I can only hope that it will be here," he drummed his fingers against his chest, "when I need it most." Seth fluttered his wings and returned to the group.

"She's amazing," Seth said once he had taken a seat on the ground at Mercury's feet. "I've never felt such," he touched his heart as he had done before, "peace."

Geoff let go of Jayne's hand and made his way over to Mother Crystal. Seth took his gaze away from Geoff, kept his eyes on the ground, and thought about what the mother of magick and life had told him. He had a loyal friend who believed in him more than he believed in himself. Seth glanced from one Guardian to the next. Although he loved these faeries and they loved him, he did not think that she had meant one of them. He sifted through his mind, thinking of all his friends, yet none of them stood out to him as more loyal than any of the others.

While Georgia and Javier took their turns communicating with Mother Crystal, Seth allowed his thoughts to roam and his heart to explore what had touched it when he came into the cavern. Yes, he had felt the darkness, as he had since his vision with Apollo. Seth knew that the darkness had not yet seeped into this cavern. Love and peace remained prominent, which of course was due to the life and the pure magick that reigned here. Although these thoughts played out in his mind, Seth had difficulty believing that only one of his friends would stay true to him.

"Now that you have all found a way in which to communicate with Mother Crystal, I would like for us to gather on the grass outside of this cavern. It is now time that I taught you about the Alexandrite and how it connects to nature," Alexander addressed the group with his usual calm voice. His hands were folded together in front of his chest. A smile played upon his lips. "Could everyone make their way up the stairwell and out into the early afternoon sunlight?"

"Is it afternoon already?" exclaimed Ryan.

"Couldn't you tell?" asked Javier. "My stomach has been rumbling for the past hour."

"Your stomach would rumble if it smelled burnt hibiscus on the fire," commented Georgia. She stepped around Javier and followed Mercury and Seth up the stairwell.

CHAPTER 14

Ryan perched upon a rock beside the purple bush outside the cavern. Georgia sat beside him while she examined her toes and rubbed off the dirt on her soles. Mercury had found a small mushroom upon which she could stand and watch everyone. Javier had planted himself on the grass and was picking at one of the blades. Geoff and Jayne stood together, holding hands and waiting for further instruction. Shoshana stood beside Seth. Sabrina was standing with her legs crossed in a yoga pose.

"Again, I would like to express how proud I am of each and every one of you with your success in communicating to Mother Crystal. When you are in need of clarification, she is able to listen and assist you in finding the right choices. Mother Crystal created this realm. She is the source of all magick and all life," remarked Alexander.

Sabrina asked, "Is that what made her so warm?"

"It is her love and her peace that make her warm," responded Alexander. "She is a life source, which in itself is warm. Her crystal could essentially be seen as her body, just as we have flesh that holds our souls and allows us to interact with biology. While we become cold or hot according to the elements of the world, Mother Crystal creates her temperature from the balance of nature."

"She really was able to calm my anxiety," offered Seth. "She knew me better than I know myself. It was like she could read my thoughts before they even entered my mind."

"Yes," agreed Jayne, "she's quite the healer. Simply being in her presence strengthened my superpowers. It was as though I were feeding off of her when I created my starlight flower. It makes me wonder if these gifts of mine truly do belong to me."

Alexander scratched his chin and searched Jayne's face. "Your superpowers do belong to you, Jayne. They were a gift from Mother Crystal. She is the source of pure magick; therefore, she is able to dispense unique magickal gifts to everyone who is destined to use them. She is also much more than just magick."

"You mentioned that she was here before the formation of our realm," interjected Geoff, "that she created our world. Can you tell us more about this?" He opened and closed his wings with a peaceful air about him.

"Mother Crystal has been around since before time existed. In a way, she brought about the beginning of time. She is part of a type of network so to speak. She is able to keep in contact with the gods, the goddesses, and other beings throughout the universes. Every life force, or energy force if you prefer, has a way of connecting with her. Because we are the realm meant to keep all other worlds in balance, she has provided us with the ability to use magick in so many ways. Some of you are able to interact with angels and gods, which is not common amongst beings of all the worlds. Granted, each world is given the opportunity to interact with such sentient beings. It is when no one believes in them any longer that they come back to us here and regenerate their life force." Alexander shuffled his feet in the dirt, stirring up a cloud of dust.

"Is that why I can see Archangel Michael and Apollo?" queried Seth. "Because I know that they exist?"

"We all know they exist, Seth," responded Alexander. "Your gift is unique to you, which reflects your ability to accept the unknown as the truth and the knowledge that things will sort themselves out. You are not like other seers whom I have come across in my millennia in this realm. You have visions that occur when your body is in its most relaxed state of being. Archangel Michael is available to all who ask for his help, but he chooses to stay around only a select few of the living on a regular basis. What you have with him is rare, Seth."

"Tell us more about the beginning of time," encouraged Georgia. "Time fascinates me."

"It would fascinate you, Georgia," stated Alexander. "To be able to freeze time and objects at your own will comes from when time began. Mother Crystal knew that time was not linear, that it moved about, twisting and turning into itself so that there was no end and no beginning, but a huge mass of cosmic strings crossing each other. She made certain that the magickal ability to freeze time would be available to certain individuals who understood how time worked."

"Why are we the first group of Guardians with whom you've chosen to share in this knowledge?" asked Javier. "Obviously, there's a darkness seeping into our realm, as Seth has informed us; but I don't understand why you wouldn't have shared this lesson before now."

Alexander paced back and forth amongst the faeries. "There was truly no need to bring any of my other Guardians to Mother Crystal. Perhaps that sounds belittling, but I assure you that had there been a need, I would certainly have introduced my other charges to her. When last I came here alone, Mother Crystal indicated that now was the time for you to be aware of her and to make an individual connection with her. All of you will need to know about her when this imminent threat reveals itself to us."

Alexander cleared his throat. "Mother Crystal has a regenerative power, which enhances your own rebirth through time. She gives clarity to your inner self and your physical self, which helps you to change our world. For example, all of the vegetation and the beings alive in our world have the ability to change and experience rebirth. A flower, which is born in the spring, grows in the summer, seeds in the fall, and rests in the winter, will be reborn again the following spring. The seasons change just as life changes."

"Caterpillars become a totally different species when they turn into butterflies," added Ryan.

"Exactly," agreed Alexander. "The alexandrite in Mother Crystal has regenerative power. She can provide a rebirth in our realm, which allows for change to occur. When we do not keep nature in balance for her, change will definitely take place; however, this change will be extremely slow."

Mercury stepped off of her mushroom. She skipped around the group and pulled at her hair. "We're all connected with nature, even when it falls out of balance," she informed the group. "We were born from our parents and we work in our community to help everyone make certain that all is well. Obviously, Mother Crystal is a part of this evolution. She must know when a change is coming. Do you think that she has found a way to let Seth know of this change, since he can feel this new darkness?"

Javier glanced over at Seth, who was still next to Shoshana. "Shouldn't Shoshana actually feel the darkness?" interrupted Javier.

"I feel it because Apollo pointed it out to me," Seth told him.

Shoshana shrugged her shoulders. "I can't always feel everything that's in this realm. I mostly have a connection to the feelings within a being and not something that's abstract, like what Seth is noticing."

"Each of you has a connection to Mother Crystal," said Alexander. "You had this connection even before you knew about her existence. So it is quite possible that Mother Crystal sent Apollo to share this information with Seth on her behalf. However, I do not think that we should speculate on the musings of Mother Crystal, the angels, and the gods. We must focus on what we do know and what we can do in each moment to assist in balancing nature."

"So what are we to do today, now that we know about the birth of magick?" asked Geoff. "Do we keep this a secret or do we share this knowledge in an attempt to balance more of nature? I guess what I want to know is, how'll this now help us to do our tasks throughout the seasons?"

"Well, I seem to have found a deeper sense of my healing powers," answered Jayne. "Like I already said, I could feel myself accessing her powers of healing, so now I know that I'm not alone in the ability to heal others. I can certainly pull from the land and thus from Mother Crystal when it comes time to mend wounds that might otherwise cause the demise of a being."

"I like the idea of rebirth," stated Ryan. "I can go from one place in space to another with only the thought of wanting to be there. What if where I went was stagnant and was in need of change? I could probably help to start that change and allow more balance into nature with such a goal in mind. Or I could even take something in abundance from one place and bring it to another place that's in desperate need of it. Wouldn't that be like a rebirth?"

Alexander held up his hands and sighed. "I am afraid that several of you are allowing your minds to take you further than was my intention in today's lesson. Rebirth comes when something dies. For change to occur and be successful, stagnation must move forward. If you were in a place of complete and utter joy, you would have no idea about sadness. Opposites must occur, as in the end, they actually complement each other."

Seth spoke up. "Honestly, Alexander, I don't quite understand everything that you're saying; however, I think that I know about opposites. Summer can only occur if winter has gone. The seasons are the basic rebirth of our realm and for all other worlds. If I examine that idea further, I know that there are faeries with basic magick and then there're those of us who have superpower magick. There must be worlds in which magick isn't prominent at all. Would our ability to use magick require that another world be unable to use magick? Wouldn't that create a balance in nature?"

Alexander nodded his head. "Yes, there are opposites playing between all the worlds that Mother Crystal created. Listen to your bodies and what is being told to you through the biology in which you live. Your chakras have an immediate connection to Mother Crystal. It is when you identify which chakra is out of balance and which one is screaming at you to listen, that you are receiving an important message from her. To keep yourself in balance will allow you to keep nature in balance. We have certainly worked on building your superpowers and using potions to assist with your skills. When we spend the Equinox at training camp every year, you are trained with other magickal creatures. All of these skills are meant to help you make better decisions when faced with controversy and imbalance."

"Are we able to come and discuss things with Mother Crystal on our own?" asked Sabrina.

"Certainly," agreed Alexander. "Now that you have made a connection with her, it is important that you continue to spend time with her. Just do not neglect your chores or your duties to your family. Remember, you can only discuss Mother Crystal amongst yourselves. Her existence is not to be shared with others in our realm."

"Why is she such a secret, when clearly she can calm us and help to build our sense of selves?" questioned Georgia. "Wouldn't knowing about her and interacting with her help everyone else too?"

"At one time, Mother Crystal was well known in this realm," admitted Alexander. "There was a seer who lived in this cavern with Mother Crystal. She protected and looked after this cavern. She went by the name of Ice Moon." He bowed his head for an instant. "She was the faerie who knew of my destiny. She trained me in all that I know about magick. When she died, I felt that it was important to keep this cavern a secret, as I did not feel it necessary to have beings coming and going at all hours. I did not want others to forget who they were and that they had a responsibility to their own lives. I think that it is important to know who you are before looking for answers to the cosmos. Perhaps I had no business hiding Mother Crystal from those living in this realm, but my intentions were honourable."

"Will there come a time when the entire realm will need to know about her again?" Javier asked tentatively. "I'm not asking because I want to tell everyone about her. I just wonder, as I think it'd be a rebirth of knowledge."

"Perhaps. Some of you may already know about her in stories that your parents told when they put you to bed. Often, what was once known to be true and real will turn into a bedtime story, which is dismissed as myth," Alexander informed them.

"Oh, I really like bedtime stories," insisted Ryan. "Sometimes, Andre and I'll stay up late and watch Luna after my mom has told us a story." He paused for a moment as his mind made a few connections. "So the story that I've heard all my life about the Lady of Ice…was that Ice Moon?"

Alexander nodded his head in ascent. "Yes, she is known now as the Lady of Ice."

"She spoke with all the gods and all the angels on a daily basis. She'd share what they had to say in order to make certain that Faerie was kept in good favour. She'd sing and dance and make poetry that whispered on the wind," said Jayne. "I remember her. My songs sometimes make me think of her story."

"Why did she die?" asked Seth.

"She had to die, my dear Seth," responded Alexander. "Rebirth can only occur when there is a death. She accomplished what she needed. Her reward was to become one with the land. She lived for an extremely long time, even by faerie standards. I assure you that she was pleased to move on from this realm. She was not afraid of what lay in the underworld. Many of those she had loved in her lifetime had already gone to the underworld. She missed them and she was ready to join them."

"Were you with her when she went to the underworld?" Seth questioned.

"Yes, I was," replied Alexander. "I was with her at that moment, as was Mother Crystal."

"It's always sad for those left behind," said Jayne.

"Let us not be sad," said Alexander. "Let us be thankful for what we have been given here today. You were all able to connect with Mother Crystal, who is the birth of life and of magick. You know that there is a way for you to reach out and access knowledge long forgotten by those who are living. You have felt an incredible sense of peace and love, the kind that can only come from she who created this realm and each of you in turn. You know about time, and that it began when Mother Crystal made it so. You are all aware of the importance of checking with your chakras so that you can be balanced physically, mentally, and spiritually. Now you are also all aware of the regenerative power that comes from this sacred land. The worlds change when there is rebirth, which can only occur through the end of stasis. Keep this knowledge with you. Do not forget how it is that you felt today inside that cavern, for it will be important when the world seems out of balance and you must find a way to rebalance nature."

"Do the other leaders from training camp know about this sacred land?" asked Seth, even though he felt that asking such a question would not give him the answer he wanted.

"I do not know if they are still aware of Mother Crystal," admitted Alexander. "It is not something that we have discussed or have had need to discuss over the years. All in this realm once knew her, so it is quite likely they know all about her and have told their own charges about her. It is not for me to ask them about what they know and what they teach. If any of them bring her up for discussion, then I am more than happy to discuss her with them."

"Are we free to go?" asked Mercury. She had not stopped skipping around the group since she had gotten off of her mushroom. "I don't think that my brain can really process anything else today."

"Yes, Mercury, your lesson for today is concluded. All of you rest well, as we will be leaving in two days for Equinox training camp," Alexander reminded them.

CHAPTER 15

The wind whipped across the land, blowing down the mountainside, circling the flats, and meeting with the sea before moving back to the land. The moon lay hidden behind dark clouds, providing no comfort on this night. The waves of the sea crashed against the cliffside, begging to climb up to where the nature spirits were gathered. No one dared to attempt a sail on this night; all would be lost in the turmoil of the sea.

The night encompassed the large group. It was comforting, allowing them to move stealthily in the evening. There was much to prepare, much to do before they were ready. A fire burned warm near a rocky hillside jutting out of the mountainside. Mercury caused the flames to dance in the night, licking each other and the air surrounding those who sought it for protection and warmth. She played with them for some time, encouraging them to grow and spark.

Ryan watched the flames as he passed by the fire. He wished that he could rest there for a few moments, but he was needed elsewhere. His gifts did not bring comfort to the large mass of beings who were gathered here tonight. He must continue to check on each nature spirit, ensuring that all were well.

A group of trolls were busy making weaponry. It was well known that these nature spirits had the gift of earth and swordsmanship. Each troll was well versed in the making of magickal swords. They had studied for centuries, passing down their knowledge to each generation. As they focused on the task at hand, it was clear that each stage of the sword making took great care and concentration.

Billy sat to the left of the sword makers, watching the process with fascination. Although he could not make a sword, he did appreciate each stage. One troll would heat and hammer the precious metal into shape. Another troll would soften the sword for grinding it into shape. He would then heat it within the flames and cool it in a vat of water. A third troll took each annealed sword, grinding out the edge and point until he was pleased with the result. He would then add an engraving to identify the sword. A fourth troll took the piece and heated it to an extremely high temperature. When he was satisfied, he would place it into a quenching tank. A fifth troll would temper the sword, heating at lower temperatures and quenching to create a strength that could not be rivalled. A final troll added a pommel, guard, and hilt to each sword so that its new owner could use the magick to defeat the enemy.

Ryan joined a group of gnomes near the cliff. They were marking a circle on the hard surface. Within the circle were various clumps of herbs. These clumps had been gathered earlier in the day. Each clump was bundled and tied with strips of soft bark, separated each from the other. Candles were placed on the etching of the circle. They would be lit and a protection spell would be cast to keep the herbs from harm.

Harum, a gnome from the south of Faerie was in charge of this circle. He waved everyone into position within and around the circle. He then snapped his fingers, lighting the candles and bringing in a warm breeze to the centre of the circle. Those who were gathered here could no longer feel the cold or hear the crashing of the waves. Energy moved within the circle, forming into ribbons of colour.

A yellow ribbon wrapped itself around Ryan. The silky feel of it was soft and caressed on his skin. His wings were left exposed. The energy of the ribbon emanated outside of Ryan, attempting to enter his own energy. He glanced around the circle and found that the others were also being wrapped in ribbons of energy. Slowly, Ryan let down his guard, allowing the energy to enter his body. His wings glowed in the moonlight as the energy became stronger within him.

The warm breeze picked up, becoming stronger and faster within the circle. The ribbons unleashed each nature spirit. They whipped in the now warm wind, creating a show of colours that entwined with each other. Sparks began to form, chasing the ribbons and touching the individuals. Ryan noted that each spark was cool, as though pulling from the elements outside of the circle.

A glow formed around each spark, which then dissipated into the ribbons. The ribbons entwined themselves together. A brilliant charge of light appeared. It expanded outside of the circle, changing the scene of the area. Ryan felt a surge of electrical power enter his being; then a popping and sizzling sound emerged. The candles blew out, the moon disappeared, and all was quiet.

Slowly, the coolness entered the circle. The sound of waves crashing against the cliffs became loud to Ryan's ears. The clanging of weaponry drifted in the air. Ryan looked around as the moon reappeared. Its glow displayed the entire cliff side and the beings working there. Groups of nature spirits were scattered about, each practicing or working on a specific talent.

Alexander appeared from within a cave that was hidden amongst coniferous trees and green leaf plants. He looked about, searching for Billy. When he spotted him sitting amongst the trolls and their swords, Alexander motioned for Billy's assistance. Billy beamed, lifted himself from the ground, and skipped over to Alexander.

"Alexander, you need me? What can I do for you?"

"Billy, it is time to feed everyone. I require your assistance with bringing out the food." Alexander gestured towards to cave.

Billy skipped into the cave. He came out carrying three large trays of raw fruits, vegetables, and edible flowers. The trays teetered on his hands and arms. With great difficulty, Billy walked over to a large wooden table. The trays balanced precariously, nearly falling to the ground with each step he took. Beads of sweat formed on Billy's forehead. Alexander shook his head. So typical of Billy to take more than he could handle in hopes of pleasing others. Once the trays were safely on the table, Billy re-entered the cave for more food. Over four trips, he produced succulent meats of venison, roast beef, pulled pork, barbequed chicken, pit-roasted lamb, and raw fish. Pitchers of various wines, nectars, and water were placed upon the table.

As the smell of food wafted in the air, the nature spirits put down their activities to join the feast. Trolls, faeries, salamanders, pixies, gnomes, and brownies gathered around the table. They sat on mushroom stools in no particular order, happy to be celebrating the day's end together. When everyone was seated, Alexander stood on his stool to address the crowd.

"Let us gather this evening to give ourselves sustenance so that we may fulfil our duty of balance. We thank those animals who have given their lives for this feast so that we in turn may be satiated to continue with assisting in the balance of worlds and realms. We give thanks for this opportunity to converse, to work together, to teach each other, and to learn from each other." The crowd murmured assents of "here, here". Alexander raised his cup; the crowd followed suit. "To a successful time together. Enjoy."

The gathering passed plates around, filled their cups, and chatted amongst each other. These were rare opportunities, ones they each cherished. Sharing of knowledge and strengthening of talents was so important during this time.

Sabrina talked animatedly to the salamander on her right. "I'm so glad that you sat next to me. I find the nights here to be extremely cold. I appreciate your heat. It's always fascinated me that you are able to emanate heat even when you aren't playing with flames."

The salamander flicked his tongue and licked his lips. "When there is cold I find that my body builds more heat, as though I am creating an internal fire for those around me. Tell me Sabrina, how far can you now throw your invisibility? I know that last year at this time you could only cloak yourself."

Sabrina chewed on a piece of lamb before she spoke. "Solomon, it really depends upon who's near me. I can cast a net to encompass up to six beings sometimes. I struggle with pulling the energy around me and using it when the others are also doing the same." She sighed, "I really want to be consistent before we're done here."

Solomon nodded. He selected several fruits and placed them on his plate. "It will come, Sabrina. When you focus on what is difficult, it makes it nearly impossible to perform what is simple. I believe in your abilities. You will accomplish your goal during this fortnight."

"Well," Sabrina raised her cup, "here's to both of our accomplishments. May they be many and varied," she drank the liquid in one gulp.

Solomon drank his nectar as well. Further down the table, Ryan moved his plate and cup back and forth. His hands remained folded on the table as he entertained Shoshana. She was tired from the day's work. Being near so many powerful nature spirits was draining when she was attempting to feel their emotions. She had not yet learned to block out unwanted emotions. Focusing on what she wanted to know was difficult with so many other nuisances impeding on her thoughts.

Shoshana watched the plate and cup move over the table. She reached out and put her right thumb in the direct path of the cup. It jammed against her nail and toppled over, crashing into the plate. "What'd you go and do that for?" asked Ryan. He picked up the cup and set it properly on the table.

"I don't know. I guess that I wanted to see what would happen," she told him. "As much fun as it is to watch items move on their own, it doesn't help me with blocking out all of these emotions." Shoshana waved her arm at the gathering of creatures.

"Haven't you been working on that for the last week?" he asked with wonder.

Shoshana sighed, "Yes, I've been working on it. I find it to be difficult with so many beings in one area. Once I block out one creature's emotions another one's infringes upon my thoughts. This morning I managed to block out two brownies, one troll, and three gnomes all at once, but then Javier stepped into the space and all of those emotions hit me at once! I found myself lying on my back when I came to. It really wasn't very pleasant. Since then, I can't seem to block any emotions from pounding at my heart and mind."

"Maybe you need to take a break and find a spot where you can be alone," suggested Ryan. "It'd give you time to regroup."

Shoshana brushed her hair out of her eyes. "I'd really like to do that, but I feel that my purpose here is to build my powers, not to hide from them."

"Regrouping is not hiding," countered Ryan. "It's recharging yourself and creating inner balance. How can you possibly help others when you aren't in balance yourself?"

"True, I see your point. Maybe after this meal I'll do just as you suggest and find a quiet spot," agreed Shoshana.

Ryan pulled the plate over to his cup. "If anyone asks of your whereabouts, I'll keep them away so that you can accomplish what you need to do."

"Thank you, Ryan. You're a true friend and a real Guardian," Shoshana responded.

"Oh look!" exclaimed Billy, interrupting Ryan and Shoshana. The two moved their heads to where Billy was pointing. The mid-section of the long table had disappeared, taking with it the nine guests and their chairs. The guests shimmered into view for a quick second before they disappeared once again. Everyone who remained around the table began to cheer and clap at the success of such a task.

"Well done, Sabrina," declared Alexander from further down the table. "This is precisely why we come together every Equinox to train together and learn from one another. The knowledge that we gain here can only benefit each and every one of you in the days and seasons to come. It has always been my pleasure to be one of the leaders who organizes this event. Although, I must admit, it no longer takes any real preparation as everything seems to flow from one Spring into another Spring."

Sabrina and those who had fallen into her invisibility net reappeared with glasses of nectar in their hands. "A toast," she called, "to our leaders!"

"Here! Here!" everyone yelled as they all gathered their glasses and took a drink. Plates continued to be passed down the table for those who were still in need of food.

CHAPTER 16

"I am telling you, Logan, something must be done about Alexander. He has had too much control over the Guardians for far too long. It is imperative that we take matters into our own hands," concluded Lillian. She took a deep breath and stared intently at the faerie in front of her. She watched as he pushed at the dirt with a bare foot.

"Not all of the council are in agreement with us," he said quietly. "It would be so much easier if we were unanimous in the decision to remove Alexander as sage of the Guardians, rather than just assist him."

"Travis is too enamoured with Alexander to know that his loyalties should lie with us. We will just have to make him see that Alexander is not the only one to follow. You and I will need to show Travis that we have the best interests of Faerie at heart, which is why we need to assist Alexander from his position."

"How do you propose that we convince Travis that our intentions are for the benefit of Faerie? I understand that he has an uncle who is a Guardian, which gives Travis cause to admire Alexander," stated Logan.

"Well," said Lillian, "I have been thinking about this dilemma for a few days now. We need to prove that Alexander has been selecting Guardians whom he prefers, rather than utilizing all of the special faeries who have been born with superpowers. I have a second cousin with autism who can cross realms, but he was eliminated from the Guardian selection during some secret test that Alexander uses to determine who will be trained and who will not be taught to strengthen his special gifts. Training all special faeries can only benefit our community."

"You need not convince me of your intentions, Lillian," insisted Logan, "for I am in complete agreement with you. What I want to know is how do you intend to convince Travis and any other sceptics in the community to follow our lead? How do you propose that we remove Alexander from his position of power with the blessing of every member residing in Faerie? Between you and I, the only way Alexander will allow us to assist him is if we find a way to remove him from his long held position."

Lillian slowly turned up the corners of her mouth. "I have discovered a secret that has been kept from many generations of faeries. I was rummaging around in the council basement when I came across an ancient parchment which refers to a cavern full of the purist magick."

Logan chewed on his inner cheek. "Like a cavern full of unicorns?"

Lillian laughed, brightening her eyes. "Oh Logan, you can be so naive. Although unicorns contain pure magick, they actually come from a purer source of magick." She glanced around the secluded glen for anyone who might be within hearing distance. "There is a cavern not too far from here, which contains the source of all magick. It was once the home of a seer who perished at least two millennia ago. It was in this large cave that she conversed with the gods and the angels. I believe that we will find the answer to all that is

Alexander and all that allows our special faeries to be born with superpowers."

"Why have we not been made aware of this cave before now?"

"It would seem, according to this parchment, that all faeries were aware of this particular cavern at one time. From what I could gather on the document, the time of Alexander's appearance in Faerie marks the end of widely known knowledge about this large cave and what it contains."

"Do you know how to access this cavern?" asked Logan eagerly.

"The document did not say, specifically. I was only able to deduce its location. As long as we work together, I believe we will be able to find a way to enter the cavern." She leaned in closer to whisper, "I think we should go now, before anyone notices that we are away from Oak Tree."

"Lead the way," Logan urged.

Lillian twitched her wings and lifted herself into the air. When she was certain that Logan was right behind her, she took to the sky above the forest trees. She zigged and zagged across the air, catching a breeze here and there, in an attempt to shake any beings who might have had the notion to follow them.

Logan kept several wing lengths behind Lillian, allowing her to lead him to this cavern full of pure magick. They flew over a tiny stream, following it north. Eventually, the stream turned into a river at the end of which housed a large waterfall that pooled at the bottom, creating a small, secluded bathing pool surrounded with lush vegetation. The two of them descended to the edge of the waterfall, resting on a slippery rock that continued to be sprayed from the falling water.

"I don't see a cavern," stated Logan. He looked in all directions for an opening hidden within the cracks of the rocks and behind the vegetation.

Lillian shook her head. "We are not there yet," she told him. "I promise that it is not far from here, now. We need only go a little ways East of here. I just thought that we should stop here in case anyone was following us."

"I'm fairly certain that no one was paying attention to us when we left the glen," Logan assured her. "They probably all assume we are in the council chambers discussing something tedious. No one could possibly imagine what we have stumbled upon here."

"Nonetheless, I think we should still take precautions. I want to be certain of everything before we take our findings of the cavern to the council and the community of Faerie. I want solid proof that not all special faeries have been utilized to their highest potential in protecting our realm. There is no doubt in my mind that we will find this proof in the depths of this long forgotten cavern. Once we can share what we find down there, then we can approach the council and it will not matter who follows us around the land," concluded Lillian.

"Then what are we waiting for?" demanded Logan. "Let's get to this secret cavern before the sun is too high in the sky."

"Follow me towards the East." She lifted her feet off the damp rock and took to the air. Her brilliant wings spread wide before slowly moving in a rhythm that carried her to a place not far to the East. Logan continued to remain two wing breadths behind her.

"Look to your left," called Lillian into the wind. "There is a purple bush that is full of tiny blue flowers. Do you see it?" She glanced behind her.

Logan squinted his eyes as he peered to where she pointed. "Yes, I see a purple bush. Is that the opening to the cavern?"

"No, I don't think so," she replied. "But I think it is a landmark indicating its nearness."

Logan began to descend first, while Lillian carried forward before she chose to get closer to the ground. Once they were both standing at the bottom of the purple bush, Lillian took a deep breath and opened her arms wide. "Can you feel the energy on the land, Logan?" she asked him.

Logan nodded his head and attempted to dig his left foot into the hard packed dirt. "Yes, it feels different here, almost…serene."

"Yes, serene and so very peaceful. It is like the dirt is vibrating under my toes." Lillian swept her arms over the land in a gesture to encompass the entire beauty of the spot. "Take a good look around us, Logan. Have you ever seen such unique plants?"

The tiny blue flowers twinkled in the sunlight, as though they were popping in and out of the purple bush. Logan reached out to touch the flowers. One of the blue petals reached up and wrapped itself around his finger. He giggled at the unexpected caress of the blue flower. "I wonder why we haven't been here before," he thought out loud.

"It doesn't really surprise me," replied Lillian. "Most faeries spend their time in Faerie and don't wander elsewhere. Why would we want to explore when we happen to have everything we need at our fingertips?"

Logan let go of the flower and spun around to examine the view further. "Other magickal creatures exist throughout our realm. Is there a particular reason we don't usually go to their land on occasion? I realise that they often come to Faerie for socials, but if we really think about it, why is that the only time we gather?"

Lillian shrugged her shoulders. "Who knows? Perhaps it has something to do with Alexander and all these secrets he has been keeping for so long. If there was a time when the council was quite aware of this hidden cavern, then it is safe to assume that at one time all magickal creatures travelled and visited amongst the many lands in our realm. Once you and I have proven to the council that Alexander requires assistance with the knowledge and training of the Guardians, then perhaps all magickal creatures will again come together throughout the lands."

"What you say makes sense," he agreed, "although I find it difficult to believe that Alexander was the root cause of magickal creatures not intermingling on a regular basis. After all, Billy the troll spends most of his time with the Guardians and Alexander."

Lillian began to walk in circles around the purple bush and Logan. "Our first priority is to locate the cavern. Once we have done that, then everything else will fall into place." She stopped in mid stride and stared at Logan. "Would you leave the flowers alone and help me find the entrance to the cavern?"

Logan pulled his hand away from the bush as though it had caught fire. "Oh, right. Do you know what it is that we are looking for exactly?"

"Yes, as a matter of fact, there should be a huge sign pointing directly at the entrance!" she huffed in exasperation. "Logan, if I knew what the entrance looked like, do you think I would be wandering around here as though I were searching for something hidden?"

"You don't have to get all upset with me," he countered. Logan walked away from the bush and began searching under rocks and sticks.

"I'm fairly certain that the entrance would be like a crevice," Lillian said as an afterthought. "Look for a crack in the ground or between some large rocks."

"I only see small rocks," came Logan's reply.

"Well, it is possible that over time the large rocks eroded into small rocks and have closed the entrance," suggested Lillian. She kept her feet on the ground, which allowed her to feel the pulsing of the land and notice any changes of the ground.

Logan spread his wings in excitement and called out, "I think I found something! Over here, Lillian, quick!"

Lillian flew to his side and peered over Logan's shoulder. "What? What do you see?" She searched the ground near his feet in an attempt to catch a glimpse of the reason for his excitement.

"The vegetation is different here," he claimed. "It is sparse in one area and quite thick in another."

Lillian scoffed, "How is that demonstrative of the cavern entrance? I could say the very same of the plants outside my home. It really depends upon the sunlight, the water, and how much I tend to them."

"No, no. Listen," insisted Logan. "You will notice that the sparse vegetation has a great deal of dry ground and small rocks between each piece. The thick vegetation is full and seems almost moist, like it has a specific water source not provided to the other plants."

"Then let's move the vegetation aside and see what is beneath it," suggested Lillian.

Logan put his arm straight out to stop her. "No, we can't disturb the vegetation. If it is hiding the cavern, then we don't want Alexander or anyone else to know that we have been here. Give me a moment to examine it closer before we decide anything."

"Okay, you look at it closely. When you see something, let me know." Lillian turned her back on Logan so that she could view the landscape and everything it contained. The wildlife consisted of birds, squirrels, and a few rabbits. She was unable to notice any magickal creatures that might be hidden somewhere near where they were searching.

"Oh, Lillian! I was correct! There is a hole here in the ground, underneath this vegetation!"

Lillian spun around and nearly fell to the ground in her haste to stand beside Logan. "Show me! Show me what it looks like!" she uttered excitedly.

Logan pried apart the thick vegetation, revealing a small hole in the ground that was worn and smooth from time. The edges of the hole glistened brilliant green. Lillian bent over and touched the edges. "They are smooth like a mineral still pure in the ground." She gasped as the brilliant green changed slightly to the pulse she could feel in the ground. "Did you see and feel that?"

"Feel what?" Logan asked.

"Don't you feel the ground pulsing like a heart?"

"Oh, that. Yes, I noticed that as soon as we arrived here. I haven't noticed any change in the pulsing, though," he admitted.

"There has been no change in the pulsing," Lillian said. "It was the brilliant green surrounding the opening of this hole that changed. It seems to be affected by the pulsing." She turned and grinned widely at Logan. "I think you found the opening to the cavern, Logan." Without thinking, she threw herself at him and wrapped him in her arms. "Oh, this is so exciting!"

"Do you want to go into the hole alone or should I follow you down?" he muffled against her embrace.

Lillian let him go and peered down into the hole. "It's dark. I can't see anything other than the walls of the crevice. I am willing to go first, but you are more than welcome to join me." She lifted her head and looked over at him. "Actually, it might be best if you did join me, just in case anyone comes along and spots you standing out here."

Logan nodded his head. "Yes, I would like to come down into the cavern with you. I want to locate the source of the pulsing and it must be down there, deep into the depths of the land."

Lillian took a deep breath. "Okay, let's go down into this hole. Oh, and be sure to put the vegetation back in place once we are in the crevice. We don't want anything to appear out of the ordinary on the surface here."

"Will do," agreed Logan.

Lillian sat on the edge of the crevice and allowed her feet to slide into the opening. She kicked at the edges and watched the brilliant green colour change slightly as she moved her legs. She giggled like a child, which of course she had not been for a very long time. Ever so carefully, Lillian slid into the hole and let her wings carry her down the walls of the cavern. At first she was able to see the rock walls as the sunlight touched them, but as soon as Logan had entered the crevice and fussed with the vegetation so that it covered the entrance, the walls glowed a deep red-violet.

"Can you see anything further down?" called Logan from above her.

Lillian shook her head and then realised that he could not see her. "No, I can only see right in front of my face and that is only the pulsing red-violet rock walls." She reached out and tentatively touched the wall in front of her. It felt moist and warm at the same time. The colour pulsed at her touch. Lillian spread her fingers out and laid her palm against the rock. "Beautiful," she whispered.

"What did you say?" asked Logan. He had not noticed that she had stopped and was touching the crevice walls. Logan's foot grazed her head before he realised that Lillian was no longer descending to the cavern. "Sorry," he mumbled.

Lillian brushed away his foot with her free hand. "Touch the wall, Logan. It feels so strange. It reminds me of something, but I can't think of what."

Logan reached out and placed both hands, palms and fingers spread wide, against the wall above Lillian. "Wow," he gasped. "It is alive. The red-violet changes slightly under my hands. The rest of the rock remains as it was before I touched anything."

"Yes. So unique," Lillian replied. She let go of the wall and continued her descent. The area widened the further down she flew. On various sides of the walls a few bats slept in hallowed out crevices of their own. Lillian brushed aside a spider as it spun a web out towards her. As she delved deeper into the land, the red-violet light became stronger, as though it were coming from a source further down. Lillian increased her wing speed until she could hear the land pulsing in her ears and the light became a source similar to the sun or moon in the sky above.

Lillian entered the cavern not long before Logan. She found herself struck mute. The beauty of the cavern enveloped her, warming her from the very inside of her soul. She lowered herself to the cavern floor and stood silent, taking in the vegetation, the flowers, the water of blue and pink, and the ever-amazing clear quartz crystal singing in the middle of the pool. Lillian felt, rather than heard, Logan come to a stand still beside her.

Neither of them spoke, yet Lillian knew they felt the same about this magickal place. There was no doubt that this was where all magick was created. Slowly, Lillian stepped forward, toward the pool of enticing water. Logan remained where he had landed, watching Lillian take the first steps within this magnificent place. When she reached the edge of the pool, Lillian gingerly dipped her left foot into the water. She pulled it out slowly, turned to Logan, and smiled widely.

"It is so warm," she told him. "The magick in here is so powerful, so potent. I have no doubt that all magick in our realm came to be in this very spot."

"It comes from that crystal," insisted Logan. "I can't explain how I know this, but I assure you it is the truth. All of our magick and magickal abilities were born here."

Lillian nodded in agreement. "Yes, I know this to be true as well. This is the source of all magick. This is where Guardians are decided. This is where special faeries fail to become Guardians." Her tone was sad as she acknowledged this truth. "Jacob was defiled here and humiliated."

"What do we do now?" questioned Logan.

Lillian turned to him. A tear slid down her left cheek. "Now, we make the decision to become Guardians."

"We become Guardians?" scoffed Logan. "That is not possible. We were not born special."

"We may not have been born special, but today I declare us special. Who else has been able to find this secret cavern in the last two millennia? Who else has dared to question Alexander and his choices regarding the Guardians? Who else deserves this more than us?"

Logan stared at her, refusing to speak. "Well?" she asked him, moving towards him and pushing her face into his.

"No one," said Logan quietly.

"Exactly," she stated. "It is here where we will become Guardians. It is here where we will be given superpowers that will help all of Faerie. It is here where you and I will change tradition and begin a new history for our kind."

Logan searched her face without backing away from her. "How do you propose we gain superpowers?"

Lillian spun around and hit Logan with her wings. "Well, the powers have something to do with this pool and crystal, obviously. Watch her closely, Logan. She pulses the red-violet that is everywhere in here. She is the source of blood, so to speak. It is she who is the heart of our realm. She moves the ground that pulses through our feet."

Logan chewed on his lower lip. "So we need to get the powers from the crystal. Should we try talking to her first?"

"I don't know," Lillian admitted. She paced back and forth at the edge of the pool. "How would we ask her? I mean, she is a crystal and doesn't appear to have a means for communicating with us."

"Not necessarily. She does seem to communicate with the pulsing throughout the land, and her colours change. If I am correct, she is red-violet down here and brilliant green on the surface."

Lillian stopped moving. "Brilliant green. The edge of the cavern hole was brilliant green. It felt strange. That must be a part of her. So if, as you say, she communicates through the pulsing and the colours, then we just need to find a way in which we can communicate on her particular wavelength."

Logan tilted his head upward and to the side as he examined the entire cavern. "What about getting into the pool and swimming over to her?"

Lillian wrinkled her nose in distaste. "Swimming? I am not dressed for swimming. What is wrong with flying over?" She looked down at her wide leaf dress.

Logan shrugged his shoulders. "Flying is too easy for us. Swimming shows how much we respect her. Of course, you don't have to get in the pool. We could always forget about this idea of yours and go back home." He beat his wings and lifted himself off the ground.

"No! Wait!" Lillian grabbed for him and pulled him back down to the floor. She grimaced. "Okay, I will go in the water and swim over to the crystal. I will probably be able to dry off on our way home. The sun is out today and the wind will help rid my dress of water beads."

Logan laughed. "I'm certain that you won't be too concerned about being in wet clothing once you have accomplished your task here."

Lillian sniffed. "Well, you might be right." She turned her back on Logan and repositioned herself at the edge of the pool. This time she placed both feet into the water and watched as the pinks and blues swirled around her ankles. She took three steps into the pool before throwing herself forward and swimming towards the crystal. She held her head above the surface, allowing only the tendrils of hair below her neck to become wet.

"You are doing great!" called Logan.

"I'd like to see you get in here," she called back.

She could hear him shuffling on the dry ground. "No, I'm fine over here," he replied.

"I'm sure you are," she mumbled. Lillian reached the crystal and paddled in one place, keeping herself afloat. The singing of the crystal was definitely louder at this close range. Lillian examined the crystal. She tilted her head to the right and then to the left. She paddled around the crystal to further view its structure and density. When she had swum a complete circle around the magnificent stone, Lillian turned to face Logan.

"She is definitely louder here in the centre of the pool," she yelled over at Logan. Her voice vibrated off the crystal and bounced against the cavern walls in an echo. "Oops. I guess I shouldn't speak so loudly in here."

"I can hear you just fine from over here," replied Logan.

"I am going to touch her. I think that might make things clear between us. Or at least, I might be able to communicate with her."

"Good idea, Lillian," Logan encouraged. He backed away a few steps from the water.

"Chicken," Lillian said under her breath.

"I heard that."

Lillian took a deep breath. She reached out her right hand and touched the clear crystal quartz. A warmth like Spring and a heart of love pulsed through her fingers. Lillian brought herself closer to the crystal and pressed her left cheek against the welcoming touch of this magickal source. The singing became a lullaby, moving through Lillian's body and out into the waves of water.

"I want to become a Guardian," Lillian whispered into the crystal. "I want to be important, as though I had been born special. My second cousin, Jacob, was born special but he was denied the privilege of becoming a Guardian. He left Faerie and has not returned in a long time. He was so ashamed. I want to envelop the superpowers that he should have received, so that I can make certain that others are not denied the status of Guardian again. I want to prove to all of Faerie that so much more is possible with magick and that, as a community, we can utilise more magick than we are able to do now."

The crystal changed her song from the soft lullaby to a deeper cord that made Lillian feel unwanted. She shook her body, attempting to repel the feeling now seeping into her. She used both of her hands to haul herself up onto the crystal and out of the water. "Do not forsake me, please," she begged. "You were so welcoming a moment ago."

The song ceased and the crystal became silent. The lack of pulsing was deafening. Lillian felt as though her soul were plummeting into nothingness. She clung harder to the crystal and pressed her body flat against it. She spread her wings out and allowed the tips of them to touch the crystal as they wrapped around her wet body. She pressed her face against the crystal and closed her eyes, searching for the pulsing to begin again. Still, the crystal remained silent.

Logan's voice penetrated her thoughts, "Why is she silent? Is she going to give you a superpower?"

Lillian tried to block his voice out, but he persisted. "What is happening, Lillian?"

"I don't know," she reluctantly replied. "She isn't communicating with me. She isn't warm anymore." Lillian could feel the heart of the crystal pulling away from her. The warmth that she had emanated was slowly cooling to Lillian's touch. "Don't leave me," she begged.

"Where is she going?" asked Logan.

Lillian lifted her face away from the crystal. She turned towards Logan and let three tears slide down her cheek before she forced them away with her hand. "Away to somewhere else."

"Can you stop her from leaving?"

"I don't know." Lillian bit her lip and lifted herself off of the crystal with a slight movement of her wet wings. When she was a few wings breadth away from the silent crystal, she soared into the air above the utmost point and hovered there. "She abandoned me, just like Alexander abandoned Jacob, and like Jacob abandoned the family and Faerie when he was rejected as a Guardian."

Anger built inside Lillian somewhere within the sadness that surrounded her heart. She set her jaw and turned abruptly to face Logan. She gritted her teeth and jutted out her chin. Her hands clenched at her sides and the blood in her veins boiled. She could feel the heat on her face and the beads of sweat threatening to drip out of her pores. "You are not going to ignore me," she stated firmly through clenched teeth. "If you won't talk to me, then I will make you at least notice that I have not gone anywhere. You will not forget me as you forgot Jacob."

Lillian plunged forward to the peak of the crystal. She grabbed hold of the silent, clear source of magick and dug at her with her fingers and fingernails. Lillian flailed her arms and legs, thrashing her body against the crystal in an attempt to be noticed. She felt like a fly blowing in the breeze, getting nowhere and yet refusing to give in to defeat. "You will not ignore me!" Frustrated, Lillian stopped thrashing and glanced about the cavern. When she spotted a sharp rock tossed away on the opposite side of where Logan stood watching her, she let go of the crystal and flew to the source of her current interest. Lillian dove down and grabbed the rock. She rushed back to the top of the crystal and began to smash the jagged rock against the silent, clear crystal quartz. Smash after smash she used all of her strength to pound the rock into the crystal that had rejected her before even listening to Lillian's heart.

With one last fling of the rock, Lillian heard the deafening sound of a scream from deep within the bowels of the cavern. It reverberated throughout the cavern and through the crystal. Lillian dropped the rock to cover her ears from the shrieking that penetrated to her very soul. The sound was the pain emitted when something is dying a painful death. The lights in the cavern faltered before emitting a soft solid glow of lavender. Lillian blinked and readjusted her eyes to the change in the cavern.

Logan lay sprawled face down on the cavern floor with his hands covering both of his ears. His legs were kicking and his body was writhing in pain from the scream. Lillian flew in his direction when a glow from the water caught her attention.

She folded her wings against her back and dove down into the pale water. She reached out her right hand and grasped at the object sinking to the bottom of the pool. It dropped out of her reach, forcing her to kick her legs hard in order to swim deeper into the pool. The object sliced through a piece of red-violet crystal and settled on the bottom of the pool. Rather than grabbing the original object she had desired, Lillian took the newly broken piece and swam to the surface.

The scream had ceased. Logan was now lying on his side breathing slowly. Lillian pulled herself out of the water and clutched the alexandrite to her chest. Her hair dripped down her face and back. Her wet feet splashed on the hard ground. When she reached Logan, Lillian knelt down before him. She held out the crystal that remained in her hand. "Look what we have, Logan."

He opened his eyes and focused on the piece she held in front of him. "What is it? It's not clear, like the crystal we can see from here."

She shook her head. "No, it was at the root of the crystal, on the bottom of the pool. The piece I had cut off her top sliced this beautiful piece off the root just before it landed on the bottom of the pool. This feels so much more alive than the clear crystal quartz ever did."

"Is it a different crystal with a different life source?"

"I think it is of the same life source. This piece is an alexandrite, although it was attached to the quartz. I think this is the root of magickal superpowers," she said excitedly.

Logan bent his right arm and lifted himself off the floor. He sat and examined the alexandrite closely, without reaching for it. "Besides more alive, how does it feel?"

Lillian rubbed the alexandrite with her thumbs. "Strong. Connected to everything magickal."

"Do you think this will bring more magick to all of Faerie?"

"Yes, definitely." Lillian gazed at the crystal, her stare mesmerized with the colours and the layers of shards within the outer alexandrite.

"Then we have what it was we came here for," stated Logan. "Perhaps it is time that we took this alexandrite and left."

Lillian looked around at the pale, nearly silent cavern. She arose from her knees and walked slowly around the cavern, coming to a stop at the bottom of a stairwell she had been too distracted to notice earlier. Without saying a word, she ascended up the stairwell with Logan following close behind her.

CHAPTER 17

Sunlight dappled across the ground and reached under the bush where Javier slept curled up beneath two leaves. The sun tickled at his nose, which he twitched and tried to brush away in his sleep. Slowly, the sun touched upon his eyelids and insisted that they open. Javier groaned and rolled over so that his back was to the sun. "Go 'way," he mumbled.

Shuffling footsteps echoed in his head, pounding at Javier's temple. "No, I'm not ready to wake up. I drank too much nectar last night at the feast." The footsteps crunched a few twigs before coming to a stop at the edge of the bush. Javier could hear heavy breathing as the culprit bent over and poked his head beneath the leaves of the bush.

"Ya up, Javier?" bellowed Billy. "I's was lookin' fer ya 'fore th' practice games begin."

Javier waved his right hand at Billy. "I was hiding from everyone. My head hurts this morning."

"Did ya bump i'?"

Javier shook his head. "No, I drank too much nectar last night. It seems to be my downfall."

Billy reached in and patted Javier on his side. "I's time ta come ou' an' star' th' day, Javier. There's lo's a do today. We's go' figh' games an' strength competitions."

"It was so quiet under here," complained Javier. He reluctantly rolled over and eyed Billy, whose nose was almost touching his own.

"How can ya find i' quiet here, Javier? You have superpower hearin' an' i's noisy this mornin'." Billy shook his head in exasperation.

Javier grinned. "I can tune them all out now, if I concentrate really hard. Last night, when I found this spot for sleep, I sent out some spells to keep any sounds from reaching and penetrating my ears. It did wonders for me. I don't remember the last time I slept so well, if I've ever slept that well."

"So's your trainin' is workin' well," commented Billy. "I's grea' ta see all of ya makin' strides in yer learnin'. Georgia froze two trolls 'afore breakfas' this mornin'. I' was funny, 'cause they was stunned when they thawed an' ev'ryone was a' a table eatin'. She told me later tha' she coulda unfroze 'em, but she wan'ed ta see how long they could stay tha' way. Think they's now avoidin' her."

Javier laughed and struggled to his feet. He swayed back and forth before managing to keep himself stationary. "Yep, I had way too much nectar last night. I don't know what it is with that stuff, but I can't seem to stop myself from drinking only three cupfuls."

"Th' sugar'll get ya ev'ry time," agreed Billy. He backed out of the bush so that he and Javier were able to stand together in the sunshine.

"It's still so quiet," Javier pointed out.

Billy glanced around the camp. "No, i's noisy. Can' ya hear th' metal swords clashin' over by th' water?"

Javier gazed beyond the trees and found a group of trolls jousting with the swords they had forged over the past two weeks. "No, I don't hear them. Oh!" he exclaimed as realisation dawned on him. "I still have the silent net cast about me." Javier lifted both of his arms into the air with his palms facing upward. "Bring back to me that which I have hidden in a net for safe keeping. Allow it to unravel and dissolve into the wind. Keep me surrounded in your white light and good health. My thanks to you who have kept me in the silence for such a time as I had asked." The glittery blue net appeared to the naked eye for a moment before it vanished into the wind.

Javier clapped his hands over his big ears as the sudden noise hit him all at once. He grimaced and then released his ears. "I don't think I was prepared for the shock of all the sounds at once," he admitted to Billy. He twitched his ears until the sounds were at a steady rhythm of which they were accustomed. "Where do we want to go first, Billy? Do we want to find Alexander and get my instructions for the day? Or do we want to take a sneak peak at what the other Guardians are up to at the moment?"

Billy scratched at the side of his head. "Oh, I think we's should go an' get ya somethin' ta eat firs', so ya don' lose yer strength when ya do them activities all mornin'. They's not makin' lunch 'til af'er a meetin' o' th' leaders. They's makin' plans fer nex' year, I think."

"Or they might be planning the final practice battle for tomorrow," suggested Javier. "Let's grab something that we can eat while we wander around camp. I'd really like to see what Seth and the others are up to at the moment. I feel like I haven't really spent much time with them over the past two weeks. We rarely spend our lessons together while here. I kind of miss them all."

"'Kay. There's some food on a small table near th' cave," said Billy. He directed Javier over to the table, where the faerie was able to select some fruit and a mullet of some sort that he placed into a bowl and carried with him. Billy grabbed a cup of water and held it for Javier. The two of them wandered through the camp, passing a group of brownies who were practicing mixing herbs in a cauldron placed over a low burning fire. Sparks of bright yellow erupted from the cauldron and all the brownies cheered in excitement.

Billy bent over and whispered to Javier, "They's been a' tha' since shortly af'er breakfas'. I's seen lo's a colours comin' from tha' couldron."

"What've the gnomes been doing?" asked Javier. "They always seem to be quiet when they work together."

"No' sure wha' they's been up to. As ya say, they's quie' with their lessons. Can' really get a sense o' their work," he admitted. "'Though I did see Geoff over with 'em a while ago. He was turnin' shapes and they's was doin' somethin' a him. I couldn' really tell what i' was they's was doin' so I kep' walkin'. 'Sides, I was lookin' fer you."

"Have you any idea where Seth and Mercury might be hiding?" Javier questioned. "Usually if I can spot those two, the others aren't far away. They seem to be like magnets, especially Mercury."

"Yeah, she's go' fire in her," joked Billy. He laughed while he gazed around the camp in search of the two faeries. "I sees Jayne and Georgia o'er near th' smeltin' 'quipmen'."

Javier looked over to where Billy indicated. He twitched his wings and increased his walking speed. "Good. Let's meet up with them and we can find out if they know what our plans are for today." Javier put a raspberry into his mouth and chewed it as he hurried over to his friends.

"Ya shouldn' eat an' walk a' th' same time, Javier," chastised Billy. "I' ain' safe. Ya could choke."

Javier ignored this comment. Once he had reached Georgia and Jayne, he shoved another two pieces into his mouth. Billy shook his head in exasperation and kept close to Javier. "How's ya two doin'? Ya been workin' hard or ya been playin'?" he asked them.

Jayne smiled at Javier and Billy. "We've been doing a little bit of both. It's so good to see you, Billy." She stepped over and gave the troll a big a hug. "Where've you been hiding, Javier? We missed you at breakfast."

"He was sleepin' under a bush since las' nigh'," Billy informed her. "I found him jus' a li'l bit ago."

Georgia eyed Javier. "I've never known you to sleep soundly before. How'd you manage to do that?"

"He cas' a spell," said Billy proudly. "Kep' out all th' sounds from th' camp."

"That's so cool," exclaimed Jayne. "Isn't what we learn here amazing? I just love to take back all my new skills and show them to everyone on our social evenings." She lowered herself to her knees and touched the bare ground. "Watch this," she said. The ground shook and opened a crack. Slowly, a green stalk began to emerge. It thickened at the base and sprouted coniferous leaves, which spread into vines and wrapped themselves around her wrist. With her other hand, Jayne touched one of the leaves. A pink light glowed from her finger and became a flower with three petals and a red centre.

"That's so beautiful," said Javier. He bent over and examined the flower closely. "Will it reproduce on its own now?"

Jayne nodded. "Yes, it's a brand new form of plant and flower. It has all the female and male parts that'll allow it to seed and grow again. Harum worked with me yesterday on this particular trick."

"Them gnomes know lo's o' stuff when i' comes to th' land," mentioned Billy.

"That's why we come here," agreed Georgia.

"Wha' have ya learned, Georgia?" Billy asked with interest. "I saws ya freezin' 'em trolls this mornin'. I' was funny."

Georgia turned slightly pink and lowered her eyes to the ground. "I don't think those trolls will forgive me anytime soon," she admitted. "I'm trying to freeze as many creatures as possible at one time. I think it might come in handy, although I couldn't tell you in what type of situation."

Javier swung his hips and moved his feet. "It'd be great to freeze a group of dancers!" He continued to listen to the music in his head and move to the beat. Georgia flicked her wrist and froze him.

Jayne laughed. "Ooh, let's study his moves before you thaw him." She scurried over to Javier and peered at his wings, his legs, and his arms. "Just a minute," she told Georgia. Jayne stood in front of Javier and positioned herself to mimic his stance. "Okay, now thaw him."

Georgia giggled. She pointed her index finger and Javier swung his hip before losing his balance and tumbling into Jayne. The two faeries landed on the ground. Jayne, Georgia, and Billy were laughing as Javier attempted to disentangle himself from Jayne. "That was uncalled for," he stated with mock sorrow. Javier rolled over and managed to find all of his limbs separate from Jayne's legs, arms, and wings.

Once Javier was back on his feet, he dusted himself off and stood back a few feet from Georgia and Jayne. "How far can you freeze something, now?" he asked wearily.

"Oh, maybe about half a mile," she said. "It really depends upon the elements, I think. It was much more difficult yesterday when the weather was windy. Today, with the sunshine and no wind, there seems to be less resistance in the distance between the object and myself."

"Tha's amazin'," said Billy.

"Does everyone have their tasks arranged for today?" Javier queried. "Since I slept through breakfast, I figured that maybe I missed out on today's instructions."

Jayne picked one her flowers and offered it to Billy. He took it from her and stuffed it into the rim of his hat, so that it peeked out of the brim. "Thanks," he murmured under his breath. She grinned at him before turning and taking a seat on a nearby rock.

"We were told to choose what we'd like to work on today, as we're leaving in two days time. Well, technically we leave the day after tomorrow," responded Jayne. "Georgia and I decided that we wanted to practice what we'd learned together, to see if we could play upon each others' powers. We might join the others later and work as a group, just like we'd do on our daily lessons in Faerie."

"That sounds like fun," remarked Javier. "Maybe I can join groups like in a round robin. Have you seen Seth or Mercury?"

Georgia shook her head. "Not since breakfast. I think that Mercury was planning to do some work with Solomon. She mentioned something about wanting to take advantage of the natural fire that burns within the salamander. Between us, I think she feels most understood around him."

"We un'erstand her," countered Billy.

"True," agreed Jayne, "but we also spend a great deal of time teasing her too. Sometimes I think she gets tired of us."

"Now, she knows how to dance," stated Georgia. She gave Javier a pointed look.

"Whose making fun of whom now?" he retorted. "My moves are perfectly good. You should see how many other faeries copy my dancing."

Jayne laughed. "Oh, believe me, I've seen them copy your dance moves. Let me tell you, Javier, they're not doing it as a complement to your skills."

Georgia laughed. "Yes, Arabella was showing two young boys your latest moves before we left to come here. They weren't too far from Oak Tree and were laughing hysterically. I think one of them even managed to put his back out. I saw him hobbling away a little while later with a look of pain on his face." She demonstrated the arm moves that she had seen, which caused her to fall backwards. She caught herself before she landed on the ground, beating her wings so that she flew upright and back onto the soles of her feet.

Billy chuckled and clapped Javier on the back. "Ya could start a comedy show, Javier."

"Ha, ha. Very funny, you three," he drolled. "Just see who comes to take you onto the dance floor next time you need a partner."

"Speaking of partners," Jayne fluttered her wings, "here comes Geoff."

Billy turned around to greet the Guardian Faerie. "Hi there, Geoff. I saws ya earlier doin' some migh'y fine things with th' brownies. I' looked like ya all was havin' fun."

"I always have fun," insisted Geoff. He quickly turned from faerie to hummingbird and back again. He reached for Jayne's hand and squeezed it. "I'm able to shape-shift as fast as I think about it now." He grinned in pleasure. "Those brownies sure know how to cast spells and use herbs to make great potions."

"Have you seen Seth since breakfast? I've been wanting to meet up with him since Billy awoke me this morning." Javier stretched out his wings and lifted his face to the warmth of the sunlight.

"I think that he went off somewhere with Mercury," said Geoff. "I might be wrong, but I think they were joining Solomon in an activity."

"See? Didn't I say that'd be the case?" exclaimed Georgia. "I'm quite intelligent, if I do say so myself."

Javier lifted his eyebrows and said into the sun, "You did say it." Georgia swatted him on the arm. "Ouch!" he said as he pulled his arm out of her way in case she went at him again. "Have you any idea where Solomon took Mercury and Seth?"

"Not really," admitted Geoff. "I wasn't really paying any attention to their plans. I was too focused on the brownies to notice anything else. Quite honestly, I didn't even know where Jayne had gone with Georgia. It wasn't until a few minutes ago that I noticed Billy talking with you, Jayne."

Javier huffed a breath of air. "Well, I'm going to leave all of you to carry on with whatever it is you have planned. I'm going in search of Mercury and Seth." He turned from the group and trekked towards the thick trees that lined the edge of the training camp.

"Gosh, he's kinda sore. How'd tha' happen?"

"Maybe we teased him too much," suggested Jayne.

Javier attempted to tune out the group he had just left. He whistled a tune as he picked up his pace. Once he had reached the edge of the thick trees, Javier took to the air and used his wings to navigate between the branches. He listened intently for the sound of voices. It was not long before he was able to locate Seth, Mercury, and Solomon. He lowered himself to the ground and took the last few yards on foot. As he came around the trunk of the last tree, Javier saw Mercury playing with flames on the end of her tongue. Her head was tilted upwards, her blond hair cascaded down her back, and her tongue was sticking out and moving the flames about.

"Wow," he gasped.

Seth turned from gazing at Mercury to the sound of Javier. He smiled and waved. "Hey there, Javier. Have you come to see the power of fire? This is the most wonderful thing I've seen Mercury do in a long time. Solomon is showing her how to play with her flames and make them dance on various objects."

Javier walked over to Seth, although his eyes never strayed from Mercury. "Can you swallow them too?"

Mercury tossed the flames into the air and caught them with her left hand. "That's an excellent suggestion, Javier." She turned to Solomon and addressed him, "Do you think that would be possible?"

Solomon flicked his forked tongue out and watched the fire faerie. "It is quite possible, although I have no idea what they would do inside of your stomach or how you would bring them back out. Am I correct in assuming that you are immune to fire?"

"Yes, fire doesn't burn me in any way," stated Mercury. "It's almost as though I've been born of fire, which in a way I suppose that I was." She glanced at Seth and Javier, but did not mention Mother Crystal, although it was clear between the three of them that she was referring to the birth of magick.

"I think that we were all born from our gifts, in a sense," rushed Seth. "When you think about it, it seems possible, right? We were born special so we were born to have superpowers. Who's to say that the two weren't intermingled at our conception?"

Solomon looked quizzically at Seth. "Absolutely," he said. "One is just as important as the other. Magick, special births, and superpowers are all intertwined. Do not forget, though, that magick is all around us and it lives in everything that exists in this realm. Nature is a form of magick. We must always remember to respect her and keep her in balance, even if we have to give up something in our lives that we hold dear."

Seth glanced at the others. "Have you felt a change in our world, Solomon?" he asked tentatively.

"A change?"

"Yes, like something is slithering into it and moving amongst everything. It feels dark."

Solomon flicked his tongue again before he replied, "Something that you might not be aware of if you were preoccupied? Something that comes and goes, depending upon your activities at the moment? Maybe something that does not feel peaceful and loving?"

Seth nodded his head. "Yes, something like that."

"Hmm." Solomon rubbed at his chin. "Now that you mention it, I did notice a shift last night, although I couldn't be certain it actually occurred. I did drink a wee bit too much nectar, I must admit."

"Me too," volunteered Javier.

Seth began to rock on the balls of his flat feet, with his hands clasped behind his back. "If you focus today, can you still feel the change?"

"I thought that you were a seer, not an empathic," stated Solomon.

"I am," agreed Seth. "It's just that one of my visions pointed out this darkness, and since then I can feel it growing."

"Perhaps it is the threat against which we are all training," suggested Solomon.

"That's what I think," said Seth.

Javier interrupted the conversation. "Well, can we continue to watch Mercury eat flames until we have to deal with this threat?"

"Certainly," concurred Seth.

CHAPTER 18

Lillian peeked her head out of her tree hole slowly. She looked from left to right before pulling herself back into the tree. Within seconds, she emerged again with a dark brown sack slung over her right shoulder. She quickly closed her door and stepped to the end of the tree branch, which was decorated with bits of various moss and carvings etched out on the bark. She pushed aside a low branch full of leaves as she moved her wings and took flight, moving amongst the trees at a horizontal angle.

Her wings moved in rhythm with her breathing. She darted her eyes back and forth as she left her home, but it did not take long before she felt comfortable enough to focus on her destination. She breathed a sigh of relief when she reached the waterfall and surrounding stream. The lush vegetation reached out to her senses. She breathed deeply of the flora and fresh water. Rushing water greeted her ears as she lowered herself to a rock near the edge of the waterfall. Dampness tugged at her clothing and bare limbs. It felt refreshing against her skin, like an unexpected cleansing.

Lillian lifted the brown sack off her right shoulder and put it gently on the rock beside her feet. With ease, she untied the knots of the white rope holding it closed. She dug around the blanket within until she grasped something hard and pulled it out of the sack to examine it in the light. The sun glinted off the crystal, causing the appearance of green to emanate from the edges and the crystal as a whole. Lillian held the crystal up to eye level and smiled widely. "You are definitely a gift from the gods," she insisted before she touched her lips to it in a kiss.

The crunch of someone stepping on a stick caused Lillian to turn quickly and hide the crystal behind her back. Her wings fluttered in agitation and fear. "No need to panic, Lillian," drawled Logan as he stepped out from behind a bush about three feet down the stream from where Lillian had landed. "You really ought to watch your surroundings more, though. I arrived before you, yet you didn't even notice my presence."

Lillian brought her hands back into view and shook her head. "How do you expect me to notice everything, Logan? It's not like I have the empathic power."

"Not yet, anyway," agreed Logan. He walked towards her. "May I?" he asked and held out his hand for the crystal.

Hesitantly, Lillian gave him the green crystal. "Be very careful with it," she cautioned. "I really don't want to have to get another one."

"You worry too much," chastised Logan. He held the crystal between his two hands, rubbing his thumbs along two of the sharp edges. "Have you noticed any new powers from it?"

"Perhaps," she carefully replied. She could feel his eyes boring into her, yet she refused to look him in the face. "It is difficult to tell exactly what is changing. I only feel more elated, more in control."

"Show me what you have gained," Logan encouraged.

She took the crystal from him and gazed into the greens that sparkled within it. "Why does it interest you so?" She continued to avoid his eyes.

"Why would it not interest me?" he countered. With a sigh of exasperation, he continued, "If this crystal can provide you with powers and gifts equal to the Guardians, then it makes sense to believe all faeries could benefit from these powers. As you mentioned before, perhaps Alexander has dismissed possible Guardians in the past when he rejected the training of all faeries born with special needs. The council scrolls indicate there was a time when all faeries born with unique abilities were trained to hone their gifts and fight for the natural balance we all hold dear."

Lillian brought her gaze away from the crystal and met Logan's stare. "I am not yet certain as to how this crystal works with the magick around us. The first time I touched it alone, I felt a surge of peacefulness and hope. My fingers vibrated and tingled. It was as though another entity were entering my body and becoming one with my soul. I could feel flames licking at my chakras. I nearly dropped the crystal. Then there was a surge through my fingertips and flames ignited, dancing on the palm of my free hand."

Logan moved closer to Lillian, his body shaking with excitement. "Did it get stronger? Can you make an entire bonfire?"

"It seemed to get stronger. I could eventually light candles, but I have not been able to light a bonfire or a kitchen fire," she admitted. At the disappointment showing on Logan's face, Lillian added, "Over the past few weeks I have noticed more abilities unrelated to fire." She remained still, waiting for his reaction.

Logan licked his lips slowly. "More abilities? Such as…what specifically?"

Lillian rubbed the crystal for a few moments before she replied, "When I am feeling alone, which is not very often," she added quickly, "I start to shimmer, as though I'm becoming translucent."

"Like Sabrina does?" he queries.

"No, not invisible, just translucent. Then I was in a hurry to get to one of our meetings last week. I had been caught up in a conversation with Sara, the faerie who makes shawls from the hemp plant, when I realised that I was going to be late for council. I left her beside the large boulder and was running down the path when suddenly I appeared in front of Oak Tree. I did not complete the journey on my own. I moved from one spot to the next, with nothing in-between." She exclaimed, "I teleported, Logan! There was no time and space for me. I was where I needed to be when I needed to be there."

"Fascinating," murmured Logan. "Are you gaining gifts? None of them are growing?"

Lillian bent over with the crystal and re-snuggled it into the deep brown sack, amongst the confines of the blanket. "No matter how hard I try, I cannot seem to increase the powers once I have gained them. There must be some way to increase their strength."

Logan chewed on the inside of his cheek. "That must be what Alexander does with the Guardians."

"What is that?"

"He must help them hone their skills, build their powers. They do meet nearly daily once they have been selected to join the elite group."

Lillian scoffed, "He could not possibly help them manipulate their powers. He has no special gift of his own, so how would he know what to do with each gift? All of these years he probably has them practice together so that they inadvertently learn from one another."

"You are forgetting, Lillian," chastised Logan, "that Alexander has been training these Guardians for millennia. According to legend, the gods chose him to guide them. He must have special gifts that we know nothing about. After all,

Alexander is not forthcoming with his knowledge or with what he does amongst the Guardians."

"Yes," she agreed, "he has many secrets that the council has been unable to extract from him. This is what I have been trying to convey to the council. We need to know more, we need to be involved in the secrecy of the Guardians. What if something were to happen to Alexander? How would we carry on with the well-being of Faerie?"

"Perhaps the answer to your questions lies within the sack at your feet," suggested Logan.

Lillian looked down at the sack harbouring the alexandrite she now possessed. "Obviously, there is a great deal to this crystal. It has allowed me to gain certain gifts that were only foretold to be given to specific faeries with special needs, those who become Guardians. You and I are not yet aware of what else will come to pass. I mean, can these powers be shared even further? Can they increase? Are there other sources hidden in our lands that would allow all faeries to become blessed with powers? Should we share this knowledge outside of the council? Or do we keep this information within the walls of our meetings until we know more?"

"So many questions, Lillian," responded Logan. "I do notice that you have not offered the crystal to me. If I were to, say, take it into my possession for a few days, perhaps we could find some answers that would inform us of the possibility that these gifts of the gods can be shared amongst Faerie and even honed with those of us not born to be Guardians."

Lillian averted her eyes away from Logan as her face flushed with a tinge of pink. "I understand what you are saying, Logan, and I do not dispute the merit in sharing the crystal with you; however, I do think we ought to first discover whether or not what I have acquired remains and if it gains in ability. Once we have established the answer to that, then we should discuss the possibility of you taking care of the crystal for a few days." She watched the water fall down the rock and crash into the pool before it was swept downstream.

"Are you documenting the changes?" queried Logan, ignoring Lillian's dismissal of his desire for the crystal.

"I hadn't really thought about documenting the changes," she admitted. "What if the written word falls into the wrong hands? What if writing these changes down somehow stagnates the power growth?"

Logan scoffed at her, "Do not be ridiculous, Lillian. You are a council member, which means you have access to some great hiding places. Besides, if the growth were to become permanent, your written documentation would show how long it takes to accrue a special gift, how long it takes for it to grow, and how long between gathering of each gift. This is like a very important scientific experiment. All experiments should be documented. Truly, you need to record everything as proof that our kind has been kept in the dark for millennia and we need to make changes to the Crystal Guardians." He rubbed his nose with his left hand, and then proceeded to scratch it with his index finger.

Lillian bent over to stretch out her back. "I hear what you are saying," she admitted with reluctance. "This evening I will begin writing down what has occurred so far since the Equinox. As of tomorrow, I will document all daily changes in detail. You are right, this is important. It is essential that we do this quickly."

"Is there anything in particular you need for me to do in order to help you speed along this process?" Logan asked eagerly.

"Tell no one about this conversation," responded Lillian. "I fear that the council might have some awareness of this crystal, but I am not yet willing to confirm its existence nor share what we know. I do not want them to be aware of what you and I did on the Equinox."

"They couldn't possibly find against us based on what we did. They would be more interested in the results rather than in the process," Logan assured them both.

"You do not know the council as I do, Logan," Lillian insisted. "They are sticklers for tradition. Anything new scares them; they fear the unknown." She paused and walked over to touch the water with her right palm. "What we did could be considered treason against all of Faerie. It was with great difficulty that I finally found the entrance to that cave. I think that most of the community believes it to be a myth, but I knew better. Something in my gut insisted that it really did exist."

"As I mentioned before," stated Logan, "I am very pleased to have been the one you invited along on the Equinox. I would not have believed in the existence of that cave if I had not seen it with my own eyes. Since that night, I have to close my eyes and I can smell the vegetation and see the pool of water changing colours."

"Well, be certain that you keep those memories to yourself and do not breathe a word of it to anyone," she seethed between her teeth.

Logan took a step away from Lillian. "I would never tell anyone what we did in that cave. How could I? Any divulgence of our actions could lead to not only being removed from the council, but it could also mean a complete ban from the confines of Faerie. Harming any form of nature is illegal amongst Faeries. What we did to that pool of water and the contents it contained… well, it makes me ill to think about it."

"Stop talking about it!" she screeched. She looked around furtively. "Someone might hear you. We can never be certain who is around listening to our conversations."

"Yet discussing what is in your sack is allowable out here in the open? What difference does it make if we discuss the cave or your newly acquired powers?" rebutted Logan. He breathed heavily and turned away from her. In a swift motion, he stepped off the rock and plunged himself through the falling water to the safety of a ledge hidden behind the waterfall. His wet feet sucked at the dry ledge, trailing wet footprints. He locked his arms across his chest and breathed deeply to calm his anger. His wings shook in frustration and his face contorted into a bundle of turned up nose and puckered lip. He ignored Lillian as she followed him into the waterfall. He could hear her wings beating and her lungs taking short breaths.

"There is no need for you to be this upset, Logan," declared Lillian. "I am the one who managed to find a way to change the distribution of powers and gifts in our realm. I am the one who convinced the council to bring Alexander to a meeting and insist that he share his knowledge of the Guardians with us, even though he refused. I took things into my own hands and took action where none has been taken before. I found the information on the hidden cave and what it contains. I spent the time around the cave area, even though you managed to find the way into its depths. I am the one who broke this crystal off of the large piece in the pool. If anyone has taken a risk here, it is I who have done so." She stopped moving her wings and thumped her feet on the rock ledge.

Logan turned around and glared at her. "You may have done all the footwork with this, Lillian, but I was along for the desecration of that large crystal. I am an accomplice. I have just as much to lose here as you do if things do not work out as we have planned. When we remove Alexander from his post, there is going to be a great deal of upheaval in the community until we can establish proper control through the council."

"We will need to establish new rules so that there is not a great deal of dissention or resistance. We need to bring the community on board with our wishes so that most of Faerie will encourage us to remove Alexander. The way it will occur is as though the community thought of removing Alexander themselves, that we are the tool used to carry out their wishes," insisted Lillian. "The only way to ensure we get our way in this matter is to make it appear as though others thought of the idea first."

"I hate to agree with you when I feel as though you are manipulating me," stated Logan, "but I must admit that what you say makes sense. Although, you may want to remember, Lillian, that I am your ally and not your enemy. If you continue to refuse me access to this crystal and these powers it provides, then I may become your enemy. Keep in mind, Lillian, that you do not want me as an enemy."

Lillian pursed her lips into a snarl. "Do not threaten me, dear Logan. If you think that I would be a simple enemy to deal with, then you are sadly mistaken. I chose you as my ally because I know that you and I have the same desires for Faerie. Just because I am taking my time with sharing the alexandrite crystal, does not mean that I have no intention of giving you access to it. I want to be certain of what we have here before we test out our theories."

Logan uncrossed his arms and rubbed at his temples. "Why are we fighting with each other, Lillian? If we cannot remain cohesive, then there is no hope in us convincing all of Faerie to agree to our plans. Let us agree to disagree. You need to test out your theories on the powers of the crystal and how they will affect you, while I am eager to try holding it in my possession for the same effect. I will acquiesce to your desires for the moment. But, do not believe that I will allow this to carry on for much longer."

Lillian nodded her head. "Agreed. Give me another week with the crystal. I promise that I will then hand it over to you for further study. By then we should be able to have some good documentation on the effects this crystal has on me. You were correct in suggesting that I record the changes that are occurring. We will carry on with writing everything down once you have the crystal. At that point, we can compare which powers it gives each of us and how those powers grow.

I think that once we have that documentation, we will approach the council again with our plan."

"Alexander and the Guardians will be home within a couple of days. Perhaps we should meet again here to exchange the crystal. Bring with you all the written records that you will be starting tonight," suggested Logan. He stretch his wings out and folded them back together.

"No, we do not want any discussion of our project reaching the wrong ears. Too many people are in allegiance with Alexander." Lillian reached out her hand and touched the falling water, allowing it to spray across and down her arm. She licked at her arm, lapping up the drips.

Logan spread his wings again and lifted himself off the ground. "Well, let us depart. Shall we meet here at this same time next week?"

"Certainly," agreed Lillian. "I will bring everything we need. Keep well," she added as an afterthought. At that, Lillian picked up her deep brown sack and quickly flew through the waterfall without looking back to see if Logan remained or left as well.

CHAPTER 19

Billy smiled as Jayne flew up and leaned in to kiss his left cheek. "I'm so glad that you came with us on our training camp this year, Billy," she gushed. A warmth moved up his neck and spread over his face. "You always make things seem so much fun," she stated, as she landed on her feet again.

"Gosh, yous is such a grea' faerie, Jayne. I had fun. I always have fun with you all," he said. He bent his head and focused on his foot pushing at the dirt. "You make me feel like I'm a Guardian too."

"Oh Billy," exclaimed Jayne, "you are a Guardian. You are more special because we chose you to be a Guardian, rather than your just being born into it like the rest of us were." She threw her arms around Billy's legs and hugged him tight. "Geoff and I are always talking about how much you mean to us, and how it seems like you should be involved in learning with us during our daily classes with Alexander."

"Geoff thinks I am a Guardian?" asked Billy in surprise.

"Oh yes, we all feel like you're a Guardian," Jayne assured him. "That's why it felt right to have you with us at the Equinox. I think you are now officially expected to attend training camp with us annually."

"Certainly, you will be attending with us each year," interrupted Alexander, as he prodded over to the two huddled just off the path. "If I could, I would have you attend our lessons as well, but alas, I cannot bend tradition to that extent."

"Tha's okay, Alexander. I understand th' importance of followin' th' words of th' gods," acknowledged Billy.

Alexander put his knobbly hand on Billy's shoulder. "You are the first magickal creature, in all my time as Saviour, who is not a Guardian Faerie, but who I think should be," he declared with great heart. "I'm certain that if Archangel Michael could break the rule, he would do so for you."

"I get ta be with th' faeries all th' time," said Billy, "which is jus' as good as bein' one. An' I help 'em too."

"You help them in so many ways, Billy," agreed Alexander. "Each day you make a difference in their lives that allows them to work more closely with nature." He pressed his hand down on Billy's shoulder before removing it and rubbing his own hands together. "We should all get back to our families before the sun sets. Guardians, I expect to see each of you tomorrow afternoon for a brief lesson before the welcome home celebrations begin. We will meet at my home, as I would like to share some items in my library with all of you."

"Should we bring anything with us?" questioned Mercury. She twisted her blond hair between her fingers, screamed in a low pitch, and kept lifting each leg one at a time off the ground.

"No, I will have everything you will need," Alexander replied. "I suggest that you all have a fun and enjoyable evening with your families. Do not stay up too late, as tomorrow night you will be bombarded with community folk wanting to bask in your presence."

Geoff laughed. "They act like we have something wonderful to give them. It always seems so strange when we come back from time away. I often feel uncomfortable recounting how exciting the trip was and mentioning the beings we spent time with. I like gatherings better once we've been home for a while. The community doesn't act strange when the weekly celebrations start; they just let us do our own thing."

"I can't wait to share my new fire power," uttered Mercury. She flicked her right thumb and index finger, causing a spark to alight. Just as quickly at it sparked, it fizzled into smoke. She attempted the movement again with the same results. Mercury creased her brow and tried it for a third time. "I don't understand," she murmured.

"What is it?" queried Ryan as he stepped closer to Mercury.

"I don't know," she admitted. "My spark isn't turning to the fireball I learned to create."

Ryan examined her fingers closely. "Are you making the same movements you were shown? In the same beat of time?"

She nodded her head furtively. "Yes, I know that I'm doing everything the same as I've been doing it. Maybe I'm tired and don't even know it."

"Or you could be excited to be home," suggested Shoshana. "I know that I'm excited. Sometimes things don't work as well when our emotions are out of control. Do something that you have always done, rather than something you just learned."

Mercury opened the palm of her hand and felt into her core. She took a deep breath and blew onto her hand. The fire erupted from within her blood and shot through her skin to form a strong flame that licked at the air. She smiled and bent to kiss the familiar orange and red fire growing from within her.

"Excellen', Mercury," commented Billy. "I like fire. Ya make i' warm when th' air is cold."

"You'll be able to perform your new abilities tomorrow just fine," encouraged Georgia. "Shoshana was right, it's all this excitement that won't allow your spark to take."

"Well, can someone else try something new, so that I know it's excitement for certain? I'm kind of disappointed in myself, especially because I don't feel super excited," begged Mercury.

"I feel excited about seeing my family," admitted Geoff. "I feel a bit off, so I'll try something for you." He bent his knees so that he was crouching on the ground. With a quick flick of his tongue, Geoff sparkled pink before he shifted into a puddle of water.

Jayne bent over and touched the puddle with the tip of a finger. The water rippled. "He is definitely water."

"I need to try now," insisted Georgia. She pushed Seth from behind without hesitation. As he stumbled forward, she whispered, "Freeze." Instantly, Seth remained air-bound, neither falling nor standing. "Can you catch him when I let him go, Javier?"

Javier flitted over to Seth and held out his arms underneath his friend. "Move," Georgia countered. As Seth tumbled into Javier's arms, Mercury flapped her arms in the air and jumped up and down.

"Something's definitely wrong with me," she exclaimed in panic. Her fingers began to twitch rapidly.

Shoshana cringed. "Mercury, your panic is enveloping my own feelings. Can you take it down a notch?" She backed away from the group, holding her hands up in front of her face.

"What happened? What did I catch? Is everything I learned going to disappear?" screeched Mercury.

Alexander deepened his voice, yet lifted it so that everyone could hear, "You all need to stop moving and talking. Mercury, stay still."

"Wha' ya think i' is?" whispered Billy into Alexander's ear. Alexander held up his hand to shush Billy, who immediately closed his mouth. Mercury continued to twitch her fingers, although the remainder of her body stayed still. Shoshana left her hands in front of her face. The puddle on the ground shrank, pulled together, and pulled upwards to twist into Geoff, who remained mute, his eyes cued to Mercury. Sabrina touched her lips to keep herself silent. Ryan glanced from Alexander to Mercury and back again.

"I do not know why you cannot create a spark, Mercury. Once you have learned a new technique with your gift, you should be able to build upon it. I have never encountered a power that becomes intermittent," admits Alexander.

"It's not intermittent!" her voice arose two octaves. "I can't even get it to work!"

"I know that you are upset," he stated with patience, "but allowing panic to take over will not help you to control your abilities. In fact, your panic will make your wishes even more difficult. I need for you to concentrate on your breathing."

Mercury started to tear up. She took a deep breath in and blew it out shakily. "That's it," encouraged Alexander. "Breath in, and breath out." Mercury followed his instructions as he continued to coach her. "In and out." It was not long before all the faeries and Billy were breathing in rhythm. Within a few minutes, Mercury was no longer teary and the others felt relaxed.

Seth shifted his short, stalking stature from one foot to the other. "Is this part of the darkness?" he asked no one in particular.

"Darkness?" repeated Jayne. Her hands glowed purple, which she placed against her heart chakra.

"Yes, the darkness," Seth stated. "There was no magick when the darkness came. It was all gone."

"No magick?" squeaked Mercury. Her fingers began to twitch again, yet she remained focused this time on her breathing.

"I do not know," replied Alexander. "I will consult my oracle once I am home. In the meantime, I suggest that you all get some rest and allow me to worry about this new development. I am here to assist you in any way I can. I promise," he added, "that I will find the root of this problem so that we can rectify it."

Seth glanced down at his feet in an attempt to avoid the stares of his peers. What Alexander said made sense, but he could not shake the vision of his time with Apollo. He could not stop the fear from seeping into his gut and spreading through his thoughts. *What if Mercury was unable to access what she had learned at training camp? What if all of their magick began to disappear one by one? What if each of them started to disappear along with their powers? What if only he and Apollo were left in a vast land of barren rock and complete darkness?*

"All of you need to go home now," instructed Alexander. "Do not mention any of this outside of the group. I will let you know what I discover when we meet tomorrow. I am certain that I will have the answer to this mystery by then."

Billy lifted his rucksack over his shoulders and nearly toppled to the ground as its weight pushed against his back. Javier struck out his arm to prevent Billy from losing his balance. Billy grinned at his friend. "Nigh' all," he said cheerily. He waved to them all and walked home.

Javier and the others collected their own belongings, departing one by one. Jayne and Geoff took to the air while the others dispersed on foot into the shrubbery. Seth was the last to leave, making his way down the path, slowly placing one foot in front of the other while his thoughts continued to wander back to the darkness.

CHAPTER 20

Seth hugged first his mother and then his father goodnight. His sister had gone to bed a few minutes earlier. She had been happy to have Seth home. Janice was two years older than Seth, yet she always treated him like an equal rather than bossing him around like some of his friends' older siblings did to them. It had been a wonderful evening with his family, but Seth was tired and the sickening feeling in his gut had not dispersed. After a warm bath and settling into his pyjamas, Seth had joined his sister and parents for a hot cup of tea before bed. Now that the tea was settling in their bellies and his sister had gone to bed, Seth knew that the time had come for him to crawl into his own bed and examine the arrival of the darkness, for he knew that the darkness was no longer seeping into Faerie. While he had been away, the darkness had become part of Faerie.

Seth took the small flight of stairs up to the second floor of their home in the cedar tree. He closed the door to his bedroom and gazed out the window into the night. The stars twinkled between the clouds that decorated the sky. The resident tree frog sang his lullaby as everyone turned in for sleep. Seth poked his head out of the window and breathed in the clear air, filling his lungs of its freshness.

A great sigh escaped his throat as Seth left the window and settled himself into bed. He pulled the warm covers up to his chin and gazed at the ceiling, counting the years of the tree embedded there. His breathing slowed and his stomach stopped turning in fear as he drifted off to sleep.

Seth could feel himself floating without the help of his wings. A lush forest spread across the land below him. The canopy of trees hid what lay beneath. As he travelled to his destination, Seth noticed the birds watching him from below, as though they were expecting his arrival. The sun was bright in the sky, touching everything with light and life. Through a break in the trees, Seth could see the rushing water before the sound of its movement touched his ears. He dropped lower in the sky toward the opening mouth of the bubbling blue and white lake below. When his feet touched the soft sand, he moved his head to the right, where a thicket of ripe, red berries were rooted in the dirt.

Seth moved his gaze from the berries to the vast empty beach surrounding the lake. At first glance it appeared deserted, yet something rustled behind a tree on the opposite part of the lake from where he stood; he almost missed the movement, it was so very subtle. Without hesitation, Seth used his wings to lift himself and fly across the lake. Once he found himself in front of the tree, he carefully stepped forward and walked around the trunk.

Sitting behind the tree, allowing the filtered sun to reach him, sat Apollo. His eyes were closed and his face was upturned into the warmth. He had a smile tapered across his face, as though he were completely content. "Hello, Seth," he greeted without opening his eyes.

Seth stopped moving at Apollo's voice. "Apollo," he acknowledged. "Can I ask what time we're in?"

"Can you not tell?" queried the sun god.

"Well, it has to be before the last time I saw you," he stated. "Although, I did see you after this time yet before this time…" his voice trailed off as his mind became confused.

"Ah, yes, the spinning of time … in its proper form of no end and no beginning. You do realise that time is not linear, don't you, Seth?" He opened his eyes and turned to face the young faerie he had summoned here.

Seth scratched at the side of his head, trying to unravel his confusion. "Yes, I know how time works," he stated. "I meant that in my life this is the third time I've spoken with you in a short bit, yet this appears to be before you speak to me later."

Apollo laughed and gestured for Seth to sit beside him. "I know what you meant. I was playing with you. You are correct in believing this to be before we meet again. I want to know if you are aware of what has seeped into Faerie?"

Seth sat down and rubbed at the ground with his fingers. "The darkness has come, as you showed me it would." He added after a pause, "Magick is still here though."

"For how long will magick remain, Seth?"

"I don't think it'll be long before magick is sucked into the darkness. I think it's started to disappear."

"How so?" encouraged Apollo.

Seth took a deep breath. "Mercury can't make a spark. She learned to make sparks and do all kinds of things with fire during our Equinox training, but when we returned late today to Faerie, she could no longer create a spark." He took another breath, this one slowly and with difficulty. "I think the darkness is taking away her gift of fire."

"The light is always the first to go," said Apollo. "Do you know what is causing this, yet?"

Seth shook his head. "No. But I think I know where it started," he suggested quietly.

Apollo moved his fingers over a clump of brown grass, causing the clump to turn green and grow an inch. Without looking at Seth, he encouraged, "Where did it start, Seth?"

"Everything began in the cavern. It has to be the cavern," he said bravely. "Mother Crystal is in that cavern. She's the source of all magick, of all life. Without her, there is no magick and there is no life. So something has infected her." He looked over at Apollo and met the god's bright blue eyes.

"I agree with some of what you say," admitted Apollo. "She is definitely the source of all magick and life. She existed before time, and before this universe and world were formed. She created all that you know here in your realm. However, I don't think she has been infected, like a virus. She cannot catch a disease. Something else must have overpowered her source or started to develop in the air."

"I disagree with you, Apollo," insisted Seth, forgetting with whom he was speaking. "She was perfect when I met her. There was nothing in the cavern and there was nothing but love and peace coming from her. Although I felt the darkness seeping in after I met with you in our desecrated realm, I didn't truly feel it in the air until our return today. Something happened while we were gone to training camp."

Apollo broke his gaze with Seth and turned again to the sky, searching out the sun. "Does Alexander have any ideas as to the source of this darkness?"

Seth shrugged his shoulders. "I don't think so. He doesn't seem too worried that Mercury is unable to use what she learned over the past three weeks. He said that he'd look up the cause and get back to us tomorrow with a solution. Between you and me, Apollo, I don't think Alexander will be able to find a solution to this. I think this is the start of what you showed me before. It's more complex than knowledge."

"The gods prophesied the coming of Alexander shortly after Faerie came to exist. Archangel Michael came to one of your own, a seer like you, and helped her to realise her purpose in training the saviour of this realm. She knew of Alexander long before he was born. She was held in the wings of Archangel Michael while she slept and was given all the knowledge she required to prepare Alexander for his position as sage of the Crystal Guardians." Apollo stretched out his arms and legs, shifting his position so that he was no longer leaning against the trunk of the tree.

A squirrel chattered from a branch above their heads, then jumped from his branch to a lower one on the tree next to them. Apollo continued, "Alexander's role has been to train all of the special faeries selected to be Crystal Guardians. His role was never intended to know the source of the threat or to fight the threat when it arrived."

Seth thought about this before he spoke again. "So Alexander has no power in this fight against the darkness."

"None," agreed Apollo.

"So, he'll come to us tomorrow with no information on the loss of Mercury's powers. Will he be disappointed with himself?" wondered Seth aloud.

"I am certain that he will feel as though he has let all of you down," said Apollo. "However, you must convey to him, Seth, that he has not let you down. You must make him understand that he does not have the knowledge he seeks and that he is not expected to have such knowledge. His role was to train the Crystal Guardians, which he has done very well. It is now time for him to let each of you prove yourselves. You all have the ability to fight this threat. He will want to gather all of the Guardians, bring them all to Faerie. Although he now focuses his time with your generation, Seth, there are many who still live and who will be required to help fight alongside you and your peers."

"Should I tell him to gather them early tomorrow? Or should I wait until lessons in the afternoon?" Seth could not even begin to imagine how Alexander would feel once he came to realise that he had no answers for Mercury regarding the loss of her powers.

"Wait until Alexander informs all of you that he cannot explain the disappearance of magick from Mercury. He needs to know that he is not responsible for solving this problem, yet he will need to take the steps necessary to come to that conclusion. Let him know that his position now is to gather all of the living Guardians. It is the Guardians who will discover the source of the threat. It is the Guardians who will plan the attack against this darkness. If you are to be successful, Seth, then you must make Alexander aware of the importance in allowing the Guardians to take control now."

"Apollo, I know that the source is somewhere in the cavern, somewhere near Mother Crystal. I just know it," he again insisted.

Apollo sighed, "You might be correct, Seth, for I cannot know everything. I only know about the light. I am not privy to the darkness, for it is everything I am not. I am of light, of healing, of Helios. I know truth and prophecy. I can heal and I can cause plague. I bring medicine to those in need. I am the leader of all muses with the gift of music and poetry."

"Who's in charge of the darkness, then?" asked Seth innocently.

"Oh, that would be Erebus," answered Apollo. "But what we are talking about doesn't really have to do with Erebus. He focuses on the underworld, not the living world. He only cares about the dead, really. He isn't interested in removing the light so much as capturing those who have passed on from life. No, the darkness we are discussing comes from something living."

Seth began to chew on his inner cheek. "Something living? How can something living feel so desolate? So creepy? So scary? I've felt the darkness. It can't possibly be something living."

"Oh, I am certain it is living," argued Apollo. "Mother Crystal is love and peace and, of course, the birth of magick. For something to destroy her it has to be alive, it has to be of her creation."

Seth began to twist his small, stubby fingers together. His tongue became thicker as his mouth became parched from fear. "Her creation is destroying her? How can that be?"

"Not all children respond positively to their parents, Seth. All children have the right to grow into their souls, to make choices and have free will. Sometimes, anger and hurt can build and become so strong, that the child can no longer feel the love and peace provided unconditionally. Mother Crystal is unconditional love and unconditional peace."

"Yes, she is. We all felt that from her when we met her in the cavern. Maybe I need to go back to the cavern and speak with her," Seth concluded. He nodded his head and stood up. "Yes, I'm going to speak with her. Maybe she knows how this darkness developed. Maybe she can help me."

Apollo smiled at Seth. "I am very pleased with you, Guardian Seth. You are the key to bringing back the magick, to preventing the darkness from taking over this realm and the worlds connected to this land. I have faith in you."

"I'll do my best, Apollo. I must say," he added as an afterthought, "you've been much more communicative today than you were the last time we met."

"Well, this is my second meeting with you, remember Seth?" he teased.

"Right. Your second meeting and my third meeting." He rubbed at his head and shifted his wings. "Are we going to meet again?"

Apollo laughed. "If I told you the answer to that, dear Seth, then how could I claim this to be our first meeting? Or rather, our second meeting?" He raised his right eyebrow in a taunt.

Seth shook his head. "You are full of confusion, Apollo. I think that now is a good time for me to leave and think about my next step and how I'll approach Mother Crystal and Alexander." He waved and lifted himself into the air. He focused on the blue sky above the treetop, moving his wings quickly. He blinked twice as the sunlight blinded his vision. Upon opening his eyes again, he found himself nestled amongst the covers in his bed. Seth turned over and sighed. He fluffed his pillow and sniffed the cool air blowing through his bedroom window. A tree frog croaked four times and Seth fell into a deep sleep.

CHAPTER 21

Seth held onto Shadow and closed his eyes. "You should open your eyes, Seth. There's so much to see from up here," Sabrina told him. She laughed and fluttered her wings. "This is the best way to fly."

"I prefer to use my own wings when flying, thank you very much," he mumbled between closed lips.

"Come on Seth, open your eyes. You've been up this high with your wings, so see what it's like upon a dragon!"

Seth took a deep breath and squinted between his closed eyelids. He could see the red scales of Shadow and the tips of Sabrina's wings. He opened his eyes further until he could see perfectly. Seth let his eyes roam without moving his head. The trees below almost appeared as though they were reaching up to grasp the two faeries and the dragon. Sabrina was grinning and her hair was blowing in the wind. Seth took two deep breaths until he was able to breathe with a regular rhythm.

"This isn't so bad," he agreed. "Shadow sure is able to move further than I can, and at a quicker rate."

"Oh yes, she's a fast dragon," said Sabrina. She bent over to scratch at her leg. "We spend a great deal of time just flying around when I'm not needed anywhere in particular. I thought you'd enjoy this flight to the social gathering. It's so different than flying with your own wings."

Seth lifted his face to the sinking sun. "I was quite leery of this idea at first, Sabrina, but I'm beginning to understand why you like to ride on Shadow. You must've missed her a great deal while we were at the Equinox training camp."

Sabrina touched Shadow ever so slightly with her hand, so that the dragon took a turn and swooped lower towards the trees and great Oak Tree. Sabrina lifted her arms into the air and threw back her head. "I love the landing!" she cried with great excitement.

Seth held onto one of Shadow's scales with a death-grip. "I don't know about this, Sabrina. She's moving so fast towards the ground!"

"I know, that's what makes it so exciting!" Sabrina laughed.

As they approached the great Oak Tree, the sun slipped behind the horizon and the faerie lights twinkled below them. The lights were strung up from one tree to the next, covering boughs and leaves throughout the neighbourhood. Faerie dust sparkled throughout the dark trees. Musical notes floated up into the sky, calling out to Seth and Sabrina. "I wonder if Jayne will be singing tonight," he pondered.

"Jayne always sings at these gatherings," Sabrina assured him. "She has such a lovely voice. Each note that comes from her throat sends energy down my spine. I could get lost in her voice on nights like these."

"I agree," concurred Seth. "It's no wonder that nature grows when she speaks."

Shadow pushed through the branches and landed upon a nobly hill of grass. She pulled her wings in and lowered her head and belly to the ground. Seth shimmied off her back. When his feet touched the ground, he dug his toes into the grass and fluttered his wings. "Thanks for the ride, Sabrina. Although it isn't my most favourite way to fly, I can sort of understand why you like it so much."

"Really?" she asked quizzically. "It wasn't until we were about to come down that you seemed to be enjoying yourself. You'll have to join us again on another day so that you can experience the amazing flight of a dragon without the apprehension you exhibited this evening."

Seth shrugged his shoulders. "Like I said, I can *sort of* understand why *you* like flying on this dragon. You can go as fast as you like."

"True," she acknowledged. "Although I do well flying on my own, sometimes my leg drags me down."

"I'd never have guessed that," said Seth. "I like taking my time getting places. It lets me enjoy everything along the way. Speed gives me an upset stomach and feels stressful."

"It's no wonder that you and Billy are such good friends," she informed him.

"Speaking of Billy, I promised to meet up with him as soon as we arrived here. Do you want to help me look for him?" asked Seth.

Sabrina limped forward and glanced around quickly. "Certainly, I can help you find Billy. My guess is that he'll be somewhere near Javier. The two of them have been spending a lot time together over the past couple of months. So, I suggest we call for Javier, as he'll be able to hear us from wherever he has chosen to plant himself."

Seth laughed. "Yeah, he might be at the refreshment table. He seems to like his nectar."

They walked across the nobly hill of grass and between two pine trees. "I like how we can grow any type of tree and plant in Faerie," commented Sabrina. "I bet there's no other place like this in all of the universes."

"None," agreed Seth. "I'm fairly certain that's why we keep everything in balance. If we weren't balanced, then I couldn't even imagine what kind of ripple effect that'd cause throughout time and space." He shuddered at the thought.

Sabrina took his hand and began to pull him towards the great Oak Tree. "Never mind such thoughts, Seth. This is a happy occasion and we are here to celebrate."

He quickened his step in order to keep up with Sabrina; although he did hold her back from the speed he had seen her take previously. "Why do you suppose we celebrate every week?"

"I don't know. Maybe we do it because everyone likes to get together with food and entertainment. It's fun, you must admit. I suppose, also, that it's tradition. When are we going to be able to see everyone in Faerie if we don't continue to gather like this every week? The past three weeks we haven't been here, so I'm sure there'll be lots of new gossip to hear about."

Seth mumbled, "I hate gossip." Sabrina ignored him and continued to pull him along at an uncomfortable speed.

Javier greeted Sabrina and Seth with a cup of nectar each as they approached the beverage table. "I heard that the two of you were on your way and desired some nectar," he teased. "To be quite honest, I haven't been able to drink any since our Equinox exertion." He grinned and handed them each the cups from his hands. "Billy hasn't arrived yet. I think that Mercury's planning on arriving late, if she even comes at all. She's still very much upset about her firepower disappearing. Last I heard, she couldn't even create a flame of any kind."

"No!" gasped Sabrina. "She must've caught something on our way back from camp. It makes no sense."

Javier leaned in and whispered to the two of them, "I also heard that Ryan is struggling with his power. He wasn't able to move something earlier today. It barely shook from where it was rooted."

"What was he trying to move?" asked Seth, with horror in his voice.

"His mother wanted a bed moved from one room on their second floor to a spot in the living room for some reason, and he was only able to shake it within its original spot. Apparently, he was exhausted and was down for the remainder of the afternoon," said Javier. "I don't know what's going on, but it's becoming quite scary."

Seth felt a knot in his abdomen twisting around. "It must have to do with the darkness. Remember when we were with Solomon and Mercury, Javier? Do you remember how I mentioned another change? I think this has something to do with that change."

Javier flicked his wings and shrugged his shoulders. "Well, I have to agree that something strange is going on around here. The last four faeries who dropped by to get some food and drink didn't say a word to me. They just gathered what they wanted and scurried away. I tried to send a net out and listen in on their conversation after that, but it was mumbled, rather than being clear enough to decipher."

Sabrina took a sip of her nectar. "We haven't come across anyone yet." She looked around the area and noted the lack of creatures. "Although, now that you mention it, Javier, it does seem awfully quiet for a social gathering."

Seth turned around on the spot. His feet shuffled one upon the other. "Where is everyone?" He placed his cup of nectar on the wooden table, untouched, and began to walk further into the canopy of trees. Javier and Sabrina followed him, keeping close and watching for anything else that might be amiss. "Has Alexander arrived yet, Javier?"

"I came straight here to the beverages. I thought this would be the best place to meet up with everyone. I haven't seen Alexander. You're the first two Guardians I've seen so far," he announced quietly.

"So what is going on?" demanded Sabrina. She stumbled on a rock and reached for Javier, who steadied her so that she did not fall to the ground.

"I'd sure like to know what is happening," said Seth. "Usually this place is buzzing with activity and you can't find a spot away from anyone. My family didn't mention anything that would be of concern to us. They seemed just as cheery, welcoming, and expectant as usual. My chores were definitely waiting for me and no one seemed to be keeping anything from me."

Sabrina chewed on her lower lip. "No differences at my home, either."

A rustling in the trees to their left caused them to stop in their tracks. "'Ey there, Javier," called out Billy as he stumbled onto the path and tripped on his feet. His arms went straight out as he fell flat on his face. "Oomph."

Javier and Sabrina jumped back just in time, but Seth found himself on the ground with his left leg underneath Billy. "Sorry 'bou' tha', Seth. Le' me ge' up an' help ya." Billy pushed his arms against the ground, causing his knee to crush Seth's leg even further into the ground.

"Ouch! Oh, stop, Billy! Let Javier and Sabrina help you up," Seth gritted between clenched teeth.

Billy turned his head to the side so that he could see Seth. "Oops. Didn' mean ta squish ya more, Seth." Billy stopped struggling.

Sabrina scurried over to Seth. "Let's just lift your one leg, Billy. Keep yourself still except for this leg." She touched his leg to indicate which one she wanted him to move.

"'Kay, can I lif' my leg now?" Billy had kept his balance on his elbows, but he was starting to breathe heavily.

Sabrina took hold of Seth's arms. "I'm going to pull you out when Billy lifts his leg, okay Seth? Let me do all the work."

"Okay," groaned Seth.

Javier nodded at Sabrina. "Lift your leg, Billy," instructed Javier. Billy lifted his leg, causing his face to fall into the ground. Sabrina yanked Seth towards her. In the process, she tumbled onto her back, although Seth was now free. Javier patted Billy on the head. "You can lower your leg now, Billy."

"Mmph," he replied as he let his leg fall to the ground. Billy lifted his face from the dirt and pushed himself back onto his knees. Seth was standing up and rubbing at his lower back. "Ya 'kay, Seth?"

Seth attempted to smile at Billy, although it came out as more of a grimace. "I'll be fine, Billy. I need to walk it out."

Billy looked at Seth for a moment, trying to figure out if the faerie wastruly all right. "Are ya sure?"

"Yes, I'm certain, Billy. There was no permanent harm done." He bent over and stretched out his back. "You came out of the trees in a hurry. What happened?"

"Yes, what's going on, Billy?" queried Javier.

Sabrina stepped over to Billy and placed her hand on his arm. "Are you in any pain from your fall?"

Billy removed his hat and began twisting it in his hands. "Oh, I's fine, Sabrina. Nothin' hur's."

"So what was the rush to get through the trees?" Javier asked him again.

"Well, I hear' some thin's tha' didn' make no sense. I though' ya migh' know why's they all sayin' these thin's." His hat was no longer identifiable as an item.

Seth looked quizzically from Sabrina to Javier, and then he rested his gaze upon Billy. "What things have you heard?"

"Jus' tha' Alexander has been keepin' secre's an' he has favouri' faeries," Billy answered as he looked down at his hands and the twisted hat.

"Who said this, Billy?" asked Sabrina.

"Some o' th' faeries. They's was talkin' in whispers when I came 'cross 'em on my way here. When I was sayin' hi, they's kinda looked a' me funny an' barely said hi back."

"So you heard what they were saying before they noticed you?" inquired Seth.

"Yep. Said he was no' bein' fair with choosin' Guardians an' he coulda had lo's more o' them trained o'r th' years. They's was wonderin' wha' ya do fer Equinox too," he told them.

"He hasn't been choosing Guardians properly? That's what they were saying?" clarified Sabrina.

"Tha's wha' they was sayin'. Sounds like they wan'ed more o' ya trained than wha' has been trained," he added.

"We were all given the opportunity to train," insisted Javier. "Every faerie born special has a consultation with Alexander. We're given a series of tests that decide whether or not we become a Guardian. Not all special faeries have the superpowers required to be a Guardian."

"No one outside of a special faerie knows about the series of tests," mentioned Seth. "It sounds like these faeries are making up information based on nothing true. Is this why there are so few people here tonight?" He met Javier and Sabrina's eyes to affirm this idea.

"Why would everyone be concerned about this all of a sudden?" contemplated Javier. "This has never been an issue before."

"I's no idea," admitted Billy. "I though' maybe ya all know's somethin'."

Javier shook his head. "The only thing we noticed was how quiet it is this evening. That in itself was enough to cause us concern, which is why we had decided to leave the food and beverage tables in search of others."

Seth stretched out his back one more time. "Let's go find the others, whether we come across Guardians, faeries, brownies, or gnomes. I'm really not fussy on who we find, as long as we can get this sorted out."

Sabrina and Seth walked under the boughs of trees twinkling with faerie lights. Billy and Javier followed close behind. Although they came across three squirrels and several birds, it remained desolated until they entered a group of maple trees housing several pixie and faerie families. Creatures scurried about between the trees and some even sat at the base of the trees conversing. As the four of them entered the area, the chatter ceased. Eyes from all angles peered at them. Seth brushed at his shoulder as the knot in his stomach spread into his chest.

Arabella came out from behind one of the maple trees at their approach. "Hi Javier!" she called. She walked across the expanse between them and gave Javier a hug. "I really missed each of you while you were away," she told them as she gave them each a hug.

"It's good to see you as well, Arabella," Javier said with relief in his voice. "We were wondering where everyone was this evening. It seems unusually quiet and we weren't sure if perhaps the festivities had been cancelled for some reason."

"Oh, nothing has been cancelled," she assured them. "I think that most everyone has decided to not participate in the gathering as they are still somewhat sore about Alexander's deception all of these millennia."

Javier took Arabella's hand and directed her over to a group of mushrooms where he, Seth, and Sabrina sat. Billy took a seat on the grass beside them and Arabella stood beside Javier. "Can you tell us what you know about this supposed deception? We are in the dark about what's been happening while we were at our Equinox celebration. We hadn't noticed anything amiss until we arrived here tonight."

"Well…" mumbled Seth. Sabrina lightly tapped his arm to keep him quiet.

Arabella glanced at each of the Guardians and then at Billy. She looked over her shoulder at the creatures silently watching from their various positions amongst the maple trees. "It became obvious while you were all away that Alexander's been keeping secrets about your training and initiation into the Guardians from all of Faerie. Councillors Lillian and Logan discovered that the superpower magick, believed to be reserved for those special faeries who become Guardians, is actually available to all magickal creatures in this realm."

"What?" exclaimed Sabrina.

"What do you mean?" asked Javier.

Seth remained silent and Billy kept his eyes upon the brownie. Arabella opened her arms and spread her hands. "Well, Lillian came across some information about the source of superpowers and how they've been allocated throughout Alexander's lifetime in Faerie. She demonstrated that she is now able to use firepower that has only ever been used by a Guardian."

Seth clapped a hand over his mouth and widened his eyes in shock. Sabrina looked around the canopy of trees at all of those watching them at this very moment. Javier got to his feet and beat his wings. Billy scratched at his head, which was still without the hat that remained in his hand from earlier. "Lillian has Mercury's firepower?" interrogated Javier.

Arabella looked at him quizzically. "No, she has her own firepower now."

"No, she doesn't," insisted Javier. "Mercury no longer has her power. When we arrived back in Faerie, she couldn't access fire, which means that Lillian has taken Mercury's firepower."

A shuffle amongst the tree boughs caught Seth's attention. A few of the faeries who had been watching silently were now flying off their perches and joining the small group around the mushrooms. Most of the magickal beings kept to their original spots and continued to listen in on the conversation. "How can Mercury no longer have firepower?" asked a female faerie with indigo wings. "All special faeries have a superpower, even if they don't end up becoming Guardians. There is no possible way of losing such a power."

"She's lost it, I assure you," stated Seth. "Something strange is happening and superpowers are diminishing."

A stout male faerie with a beard said, "We have all been assured by Councillors Lillian and Logan that all of Faerie will have more access to superpowers. It may even be that all magickal creatures will soon be able to have such gifts in our realm, so that we can all help in creating further balance between worlds."

"Yes," agreed another female faerie. "Now everyone will have the opportunity to become like a Guardian. No one will have to be born special to do the amazing work that has always been reserved for those of you who are Guardians. Becoming a Guardian will be a choice available to everyone."

"This makes no sense," stated Sabrina. "There're many tests that must be taken and passed for a special faerie to become a Guardian. Being born special doesn't guarantee a place amongst the Guardians. So really, it's not possible for any and every magickal creature to gain a superpower and become a Guardian."

"Take Mercury, for instance," said Seth. "She's a Guardian, yet her superpower has been stolen, obviously."

"No one is stealing superpowers," denied the faerie with indigo wings. "The Faerie Council would not steal powers. They are more concerned with the fact that not all special faeries have become Guardians, which means that perhaps superpowers have not been allocated appropriately."

"You have to be born with a superpower," insisted Javier. "All special faeries are born with a superpower. Just because you have a superpower doesn't make one a Guardian!"

"Really?" demanded the male faerie. "Is this something that Alexander told you or is it something you came up with on your own?"

"What do you mean?" asked Seth. "This has always been the way of Guardians."

"Councillor Lillian believes that the ways of the Guardians may have been misleading, since Alexander became your sage. Many faeries are in agreement with Lillian. Perhaps it is time that all of the special faeries who did not become Guardians are retested. If Lillian can have a superpower of fire, then certainly all special faeries could have been Guardians," declared the other female faerie. "Once all of those faeries are given their rightful place as Guardians, then the Faerie Council can make sure other faeries also have access to superpowers."

"But that would mean taking away the superpowers of faeries who are Guardians, just like what's happened to Mercury," insisted Seth.

"And to Ryan," added Sabrina.

"I think we should go," suggested Arabella. "There doesn't seem to be a great crowd tonight, and I think everyone needs to think about what the council is proposing."

"Jayne and Geoff haven't arrived yet," protested Sabrina. "Shoshana and Georgia will be expecting us here as well."

"Then we'll go find them first," Arabella said. "Come on, Billy. Let's take these three away from here, so that they are able to think about the changes that are bound to come since the discovery that superpowers can be shared with non special faeries."

"Yeah, tha's a good idea, 'bella. We's gonna go find th' others. They gotta be somewhere's 'round here," agreed Billy. He picked Javier up by a wing and backed out of the small clearing. "Le's go find th' others 'fore they arrive."

Sabrina and Seth turned from the three faeries and followed the others into the trees. "We left Shadow over near Oak Tree," Sabrina told them. "We need to go get her first."

"Okay, lead us to her," said Arabella.

"Once we get out of here," stated Seth, "I need to go run an errand."

CHAPTER 22

Lillian paced back and forth in front of the small pond containing Mother Crystal, holding onto the piece of alexandrite in both of her hands. She turned at the sound of Alexander's footsteps on the staircase and watched him descend into the small room. He looked old, not at all like he usually looked when in the presence of others. She stopped pacing and waited for him to acknowledge her. Alexander stood at the bottom of the stairs watching her, his eyes piercing into her. He did not say a word.

Lillian let out her breath in frustration. "Well?" she demanded of him.

"Well, what, Lillian?" he asked quietly and slowly.

"Well, what have you to say for yourself, Alexander?" She held tight to the crystal in her hands.

Alexander took two steps forward and then stopped. "I really have no idea what you would like me to say, Lillian. I am here, where it seems you have brought me. I am at your mercy. I am here for your sake, not for my own," he insisted.

Lillian laughed in derision. "So you admit it, do you? You admit that you have been wrong about the Guardians all of these years? Obviously, I have proven to you and all of Faerie that more faeries could have been trained in the sacred magick that you have reserved for a few of your favourites. What do you have to say about that?"

Alexander moved his gaze from her face to Mother Crystal who remained silent within the pool. Her colour was muted, pale since the last time he had been here. "I was never meant to train all of the faeries born special. Through specific testing devised from our gods, each and every special faerie was given the opportunity to prove that their abilities met specific criteria. Certainly, faeries not born special were not even to be considered for training, let alone for testing of becoming Guardians."

"It is only your word that this is the rule," declared Lillian. "You cannot claim that the gods wanted this to be so, as I now have the powers of a Guardian. I am absolute proof that you have been wrong all of these years. I was not born special, yet I can now access superpowers that have been kept within this cavern."

"No, Lillian, you are mistaken," assured Alexander. "The piece of alexandrite crystal that you hold so tightly in your hands does not belong to you. It belongs to Mother Crystal here." He pointed to the crystal quartz damage of Mother Crystal. "She is the source of all magick, she is the one who truly holds all of the superpowers that have been bestowed upon a certain number of special faeries."

"She is full of magick, yes, but if everyone had access to her, then there would be so many of us who could have superpowers," insisted Lillian. "With this small piece," she held up the crystal in her hands, "I was able to gain access to powers and to share those powers with Logan."

Alexander sighed and rubbed at his forehead. "You do not truly have the powers you are using, Lillian. You have stolen those powers from other faeries. As you continue to use the alexandrite, then you continue to deepen the unbalance in our realm and in other worlds throughout the universe and beyond. No new powers are created with the piece of crystal you now possess."

"You lie!" she screamed at him. "You want to keep all the powers to yourself and your select group. My second cousin was born with superpowers, yet you eliminated him from becoming part of your precious Guardians. He was humiliated amongst our family members, but I never forgot who was truly responsible for his fall within the family. It was your fault, Alexander, your fault that my favourite cousin was unable to become one of the prestigious Guardians and bring great pride to our family."

"Is that what all of this is about, Lillian, to repair your cousin's reputation? If I remember correctly, his name was Jacob and he was born with autism. He was a very talented faerie," Alexander said with pride. "What was it he could do? It had something to do with time, wasn't it?"

"Jacob was able to cross realms," Lillian spat at him. "Before you rejected him from being a Guardian, he would take me to other realms a few times each year. Once he failed to be in your favour, he stopped crossing realms and resigned himself to travelling over the lands of our world. You broke his spirit!" she exclaimed.

Alexander slowly shuffled his feet over to the edge of the pond. He bent down and touched the lavender water. "Are you certain that it was his spirit I broke, and not your own?"

"It wasn't me who stopped jumping from realm to realm," she seethed.

"Perhaps when Jacob decided that moving between realms was no longer necessary for him, you took it personally. Was the moment that he chose to leave faerie the moment when you no longer felt important, Lillian?" he asked calmly. "Was that the real fall of the family?"

Lillian beat her wings rapidly in anger. "How dare you make this about me?" she screamed at him. "This is about all of those special faeries that you chose to reject. How many of them left Faerie because they were no longer revered in our society?"

"None," stated Alexander. "Being born special does not guarantee that a faerie will become a Guardian, yet it does guarantee that such a faerie is unique and loved unconditionally by all."

"I know that this alexandrite," she held up the crystal in her hand, "is just the beginning of helping all of those special faeries to use their talents beyond what you decide for them."

"How do you propose to change what the gods have decided since the beginning of their time?" queried Alexander.

Lillian sneered at him. "Again, you claim to speak for the gods. You may have been their chosen saviour, but I certainly do not believe that you are following all that the gods wish to happen. How could the gods and angels want this cavern to be kept a secret? Before you were appointed the sage of Guardians, everyone in Faerie was aware of this cavern and what it contained. Now, this cavern is a secret from everyone but you!"

"I could not have kept it as a secret that well," admitted Alexander, "for it seems you have discovered this place."

"Then you admit that you do not want others to know about this cavern?"

"Yes, I admit that I am not at all interested in having everyone know of this sacred ground. It is not that I want to keep this place for myself, but I feel that times have changed and not everyone is able to respect the need for privacy here." He walked along the edge of the pool, careful to keep his feet from getting wet. "Let's take you, for example, Lillian. Once you discovered this cavern, did you not enter it and take something from here that did not belong to you?"

Lillian looked from the crystal in her hand to Mother Crystal resting in the middle of the pond. "I only took this piece as proof that you have not been doing all that you should with the Guardians."

"How long did it take for you to share what you learned with that piece of alexandrite?" he asked.

"I immediately told Logan about the possible existence of this cavern. I brought him along to help locate it, and we entered together," she replied with triumph.

"Did you share the magick with him?"

"Of course I did," she claimed. "How else was I to prove that more than one faerie could use the magick from this crystal?"

"Have you noticed any of the changes in Faerie since you found this magick?" he asked wearily.

Lillian turned around and watched Alexander pace from one end of the pool edge to the other end. "Obviously, I have noticed changes. Isn't this exactly what we are talking about? I now have access to superpowers and so does Logan. Magick is changing so that all faeries can have superpowers."

"No, that is not the magick I am referring to," he stated. "When you are not so focused on the powers you have gained, can you feel the change in our realm? Have you noticed little things that do not seem right?"

Lillian stood still without saying a word. She rubbed the crystal in her hands while Alexander continued to move back and forth. "I will agree that magick is changing, but it isn't that things are wrong. On the contrary, things are beginning to align correctly. More magick is being accessed and used. It is no longer being hidden away from everyone so that you can control it."

"Lillian, forget about what I might have been doing wrong all these years and focus on how you feel in nature. Put aside how good it feels to access powerful magick, if you can. I want you to focus on the changes in nature and the vibrations those changes are sending into our realm," insisted Alexander.

She let her wings rest against her back, closed together. Without a sound, Lillian turned her head to the side and listened to the sounds in the cavern and those seeping through the rocks from above. She shivered slightly before looking intently at Alexander. Lillian took a deep breath and held tighter to the crystal. "You are trying to distract me, Alexander. You are a fool if you think that I am going to ignore what I have found in this cavern, if you think that I am going to keep secrets from all of Faerie so that you can continue to eliminate viable special faeries from becoming Guardians. In fact," she raised her voice in strength, "I do believe that what is hidden here in this cavern can actually allow all faeries to become Guardians if they so wish."

"You are too focused on the new magick, Lillian," Alexander sighed. "I need for you to realise that I am not choosing only a few special faeries to become Guardians. If it were strictly up to me, I would certainly train all special faeries to become Guardians of this crystal." He gestured again to Mother Crystal, whose light had faded even more since their arrival in the cavern. "I do conduct testing on each and every faerie born with special needs and special gifts, but it is not I who makes the final decision on which of these faeries will become Guardians. I leave that up to Archangel Michael."

A gasp escaped from a crevice in the cave. Lillian and Alexander spun around to find Seth climbing out from between two walls that had merged together over time. Shock registered on Seth's round, flat face. He walked over to the edge of the pool, keeping his distance from the gnome and the faerie. Lillian backed up and tripped over Alexander. As she fell backwards, her grasp on the crystal faltered. She attempted to grab hold of the piece, twisting her body to catch it before it fell to the solid ground and shattered.

"No!" she screamed, her voice echoing on the walls of the cavern as the crystal smashed. Lillian reached for the nearest shard, pulling it to her chest. She clutched the shard between her thumb and index finger. "Look at what you have done!" she accused Seth. Tears welled in her eyes, threatening to come loose and spill down her cheeks. She blinked them away hurriedly.

"I didn't mean to…I didn't mean to hurt your piece of Mother Crystal," stammered Seth. He looked from the shards scattered over the ground to the one piece she clung to desperately. "I…when Alexander mentioned Archangel Michael…I saw him in the pond, touching Mother Crystal."

Alexander walked around Lillian as she continued to lie on the ground. He reached for Seth's shoulder, but Seth pulled away from the gnome. "No, don't touch me," he instructed. "I'm confused. I came to you about the darkness, but you didn't make it go away. You told me not to worry about it even when I knew it was getting stronger."

Alexander sighed, "Seth, it is my job to worry about the magick. It is your job to learn and to build your powers."

"I have been building my powers," Seth replied. "Yet, some of our powers are diminishing. The darkness is encompassing our superpowers and there's nothing you can do about it."

"So the Guardians are losing their powers?" asked Lillian. She turned to view Alexander. He did not speak. "You are allowing something to take the powers of our superheroes? Is this not what I have been trying to tell you? Don't you see how important it is that all special faeries be trained and nurtured to hone their skills and use them for the good of all Faerie?" She shook her head in disgust. "You are too stuck in your old ways, Alexander. You are unable to see the need for sharing your knowledge of our Guardians."

"Neither one of you understands what it is that I am here to do," countered Alexander quietly. He rubbed at his right ear. "I am not here to train every faerie about their magick. I am here to help strengthen the powers of certain faeries. I am here to teach the ways of the ancient magick. What the Guardians choose to do with the limited knowledge

I can share is purely up to them. I can only guide you, Seth. I cannot make choices for you."

"Do we have to hear more of your dribble regarding why there are a limited number of Guardians?" demanded Lillian. "It is because of you, Alexander, that the darkness is encroaching upon Faerie. Had you helped all of our special faeries over the millennia, then this crystal," she held up the shard between her fingers, "would still be whole."

Seth examined the crystal shard before focusing his attention on Alexander. "The darkness is no longer encroaching upon Faerie. It's taken root in our realm, Alexander. The darkness is everywhere now. Mercury is now limited in her firepower. Ryan can't move things from great distances. It takes Sabrina all of her strength to encase the nine of us Guardians into her invisibility." He paused to let the words sink in as he finally spoke them aloud. "You never did find out why our powers were diminishing."

Lillian snorted, "Even your own charges have noticed that you are not fulfilling your requirements as their sage. Are you so arrogant as to believe that your own thoughts and ways are not to being questioned?"

"Don't," Seth told her. "Don't put words in my mouth to justify what you've done, Councillor Lillian."

"What I have done?" she retorted indignantly. "I have only tried to prove that more magick can be utilized in our community. I want all special faeries to become Guardians, unlike Alexander here."

"As I said before, Lillian, it is not my choice to eliminate special faeries from taking a spot as Guardians. It is Archangel Michael who makes the final decision," insisted Alexander. He again rubbed at his forehead, creasing the folds of his leathery skin. "How can you possibly argue with Archangel Michael? He knows so much more than we do."

"He looked sad," whispered Seth, as he bowed his head in memory of the few minutes previously when he had seen the angel.

"Archangel Michael looked sad?" asked Alexander.

"Yes, he looked very sad, like we had all let him down," stated Seth. "He was in the pond, touching Mother Crystal where she's wounded." Seth pointed to the crystal who continued to pulse with faded colour.

Lillian licked her lips. "You saw Archangel Michael touching the wound on that large crystal?"

Seth nodded. "Did neither one of you see him?"

"No, we cannot see Archangel Michael," admitted Alexander. "It is only the special faeries and those who are born as seers who can communicate and view the angels and gods. Lillian and I are neither seers nor special faeries; therefore, we do not have the privilege of communicating directly with such beings. We can access the gods and angels only through Mother Crystal."

"Well, I should be able to see them now," declared Lillian. "Obviously, I did not see Archangel Michael, as I was not looking in the right direction at the time he appeared."

"Why do you think that you would be able to see what so few can?" Alexander asked her.

"I am a new type of Guardian, one who was not born special but who is able to access superpowers usually reserved for Guardians." She spread her wings out behind her, causing her to appear larger.

"The powers that you possess do not truly belong to you, Lillian," insisted Alexander. "You have stolen those powers through the desecration of Mother Crystal."

"I did not desecrate anything!" she denied. Lillian began to flap her wings furiously.

Seth watched her with curiosity. "You caused the wound in Mother Crystal?" He moved his gaze from her to the shattered crystal on the ground. "Is that a second piece that you just broke? That's one of the missing pieces that Archangel Michael was trying to heal?" He allowed the sadness to encase him and tangle with the darkness.

"It is a rock full of magick, it does not need healing," Lillian stated. "You must have been mistaken with what you saw on Archangel Michael's face. He would only be pleased that I have found a way to spread more magick and create more superpowers in our realm."

"No," whispered Seth. "He wasn't at all pleased, but he didn't seem angry either." He waddled forward to stand in front of Lillian so that she could not look anywhere but at him. "Archangel Michael was very sad. He was focused on the wound you caused, he wasn't paying any attention to you and Alexander."

Alexander cleared his throat. "I believe you, Seth. There must have been great sadness within Archangel Michael, as it is he who chooses the Guardians and it is he who prophesied my arrival to this land. I was supposed to protect Mother Crystal and all of magick from a threat long ago expected."

"It would seem that you failed in your duty," sneered Lillian. "It must be that Archangel Michael is disappointed in you, Alexander."

"Yes, it would seem so," he admitted.

"No, he didn't seem to be disappointed in anyone," countered Seth. "He was so focused on Mother Crystal, it was for her that he felt sad."

Alexander turned his back on Lillian and Seth. He took a few slow steps over to the edge of the pond. "He may not have indicated that it was me with whom he harboured disappointment, but I can assure the two of you that it was my failure at preventing the threat from growing that has ultimately made Archangel Michael sad. I did not listen to the signs of the imminent threat. I have become too complacent over the years. I should have known that you were part of the threat, Lillian, the day you confronted me at the council meeting. You all but told me that you would do anything and everything possible to take over as sage of the Guardians. It was my responsibility to stop you at that moment. I was not paying enough attention."

"It is not me who is the threat," Lillian said. "The archangel must have thought you to be the threat, as you were the one who did not try hard enough to train all of the superheroes properly. If it was a test that determined whether or not these faeries became Guardians, then you were the one who failed in training them properly."

Seth lifted his hands to his ears and covered them, blocking out the discussion between Lillian and Alexander. "Stop!" he cried. "Don't you understand that what's happening right here and now is affecting the balance of nature? We need to work together to fix this darkness and sadness."

"What is it that you propose we do, Seth?" asked Alexander. "I am now listening to possibilities."

"I don't know what we should do," admitted Seth. "I know that this," he gestured to the two of them, "isn't working. We need to fix Mother Crystal."

"She cannot be fixed, my dear Seth," Alexander stated. "She has been desecrated. Once magick is harmed, there is no way to heal it."

"Maybe she doesn't want to be fixed," countered Lillian. "She has all this magick stored inside her. When I came across her and was able to use a piece of her, the magick seemed to spread everywhere I went. Perhaps she wants to be free from this dark cavern where she is forgotten."

"No," Seth shook his head. "She is harmed. When you took a piece of her, you damaged her magick. She was pure before you hurt her. She holds all magick. She is the birth of magick. If we take away her birth, then we eliminate all that is beautiful in our world. We take away the light. I think you need to give Mother Crystal back the magick you stole from her, Lillian."

Lillian backed away from Seth. "I am not giving back this powerful magick. I am not giving up becoming a Guardian. Do you not understand what this has done for me? For all of Faerie?" she spat.

"I do know what it has done," affirmed Seth. "Because Mother Crystal is no longer whole, the darkness has entered our realm and is breeding throughout the land. Soon there'll be no vegetation and no life. Helios will not rise and the stars will not sparkle. Luna will lose her pull on the world. As Guardians, we don't take from Mother Crystal. She gives to us freely before we are born. She knows that we will be chosen to help balance all of nature and all of the worlds throughout the universes. What you've taken from her does not belong to you, Councillor Lillian. What you've taken comes from other Guardian Faeries who've been selected to keep the balance we so desperately need in Faerie."

Lillian held out the palm of her right hand, where the crystal shard lay silent and broken. "I will not allow either of you to take from me what I have worked so hard to acquire." A flame sparked on her palm, dancing from one finger to the next. It grew steadily upwards, reaching for the sky outside of the cavern. She flicked her wrist, causing the flame to shoot out of her hand and onto the ground in front of Alexander. "Do not come a step closer to me, or I will create more flames, the likes of which you have never seen."

The swishing of wings distracted Seth from the flame and the faerie who produced it. He turned his head towards the sound, across the pond where a small ledge jutted out of the cavern wall. The magnificent blue wings of the archangel were spread wide, keeping him above the ground and inches from the ledge, for which he was too large to sit upon. His face was sad, yet astonishingly beautiful and caring. Seth took a step towards the angel, eager to be near him and needing to understand the sadness.

Before Seth could move any closer, a ball of fire zoomed past his ear and hit the wall holding the crevice in which he had been hidden. The flame fizzled out against the rock. Seth ducked this time and moved towards the pond. Flashes of light bounced off the walls as flames were hurled about haphazardly. He could smell the burning vegetation that grew in one corner of the cavern. Seth kept his eyes focused on Archangel Michael, who did not stir from his spot across the pond. Seth stepped into the iridescent pond and swam across its width. Heat pulsed against his head and arms as he swam towards the archangel.

A loud thud reverberated through the cavern. Seth glanced back to see Alexander laying face down on the floor. This distraction resulted in a fireball nearly hitting his head. Flames danced upon the surface of the water beside him. Seth took a deep breath and pushed himself under the water. He used all of his muscles, those that were soft and those that were toned, to swim as fast as he could to his destination, to where Archangel Michael waited. He scratched his hands against the edge of the pool before giving one strong kick to propel his body to the surface of the pool.

A great flash of light blinded Seth as he blinked away the drops of water flowing down his face. He raised his arm to shield his eyes from further exposure to the light. The pool glistened deep red and orange. Seth kept his eyes covered as best he could while he groped around for a dry spot on the ledge where he could hoist himself out of the water. He kept his wings flat against his back, in an attempt to wrap them around his body. With great effort, Seth lifted himself out of the water and lay on the edge of the pool at the feet of Archangel Michael, who had lowered himself to the floor.

"Stay where you are, Seth," suggested Archangel Michael. "Do not raise your head from the cavern floor. There is too much danger at this moment. I will protect you."

Seth breathed a sigh of relief and kept his cheek against the ground. His wet clothing clung to his body and dripped onto the floor, pooling around him as he remained still. He could hear the crackling of fire on the other side of the cavern. His heart pounded in his ears, causing the blood to rush through his arteries and veins.

A large crash shook through Seth's body. He kept to the ground, yet managed to turn his head so that he could see what was happening across the pond. He gasped at the scene before him. The pond was on fire and the flames licked at Mother Crystal. The cavern walls were charred black. Alexander had gotten to his feet at some point, and he now limped backwards towards the stairwell, while he continued to watch Lillian angrily throwing fireballs in all directions.

"Shall I tell everyone what a coward you truly are, Alexander? What kind of sage abandons his charge in a cavern of fire? Do you arrogantly think that once you surface from these depths that all will be forgotten down here? What will you reply when everyone asks about Seth? Are you going to blame his loss of life upon me or upon himself?" She hurled a large orange flame at his head, grazing the top of it. She leapt forward and quickly threw another one before he took the first stair to freedom.

"Seth is well protected," replied Alexander between gasps for air. He touched the grey singing hair on his head. He noticed his hat laying not far from where he had fallen, before Seth had plunged into the waiting pool of water. "He does not need me to save him. He is a Guardian, after all."

Lillian flew into the air and aimed another ball of fire at Alexander. She hesitated a mere second, which gave him the opportunity to climb one more step. "Coward!" she yelled at him. As he turned to look back at her, Lillian smiled maliciously. She feigned throwing the fireball at him, then spun around quickly and hurled it at Seth, who now lay beneath the wings of Archangel Michael.

Seth flinched but managed to remain still. Although he knew the others could not see Archangel Michael, he still felt the need to protect the angel. Seth knew that Michael could hear his thoughts, as the angel pushed slightly with his wings to keep Seth against the ground. The fireball turned to flames, which spread against Archangel Michael and licked at the wings protecting Seth.

"You are going to burn!" Seth exclaimed. He struggled against the archangel, who would not give an inch.

"Stop struggling, Seth. I will not burn. You need to remain still until it is safe to move," Archangel Michael instructed.

Seth watched the flames lick at his protector. Each flame moved across the bones in the wings and danced from the orange and red to the blue of Archangel Michael's wings.

"Why is he not burning?" Lillian yelled as she prepared another ball of fire.

"As I said," responded Alexander, "I am not leaving Seth to die. He is more protected at this moment than he would ever be if he were to come with me now."

Lillian moved her wings rapidly in frustration. "So he knew that I could not touch him when he decided to enter the pool? Then I blame what I am about to do on your precious Guardian, Alexander." With one swift movement, Lillian turned and threw the ball of fire at the fading Mother Crystal, who remained unprotected in the middle of the pool.

"No!" screamed Seth as he struggled against the wings of Archangel Michael.

"Stop!" Alexander cried as he stumbled forward and fell to the cavern floor.

Lillian held out her palm and materialized another orange flame. She allowed it to dance on her fingers before she flicked it across the distance between Alexander and herself. The flame took to life and surrounded Alexander, preventing him from exiting the circle in which he was now encased.

Seth watched in horror as the first fireball penetrated Mother Crystal. Her pulsing colours faltered, reducing the light within the cavern. "She's on fire," moaned Seth in despair. The flames licked at her from the inside, leaving damage in their wake. Seth could not see where the flame had penetrated her from his position, but he knew it would have left a devastating hole. The strange smell of melting and smouldering crystal filled his nostrils.

Seth and Archangel Michael could not take their eyes away from Mother Crystal. It was not long before she stopped pulsing with life all together. She became a clouded white and the pool, an even paler lavender. There was no longer any sign that she had once been a clear crystal quartz with roots of deep red-violet colour pulsing with life and magick. "She's dying," Seth whispered in pain.

"No, Seth, she is not dying, for she is everywhere. It is the magick which is dying," Archangel Michael told him.

"Apollo," Seth said. "Apollo warned me of a threat that would destroy all magick and plunge our world into darkness. He said that once the magick was gone, there was no way to get it back." He paused. "Or was it Alexander who said there would be no way to get the magick back?"

"Look inside yourself, Seth. What do you hear from your inner voice? What is it telling you?" queried Archangel Michael.

"I don't know. There's too much fear inside me. I'm so confused," he moaned.

"Let's start from the beginning," encouraged Archangel Michael.

"Can't we start from the end? I figure things out much better if we start at the end and work our way backwards," insisted Seth.

Michael sighed. "Start where you feel is best. Where does your mind take you first?"

Seth let his mind wander from the cavern. It was difficult at first, as fire continued to ignite throughout the room. The sadness that had touched him the first time he met with Apollo deepened in his core, making him want to vomit. He took a deep breath and settled his stomach. Seth followed his thoughts to a vision that contained several faeries wearing costumes and waiting for Alexander to arrive. It had seemed like a helpful group, but Seth had not felt good about what was happening. He gasped as realisation dawned on him. "It was Lillian. She was the one who spoke at that party." He glanced quickly at Archangel Michael. "Only it wasn't a party, was it? It was a council meeting. That was when Lillian wanted to become a Guardian. She didn't want the knowledge of us for the good of Faerie, she wanted the knowledge so that she could become one of us."

"She has always wanted to become a Guardian," said the angel. "It was at that point in time when she was looking for a way to make it happen."

"Alexander knew who she was and what they were doing when I revealed my vision. He didn't say anything."

"He was hoping to solve this problem without having to worry you and your colleagues. What he did not know," continued Archangel Michael, "was that it was not his knowledge which was required to stop this threat. His job was to train all of you and allow the Guardians to fight the threat."

"She is more than a threat now," declared Seth. "She has destroyed Mother Crystal and all magick that was born of her."

"Not all," cautioned Archangel Michael.

"Oh, what are we to do?" cried Seth. He buried his head into his hands. "The light has all gone. Apollo was right about the darkness seeping into our realm. I felt the darkness and yet I could do nothing to stop it."

"Fear not, Seth," cautioned Archangel Michael. "The darkness has not encompassed everything yet. Your heart is still pure and there is a way in which to fix this still."

"How can you be so certain, Archangel Michael? Apollo insisted that once the magick was gone, it couldn't be brought back. He was very clear when he informed me that I must stop the threat before it blocked out all the light."

"Exactly," agreed Archangel Michael. "Apollo said that you must fight this darkness before the light was blocked out completely. There is still light in this world. You will find a way to heal this land yet, my dear Seth."

Seth stared at Mother Crystal, or what was left of her. He groaned in despair. "I'm not a healer. I'm a seer. Jayne is the healer. She's the one who should be able to heal the land. Yes," he said as he struggled to sit up properly, "Jayne is the one who can help heal this land. She's full of life, just like Mother Crystal was before…before…well, you know."

"It is important that you gather all of the Guardians, Seth. Make certain to bring those who are currently training under Alexander together with those who have trained in the past and are now balancing nature on their own. Whatever you do," stated Archangel Michael, "do not forget that you are essential in this quest to bring back the light in full force. Do not despair when you come to realise that a part of the darkness will always remain, for nothing will ever be as it once was, before Mother Crystal was destroyed here."

Seth got to his feet and moved away from Archangel Michael. He squinted across the pool to where Alexander still lay in a swath of fire. Lillian was dancing like a madwoman. It was as though all sense had left her being and she was a shell of delirium. Seth watched her for a moment before he took to the air and flew in her direction. Just before he reached the shore near where she stood, Lillian looked up and noticed Seth. She screamed and flapped her wings fervently. "How are you still alive? Were you not destroyed when I burned that crystal you seemed to enjoy so much?"

Seth hovered above her and a few feet away. "You can't destroy all that is good, Lillian. What you've done here today is shameful, even despicable. However, I'll give you one more chance to make right what you have done, before I seek the other Guardians."

Lillian scoffed, "Guardians? What makes you think that I am not one of you now? Have you not seen what my superpower can do? I have the power of fire! I can now help to balance all of nature and be revered throughout our realm. The council will be very pleased at what I have accomplished here. They will listen to me now when I inform them that Alexander was keeping vital information and magick from them and from our community."

"You think that you're a Guardian?" queried Seth. He ignored the ache in his heart for what he had witnessed her do to Mother Crystal. "Is everything you did here," he gestured to the pool, the destroyed crystal, and to Alexander still encased in flames, "because you want to be a Guardian?"

"Of course," she answered. "I have seen the benefits of the crystal that gave me these powers. I know that not faeries born special can have superpowers and become Guardians. I have proven that Alexander only chose his favourites to become Guardians. There was no excuse for him to have denied my second cousin a place as a Guardian. How many other faeries did he refuse to train because he did not find them as appealing? This cavern was well known to all of Faerie before Alexander became your sage. Once he took his place as the saviour, the knowledge of this cavern faded into the past, as all the training knowledge about Guardians faded from the ordinary faerie."

"I am a true Guardian," declared Seth. "I know the teachings of my sage. I know the secrets of the Guardians, for I've been well versed in them. I'm aware of all that has been known and all that will be known about my kind. I can assure you that Alexander doesn't have favourites and that he isn't keeping important secrets from all of Faerie. Being a Guardian is a sacred trust that the gods bestowed upon us who have been born special. I didn't decide to become what I am," insisted Seth. "I was born with superpowers and needs that are special and unique. It may look like my life is easy from where you stand, but I can assure you that I struggle everyday with the challenges my body and mind face because of an extra chromosome in my genetic makeup."

"Enough!" yelled Lillian. "Do you think it is easy for me to have been born in this body? There is nothing special about me! I am not at all unique and loved by all. I could get lost in a crowd and no one would notice, but if you and your kind were to get lost, everyone would miss you and go searching for you until you were found."

"Mother Crystal loved everyone, no matter how different or how same they might appear on the surface. You weren't happy with the gifts given to you by the gods," said Seth. "Because you don't have a superpower doesn't make you any less loved and needed in our realm." He chewed at his inner cheek. "Perhaps you don't see your own special gifts."

Lillian flew to his level and placed her nose against Seth's nose. "You think that Mother Crystal loved me? When I came to her and asked that she make me a Guardian, do you know what she did?" When Seth did not answer, she continued, "She turned her love away from me! She ignored me. She stopped beating and pulsing with love. Has she ever done that to you, dear Guardian?"

"No," Seth whispered.

Lillian smacked her forehead against Seth and pushed him away with her arms. "Let me tell you, Seth, that Mother Crystal also has favourites. She chooses who to love and who to ignore. Well I will not stand for it any longer!"

With that declaration, Lillian raised her right arm, formed a fireball larger than her own body, and hurled it at the remains of the crystal protruding out of the desolate pool. The flames grew larger the further they travelled, gaining speed with every lick of the flame. The bottom half of the fireball exploded as it came in contact with what was left of Mother Crystal. The top half continued to hurtle across the pool where it came into contact with Archangel Michael. His wings went from their beautiful blue to the colour of hot white flames. The fireball broke into a million tiny pieces and shot away from the archangel and onto the walls of the cavern, bouncing from one rock wall to the next.

An explosion erupted from above and from far below the cavern. The sound was so deafening that Seth's eardrums rang once and then became silent. He covered his eyes from the blinding light that erupted and felt himself fall to the ground. All he could feel was his own heartbeat, yet he could no longer hear it pound through his ears. He knew that he was drawing breath, but he did not feel a complete part of his body. It was as though his soul had detached from his body and was now floating between realms. Time and space no longer existed. He could not see, he could not hear, and he could no longer feel the existence of anything but his own thoughts.

Moments seemed to stretch into hours. He no longer had a sense of time. Was he even a part of anything anymore? Where had he been? Who was he? Where did he belong? How long had he been nothing?

A searing pain awoke him. He was covered in sweat and his head pounded. Seth rolled over and onto his side. The pain pulsed in his chest. He clutched at his heart and came to realise that the pain was located in his lungs. He needed air. Seth gasped for the oxygen until his lungs felt full and no longer ached. He felt the bile and began to retch, heaving his body in convulsions. His wings twitched. His legs constricted. He clung to his chest until his breathing slowed and he could open his eyes.

Slowly, Seth rolled his eyes across what was left of the cavern. The rock walls were all singed from the fire that had encompassed the entire cavern. Although the stairwell remained, there was no longer any sign that vegetation had once grown in this place where magick had been born. What remained of the pool was a puddle of murky liquid. Mother Crystal had been desecrated to a small shard of red-violet alexandrite. If he had not met her before this moment, Seth was sure that he would not have know her beauty, her grandeur, and her existence as the source of all magick.

The chard remains of a green hat lay alone, where once there had been the gnome trapped within a fiery circle. A blue feather floated in the air and over to Seth. It hovered above his vision before slowly floating to rest beside his right hand. He reached for the beautiful piece of Archangel Michael, the angel who had held and protected him from balls of fire and certain death.

Seth squinted against the darkness as a cold wind whipped through the cavern and chilled him to his very bones. He shivered and held firm to the feather in his hand. The cavern rippled in his vision. Seth blinked and shook his head. When he opened his eyes again, the ripple was larger, moving across the cavern like a wave across the ocean. He watched as it moved in one direction and then in the opposite direction. It was as though the realm were moving but at the same time staying still. He pushed himself into a sitting position and watched more intently. The ripples began to widen and become more prominent. They were small at first, and then appeared as a large tear in a blanket.

"Yes," he whispered, "a large tear in a blanket. But this isn't a blanket." It took a few moments before he came to realise that the ripple and the tear were the same thing. "It's a tear in the realm." He sucked in his breath and clutched the feather to his chest. Fervently, Seth looked around the cavern as panic began to build inside his soul. There were several tears that appeared as ripples. There was a moment when he thought that he saw Apollo, but the god was gone before he could be certain. He began to count, "One, two, three, four, five, six...thirteen tears." A tear slid down his cheek, as Seth came to realise the significance of these ripples and tears. "The world is no longer whole. It has been ripped apart."

CHAPTER 23

It was not easy to fly against the wind. It was blowing in gales, acting in response to the gods' anger. Sabrina was physically fit, but even she was having difficulty staying on course. Such turmoil had not been seen in her lifetime; she doubted that such had occurred in anyone's lifetime. She had been playing with a tree faerie when the call had come. Alexander had been extremely specific that her presence and those of her colleagues were needed immediately. There was to be no delay and no explanation until they arrived at the meeting place.

It had not taken long for Sabrina and the others to realise that something terrifying had occurred. Certainly they had been training to fight for nature and balance, but none of them had really believed they would be called to such a catastrophe. The Guardians had gathered in the meadow with supplies, checking that everyone was ready to leave.

Ryan had informed Billy the troll that the superheroes were leaving on important business and were unaware of a return date. They could not find Seth, so it was important that when he did show up, that Billy tell Seth where everyone had gone. Ryan had indicated that this sudden windstorm was causing concern in Faerie, where everyone was used to a relatively calm existence in regards to weather.

Javier was the most relaxed, taking his time arriving with his pack. He informed everyone that they would need to double check supplies. This was done with one faerie checking another faerie's pack, as this was the most efficient way of ensuring that no one had forgotten anything in the rush. Of course, as Georgia pointed out, their packs were always ready in case of an emergency. Ryan spent his time checking packs by transporting from one to pack to the next, until finally he found himself back with his own well-packed rucksack.

Once it was confirmed that everyone had the required supplies, the superheroes set off to meet Alexander at the mountain training camp. The wind had been minor when they began to fly; yet it hadn't taken long before it picked up and fought against the group of Guardians. Georgia moved into the lead. Her face was flushed with determination and sweat from the struggle to keep moving towards their destination. As she flew into the clouds, the others followed. There would be safety amidst the cloud-cover, where they could hide and fly without being seen.

Being amongst the mist and drizzle that made up each cloud would also muffle any discussions between them, and allow them to perform magick known only to Guardians on their journey South. It was best to fly a great distance before performing any magick that might alert beings on the ground.

Shoshana flew between the group members. She preferred this position, as it gave her the ability to focus on her colleagues' feelings, while at the same time blocking out unwanted and unnecessary emotions from other creatures in the vicinity. Her peers were anxious and only a touch fearful. Certainly they had trained for this, but it was one thing to train and one thing to actually be in a situation with no knowledge of what was occurring. Of course, Shoshana was certain that Alexander would only call upon them if he felt they were ready to execute the proper magick required in this unknown situation. It wasn't as though this particular group of superheroes were the only group of Guardians in all of Faerie.

Mercury flew beside Ryan. She felt chilly in the clouds. The mist soaked through her skin. Her bones ached. Although her inner core still burned with fire, Mercury was still not able to produce the element. Mercury sighed in frustration and glanced over at Ryan.

Ryan fidgeted with the strap on his pack. He kept moving the cords up and down with his hands, causing the strap to lengthen and shorten. His eyes continually darted backwards and forwards. He was on constant lookout for danger and any sign of what might come. Reaction time was important; he did not want to be caught off guard. Although he could not move objects mentally, he still believed that he could teleport everyone to safety.

Geoff and Jayne flew close together. They did not need to speak, for they both felt the same emotions as the others. They were anxious, tense, and fearful. Geoff brushed his swollen hand against Jayne's tiny one. The mere gesture provided some reassurance.

No one was in this alone. Except for Seth, they were all here together. There would be support and protection if the superheroes remained together, yet they had decided that Ryan would teleport the group once they were far enough away from Faerie so they could arrive at their destination quicker than if they continued to fly. During the teleporting they would be separated for a short time while Ryan transported back and forth. Ryan had not been able to take more than four of them at a time on his transports, and with his telekinesis powers diminishing, this was not the time to attempt a transport containing a larger group.

The wind picked up and rushed past the group then circled back around them. Ryan moved his wings faster in an effort to keep at his current pace. The dampness from the clouds made his clothes and skin wet. He brushed away his bangs from his face while drips began to form and run down his face. Ryan blinked away the raindrops.

The wind became even stronger. Raindrops from other clouds fell sideways and came in waves. Clouds moved fast, yet there was no end to them. Even though the wind was strong, the clouds thickened rather than dispersed. The faeries continued to fly within the storm, their wings moving rapidly. It wasn't until Ryan fell backwards into Shoshana that it became obvious the group was no longer making progress. The storm prevented them from flying more than a few inches every minute.

Ryan addressed the group, "I think we have no choice but to teleport. I'd rather we be closer to our destination first, but that isn't going to happen in this storm." His voice was carried away almost before it reached the ears around him.

The group huddled closer together. Shoshana felt the beginnings of panic coming from most of the faeries. Ryan spoke again. His raised his voice as loud as he could in hopes that everyone would hear clearly. "I'm going to take two of you at a time. It's important that those of you who are waiting for your turn remain in this spot." He looked around at each of his colleagues. "I know this will be difficult, but it must be done to ensure that we meet up without delay when I return from the mountain camp."

Mercury shook from the cold. She moved closer to Javier for some warmth and looked around at her colleagues. Their wings were moving rapidly to keep themselves in one spot. "Maybe we should hold hands and form a bird flight shape, even though we won't be moving forward. It might cut some of the wind from beating us around," she suggested.

Javier nodded his head. "A great suggestion, Mercury. I'll take the middle lead."

Javier took hold of Mercury and Sabrina, who held Georgia. Mercury grasped the hand of Geoff. He smiled at

Jayne, knowing she would be one of the first to leave with Ryan. Shoshana reached for Jayne then moved towards Ryan. Although Shoshana did not feel right about being one of the first to go, she knew that arguing would delay them all even further.

Ryan opened his hands and took those of Jayne and Shoshana. He looked at the group and then around their cloud cover. The wind and rain were dropping in temperature. Some of the rain drops turned to hail and snow. He felt awful that he could only take two of the group at a time, but attempting to bring one more to make his usual four was a risk, since he was uncertain of his powers. Ryan felt the squeeze of Shoshana's hand. It gave him courage and allowed him to remove the negative and fearful thoughts from his mind.

With one last look at the superheroes, Ryan pulled from his core. The strength grew until it moved into the bodies of Shoshana and Jayne. He focused all of his strength on their destination. A pop sounded. Ryan felt a tug and the three of them swirled into a vortex. The cold disappeared. Deep warmth spread through the three faeries. Ryan felt the dampness of Jayne's hand. Her fingers were knobby and short. The wet from the rain and from the sudden warmth of the teleport pooled in the folds of her skin. Ryan held tighter to her hand.

Shoshana felt no emotions aside from her own. The focus on her inner self was strange and somewhat disconcerting. She was not used to being alone in her head; she always had others' feelings infringing on her space. She could feel Ryan's hand in her own, yet she received nothing from him other than his body warmth. In the vortex, there was no sense aside from touch. She could not see, she could not hear, she could not speak.

Although Jayne was warm to the touch, she could not feel the warmth within her core. It was as though she had lost a part of herself; there was no way to access her healing warmth at this moment. She felt lost and alone. Her thoughts strayed to Geoff and the others. Even though Jayne knew she would reach safety soon, at which point she would again feel and be able to access her healing powers, a large part of her soul felt fear for the group awaiting Ryan's return. If it had been up to her, Jayne would have waited with Geoff and have been one of the last to teleport to safety.

Ryan touched ground first. The suck and pull into the space upon the cliffside of the mountain camp was a relief. When Jayne and Shoshana touched the ground after him, Ryan released their hands. The three of them looked around the familiar surroundings. It only took a moment to realise that their training grounds were quickly filling up with magickal creatures from across the realm. There was a military-like arrangement to the proceedings, which was significantly different from the supportive camaraderie of their last training session.

Ryan spoke quickly, "I'll leave you now and return immediately with the next group. Find Alexander and let him know that we are arriving as quickly as is possible. Let him know about the storm and that we were unable to locate Seth before we left Faerie."

Shoshana nodded. "We will. You go Ryan. Don't worry about us. We know what to do." She gave him a pat on the back before turning in search of Alexander.

Jayne looked pleadingly at Ryan. "Be safe. Get them all here as soon as possible." She wiped at a tear as it slid down her cheek. Ryan took her hand and squeezed it gently. Then he was gone. Jayne took a deep breath. She looked around at the bustling activity. Jayne walked towards the cave on the far side of the camp because she could see Shoshana heading in that direction. As an empath, Jayne was confident that Shoshana could locate Alexander within minutes.

Shoshana and Jayne stopped in front of the cave where they knew Alexander was located. The coniferous trees had lost their leaves and the green plants had withered up. There were several trolls guarding the entrance. Their massive build and menacing stares were daunting. Shoshana was certain that she had met these particular trolls on one of their training camps. She could feel Jayne recognize the group as well. Shoshana waved to the four guards and smiled up at them. When they did not respond, she bit her lip and looked to Jayne for assistance. Jayne shrugged her shoulders, bewildered at such a cold response.

Biting her lip further, Shoshana flew to eye level with the one who appeared in charge. "Hello." She cleared her throat. "We," she gestured toward Jayne, who waved feebly, "are here to meet with Alexander. He has sent for us."

The troll squared his shoulders. He crossed his chest with a mighty sword. "No one enters." The others formed a strong hold, preventing any penetration into the cave.

Shoshana attempted to reach for their emotions. She let the tendrils leave her body, searching for the emotional tendrils coming from the lead troll. When she felt the end of his emotion, she began to wrap her tendrils around his own. Yet, she found resistance. Or rather, there was a force field surrounding his emotions. Shoshana brought her tendrils back slightly. Confusion masked her thoughts. A frown played upon her face. She refocused, pulling in her own energy and erasing her thoughts from her physical self.

Shoshana again sent the tendrils of her emotions forward. They snaked upon the ground, moving amongst the insects, the earth, the rocks, and the bare grass left from days when it had been abundant in this area. She let the tendrils touch the air around the lead troll. They wrapped the air, growing like a vine around the trunk of the creature. She dared not attempt to touch his emotions too quickly. This time, she let her own emotions rest about him, giving a sense of vulnerability while she waited for his tendrils to accept her own as familiar.

As his emotional tendrils began to stretch out, Shoshana slowly moved hers forward. They touched the outside barrier of his emotions; he moved back slightly, but then relented and allowed her emotions to wrap around his. There was warmth; yet it was not alone. Something quite different lay amongst the emotions. Shoshana could not grasp a word or a feeling to describe this new sensation. As she probed further, a vibration touched her. It was low at first, and then it quickly picked up speed. It was so sudden and so unexpected, that Shoshana was unprepared when it reached out and sucked her emotions from within her core.

With a force unmatched, Shoshana felt searing pain. Blackness engulfed her before she could scream. A soft white light appeared. It was small at first. As it swam closer to her, Shoshana noted the light expanding. She was uncertain of its destination, yet she felt comfort emanating from it. She felt her own emotions and let the tendrils move towards the light. As they touched, Shoshana felt warmth, love, and peace. There was no pain. There was no darkness. There was no suffering. She allowed the light to encompass her whole self. Just as quickly as the pain and darkness had come, the light shone bright and brought her back to the cave entrance.

* * *

Alexander was quite distraught. He kept mumbling something about not having taken the situation seriously. He should have done something when the rumblings had begun; yet he had believed that with time the council would have ceased their enquiry into the secrets of faerie superheroes. Oh, how he had been wrong. Now it appeared there would be repercussions for a great long time to come. There was no telling how this would be fixed or how far reaching the damage; there would be a great deal to do before anything would settle to some semblance of order.

He could hear chatter outside the cave, yet he paid no heed to the discussions. Alexander looked at his feet; they had worn a path on the dirt floor. He stopped for a moment and refocused his thoughts on his current surroundings. He breathed in the scent of rock and dirt. He could not keep his thoughts focused as much as he tried to do so. It had been a very long time since he had no control over his thoughts and actions. Alexander did not like this feeling, this sense of loss and … fear. Yes, he felt fear. Not only did he feel it, but he could taste it too.

Alexander knew that he required assistance from all of those who trained yearly at this camp. He had no idea how they would react once they found out that the cause of this threat was from one of the members of the faerie council. He also was not certain what to do about Seth. He had left the young Guardian in the cavern, even though he knew it was best at that particular moment. Lillian had nearly killed Alexander. His focus when he had managed to leave the cavern was on the remainder of the Guardians and gathering all of those who would be able to fight Lillian and her followers.

The commotion beyond the cave brought Alexander back to his current situation. It was becoming more and more difficult to tune out the ruckus. The guards were under strict orders to keep others away while he figured out the next step in saving this situation. Was there a way to save it? A flash of light blinded the corner of his eye. Alexander turned when the stick of fire flew into the cave. The flames licked the stick, smouldering on the damp leaves and dry dirt of the cave floor. Something must need his attention. His feet moved from his path towards the cave entrance.

The cold chilled him as he stepped outside. Shouts and whistling wind greeted Alexander. Before him were several beings in combat, or what appeared to be a great fight. Alexander glanced about, searching for a reason, a glimmer of the cause. Shoshana was in the midst of the battle, doing what she could to repel the trolls. Jayne cowered against the wall of foliage, holding herself for comfort. Alexander lifted his arms. He spoke a tongue unfamiliar to those around him. A great warmth grew from the ground. It swelled and burst forth to the fight. A rumble could be heard from great distances, penetrating the air, the earth, the water, and the fires at camp. Each member of the battle was thrown across the ground, frozen in place with the shame of fighting with allies.

Javier ran towards the dispersed fight. He was dishevelled and in a panic. He stopped in his tracks when he noticed Alexander glaring at those heaped on the ground. Within seconds, Mercury and Sabrina stood three feet from the cave entrance. Javier saw a flash of Ryan as he teleported one last time from the camp. "This is not the time nor the place to fight amongst ourselves," Alexander announced to the captive audience. "We have come together so that we may fight against she who has caused a destruction so brutal that our world is no longer safe and balanced. There is much to be done to prepare for what lays ahead."

Gideon, leader of the trolls, marched from across the camp. His jaw was set in a hard line and he was carrying a newly hammered sword. "There was no need for this altercation to occur," he addressed the trolls who had been guarding the cave for Alexander. "You know these Guardians and that they are Alexander's charges. There was no need to preventing their entrance into the cave. Next time you feel the need to cause havoc, come see me first."

The wind picked up and blew swirls of dirt around the camp. Within one of the swirls, Ryan appeared with Geoff and Georgia. An open gash cut across Geoff's forehead. He held his hand to the wound, as the blood oozed between his fingers and trickled down the side of his face. Jayne pushed her way through the group of magickal creatures and reached up to touch his forehead. She whispered in the wind and white light appeared on the palm of her hand. It pulsed three times before she removed her hands from Geoff's forehead, where his skin had stopped bleeding and sealed. "You'll be fine now," she assured him. She took his hand in hers and led him over to where Javier stood.

"It is time that I spoke with the leaders who represent each magickal being at this camp," voiced Alexander to the huddled group trying to keep warm. "Once we have spoken alone, we will begin gathering in small groups and giving instructions on our strategy to move out and prevent further destruction of our realm." With that, Alexander and the other leaders withdrew to the cave.

CHAPTER 24

Seth sat huddled against a tree, holding a warm cup of nectar. He shivered as the wind whipped around him and blew sprays of the ocean at him. It had taken him quite a while to reach the training camp, since he had not met up with the other Guardians on their initial transport there. He could not face Alexander yet. While the others tried in vain to access the cave holding the sage, Seth had remained as far from the entrance as was possible without seeming downtrodden.

Billy had been at home fretting when Seth had returned from the cavern. His flight had been long and painful. The sun had been hidden behind dark clouds and was slowly taking back its light as Seth had flown straight to Billy. The troll had been beside himself with concern. When the Guardians had received a distress call from Alexander to meet him at the training camp, they had been in a panic when they were unable to locate Seth.

The troll had explained that something had entered Faerie and required the immediate attention of the Guardians. Alexander had not given anyone information about what had occurred or what the threat could be, but everyone knew it was bad. The winds had come and darkness had fallen suddenly. No one could decipher how this came about or when it would cease to be. Seth had asked for hot tea, which Billy had happily supplied after much discourse in the kitchen.

Over a steaming cup of peppermint tea, Seth had informed Billy that the world had been ripped apart and that the cause of the threat was one of their very own council members. He had not mentioned details, as he was not yet certain how Alexander and Lillian had escaped the cavern or how it was that they were both alive. Billy had mentioned that the council was out in full force to fight against Alexander. Gossip had spread that Alexander had caused the darkness enveloping Faerie.

Billy had agreed to accompany Seth to the training camp. Because Billy could not fly, Seth and he had walked over the land and travelled by raft to the rock island where everyone was now gathered. Billy had been proud of supplying the raft, although he would not share when it had been built. They had taken very few provisions with them, hoping to travel light so that they could reach the camp within a day.

Seth glanced around the camp now, watching the trolls sharpen their metal weapons and the gnomes cast spells of protection. He had not eaten the food that was provided earlier. His stomach was in knots and he was unsure as to how he was going to approach his colleagues when it came time to tell them of what took place in that cavern. Seth took a long, deep breath of the crisp air.

Footsteps crunched on the ground as they approached from the north. Georgia sat down on the hard, cold ground beside Seth. She placed her arm around his shoulder. "You haven't said a word since you arrived," she mentioned. "Are you upset with us because we couldn't wait for you in the meadow?"

Seth leaned his head on her shoulder. "No, I'm not upset with any of you. It was smart of you all to leave together. I appreciate so much that you left word with Billy, knowing that I'd seek him out when I couldn't find any of you."

"Then why are you over here alone? What can I do to encourage you to join us?" she asked with concern.

Seth shook his head. "I wish that I could tell you," he replied, "but I'm not sure what words to use or exactly what it is that I have to say. It's...."

Georgia rubbed his head softly. "When you're ready to share, know that I'll listen with an open heart."

"Thank you."

They sat in silence and watched the activity of the camp. After a while, Billy strolled over with a bowl of greens that he placed in Seth's lap. "I noticed ya hadn't eaten anything, Seth. So I got ya some dinner." He lowered himself to the ground and sat beside Seth.

"You are a truly great friend, Billy." Seth smiled at him and began to pick at the food. His senses were numb so that he could not taste the greens, yet he chewed and swallowed until the bowl was empty.

"How's was your's flight here, Georgia?" Billy asked after the long silence.

She brushed a strand of hair out of her eyes. "It was turbulent and scary as we didn't have any idea what had happened. We still don't know what's occurred, but at least we're all here together now." She patted Seth's hand in reassurance.

"Yep, we's all together now," agreed Billy. "Though th' leaders is still meetin' in the' cave. Don' know when they's comin' out and speakin' to us."

"Alexander will gather us soon, I'm certain," insisted Georgia.

Seth remained silent. He did not know what to think of Alexander at the moment. It was not Alexander's fault that the world had been ripped apart and Mother Crystal destroyed, but somewhere in his heart Seth was unable to convince himself of this truth. He really wondered why it was that Alexander had left him alone in the cavern, not knowing if Seth was alive. Seth still had the feather from Archangel Michael just inside his pants. He had no idea what had happened to the angel, and he felt uneasy that there were so many blank memories regarding what had occurred in that cavern.

"Javier was trying to listen at the cave," Georgia was saying, "but the trolls wouldn't let him get too close. Between the wind and the ocean he wasn't able to hear anything from within the cave walls."

"Did Shoshana get any feelin's?" Billy asked.

"She's having trouble focusing at the moment. There's so much turmoil from everywhere that all she's feeling is apprehension and fear. She isn't able to decipher anything individual. Geoff and Jayne are keeping quite close to Ryan. Because Mercury isn't able to create any type of fire, the bonfires we have burning here were created by hand."

"Still no fire?" exclaimed Billy. "Wha's wrong with her?"

"Her powers have been stolen," murmured Seth. He ignored the clenching in his stomach and the stares of Billy and Georgia at his revelation.

"What do you mean her powers were stolen?" asked Georgia. Her chin dropped and her eyes widened. "No one can steal powers. We're born with our superpowers. We can't give them away and no one can take them from us."

"Not true," argued Seth. "Remember when she was having trouble with sparking when we returned from Equinox training camp?"

Georgia nodded her head. "Yes, but Alexander figured it had something to do with not yet sharpening on her new skill."

"It has nothing to do with that," stated Seth. "Her superpowers have been stolen. I know how it happened." He bowed his head to avoid Georgia's eyes.

"Stolen powers?" interrupted Billy. "How'd her powers get stolen?"

"Councillor Lillian stole Mercury's fire power," whispered Seth.

"No!" exclaimed Georgia. "A council member would never do such a thing. And besides, how could it be possible to steal something innate? You need to explain yourself, Seth! What is it that you know and the rest of us don't?"

Billy said, "He'll tell ya when he's ready. Don' make 'im say what he can'."

Seth lifted his chin and smiled warmly at Billy. "It's okay, Billy. I need to tell Georgia and the other Guardians what happened. It's that I don't know everything." He took a deep breath, "Alexander might know more than I do."

Georgia pulled on Seth's arm, forcing him to look at her. "You know why Alexander brought us here? You know why the light is gone?"

"Yes, I know." He did not offer any more information. Seth still felt sick to his stomach.

"Should I gather everyone here, then? So that you can tell us what we're fighting?"

Seth nodded his head. "Georgia, bring our group here, but don't tell them why. I need to think of how to say what I know without confusing my thoughts. I'm having trouble believing what happened and I have some spaces in my memory that are blank. I don't know if I blacked out or if I saw what happened and just can't remember. And Georgia?"

"Yes, Seth?"

"Don't take Billy with you. I want him to stay here with me." His eyes begged her to comply with his request.

"Seth, you can count on me," she assured him. "I'll be back soon with the others." She walked away quickly.

"I's all gonna' be 'kay, Seth. Ya Guardians bin trained well. Jus' go with yer gut an you's be well," encouraged Billy. "I knows ya have it in ya ta do wha' needs doin'."

Seth reached out and grasped Billy's hand. "You're a very good friend, Billy. I don't know what I'd do without you."

Billy blushed, "Awe, shucks, Seth. Yer a good friend too."

The two stopped talking and silently watched the proceedings around camp. There were three bonfires, one of which was being stoked by a middle-aged brownie in purple clothing. One of the trolls was cutting wood with an axe and shaking his head at the manual labour required when a faerie known for her firepower was within the vicinity. Pixies were sitting around the fires chatting about strategy and deciding what was required for the next meal. It was not easy to feed such a large group when there had been no warning or preparation for such a gathering.

Ryan lumbered towards Seth and Billy. Obviously, Georgia had spotted him first on her quest to gather the group together. Jayne and Geoff were not far behind the two of them. Georgia came with the others. Once they were all sitting around Seth and Billy, Georgia said to the group, "Seth was with Alexander when the darkness descended. He knows what occurred and why we are here. Seth, will you tell us what you know?"

Seth took a sip of his now cool nectar. "Remember the cavern where we met Mother Crystal?"

"Yes."

"Of course."

"What about it?"

Seth took a deep breath to calm his nerves. "I went there because of a vision. The darkness that I was feeling was getting stronger. Since I knew that Mother Crystal was where magick was born, I figured that the cavern would be a good place to start finding the answers I needed. When I arrived,

Mother Crystal was quiet. She was so pale and clouded. Before I could speak with her, Lillian arrived. She was holding a piece of Alexandrite. I've no idea how it was that she had that piece. It looked different than what Alexander possessed."

"I thought that only Alexander knew about the cavern before he shared it with us," interrupted Jayne.

"Yes, he mentioned that we were the first group of Guardians with whom he shared the sacred land. How could Lillian possibly have known about the cavern and have come in possession of a piece from Mother Crystal?" queried Sabrina.

"Wha's th' alexandrite look like?" asked Billy, curiosity plaguing him.

"Oh, it's absolutely beautiful," gushed Georgia. "When in the sunlight it becomes a brilliant green that shimmers and changes. Once you bring it into the dark, the alexandrite becomes a deep red-violet. It has such warmth and pure magick emanating from it. Of course, it's from Mother Crystal herself, so it's made of pure love." Georgia sighed with contentment as she thought about her time with the crystal.

Billy watched Georgia light up as she spoke. "I' sounds pretty," he acknowledged.

Ryan cleared his throat. "What'd she do with the alexandrite?"

Seth shook his head. "She held it up and asked for more superpowers. She kept talking about how her firepower was growing in strength and that she'd even been able to share the power with another member of the council." He bent his head in thought. "I can't remember his name."

"She has my power?" shrieked Mercury. She jumped up and began to move her fingers rapidly above her head. She bounced on her feet and then skipped in a circle, gaining speed as she created a dust storm around the group. "My power. My power. My power," she chanted. She twitched her neck from one side to the other and turned inward.

Shoshana looked from Mercury to Seth and back again. "One of the council members has Mercury's fire power? Does that mean all of our powers are going to be stolen from each of us?" She could feel the panic rising amongst the group as each member contemplated this possibility.

"That isn't possible, to steal our powers," argued Ryan. "Besides, only Mercury, Sabrina, and myself have been struggling with our superpowers. No one else is missing powers, are they?" He searched the group for affirmation.

"Mine are good," confirmed Geoff. To prove his point, he transformed into a replica of Billy and then back into himself.

Georgia shrugged her shoulders. "I haven't noticed anything odd about my abilities," she declared.

Jayne nodded her head in agreement and produced a flower, although it did appear less fragrant than usual. "Must be due to the storm," she murmured.

Javier rose to his feet and followed Mercury as she continued to move amongst the group. "Something must be wrong with my super hearing. I tried several times to listen in on the cave where Alexander is keeping himself and I couldn't catch a single sound. I've always been able to hear everything in the vicinity. I can even hear things I'd rather not. So maybe this Lillian has started to steal my powers as well!" His voice raised an octave in volume as the panic began to take hold in his chest.

"No, so far Lillian only has fire power," Seth said above the wind and the murmurings of his colleagues. "She did mention that the other councillor had some of the firepower as well. It's possible that they might have access to cloaking and telekinesis and not even know it. I don't think she has your hearing, though Javier, because she had no idea that I was in the cavern. Also, I haven't finished my story."

"Ya all needs ta listen ta what Seth 'as ta say," Billy insisted. It took a few moments for everyone to quiet down and refocus on Seth and his tale.

"Alexander had come down the stairwell while Lillian paced in front of the pond. Neither one of them noticed me, as I was hidden in a crevice. When I'd heard someone coming down the centre of the cavern, I hid quickly as it was strange that one of you would be there as well." Seth looked at each member of the group before he carried on. "She'd been expecting Alexander. He didn't look well. He looked very old," added Seth.

"Well, he is old, isn't he?" interjected Ryan without thinking.

There were a few snickers, although Seth ignored them. "He was tired, as though he hadn't slept in a long time. My heart went out to him at that moment, but I didn't dare reveal myself to them. My gut told me to stay hidden."

"So they'd arranged to meet up in the cavern," Jayne contemplated aloud. "Alexander was aware that Lillian had knowledge of the sacred land."

Seth nodded his head in ascent. "She accused him of refusing to train all special faeries to become Guardians. Lillian talked about her second cousin who could cross realms and insisted that Alexander favoured some faeries over others. They argued for quite some time, then…then…" Seth faltered. "She started throwing fire when I came out of the crevice. After that she really lost it. There was fire everywhere. Archangel Michael was there. He kept me safe, but I don't know what happened to him."

Mercury stopped skipping and moving her fingers at the mention of Archangel Michael. Although she did not sit down amongst the group, she held still for the remainder of Seth's story. Jayne took hold of Geoff's hand and squeezed his fingers. Javier stood still behind Mercury.

"She encased Alexander in a ring of fire. This is where things become confusing for me, as there was so much going on and I'm not sure of everything. I can't remember everything, or else I'd passed out. Lillian threw the largest fireball I've ever seen right at Mother Crystal."

Gasps of horror and declarations of "No!" came from the others. Seth continued, "In the end, Alexander and Lillian were gone. I don't know when they left or how. I have a feather from Archangel Michael's wings." He produced the single feather for all to see. "What was left of the cavern was devastating. Mother Crystal was a small shard of red-violet alexandrite and what was left of the pond had become a murky liquid. There were burn marks everywhere and the beautiful vegetation was gone. I saw things that rippled in the air." Seth shuddered at the memory. "There were rips in what I could see. Although I'd no idea what had happened to Archangel Michael, Alexander, and Lillian, I knew beyond a doubt that the world had been ripped apart."

"Ripped apart?" said Georgia.

"Yes, ripped apart. I could see the tears in our realm. I can still see the tears when I look for them," admitted Seth. "I try not to look."

Jayne let go of Geoff's hand. "Are you sure there are tears in our realm? Maybe the storm is making it seem as though our realm has tears in it."

"I see 'em too," piped up Billy. "They's ev'rywhere." He reached out in front of his face and touched what the others could not yet see.

Seth smiled at Billy, thankful for the support of his friend. "The storm is coming from the missing pieces in our realm. I don't know how much damage this is causing in other worlds."

Mercury sighed, "Our realm keeps all worlds in balance. If our world is out of balance, then it's fair to say that all other worlds are also out of balance."

"This is what Apollo was trying to show me. I had focused on the darkness when I was with him. I didn't see the rips in the realm, because I didn't know to look for them."

"Did Apollo know what was going to cause this desecration of Mother Crystal?" inquired Jayne, bringing everyone back to the reminder that the birth of magick and all life as they knew it, was now a shard in a place far from where they were now gathered.

"If he knew, he didn't share any of that with me," admitted Seth. "Apollo was so sad and scared. He must've known that things would change immediately. I found it confusing to speak with him. It was -"

A loud drum echoed throughout the camp, indicating that everyone was to take a station and await further instruction. Javier, Ryan, and Georgia immediately flew away from the group. Shoshana got to her feet slowly and held her hand out for Seth. "Come with me, Seth. I won't leave you here alone with your fear."

Seth shook his head. "I can't join you. I need to stay here with Billy."

"I's 'kay, Seth. Ya go do wha' ya need an' I'll wait here fer ya."

"No, I'm not leaving you, Billy. You were kind enough to come here with me, so I assure you that where you stay, I will stay, and where you go, I will go," Seth informed him. "So we'll wait here." Seth reached for Billy rather than taking the hand Soshana held out for him.

Shoshana pulled her hand back as though she had been slapped. She turned on her heel and swiftly walked away. Sabrina and Mercury joined Jayne and Geoff, walking towards their station. When it was Billy and Seth alone again, Seth turned to his friend. "I can't join them yet, Billy. I know that it's my job as a Guardian to follow with them into the fold, but I can't. Not yet."

Quietly, Billy said, "I's Alexander, ain' i'?"

Seth watched the pixies and the brownies hurry towards the cave. The trolls had abandoned their work on weaponry and spoke in low voices at the back of the gathering. "He left me alone in that cavern. He didn't bring me with him and he didn't tell anyone where I was. If it hadn't been for you, Billy, I'd still be in Faerie while everyone else was here."

"Th' others looked fer ya, but they'd no idea where ya'd gone. So's they told me ta wait fer ya," Billy said with pride.

Seth eyed the troll. "Would you have waited for me even if the others hadn't asked you to do so?"

Billy patted Seth on the back, causing the faerie to fall forward onto his crossed knees. "'Course I'd a waited fer ya, Seth. No way I was gonna leave ya alone an' not know where every'n'd gone. Tha's wha' friends do fer each other."

Seth did not point out that he had considered the Guardians to have been his friends, yet they had not waited for him. Although, to be fair, the others had not witnessed the proceedings within the cavern and they were following the instructions of Alexander. They had no way of realising that Alexander had known where Seth lay and that the gnome had left him sprawled on the ground of the burnt cavern. Seth shivered at the memory. His heart ached, and except for the troll sitting beside him, Seth felt alone.

Billy shifted his weight and leaned against the tree. "Does Alexander know you's here now?"

"I have no idea, Billy," Seth admitted. He felt a new type of loss in his heart. He had always looked up to Alexander and believed that the gnome would always put his safety and that of his colleagues before anything else. Perhaps Seth had been naive, yet he could not help but feel betrayed by his sage. "Honestly, I don't know what to think right now."

"Then don' think. Jus' be," encouraged Billy. "We'll wai' here and sees wha' happens with 'em all goin' ta the call jus' now. 'Sides, we have's a good view o' th' action."

"You always know the right thing to say, Billy. Thank you."

They watched the activity together. From their position, it was impossible to hear any instructions or discussions related to the sudden call to attention. Seth imagined that the sage would be giving information about Lillian and her cohort. Of course, there had been whisperings in Faerie about the council and some others questioning Alexander's position. Seth figured that this meant there was no longer solidarity behind Alexander and the Guardians. He could understand the desire for changing alliances, yet he was unwilling to go there himself. He still believed in all the good Alexander had done and all that he had taught Seth. It was certainly not easy to remain at the trunk of this tree while everyone else organized into military position to fight Lillian and her following.

"Ah, see them groups? They's all gettin' organized into teams," Billy pointed out. "Ev'ry magickal creature's in each group. Guess they's sep'ratin' you Guardians. 'Course, there's more 'n jus' your group here."

"Yes, I'd imagine that all Guardians living were called to arms," said Seth. "I wonder what the special faeries who tested and failed to become Guardians are doing."

"Wha's 'at?"

"Well, not all faeries born special become Guardians, Billy, but they all have superpowers. I wonder if they're recruited in times like these, or do they carry on with whatever it is they do as adults who aren't Guardians?"

"Them's good questions. Do ya know any of 'em faeries?"

"I've come across such faeries in Faerie, but I've never actually had a conversation with one regarding what life's like when one isn't selected as a Guardian. It must be difficult when such a faerie was expected to become a Guardian at birth. I've met other Guardians here during Equinox training camp, so I know that they're somewhere around here." Seth rubbed at his temple, where his head had been pounding since their arrival on the rock island.

"Do ya think Alexander is tellin' everyone 'bout what happened in the cavern?" asked Billy, as he watched the now selected groups begin to assign tasks to each member.

"Yesterday I would probably have thought Alexander would be telling the camp about what happened in the cavern with Mother Crystal. At this moment, though," he struggled for a breath of air, "I have no idea what Alexander will do. I'm sure that he's doing everything he can to assure the camp that all will be well again."

"Do ya believe i' will all be good 'gain, Seth?" Billy filled his question with hope, begging Seth to tell him that this was only temporary.

Seth watched the crowds as he contemplated an answer. "It's hard to say, Billy. Do I think we can stop Lillian and her cohort? I think it's possible. Will life in this realm be as it was before she desecrated and then destroyed Mother Crystal? No. After what I saw, I can guarantee that life will never again be so peaceful and balanced. I will never again be the same," he concluded.

Billy licked his lips and kept silent. Seth uncrossed his legs and got to his feet. He held out his hand for Billy to join him. The troll struggled to his feet and readjusted his hat. "It's time that we join the group and hear what's to take place," Seth stated with forced conviction. "I can't wallow in my confusion and sadness, while my peers fight against something they may not understand."

"I's with ya," declared Billy.

"Great!" Seth took two tentative steps forward, then hesitated.

Billy picked Seth up at the back of his neck and dangled him as the troll walked forward. "I help ya, lil buddy."

Seth laughed at the situation. He swung back and forth under the strength of Billy's hand. "We should get close to the front, so that we can hear everything being said. Once we know Alexander's plan and what everyone here will be doing, you and I can integrate it with what I know to be true and with what we need to do to remedy the situation."

"'Kay, I take us to th' front," agreed Billy. He weaved his way through the various groupings of creatures. No one paid any attention to Billy and Seth, although a few of his colleagues did glance at Seth's situation. When they were within ear shot of Alexander, but hidden amongst one of the groups, Billy dropped Seth onto the cold ground. The wind was picking up again, even though it had never really stopped.

Seth looked around the group within which he and Billy were hidden from Alexander. He felt a pang of shame at hiding from his sage, but Seth pushed it down into his core and ignored it for now. Georgia was amongst this particular group. Seth scurried over to her. "What do you know so far?" he asked her.

"I wondered when you'd join us," she replied. Georgia brushed a strand of hair out of her eyes. "Alexander has instructed everyone to create strong groups, which we've done. The best way for this was to be certain that every magickal creature is represented within a grouping. This allows us to play upon all of our strengths. I have to say though," she lowered her voice, "it makes me uneasy to be separated from the rest of the Guardians. We've always trained together and work best on each others' strengths."

Seth kept his voice at a level similar to Georgia's. "Yes, I agree with you. I don't think we should be separated. It was difficult enough for me when all of you had left Faerie together and I was alone. If it weren't for Billy, I don't know how I'd have gotten here on my own."

"I'm sorry that we couldn't wait for you, Seth. We really had no idea where you were. Even Shoshana couldn't sense you."

"I know," Seth said reassuringly. "That isn't why I'm saying this. I think we need to stay together. I like the idea of everyone else being placed into mixed groups. I'd rather that we move amongst the groups as needed."

Georgia nodded her head in agreement. "However, Alexander has instructed us to be in different groups."

"What did he say happened?"

"He didn't specify anything in particular. He told us that Councillor Lillian and Councillor Logan have moved against the balance of our realm. They've collected a following from within Faerie and are attempting to take over as sages for the Guardians. Alexander also mentioned that the gods are not happy with this, which is why we have this awful storm."

Billy shifted in beside Georgia. "He din't say nothin' 'bout the world bein' ripped 'part?"

"No, nothing about what Seth told us. I think he doesn't want to alarm everyone too much," she said in defence of her sage. "Alexander is focusing on the imminent threat to us, which is Lillian and her following. Most likely we'll be dispersed soon, to fight against her and her group."

"This storm is more than a fight against Lillian," insisted Seth. "The realm is out of balance and the magick is dying. We need to save the magick before it's gone completely. Once it's gone, we can't get it back." He could feel the panic rising in his heart chakra.

"Maybe Alexander thinks it would be easier to save magick once Lillian has been neutralized," suggested Georgia.

"If that's what he thinks, then he's wrong." Seth shook his head at the lack of focus on Mother Crystal.

"You don't know that, Seth," she said. "Alexander knows what he's doing."

Seth did not believe this. "Why did he leave me alone in the cavern?"

"I don't know," admitted Georgia. "You even said yourself that you have no idea how and when Alexander and Lillian left the cavern. Maybe leaving you there was safer than taking you with him."

"For whom?"

"Oh, Seth –"

"Can I have your attention again?" Alexander called out to the members in the camp. "Now that you have organized into your groups, I have further instructions on what will take place shortly." His voice carried across the desolate land, although it remained soft and comforting. Seth struggled with the desire to allow Alexander's voice to give comfort.

Billy bobbed his head up and down in an attempt to get a glimpse of the gnome speaking. "Yep, there he's is."

Alexander addressed the crowd, "My sources have informed me that Lillian has been spotted in the South, near the caves of Gonia. We need to move in various directions, so that we have the area surrounded when we descend upon her and her followers. She will not relent without a fight. We do not want to kill her, as that is not the way of faeries. If you are successful in neutralizing her, then it is imperative that you bring her back here, where we have the ability to keep her from causing more damage to our realm."

Seth squeezed between a troll and a brownie. He hurried forward and stopped in front of Alexander. The gnome acknowledged the faerie with a slight nod of his head. "Aren't you going to tell them why there's such a storm? Shouldn't we be fighting to save magick rather than neutralizing Lillian? Once the magick is gone, it's gone forever. We can deal with Lillian once we've saved magick," Seth declared.

"What is he talking about?"

"What's wrong with magick?"

"We need to get the rogue faerie to please the gods, so that the storm ends."

"How dare he question the sage of Guardians?"

Alexander looked sadly at Seth. "Our focus at the moment, Seth, is to neutralize Lillian and her cohorts before more damage is done."

"No, Alexander," disagreed Seth. "The damage has already been done. If we don't stop the magick from dying, then what happened to Mother Crystal will be permanent. It won't matter what else Lillian does. The world has been ripped apart. This storm is not the result of angry gods; it is the result of destruction to Mother Crystal and all that is magickal. How can everyone here fight for the return of magick if they don't even know it's dying? You aren't giving them enough information, Alexander." Seth turned to examine the groups of warriors, for that was what they were now becoming.

"You do not understand, Seth," countered Alexander. His voice continued to be warm and inviting.

"I do understand, Alexander. You left me in that cavern. You know what happened to Mother Crystal and you know that our realm is irrevocably damaged. If our realm is under such distress, then it must be true that all worlds are in turmoil. This is the darkness that I told you about. You ignored me then, relying instead on your knowledge from the past. I am telling you, though, our focus needs to be on saving magick or what we are all doing here is pointless." Seth felt the strength build within his core as he fought with words against the one who had taught him about being a Guardian, and about following his own gut instincts.

"We cannot fight against what we do not have in front of us," stated Alexander. "There was nothing left in that cavern that could be saved, so now we move forward to fight against what is concrete."

Seth sucked in his breath at these words. His heart ached and he felt like something died within his soul. He was barely able to whisper the words, "I was left in that cave." He felt the tears sting at the back of his eyes before they fell down his cheeks. It was in that moment when he knew what Archangel Michael had told him without words. Seth needed to save magick without this gnome and without those who continued to believe in the knowledge of this great sage who had been around for millennia. Seth folded his wings and turned his back on Alexander. He walked slowly into the crowd and found Billy standing with Georgia.

"I'm sorry, Seth," Georgia said with love. "I know that you truly believe the world is ripped apart and that we must focus on saving magick, but Alexander is right, we need to stop Lillian from doing more damage."

Seth met her eyes. "I am going to find a way to stop the magick from dying completely. You can go with Alexander and fight against Lillian, or you can come with me, Georgia. I could really use your help."

Georgia fluttered her wings. She turned her head towards where Alexander stood and back to her friend. "I want to help you, Seth. I really do, but Alexander knows what he's doing. He was chosen to be our sage, by the gods no-less."

"Are you certain that you don't want to join me, Georgia?"

She bit at her inner cheek. "Oh, Seth. I wish that I could be with you and with Alexander at the same time, but I can't. I wish you well." She leaned over and kissed him on his left cheek.

Seth squeezed her hand and turned to Billy. "Shall we go, Billy? They don't need us here anymore. You and I have somewhere else to be."

"Yep, le's get th' rucksack and we can go." Billy smiled at Seth and readjusted his hat. "See ya, Georgia."

"Bye Billy," she said sadly.

Billy and Seth weaved their way through the groups. One by one, Seth and Billy came across the Guardians nestled within groups ready to leave for the south. Geoff and Jayne had been placed together, as they had refused to be separated at such a hostile time. Jayne had wanted to join Seth and Billy, but Geoff insisted that they remain with the others. Shoshana had a difficult time making her decision, but in the end, she chose to remain, as this was what she believed she had been trained to fight. Sabrina had suggested that Seth take Shadow with him, as she was certain the dragon would be more useful with Billy and he than with herself. With one last look back at the bonfires and the magickal creatures at the camp, Seth and Billy climbed upon Shadow with their rucksack and took to the stormy sky.

CHAPTER 25

They climbed higher into the sky above the camp. Shadow was slow with her ascent, as the wind was cold and cruel. She fought against the power of the storm, angling from one side to the other in an attempt to rise higher where Seth thought would be less wind. He was not yet ready to leave the area completely, as he felt the need to watch the warriors' head off on their quest to capture Lillian. Billy had not questioned Seth's decision to leave on their own and follow what Seth believed to be the most beneficial course of action for their realm.

"Billy, why didn't you choose to stay with Alexander? What made you decide to come with me?" Seth asked with wonder.

"'S easy," replied Billy. "Ya need me. Alexander has ev'ryone else ta help 'im. 'Sides, you's doin' the righ' thin'. Alexander don' know that you's the true Crystal Guardian."

"I'm the what?" Seth was surprised at this revelation.

"Th' true Crystal Guardian. Tha's the name of ya. I heard 'em gods say so when I firs' met ya. They was gathered 'round yer like they always is. Sometimes I sees 'em an' sometimes I don'."

"I had no idea that you could see the gods, Billy."

"Ya, since I was born. They said not ta tell no one, but I think it's 'kay ta tell ya now," he stated.

Seth thought about how this would help with finding a way to heal Mother Crystal. There was no doubt that she needed to be healed, and soon. "Do you see any of the gods right now, Billy?"

"No. I hasn' seen 'em since we was back in Faerie, 'afore ya came and got me." He leaned forward and shifted his weight on Shadow. "I think they's angry a' wha' happened to ya and Mother Crystal."

"I agree with you, Billy. The gods must not be pleased with what has happened. Apollo tried to tell me a few times that this would happen. He was somewhat vague, though."

"Oh yeah, Apollo is a funny one. Spends lots o' time playin' and not much workin'. I likes him though," agreed Billy.

The wind continued to blow and whip through their bodies to chill them to the bone. The higher they flew, the colder the air became. "I thought that hot hair was supposed to rise," said Seth.

"Then le's go down again," suggested Billy. "We'd see 'em all better from lower. They gonna leave camp soon."

"Shadow, take us lower, but keep us out of the view of the newly appointed warriors," instructed Seth.

The dragon turned to her left, angling towards the ground. Seth and Billy clutched at her as they felt the tilt. She soared with the wind, catching it in waves on their descent. The wind currents were strong, causing Shadow to struggle against them when she wanted to move in a different direction. She turned as best she could, causing Billy and Seth to hold tightly to her scales to prevent a mishap. With a swoop and a dive, Shadow finally found a current that kept them floating in one position not too far from the camp.

Seth leaned forward, so that his body was flat against Shadow. In this position, he was able to move his head slightly to the left and observe the camp below. He felt nauseated at spying on his colleagues and the magickal creatures who were about to start a war.

"I sees th' group with Sabrina," said Billy. "I' jus' shimmered. She mus' be tryin' ta cloak th' whole group. Keep 'em hidden from th' enemy."

"Lillian isn't really the enemy, Billy. They all want to believe that she's the enemy, so that they have someone to fight. We should all be focused on healing the land, not causing more destruction. I agree that Lillian needs to be held responsible for her actions, but to put all this effort into capturing her isn't going to save our realm. If my peers were to help you and me, then I'm certain that we could heal our realm and save magick."

"Maybe they's gonna have some success too," suggested Billy. "Ooh, look. Sabrina's group shimmered 'gain. She's got it. They cloaked." He clapped his hands together and lost his balance. Billy slid to the right and grasped for something concrete to hold onto. He managed to grab hold of Seth's leg, pulling the faerie down with him.

Seth felt himself slipping from the weight of Billy. He tried to keep hold of the scale and hook his arm beneath it for security, but Billy was too heavy for his little body to hold. "Shadow!" he screamed as the two slipped off the dragon and spiralled down in a freefall. Seth beat his wings in an attempt to slow their fall, but the wind was too strong for him to make any progress. A great gust picked up the two flailing magickal creatures and carried them to the north, over the dark and tumultuous ocean. A dark object darted below them and swooped up to gather Billy and Seth between two claws. Seth breathed a sigh of relief when he opened his eyes to discover that Shadow had made a dive, and come from beneath them, to catch them with her front legs.

"Oops, guess I shouldn' move so much on th' dragon," said Billy.

Seth laughed out loud, his body shaking from shear relief and the much needed laughter. "Whatever would I do without you, Billy?" he laughed even harder.

"Ya'd prob'ly stay on th' dragon," grinned the troll. He laughed too, causing Shadow to grip her claws into his clothing even tighter.

"How do we plan on climbing onto Shadow's back? Do you have a suggestion?" Seth was beginning to feel a bit queasy from swinging in Shadow's claws at such a height. He much preferred to ride on her back, where it was relatively safe.

"I sees a pen'sula o'r there. Wanna land down there, Shadow? An' we can climb on yer back agin." The dragon turned her body and soared in the direction Billy had mentioned. The wind whipped at Seth and the spray from the ocean dampened his skin and clothing. He felt as though he had been for a swim in the icy waters. If Billy was cold, he certainly never mentioned it, nor did he complain.

Shadow dropped the troll first then she let Seth fly to the ground once they were safely on the desolate peninsula. The waves crashed at the land, swallowing most of it into the mouth of the angry water. The dragon selected a place for landing and timidly placed her feet on the wet rock. Her claws dug into the surface. Billy readjusted the rucksack on his back and stumbled over to the left side of Shadow. He touched her scales and glanced into her large blue eyes. "I's sorry 'bout earlier. Won' happen agin," he promised. She bowed her head and lowered herself onto her belly so that he could climb upon her back.

Seth flew over to the dragon and the troll. He hovered near the two, until Billy was securely in place, at which point the faerie found a nitch not far from where he had originally sat before he and Billy had fallen off the dragon. Seth held on and lay flat against Shadow's back. Shadow took to the sky again, although this time Seth could see the tears in the realm rippling everywhere they turned. The dragon clearly either sensed them or was able to see them. She turned and twisted to avoid colliding with them, causing her to lose balance and drop several times with the power of the wind.

"Do you see the tears in the realm, Billy?" Seth pointed one out to the troll who had not moved from his position upon the dragon.

Billy followed Seth's finger to where a particularly large tear flapped in the wind and moved across the space. "Yep, I sees i'." He averted his vision from the large tear and began searching for other ones in their vicinity. "Two o'er there," he pointed in the opposite direction of where they were attempting to fly.

Seth counted the tears, although the constant turning in the sky made it difficult. "When I first noticed the tears in the realm, Billy, I counted thirteen of them. Now I can't keep track of how many have been created. The tears are multiplying and becoming larger. Do you think they can see them from the camp?"

"They mus' see 'em," said Billy. "They's big tears an' lots of 'em. Hafta be keepin' yer eyes closed not ta see 'em."

"Whatever you do, Shadow," Seth told her, "avoid entering one of those tears. I don't know what will happen to us if we end up in one of them. Keep us in our realm no matter where that might take us."

The dragon lifted her head and turned to glance back at the faerie and troll clinging to her back. She varied her height in flight, yet did not make any progress towards the north. Seth squinted through the wind as raindrops began to fall. He could still locate the camp due to the burning bonfires that remained strong. Boats had been deployed into the rough ocean. It appeared as though there was great difficulty loading the boats to carry the warriors south.

Within one blink, Seth lost track of an entire group of warriors who had not been far from the tree where he had found safety. "It looks like Ryan has transported his group. They're no longer on the island."

"Don' know how they's gonna get in dem boats," Billy stated. "They all needs a Ryan ta take 'em where they wanna go."

"As long as they don't step into one of those tears, they should be safe enough. Although, I'd much rather see them stay on the island than go and fight against Lillian. I don't think the gods are pleased with the choice to take up arms. The weather's certainly not improving."

"The' weather's gonna get worse, Seth," claimed Billy. "'Til we save magick, th' realm will keep breakin'."

As these words reached his ears, Seth felt his heart chakra tighten in the realisation of this truth. He could really use his peers with this task, but he knew in his soul that it was up to Billy and himself to find a way to stop the magick from dying. "Shadow, we need to get away from here. Take us somewhere safe, where we can land and develop a plan of action that'll be more productive than what's occurring below us on that island," instructed Seth.

As Shadow flew north, a great streak of lightening struck from the east and tore at the realm, opening a great hole that flapped against itself in the storm. The god of thunder appeared, banging his hammer against the dark clouds. Thor was magnificent to behold, yet he paled in comparison to Archangel Michael. The god's long, blond hair blew in the storm, touching his smooth cheeks and chiselled jaw. Thor did not smile, rather he clanged his hammer again and again in anger at the breach of this realm.

Shadow flew lower and back in the direction of the camp, as the god of thunder and more tears in the realm prevented them from flying to the north. The rain pelted at them, stinging like shards of ice. Between the wind, the rain, and the ocean, it was no longer clear in what direction they were flying, whether towards the sky, the ocean, or land. Seth could feel the dragon panic beneath his fingers. He rubbed at her scales in an attempt to calm her. "Find land, any kind of land," he crooned against her body.

He could feel her respond as she shuddered and dropped again. On a crest of a mountain they landed, far above the surface of the ocean. The jagged rocks were slippery from the storm and the vegetation was sparse. What had been growing to feed the wildlife was now ripped from the roots and blowing about the mountainside. Seth climbed down off of Shadow. He stumbled as he walked, unable to find the balance that had been obsolete while in flight. He stood as tall as he could and kept his feet planted on the ground. At the sound of Billy's footsteps, Seth turned to his faithful friend.

"I don't know how we're going to reach Faerie and the cavern in this storm, Billy. The realm is shredding as we speak. I'm at a loss as to how we'll proceed on our journey," admitted Seth.

Another large crack of thunder drew their attention once again to the sky. The great tear that they had managed to avoid opened further, turning dark and circular. It spun into a funnel and opened wider, causing more darkness to descend upon the realm. Shadow nuzzled Seth and Billy with her neck, pulling them close to her. She whimpered only once, as the funnel widened into a vortex of many colours. The drifting vegetation was pulled toward the vortex and swallowed into its black depths. Trees that had been sturdy throughout this storm were uprooted.

As the rocky land became more desolate, the bonfires in the camp flickered once, twice, and then were snuffed out completely. Although it had been dark for some time now, it seemed to Seth as though the light had gone out. The only light visible to the naked eye came from within the vortex. Deep blues swirled within its eye. He kept his vision focused on the eye of that vortex, which was the only reason he was able to decipher what was happening.

One by one the boats were pulled from the sea and brought into the vortex. Weapons made at the hands of trolls were sucked in as well. Seth and Billy watched in horror as they recognized the magickal creatures who were picked up from the camp and swirled in the vortex before disappearing into its depths. He felt a part of his soul die as each and every Guardian he had grown to love was taken from him. Seth looked away when the sage he had followed so blindly for so long joined his friends in the indiscriminate vortex. He buried his head in the arms of his friend, who held him and cried with him silently. Shadow lowered her head and let a tear slide down her face and drop to the ground.

The three of them stood still on the mountaintop and watched the vortex suck everything living into its eye. It came no closer to the dragon, the troll, and the faerie, yet the winds were forceful and the rain continued to drench them to the bone. Their teeth chattered and their bodies ached. One by one the bright stars went out, as though flames had once been the source of their light. There was no longer a sign that any moon had shone in the night skies. The vortex shimmered amongst the tears in the realm. Seth was unable to identify what was happening, until it closed and disappeared. Slowly, the wind died down and the rain became a drizzle.

Seth blinked in the deep darkness. He lifted his hands to his face, yet he was unable to see beyond his nose. "Billy, are you there? Shadow?"

A shuffling of feet met his ears and then he could feel Billy's hand groping at his arm. "I don' see. There's no ligh'. Is 'at you, Seth?"

"Yes, this is my arm," he replied and squeezed Billy's hand for reassurance. "Do we know where Shadow went?"

"Nope, can' see her neither."

A rough, wet tongue ran itself along Seth's head. "Ah, she's here. She can see us."

The dragon sneezed on the two of them, raining bits of snot onto their heads. "Yep, she smells us, too," confirmed Billy.

"I think we need to climb upon her back again, Billy. Shadow, once we're safely on your back, I need you to take us home to Faerie," insisted Seth. He turned to the troll beside him, even though he could not see in the darkness. "Billy, can you feel your way onto Shadow?"

"O' course I can," Billy replied, as he walked forward with one arm outstretched in front of him and the other still holding onto Seth. "I ain' losin' ya too, so we goes together."

Seth attempted to keep up with Billy, yet found himself tripping along the way. There were stones and debris on the ground, which the two of them continued to stumble upon as they made their way in the direction of Shadow. She was now licking her body to clean off the rain, which allowed them to hear her location. As they reached her, Seth and Billy carefully climbed upon her and found secure seating.

"Dragons are able to see without any light," mentioned Seth. "Shadow, we're ready to go home any time you'd like to take us there." The dragon spread her wings and lifted into the dark sky. She turned toward north and began their smooth, lonely journey to Faerie.

CHAPTER 26

As they touched down in front of Billy's home, Seth breathed a sigh of relief. His eyes had adjusted enough to see within four feet of his nose. It took a while to notice that his wings still glittered in the dark. Billy had hooted and hollered when Seth's wings began to shine and sparkle. It was the first indication that their eyes were finally adjusting and that magick had not yet died. They clambered off of Shadow and Billy opened the door to his small home nestled in the hill mound.

"I thinks you can get in ta th' livin' room, Shadow," stated Billy. He opened the door as wide as it would go. "Jus' let Seth an' me get in here's firs'." Billy shuffled into the one room home and hurried over to where his frog would be waiting for him. The water bowl was empty and there was no sign of his pet. "Guess he wen' with th' others in th' vortex," he said with sadness in his voice.

"It'll be okay, Billy," Seth assured him. "We'll find a way to get everyone back and we'll keep magick from disappearing completely. Even you said that my glittering wings are a good sign."

"Ya, I guess so," he replied without much belief. "Ya two thirsty? Wan' water?"

Seth licked at his lips. "Water would be wonderful, Billy. I didn't realise how much I was missing a drink until now. You'd have thought that with all the rain we were immersed in that we wouldn't be thirsty at all."

"Well, rains on th' outside. We needs water on th' inside," Billy informed him. "Lot's a water is good fer us." Billy rummaged in the kitchen while Shadow budged her way through the door and into the living space.

"I gots water fer ya, Shadow." Billy placed a large bowl filled with water on the floor in front of her snout. Spots of water trailed from the kitchen sink. "Tha's be good fer ya. I don' know wha' dragons eat, so not sure wha' ta give ya other 'an water." He shuffled back to the kitchen and handed Seth a glass and began to drink one himself.

"We need a plan," Seth said. "I didn't see any lights when we came into Faerie, and what I could see in the dark looked desolate. I think it's safe to assume that everyone here has also been taken into the vortex."

"Yep, I's agrees with ya, Seth. I didn' see a thin' and there's no Hermy here. He wouldn' a lef' withou' me." Billy refilled his water glass and began to drink from it again. "Safe ta say is jus' us three."

Shadow pushed her water bowl across the floor to where Billy stood. "Ah, ya wan's more." He put his own water down, filled up the bowl and put it back down for her to drink from at her leisure.

"I think we should rest for a bit, and then we need to decide where to go from here," stated Seth. "I don't think we can make any wise or large decisions at the moment. I feel exhausted and my heart aches from everything that has happened."

Billy put his glass in the sink. "I's tired too. Ya can have m' bed, Seth. I can sleep on th' floor. I got extra blankets and pillows in th' closet. Shadow can jus' lay where she finds room. In th' mornin' we can gather food ta eat. 'Though I don' think there'd be much lef' ta eat ou' there."

Seth walked over to Billy and gave his friend a hug. "We'll find something to eat, I'm certain. We've survived this far, so I'm sure that the gods and angels will provide for us. As you said to me earlier, Billy, I am the Crystal Guardian. Between you, Shadow, and myself, I know that we can survive and somehow find a way to make things better than they are at this moment. Once we're well rested, we'll worry about our next move. It's very kind of you to offer me your bed, but I'll be very comfortable on your couch."

"'Kay. I'll get ya a blanke' 'nd pillow." Billy went to the closet and produced the items for Seth, who took them to the couch and arranged himself horizontally. Billy provided a pillow and blanket for Shadow, although she had already lain herself on the floor and was sound asleep. "Sees ya two in th' mornin'."

* * *

Seth struggled to fly higher, but his wings were not cooperating. He could barely skim above the sharp pebbles strewn in his path. The further he went, the better he could see, as though the darkness were subsiding. There were no sounds aside from his own breathing. Seth let his wings fold against his body as he came to the familiar spot where he had met Apollo in the darkness several weeks ago. His bare feet touched the barren ground. He took a few steps forward, searching for the sun god who had to be somewhere near. "Apollo?"

A shuffling behind a large boulder came in response. "Over here, Seth." Seth hurried over and around the boulder. This time Apollo was draped in a long white robe. He sat with his back against the boulder and his legs straight out in front of him. The god picked at the dirt under his fingernails. "Did I not warn you about the darkness?" he asked nonchalantly.

Seth kneeled in front of Apollo. "The last time I saw you in this spot you were weeping and difficult to understand. I've seen you since then, of course. Or…never mind." Seth waved his hand to brush away the words he left unsaid. "I need your help, Apollo."

"Everyone needs something from me, dear Seth. The life of a god is not as leisurely as one would like to believe. I think that now is before later and later was a while ago."

"Please don't talk in riddles," the faerie begged. "My head is too full at the moment to even begin deciphering what your words mean."

"Very well," stated Apollo. "I'm sure you can take the time later to think about what I have suggested. How's the light for you? Can you see enough?"

Seth rubbed at his head and beat his wings. "I'm learning to adjust to the darkness, although there does seem to be a bit of light here. Or rather, there's less darkness here than there is in Faerie."

"This is Faerie, Seth. I thought we had established that one other time."

"Yes, I know," replied Seth. "I think this is the same time as before, except that you aren't as self absorbed. I was able to identify the threat, but obviously I couldn't stop it. I knew that Mother Crystal was the answer to everything, so I went to the cavern to speak with her. When I arrived, there was no time to connect before the world was ripped apart and she was destroyed. I'm unclear on what really happened next, but I know that it couldn't have been good."

"It was certainly not good," agreed Apollo.

"Mother Crystal was the birth of all magick," continued Seth. "So she was pure magick and all of us magickal creatures came from her."

"You did indeed."

"I need to find a way to heal Mother Crystal. I know that magick isn't all dead yet, but it is dying rapidly."

"Oh, lots of things are dying."

"Billy came with me. He says that I am the true Crystal Guardian."

"So you are."

"I don't really understand what that means," mentioned Seth.

Apollo bent one leg at the knee and scratched at his foot. "You are the one for whom Alexander was chosen to train. You are the seer who was born to save magick."

Seth watched the sun god. "Can you bring back the sun even without my help?"

Apollo shook his head, "No."

"This is what I know," Seth began. "Mother Crystal is who created all magick."

"True."

"Therefore, she is pure magick."

"Yes, she was," agreed Apollo.

Seth ignored the god as he continued with his commentary. "I still have magick, as my wings sparkle and glow in the darkness."

"Very observant."

"This is how I know that not all magick is yet gone."

"Of course."

Seth gritted his teeth and tried once again to ignore Apollo's remarks. "To save magick, one needs to have magick."

"True, yet again."

"From what I saw of Mother Crystal when I left the cavern, she is in great need of pure magick, as of course she was pure herself."

"Pure magick is extraordinary."

"Are you made of pure magick, Apollo?" queried Seth, continuing to let his mind place the pieces together.

"Not at all, my good faerie. I am not made of any type of magick whatsoever. I am a god, which does not require magick of any sort," replied the sun god.

"I need to find some pure magick and bring it to Mother Crystal. Only pure magick can heal another source of pure magick."

Apollo brought his feet together and sat in the position of meditation. "Need we talk about magick? It really is getting on my last nerve."

Seth got up from his knees and began to pace back and forth in front of the annoying god. "The only life I know that's left in my realm includes Shadow, Billy, and myself. Everything else was sucked into the vortex, which is where your sun has gone as well."

Apollo snapped his head up. "My sun? You have found Helios?" He watched Seth carefully now, never allowing his eyes to wander away from the Crystal Guardian.

"Have you no idea as to where your sun has gone? You must've seen it disappear," said Seth in exasperation.

Apollo looked sheepish. "Well, technically, I wasn't exactly watching my precious Helios at the moment it disappeared. I was chasing...I was chasing something across the sky."

Seth raised his left eyebrow. "You were chasing something across the sky? Or do you mean to say that you were chasing *someone* across the sky?"

Apollo waved his hands in the air. "Someone. Something. What's the difference really? The important thing, at this very moment, is that you saw my Helios disappear, which means you can probably bring it back to me."

Seth stared at the sun god with disbelief. "Haven't you been listening to anything I've been saying, Apollo?"

"Of course I have been listening! You said that you know where Helios has gone!" The sun god stood up and stamped his foot to make his point.

Seth shook his head and closed his eyes to block out the vision in front of him, even though he could not block Apollo out of his thoughts. "Apollo, everything living went into the vortex. This included Luna, the stars, and Helios. If you'll just focus for one moment –"

"I am focusing!" yelled the god. "All I care about is getting back my sun! I cannot ride my chariot across the sky until Helios is back with me!"

Seth lowered himself to the ground. He crossed his legs and placed his chin in his hands. He watched Apollo continue to stomp his feet and walk around in a circle, creating a bit of a dust storm, even though the rain had not completely soaked the dirt. Seth closed his mouth and let his voice remain silent. There really was no point in continuing to discuss the matter with Apollo, while the sun god was unable to focus on the loss of magick and Mother Crystal.

Seth still could not figure out how Apollo was creating light in this deep darkness. He examined the god, as he continued to make circles in the dirt and rant about the importance of racing his chariot across the sun dappled sky. Apollo certainly did not glow like the sun, although, to be fair, the sun had been pulled into a vortex. His muscles were not as well built, as Seth would imagine pulling a chariot would require. In fact, the god was somewhat similar to an adolescent who had not yet known physical labour.

"You need to bring my sun back to me, young Seth," Apollo affirmed. "There is no doubt about it, without Helios nothing can live here." Seth continued to watch the god and remained mute by choice. "In fact, without life, there is no food for you to eat; therefore it is essential for your own existence that you bring Helios to me." Apollo stopped walking in a circle and smiled down at Seth triumphantly.

"Are you done talking about your sun and your chariot, and what I need to do for you, Apollo?" asked Seth in a slow monotone, so that the god would be forced to listen.

"You are the one who came to me," he pointed out. "The least you can do is show some respect for what I have to offer."

"So far," replied Seth with trepidation, "all you've given me is a headache. I'm trying to locate another source of pure magick so that I can heal Mother Crystal. It'll take both of us to come up with the solution to our problem of being stuck in this realm of dying magick."

"Well, there is another source of pure magick, although it may have been sucked into the vortex that you keep talking about," said Apollo.

Seth lifted his head and looked eagerly at the sun god. "So there is another source of pure magick in this realm? It couldn't possibly have been taken into the vortex, unless of course," his voice began to falter, "it was living."

"It's not that you need the magick to come from the living creature so much as from a part of this particular magickal creature. As long as you can find this creature in this realm, then you should be able to procure the pure magick from within the creature," stated Apollo.

"What type of magickal creature has pure magick within it?" questioned Seth aloud, as his mind searched through all the names of magickal creatures he knew. "Shadow is a dragon, and they are associated with treasures and shiny objects. However, I don't think dragons are pure, especially considering the fact that they contain fire and can turn from good to bad given the right circumstances."

"Dragons? Oh, dragons are great for taking on a flight and keeping you warm on a cold winter night, but they certainly do not contain pure magick. No, the creature I am referring to can be found at the source of a waterfall and is the most beautiful sight to behold," insisted Apollo.

"A beautiful creature made of pure magick or containing pure magick, as you say, can be found near a waterfall? There's a lovely waterfall near the cavern where Mother Crystal is located. I've noticed that rainbows like to dance in that particular waterfall."

"Actually, there is one source, of what you are seeking, hidden amongst the waterfall. I know this, as I hid it there myself not too long ago," said Apollo. "Of course, I did this before the darkness came and took away Mother Crystal."

"To be more accurate," interjected Seth, "Mother Crystal was taken first, which then allowed the darkness to take over."

"Did the darkness not seep into this realm before Mother Crystal was desecrated? I took precautions, although I could not prevent what has occurred. I could only set things up, in hopes that you would be able to put the pieces together and find a way to save magick," insisted Apollo. "Now go and find that which you seek. I am certain that when you come upon this beautiful creature, you will recognize her and find a way to bring her purity out to save some of what has been lost."

Seth stood and began to walk away from Apollo. He thought at first that the further he moved away from the sun god, the more difficult it would be to see in the darkness. To his surprise, he was now able to see with his inner sight as though his eyes were made to view the world without light. He continued to walk until his fingers tingled and his feet were sore. Seth stretched and found himself lying on Billy's couch, with Shadow sound asleep and his host snoring from the other side of the room.

CHAPTER 27

The clanging and banging coming from the kitchen penetrated into Seth's slumber and pulled him out of sleep. He yawned and turned from his back onto his side so that he could view the kitchen from his makeshift bed on the couch. He let his eyes roam around the room, even though there was no morning light, if it even was morning. Another crash vibrated through his bones and forced Seth to sit up. "What is all that ruckus?" he inquired.

The sounds ceased and Billy said, "Sorry 'bout that, Seth. I was lookin' fer some food fer us ta eat. I's kinda hungry so's I figure Shadow an' ya mus' be too. All's I've found is some dry biscuit an' some ol' dried meat."

Seth climbed off the couch and managed to find his way around the kitchen clutter to the table. "I'll eat anything you have. I'm not at all fussy about what we eat at the moment. Where's Shadow?" he asked once he realised that she was not in the room with them.

Billy began to lay out the food on two plates. "Oh, she wen' ou'side ta muster some food she can eat. Don' know wha' dragons eat. I's glad my home's still here. Not much left o' th' rest o' Faerie far's I can tell." Billy placed one plate of food in front of Seth and the other he put in front of his own chair as he sat down.

Seth took a bite of the unknown dried meat and chewed slowly. He savoured the salty flavour and the taste of real food. Once he had swallowed his first mouthful, Seth spoke, "I met with Apollo again through the night. Or rather, when I slept I had a vision with Apollo. I really have no idea if it's day or night anymore."

"Yeah, nigh' an' day is not importan' now that i's dark all th' time," agreed Billy.

"Right. Well, as I was saying, I did have a vision with Apollo again. He was a bit more helpful this time, although he still had difficulty focusing. The god kept talking about riding his chariot. He had absolutely no idea that the sun had been sucked into the vortex, as he had been chasing someone across the sky at the time the darkness descended."

Billy crunched on his dry biscuit. "Ya need some water, Seth? I can get some from th' pitcher on th' counter." He got up from his stool and poured water into cups before Seth had a chance to respond. "These biscui's is dry. Needs water ta wash 'em down. Did ya find wha' ya wanted though, from th' sun god, even though he wasn' focused?"

Seth swallowed another mouthful of meat. "Before I met with him, I already knew that what we need to find is pure magick. I kept asking him if there was a source of pure magick other than Mother Crystal. My theory is that it'll take the purity of magick to heal pure magick, if that makes sense."

"Yep, makes sense ta me." Billy gulped back half of the water in his cup.

"Apollo was vague, as usual, about another source of such magick. He did mention that what I seek will be found hidden in a waterfall, not far from the cavern where Mother Crystal existed."

"So is thi' source livin' or an objec'?"

Seth dipped a piece of the biscuit into his cup of water. "Apollo described it as a beautiful creature, so it must be living, which means that there are four of us still alive in this realm." He took a bite of the damp biscuit.

"We gonna fly there on Shadow? 'Cause I think i' migh' be faster than walkin'. Though af'er las' nigh', I am glad I don' have wings. There's some crazy flyin' in tha' wind and rain." Billy ripped a piece of the meat with his front teeth.

"I believe that the three of us need to stay together at all costs," said Seth. "I don't think we should be more than a few feet away from each other at all times. We should definitely take supplies with us if you have any that we could use."

"What we gonna need?" Billy ate another piece of the meat. He licked his fingers and then lifted the empty plate and licked it as well.

"Do you have water skins?"

"Yep, got four of 'em."

"We'll want blankets and a change of clothing in case it rains again. I was so cold, and I couldn't get warm, until I had snuggled onto your couch. I don't want us to be forced to wear wet clothes and have no blankets again."

"I got lots o' those."

"Whatever food you have left in here, we should take as well. I don't know what we'll find to eat on our journey. If all of the life has been removed from our realm, then we'll go hungry soon."

"Can we find food in th' lake? There's gotta be fish an' seaweed in th' water still," Billy said as he put his plate in the sink.

Seth stopped chewing the last of his food and stared at Billy. He twitched his wings and smiled widely. "You are absolutely brilliant, Billy!" Seth flew into the air and threw his arms around the troll as best he could. "Of course there would be food in the lake! The water wasn't sucked into the vortex, so what was under the surface must still be there! Oh, Billy!

This means we won't starve to death before we find the source of pure magick!"

Billy laughed and spun around with the faerie attached to him. "I likes eatin' fish. Them's good eats. Lot's a variety."

Seth let go of Billy and kept himself levitating in the air. "This means that we're going to need a few packs in which to carry what we collect from the lake. Let's get everything packed up so that we're ready to go once Shadow returns from her feed."

"'Kay. I got packs in th' cupboard near my bed." Billy turned and walked across the room to open the wooden doors beside his bed. He pulled out items and toss them one at a time behind him. As he found three blankets and two packs, he dropped these on the unmade bed. "Seth," he called as he continued to empty the cupboard, "ya can find th' water skins under th' ice box."

Seth flew over to the icebox and pulled open the drawer beneath it. Once he had the skins in his hands, he took them over to the bed and placed them atop the items Billy had already selected from his now empty cupboard. Seth ducked as Billy threw the last item in his hands on the floor at the foot of his bed. "Well, tha's everythin', Seth. We can packs 'er all up an' be gone soon." Billy closed one side of the cupboard and picked up the first blanket he could reach off of the bed. He rolled it up and placed it in one of the packs. As he continued to roll up the items and place them in the packs, Seth watched him work.

Seth could smell her breath before she entered the hill mound home. It was a mixture of rancid and sweet. Shadow poked her head into the home and shimmied her body into the living area. She opened her mouth and licked at the wall behind the couch where Seth had slept. A green stain remained where she had licked.

"Shadow, we're going to leave soon. Our first stop will be the lake, so that we can gather food to eat on our journey. The plan is for Billy and I to fly again upon your back. This'll ensure that we don't lose each other. We're going to find a living creature, which will allow us to stop magick from dying completely," Seth informed the dragon. She blinked at him and gave him a nod of understanding.

"Everythin's packed and ready ta go, Seth," stated Billy, as he swung one of the packs onto his back and carried the other two with his hands. He stumbled forward as he attempted to cross the room.

Seth flew over to the troll and held up his hand. "Wait, Billy. You can't possibly carry all of that yourself. You need to let me help you carry at least one of those packs."

Billy looked at the faerie and then at the two packs in his hands. "These are big an' heavy, Seth. Once we get outside, I's gonna put 'em on Shadow. She's strong and can carry these while we travel. Y' are too small ta take any o' these. You's needs a faerie size pack an' I don' have one o' those."

Seth flew out of Billy's way and relented. "Fair enough, Billy. Is there any room in those for food?"

Billy lifted one of the packs. "Oh yeah. This one has lots o' room fer the food from th' lake. We need ta go now, though." Billy secured the packs on Shadow, walked towards the door, and exited his home. Seth followed his friend, with Shadow carrying up the rear. No one closed the door and no one looked back at the misshapen home in the hill mound. They walked down the path and around where the trees of Faerie would have been growing and down to the lake. Although there were no trees and homes to obstruct their taking a direct route to the lake, no one suggested that they veer off the path.

Once they reached the edge of the lake, Shadow put her head under the water and took a long drink. Seth flew over the surface of the water and hummed a tune that Jayne used to sing on the days when they would all gather and play at the lake. Soon, his humming turned to words, even though his voice was not nearly as healing and soothing as Jayne's.

"Learned were the few he chose
To help in the saving of them all
So that one day each would know
The purpose of their gift

Come to me all my friends
Give thanks and praise to one we admire
One whose selfless acts are many
Asking nothing in return

For he is our true keeper still
Happy to be amongst us few
Joining in our search for balance
Of fire, water, earth, and air."

Seth kept an eye on the lake, viewing far below the surface for any sign of fish. The instant that one jumped, he moved his wings in a dance and let the faerie dust fall to touch the fish. At once, the fish became limp and floated over to where Billy waited to wrap it up and place it in the sack he had designated for food. After Seth was able to catch several fish in this way, he flew back to the dragon and the troll. "Do you want me to swim down and harvest some seaweed?" he asked his friend.

"Tha'd be good, Seth. Then we's have 'nough fer a few days eatin'," Billy agreed.

At once Seth stripped off his clothing and plunged into the lake. He kicked his legs and moved his arms so that he was near a thick selection of seaweed within moments. He pulled at the vegetation so that it came out by the roots. With two handfuls of the greens, he used his wings and legs to swim to the surface. Seth stepped onto the sandy beach and handed the seaweed to Billy. Quickly, Seth shook himself dry and donned his clothing once again.

Shadow waited patiently as Billy secured the pack to her back before climbing upon her. Seth flew to a spot close to Billy and settled himself into her scales. "Shadow, we're going to fly along the river to a place where it meets with a hidden waterfall. The land where we're going is sacred and not well travelled. Do you know where this is, or should I direct you to within the vicinity?"

The dragon spread her wings and lifted into the sky as her response to his question. Seth sighed in relief. "I know the location of this waterfall, but I haven't been there myself," he told Billy and Shadow.

Shadow soared in the sky, becoming one with the air and the freedom from gravity. She turned slightly and with one movement of her strong wings, pushed forward to catch a wind current. She stretched out her tail and let her body become long and strong. Her body shivered in anticipation of the flight and in her ability to take her charges to the sacred land. Seth sighed at the warmth coming from her, feeling as though he were at home for just a moment, snuggled into the safety of his family.

Seth blinked away the wind from his eyes. He looked over at Billy, who seemed content upon the dragon, as though there were nowhere else he would rather be in the realm. Seth felt a warmth of love for his loyal friend and he was thankful that he was not left alone to search for the waterfall and the beautiful creature hidden behind it.

It seemed as though they had just risen into the air when Shadow began a slow descent. The shift in height altered the feel of the air. The further to the ground they went, the warmer the temperature was, even though it was difficult to find warmth anywhere without the sun. Seth periodically shook his wings to see the light glow from them. Sparkles appeared like fireworks, which entertained Billy and kept him focused on staying seated in one spot.

As Seth let the dust from his wings spread across the scales between where he and Billy sat, Shadow took a sudden deep drop in her flight. Seth lurched forward and Billy tipped to the side. The faerie dust scattered in the wind and left a streak of green across the sky as they landed at the end of the river, where it became a small pool hidden amongst the crevices of rocks. Seth could hear the waterfall rushing downwards and splashing into the pool. The smell of fresh water and the damp soil tickled his senses.

Billy slid off of Shadow and landed on the ground with a huge thump. "Ooh, my butt hit somethin' sharp."

"Can you smell the soil, Billy? It's like the remnants of plants. This place must've been covered in a variety of vegetation before the vortex," said Seth. He flew off of the dragon and stood beside Billy. He breathed deeply. His fingers and toes tingled as though magick were moving through his body. "I can feel the beautiful creature we're seeking. She's definitely here."

"Maybe she is watchin' us now," suggested Billy. "She migh' be in charge o' th' soil, keepin' it fertile for when the plan's come back."

Shadow dipped her head and cocked her ears to the sounds emanating from the land. She sniffed the air and bared her teeth. Her voice rumbled in her throat, calling out to the living creature hiding from their limited view in the darkness. She swished her tail back and forth, back and forth against the ground. She held her powerful wings against her sides and shifted the weight of the three packs still strapped to her back.

"Do you know where she's hidden, Shadow?" asked Seth. He moved close to her and placed one of his hands on her wing. "Can you take us to her? Billy and I can follow you."

Shadow bent her head and touched Seth with her nose. She turned and licked Billy from his chin to the top of his head, causing his hat to fall off and his hair to stand on end with the help of her saliva. She brushed passed the two of them, her feet padding on the ground and her nails digging into the recently harvested soil. She stopped at the edge of the pond and took a long drink to quench her thirst.

"Goo' idea, Shadow." Billy pulled out a water skin from his pocket and dipped it into the pond. He took a drink and handed the skin to Seth. Once Seth had finished wetting his palate, he filled the skin with water again and gave it back to Billy for safekeeping. Billy quickly put it back in his pocket.

Shadow eyed the two before she continued walking along the edge of the pond towards the waterfall. When they could go no farther along the shoreline, Shadow slipped the packs off her back, stepped into the pond and submerged herself beneath the water's surface. Billy glanced over at Seth and then at the pond where Shadow had disappeared. "Ya think the creature is under th' water?"

Seth shrugged his shoulders. "I don't know what type of creature we're looking for, so it's possible that she's a native of the water. It makes sense, really, if you think about it. Apollo said that he brought her here and hid her near the waterfall. The pond is essentially near the waterfall. The waterfall actually becomes the pond."

"'Kay, so's we need ta get in th' pond an' find her," said Billy. He took off his shoes and socks. "I's not gettin' my clothes and shoes wet. Best go in without 'em."

Seth watched the troll for a minute before he too undressed for the imminent swim. When they were both ready, they stepped into the pond and let the water surround their bodies as they slowly lowered themselves into its depths. The water was soft and warm, much more so than they had expected considering the cool air. It was a relief to feel the warmth lap at their bodies. Seth swam in a circle and then did laps from one end of the pond to the other. Billy splashed around in one spot and waited for Shadow to resurface. He knew she would join him shortly.

Seth's wings continued to glow as he swam. When he dove under the surface the water glowed green. As he resurfaced, the darkness sparkled around him. He swam on his back and gazed up at the dark sky. He felt as though he were in a dark hole, rather than being one of four left in the realm where he was born and where he would one day die. He refused to allow himself to think that death was a possibility in the near future. Seth flipped over onto his stomach and paddled back over to where Billy and Shadow were located.

"Did you find the creature under the water?" Seth asked Shadow. She turned her head away from him and lowered her chin in response. "Oh, so she isn't in the pond. How should we begin to look for her then?"

Billy stepped out of the pond and shivered at the sudden drop in temperature. "Ooh, i's cold outta th' water." He rummaged in one of the packs and pulled out a blanket, which he wrapped around his wet body. "Can' we jus' call fer her? She prob'ly can hear us. Maybe we offer food, cause she migh' not fish."

Seth joined Billy on the shoreline and found another blanket in the pack. He rubbed himself down with it and then wrapped himself within its great big width. The blanket glowed from his wings. "I say we get dressed and then walk around the pond and call out for her. We don't know her name or even what type of magickal creature she might be, so perhaps we can ask if anyone living is around. Maybe the sound of our voices will entice her to reveal herself to us."

Billy dropped his blanket and hurriedly dressed in the clothes he had discarded on the soil. He sat down to pull on his shoes and socks. "Have ya seen my ha'? I don' know where i' wen'."

"I saw it fall off your head when Shadow licked you, but I didn't see where it landed," replied Seth. It took him longer to dress, as he had to locate the clothes he had thrown about when preparing for the swim. Seth layed out both wet blankets on the soil in hopes that they would dry. "Maybe we can find it later. If we leave everything here in a pile, we should be able to find it all again. It'll be much easier to move around the pond and waterfall without the extra weight."

Billy sighed, "I 'spose we can find i' later. Are we gonna star' walkin' now or wait fer Shadow ta come outta th' water?"

"We can leave her here for now." Seth walked to the edge of the pond and addressed the dragon, "Billy and I are going to take a walk around the pond and see if we can't find the beautiful creature. We'll meet you back here once we've either found her or we've done a complete search of the area."

Shadow swam a few feet away from Seth and turned onto her back. She watched him closely and snorted at him. "Good, I'm glad you agree with us," he told her. Seth turned to Billy. "Are you ready?"

"As ready as ever," he replied. Seth led the trek around the pond, heading in the direction of the waterfall. Billy walked beside Seth, taking small steps so as to keep close to his friend.

They were silent for a few minutes, while they listened to the water and any sounds that might indicate another living creature in the vicinity. Except for their footsteps and their own breathing, there was no indication of another. Seth kept close to the edge of the pond. When they reached the cliff rocks that nestled the waterfall, the two of them climbed up the rocks and began the ascent above the water source. Seth struggled with the rocks rather than using his wings to fly. He used his hands to haul himself up on the particularly large rocks. He could hear Billy slipping and stumbling as the rocks became more smooth and uneven.

When they finally reached the top of the cliffside, Seth breathed a sigh of relief. "That was some workout," he said.

Billy moved his right hand up and down his outer calf muscle. "I hopes we only do tha' once. I' woulda been easier ta have gone out from th' cliff and walked on the grasses." He paused and then said, "Well, where th' grasses shoul' be."

"I agree," puffed Seth, "but I think we need to keep as close to the waterfall as possible, as we need all of our senses to find the pure magickal creature. Since we can only see a few feet in front of us, being further away wouldn't help us in our search. Apollo was very precise when he mentioned the waterfall. He told me that what we want is hidden near the waterfall, so we can't widen our search yet."

Billy took a few deep breaths of the fresh breeze that had come from below. "Are we's gonna cross the water here where th' waterfall comes?"

Seth examined what he could of the water advancing towards the cliff. The mouth of it was nestled between two large, peaked boulders. The space between was wide and appeared precarious. "I can fly across the water, but unfortunately, you can't," he deduced.

Billy stepped to the right and to the left as he examined the expanse between the boulders. "I coul' prob'ly climb down to the mouth and walk 'cross the water."

"Let me check first," Seth cautioned. "I'll fly above and see if it's safe for you to cross on foot." He lifted his wings and fluttered them as he took to the air. They continued to glow green and leave speckles of dust where he had been. When he reached the edge of the first boulder, Seth lowered his feet to the rock and leaned over the side to catch a glimpse of the water below. It was calm from the original source, but soon became rough and treacherous once it reached the mouth of the fall. Foam spewed upon the surface and grabbed at the boulders before it plummeted down the fall.

"I don't think it's safe for you to walk over, Billy," he yelled back to the troll he had left waiting on the other side of the boulder. Seth turned around to begin his flight back to Billy. His heart beat rapidly as he saw Billy scrambling upon the boulder behind Seth. The surface was smoother than it had appeared from below.

Once he was upon the boulder, Billy raised himself to his feet and stepped towards Seth. "I's decided ta join ya as we gotta cross here even if i' be difficult. So here's I am." He grinned with pride and placed each hand upon a hip.

Seth held up his hands. "I don't think you want to come any closer, Billy. I've looked at the water and it's going to be too difficult to manoeuvre. It'll toss you and turn you around until you no longer know which way is up and which way is down. It's a definite death trap."

Billy's grin faltered. "I's very strong, Seth. I can swim well. 'Sides, I can' leave ya ta do this on yer own." He took a step forward. As his left foot went out from under him, Billy flailed his arms and grabbed at anything he might hang onto. As he tumbled forward, Seth jumped out of the way. Billy grasped at the rock surface, yet his fingers managed to only scrape across the hard stone. Down he slid, falling from the boulder feet first.

"Billy!" screamed Seth as he few to his friend's rescue. He watched in horror as Billy plunged into the roaring surf at the mouth of the waterfall. Seth swooped down from the edge of the boulder and hovered above the turning water, searching everywhere for a sign of the troll. He flitted back and forth, using the green glow of his wings to cast light upon the surface of the water.

A great roar erupted from the pond below. Seth could feel the pounding of her wings as Shadow took to the sky and flew in a circle. She worked her way to where Seth hovered in fear. Her tail swished back and forth as she propelled herself to the mouth of the waterfall where Billy had last been seen. Seth had no need to tell her what had happened, for she knew instinctually that one of them was in danger and that her assistance was required.

Seth watched her assess the perilous situation. She turned quickly. He froze in the air as he realised that he was useless at this very moment, when strength and bravery were everything in being able to save his loyal friend. Shadow suddenly dipped sharply down the waterfall. As her tail disappeared from his view, Seth refocused and flew towards where he had last seen her.

Shadow turned a summersault and plunged into the crashing water as it sped to the pond below. Time stood still, as though Georgia were here freezing moments for their entertainment. Seth could feel his stomach turn as he thought of Georgia and the others who had been taken into the vortex the night before. It was difficult to believe that it was only a few hours ago when they were all gathered at the mountain camp. He kept his eyes glued to the waterfall, waiting for a sign of Shadow or Billy. He felt like his heart beat at a slower pace than usual, yet he knew somewhere within his mind that it wasn't really slow, that his mind was playing tricks on him. He knew this moment was testing his mind, his body, and whatever else was part of him. Seth took one shuddering breath and then flew down the side of the waterfall, looking for any sign of life.

The spray caught him in the mouth and he sputtered before pulling further away from the water. He stopped moving when he caught a glimpse of something red. It was for only a moment, but he was certain that he had seen a part of Shadow. He waited, beating his wings in anticipation. He dared not move, just in case this was the only glimpse he would get before having to believe that they were not going to return to him. Seth shook his head to remove such negative thoughts.

At first he was not sure he could believe his eyes, yet there she was, flying at full speed out of the water and towards the ground. Shadow was such a magnificent sight, as she held an object in her mouth with her wings spread wide and her tail straight out behind her. She landed smoothly on the soil beside the pond and dropped the package she was carrying. Her head bent over her prey, hiding it from Seth's view. He dared not let his relief surround him completely, not until he was certain of what he had seen.

Seth beat his wings as fast as he could, flying over the pond and down to where the dragon was licking her catch. Seth pushed against her head with his hands, trying to see what she had brought out of the waterfall. She blinked at him but did not move her head. "Is it Billy? Did you save Billy? Can I see him? Let me see him!" he begged like a child.

Seth ran around her head and squeezed between her front legs and snout. There, lying on the ground, getting bathed with Shadow's tongue was Billy. He had his eyes closed and was completely still. Seth rushed over to him and threw himself atop the troll. He sobbed as his heart broke into another piece. "I'm so sorry, Billy. It's all my fault! I shouldn't have suggested that we climb up the cliff."

He was not aware at first of the arm slipping around him and the fingers spreading against his wings. "I's 'kay, Seth. I's all righ'. Shadow caugh' me. I wasn' gonna leave ya, li'l friend."

Seth's heart skipped a beat. He raised his head to look into the warm eyes staring at him. His heart soared at the look on Billy's face. "You are alive!" Seth kissed Billy's forehead over and over with relief. He began to feel the warmth spread through his body and out to the tips of his fingers. "Thank goodness you are alive!"

A wet tongue slicked his back. Seth laughed and pushed himself onto his knees. He reached out for Shadow who allowed him to touch her nose. "Ya gonna get off me? She keeps lickin' me like a mother bird." Seth scrambled off Billy and found himself skipping on the ground in pleasure, much like Mercury when she is happy. Billy used his elbows to prop himself into a sitting position. Shadow licked him one last time and let him be.

Once Billy was on his feet, he hobbled over to Seth. "I though' I was a gonner. I couldn' breathe an' I jus' kep' tumblin' in th' water. Then Shadow came outta no where an' had me in her teeth. I knew I'd be 'kay when she had me. But, Seth, I think I saw somethin' in the fall."

Seth remained still as he listened to Billy. "What did you see?"

"Shiny, like yer wings. I saw the shiny glitter an' it was pretty. It sparkled in the water an' i' was lots a colours," he replied. "Kinda like a rainbow af'er a spring rain. Yeah, i' was a rainbow of glittery shine. Real beautiful." He closed his eyes at the memory, a smile playing on his lips. He seemed calmer, as though he had witnessed something sacred.

Seth watched Billy in his reverie. He knew that what Billy had seen was the source of pure magick Apollo had hidden in this place. He knew beyond a doubt that they now had a chance to save the life that had been destroyed in this realm and to rebalance nature once again. As though Billy were channelling the calm that had overcome him, Seth felt the hope that had eluded him up until this point. He could not remember the last time this feeling was so powerful, so real, and so unobstructed.

"Were you able to identify what type of creature this was? Do you know where in the waterfall she's hiding? Do you have any idea how we can get to her now?" Seth's questions tumbled out of his mouth in rapid succession.

Billy placed his hand on Seth's shoulder. "Slow down li'l friend. We's gonna get to her. She ain' goin' nowhere. I's no' sure wha' she is, though. There was so much sparkle and glitter comin' from in there." He pointed to the waterfall, yet kept his eyes focused on Seth. "I don' know if she saw me an' Shadow, bu' we know where ta look fer her now."

Seth nodded his head and looked deep into Billy's eyes. "You're right, Billy. If Apollo placed her here at some point and she's still here, then it's safe to say that she'll be waiting for us once we get into the waterfall." He bit at the inside of his cheek. "Is she a part of the water?"

"Wha' ya mean?" Billy asked quizzically. He tilted his head and furrowed his eyebrows.

"Was she a part of the water, like a water nymph? Do we need to find a way to become one with the water to find her again?" Seth felt a touch of impatience at himself for not knowing what she might be and how she might be captured in the water.

"Th' water moves," said Billy. "She ain' th' water. So, no, she's not a water nymph. I' was like she were in th' water, but a' th' same time she was away from th' water. 'Sides, I didn' see her th' whole time I was fallin' down an' tumblin' in th' rush o' water. I' was quick when I saw her. I barely regist'rd wha'd seen when Shadow had me."

Seth's mind spun with too many thoughts and ideas to keep track of where his brain was taking him. Visual images flashed from rainbows to sunshine, from Georgia freezing water to Mercury burning wood, from Mother Crystal to Alexander, from Apollo to Shadow. He pressed his hand to his forehead in an attempt to sort out the images and take control of his thoughts.

Shadow shifted behind Seth and Billy. She swished her tail and extended her wings in a stretch as she yawned. Seth turned to her and touched her nose again, which was warm. "You are a truly amazing dragon, Shadow. I'm so glad that Sabrina sent you with us on this quest. I know that you must miss her greatly."

Shadow licked at his hand and blinked at the mention of her faerie's name. She snorted a puff of smoke from her nostrils and bent her head low to the ground. Billy hobbled over and ran her ear through his fingers. It was a moment of silence and contemplation for those whom they loved. Like Seth, neither of them were able to spend any time thinking about what might have occurred once everyone had been taken into the vortex. Seth could only hope that they were safe somewhere in suspended time. The thought of that made him smile.

"We's gonna get 'em all back," murmured Billy. "Bu' firs' we need ta go inta th' waterfall, this time on purpose." He smiled sheepishly.

"Yes, we need to focus on entering the waterfall," agreed Seth. "How should we go about getting into it without drowning?"

"Well, we's already swam in the pond and din' get close enough. We went above i', an' tha' wasn' successful. Maybe we's need ta somehow get under or behind it," Billy suggested.

"Behind it?" Seth's eyes lit up with excitement. "That's it, Billy. We need to get behind the waterfall. There must be a cave or a ledge of some sort that's used as a safe place for this rainbow coloured creature." He threw himself at Billy and hugged the troll with all of his strength. "Oh, Billy! Whatever would I have done here without you? Have I told you how glad I am that you chose to come with me rather than stay with the other Guardians?"

Billy grinned from ear to ear. "Awe, shucks, Seth. I's glad too." Seth thought that he saw a touch of red on Billy's cheeks, but he could not be sure in this darkness.

"Should we fly into the waterfall on Shadow's back? I think that we would have to decide at what height the ledge might be. I wouldn't want Shadow to have to fly up and down in the falling water, searching, while we all get soaked and struggle to breathe." He turned to Shadow and asked her, "Do you have any idea where you managed to grab Billy in the waterfall? Maybe that's where we need to start our search."

Shadow shook her head slightly in response, yet managed to keep her chin on the ground. Billy walked to the edge of the pool. He lifted his head and looked the waterfall up and down. "I think we was 'bout five feet 'bove th' surface o' th' pond. So's I say we star' there."

Seth examined the shoreline to the point at which Billy suggested, compared to the pond surface. "Agreed. Shadow, are you ready to start now, or do you need to rest a bit after all this sudden flying?"

Shadow slowly got to her feet and lumbered towards the pond. She found a soft spot in the soil where she curled up in a somewhat fetal position and closed her eyes.

Seth laughed. "I guess that's our answer. Billy, do you want to rest as well? I know it wasn't very long ago since we left your home, but it seems like it was ages. Since Shadow's going to have a sleep, we might as well do the same. We can't be sure as to when we'll next be able to rest."

Billy was already rummaging in one of the packs and pulling out dry blankets. "Yep, I coul' use a nap. Migh' as well all sleep a' th' same time." He took two blankets over to Shadow and propped his back against her warm belly. Seth flew over and nestled in beside the two. Billy arranged the blankets so that they covered both him and Seth.

CHAPTER 28

"Wake up, Seth. We needs a get inta th' waterfall," Billy's voice penetrated his sleep. Seth shifted, yet did not open his eyes. "Come on, lil frien' we gotta go get th' magick now."

Seth shivered as the blanket was pulled away from his body. Seth reluctantly opened his eyes to find the troll's face inches from Seth's sleepy form. "I wasn't done sleeping, though," he yawned in protest.

"I' don' matter if you's was still wantin' a sleep. We needs ta get th' rainbow critter from th' waterfall. Shadow's 'wake too." Billy pulled Seth to his feet and patted the faerie on his back.

Seth rubbed at his sleep worn eyes and blinked. He attempted to open them wide, which he found to be easy as there was, of course, no light to touch them with brightness. "Okay, we'll go soon. Can I have some water first, though? My throat is parched."

"Sure ya can." Billy pulled out the water skin, opened the lid, and handed it to Seth, who took a deep drink of the refreshing liquid. He handed the water skin back to Billy, who placed it into his pocket for safekeeping.

Shadow lumbered to her feet and shook her body to loosen her muscles. Billy limped over to the dragon and carefully climbed upon her back. It took him a few minutes to get settled, but once he did he called out, "Le's go, Seth."

Seth scratched at his back and flew up to sit beside Billy. Shadow spread her wings and took to the air. She flew high and circled around in the sky to help limber her muscles. Her wings created a wind that teased at Seth and Billy. She dove toward the pond and lifted back up just before she touched the enticing water. Seth and Billy fell to the side, yet managed to continue holding onto the dragon's scales.

"What are you doing, Shadow? Didn't we agree that we'd enter the waterfall at about five feet above the water surface? Why are you doing loop de loops instead of taking us through the waterfall?"

"She's jus' warmin' up, I thinks," said Billy. He smiled and closed his eyes. "'Sides, this's fun. Now I knows why Sabrina always flies th' dragon throughou' Faerie. When we get back ta Faerie an' ev'ryone is home, I'm gonna find me my own dragon. I think Hermy'll like havin' one 'round."

Seth thought about it and asked, "Where would you keep her? Shadow could barely fit in your home as it was."

"I could make 'er a bed ou'side. Or I could star' diggin' out more dir' from th' wall in th' livin' room." He grinned at the idea of a dragon living with him and his pet frog.

Shadow took one last swoop around the area before she flew towards the waterfall. Once she faced the rushing water, she angled herself so that the waterfall was on their left side. As she adjusted their height compared to the water surface below, Seth stretched out to examine the water falling from above. He squinted his eyes and he set his mind to neutral so that his vision blurred. These two techniques yielded no sign of anything glittery or like a rainbow.

"Can you see what we're looking for, Billy? I can't seem to catch a glimpse of anything like what you saw," Seth complained.

Billy craned his neck to get a closer look at the waterfall. The steady stream of fresh water falling from above and crashing to the pond below did not allow anyone to see into the waterfall itself. "No use, Seth. We gotta jus' go inta th' thing."

Seth took a deep breath. "Shadow, are you ready to go forth into the depths of this waterfall again? If we're unsuccessful at the first try, we'll come out here and regroup." He shook his wings to spray faerie dust on the dragon as an extra precaution.

Shadow turned and circled the pond one last time. She angled to the right and swished her wings as she headed straight towards the waterfall. As her head broke through the downpour, Seth and Billy shielded their eyes with their hands to prevent the water from blinding them completely. Seth blinked and examined the water falling all around them. He opened his left hand and let the water pour onto and off of it. His wings brightened and changed colours.

Billy reached out and touched Seth's wings. "Pretty, like th' rainbow I saw when I fell into th's earlier."

"Just like it?" Seth queried.

"Yeah, jus' like i'. Only your wings is movin' rather than stayin' still."

"The other rainbow didn't move?"

"Nope. It jus' was in one spo' th' whole time," Billy affirmed.

Seth contemplated this revelation and thought about what would create a rainbow and not move. He was able to make a rainbow and move it with his wings, so whatever was here in the waterfall did not have wings or else the glittery colours were part of something that stayed still. He thought of all the magickal creatures he knew who were not born with wings. There was Billy, of course, which would also include all trolls. Brownies did not have wings, nor did gnomes and salamanders. Goblins certainly did not have wings, although he did not know any personally. He had heard of centaurs, but had never actually known any to exist in this realm, although that was not to say they did not exist. They probably kept to their own kind.

"We need to go further into the waterfall, Shadow. Take us to the other side here, against the rock surface," instructed Seth.

Shadow flew forward, taking them further into the waterfall before coming out the other side, where the water did not fall and the rock surface was solid. It did seem as dark in here as it had on the other side of the waterfall. Seth's wing colours increased in strength. They provided more light here, as though they were in contact with something else which was able to extract the light from within his wings.

Billy stared at Seth and the glittery glow he gave off in this new environment. "You's pretty, Seth, jus' like she is," he said in awe. Billy moved his head to look from Seth to the beautiful unicorn standing on the rock ledge, watching the three of them enter her protective space.

Shadow landed gently on the ledge behind the waterfall, where it was dry and the water was unable to touch, even with the spray. Seth slid off of Shadow's back and touched his bare feet to the rock ledge. He gaped at the unicorn standing a few feet away. She was snow white, with not a blemish of any kind on her perfect figure. Her muscles were toned and her mane was full. Seth was mesmerized by the twisted horn set upon her forehead. Her horn glittered from all the rainbow colours emanating within and around it.

"She is pure magick," breathed Seth. "The magick from a unicorn horn is pure magickal dust. That's why she contains all the colours of the rainbow in her single horn. She's the most beautiful being I've ever seen." He walked tentatively forward, careful not to startle the unicorn more than they had with their sudden arrival.

Billy stayed upon Shadow, who did not move an inch. The dragon was as awestruck as did the troll. Both were smiling at the creature before them. Seth held out his hand to the unicorn in good faith. When he was below her head, she bent forward and touched his hand with her nose. A peaceful and loving sensation spread through Seth's fingers and into his body, tingling all over as it moved into each cell of his being. The sensation was alive and pulsing. He felt happiness and for a brief moment the darkness faded completely.

Seth could feel the power of the unicorn and the magick that lived within her. His wings began to sing like those of a cricket, bouncing off the rock and wall of water. He jumped at this sudden change in his wings, at this new experience in his body. A rainbow streamed from the horn of the unicorn to the tips of his wings. Butterflies danced within its bands of colour. Seth fluttered his wings and watched as his faerie dust fell and entered into the rainbow. The butterflies picked up the dust and carried it to all parts of the rainbow.

"Wow," whispered Billy. He climbed off of Shadow and stood beside her, watching the magick connect and grow between Seth and the unicorn.

Seth flew upwards and stopped at eye level with the unicorn. "We've come to you in hopes that you'll help us save magick. Outside of here," he gestured to the waterfall, "all is in darkness. Mother Crystal has been destroyed and the light has receded from our realm. Only the three of us, and you, remain alive in this world. Everything else living was taken into a black vortex. We came in search of you, because you are our only hope in bringing back a balance to nature and allowing the light to once again touch upon our realm."

The unicorn blinked at Seth and turned to view Billy and Shadow. She then glanced at the rainbow and its continued connection to Seth and herself. She stepped back one hoof-length. The rainbow did not break between them, but rather it lengthened and shimmered. She bowed her head and touched Seth with the tip of her horn. He reached out his hand and grasped the end of it. The calmness that he was experiencing deepened and sang within his soul. When he removed his hand from this magnificent creature, Seth noticed that his hand glittered and glowed with light. He shook his hand and watched the beautiful dust particles sway from side to side as they fell to the ground. Before they touched the rock ledge, a few of them grew larger and brighter. These particles took on a mind of their own and blew over to Billy and Shadow, where they chose to fall and rest on the two of them.

Seth turned around and broke eye connection with the unicorn. The rainbow remained connected between them, as though they were now one magickal being in this desecrated realm. "She is willing to go with us. I can't read her mind, as that is not my gift, but I can feel her emotions and her thoughts as though they are part of me. When the vortex came, she felt it and has been scared ever since, even though she still feels the peace and calmness that comes with pure magick."

Shadow stretched her head forward and came nose to nose with the unicorn. She sniffed the white creature and then licked her forehead, leaving the horn untouched. The unicorn shook her mane and shifted forward several steps. "Looks' though they like each other," Billy uttered. "This a good thing. Do ya think we gonna all ride t'gether? Or do ya wanna ride th' unicorn an' I'll ride on Shadow?"

Seth put his hand out and touched the hoof of the unicorn. "I think we should walk to the cavern. This is a unicorn, not a Pegasus; therefore she has no way of getting there by flight. The cavern isn't too far from here, so it shouldn't take us very long to reach our destination."

"How we gonna get th' unicorn outta here?" Billy walked from one end of the ledge to the other. He stuck his head around each corner to see if there was a secret way out from under the waterfall. On his way back from one end, he leaned forward and put his head into the fall of water. When his head re-emerged, dripping wet, he shook it and stated, "No ways out here."

"Well, if it hadn't been for Shadow, it would've been extremely difficult for us to have gotten here to begin with, coming through the fall. Let's figure out what we do know and maybe we can deduce a plan from that."

"'Kay. We knows tha' we flew in here with Shadow. She has powerful wings an' grea' strength. When I's was fallin' down, I saws the unicorn's rainbow."

"We didn't see the unicorn or her rainbow colours until we had actually passed through the waterfall this time," mentioned Seth.

"So's maybe angle has ta do with wha' we can see from in here." Billy shook his head to dispel some of the water drops.

Seth paced back and forth between Shadow and the unicorn. "Apollo brought the unicorn here, so he obviously didn't use customary mortal methods. He had to have used powers only bestowed upon the gods."

"Did he use magick or somethin' else jus' for gods?"

"Apollo has no magick. He told me that he's a god and gods don't need or have access to magick. So, although we are going to need to use some type of magick, we can't base it upon Apollo's actions." Seth twitched his wings as he thought. "We know that we couldn't access this ledge from when we were in the pond, so coming from below won't give us a way out."

"We got no access from th' sides and none from 'bove nor 'low. So's tha' jus' leaves through th' fallin' water," Billy stated. He sat down and crossed his legs. "Don' know how we's gonna get ou' withou' flyin'."

Seth stopped moving and stared at Billy sitting on the ledge with his chin in his hands. He flew over to the troll and sat down in front of him. "Basically, we know there's only one way in and one way out of here. We have Shadow, a dragon who's strong. We have you, a troll who's able to ride upon the dragon. We have me, who has wings and can fly solo. And finally, we have a unicorn full of pure magick who can't ride a dragon and doesn't have wings with which to fly." He put his right cheek against his right hand and groaned.

Billy sighed, "Yep, seems there's no way outta here with th' unicorn."

"There has to be a way!" exclaimed Seth. "If there was no possibility of taking this unicorn out of here and to the cavern, then Apollo wouldn't have placed her here to await for our arrival." He pushed his wings all the way back and clapped them together in frustration. Faerie dust billowed from his wings and settled on the ground around him.

Billy lifted his head from his hands and examined Seth with wonder. "Wa's yer faerie dus' do, 'sides glitter an' glow?"

"Why does that matter right now, Billy?" Seth asked with a touch of irritation in his voice.

"'Cause I needa know. I's jus' thinkin' 'bout..." his voice trailed off.

"Without the faerie dust, I wouldn't be able to fly," admitted Seth. "It's a natural part of my wings, just like all moths have a coating of fine, soft, dust-like substance. It's also what gives my wings their colour." He moved them to prove his point.

Billy leaned forward on his crossed knees. His eyes began to twinkle. "So wha' would happen if ye were to take th' dus' from yer wings and put i' on th' unicorn? Would she fly?"

Seth's head snapped up and he looked from Billy to the unicorn standing behind his own back. "Billy, you are brilliant! My faerie dust would allow her to fly!" He jumped up, danced and clapped his hands. "Oh, however did you think of that?"

Billy's face turned scarlet and he grinned from ear to ear. "Oh, i' jus' was in my though's. So I le' it come ou' my mouth." He sat up straight and stretched his back and arms.

"Oh, ho! We have a way out of here with the unicorn!" Seth continued to dance around on the spot. Shadow tilted her head and eyed him suspiciously. The unicorn turned around and swished her tail at him. Seth scurried over to the unicorn. He ran between her legs until he had reached her front hooves. He let his wings carry him up to eye level with the beautiful creature. "We're going to get out of here and take you with us."

She closed her eyes and bowed her head to Seth. At this gesture, Seth touched her beautiful horn and held onto her. He could feel her reassurance and her gratefulness at his arrival. She had been lonely since Apollo brought her here. She missed her kind and those who understood the importance of community. The bond that formed between them was strong and it felt as though they had always been meant for each other. Seth asked her silently for her name.

"Una," he whispered. Seth let her go and flew onto her neck, where her thick mane cascaded over both sides and down the beginning of her back. He let his fingers play with her mane. She was soft and yet her muscles indicated solid strength. Seth spread his wings wide and closed his eyes. He pulled from his core and could feel the magick from within enter his wings. He closed and opened his wings, yet allowed his feet to remain on Una's neck.

Billy gasped with surprise and pleasure. "I's workin', Seth. Yer wings is as green and glittery as never 'efore. Th' dus' is fallin' on her an' makin' her neck an' back glow green."

Seth did not respond to this vocal revelation. He knew that he was sharing the magick from his faerie dust with this beautiful, white unicorn. He could feel their connection strengthening and building across the rainbow that they shared. He kept his eyes closed and his mind and body focused on sharing his faerie dust with this source of pure magick. His heart beat loudly in his ears as the blood in his body pumped it through to feed his magick. It was not long before he could hear Una's heart beat as well. The rhythm of their two hearts began to beat as one, pumping their blood forth through their bodies and spreading the shared magick across each soul and body.

Seth let go of Una and opened his eyes. His feet and his legs glowed. All across Una's white fur coat was a dusting of his faerie magick. "You should be able to fly now," he told her, "although I've no idea how this'll work without wings on your body."

"I thinks you have ta stay on her when she star's ta fly," Billy stated from the ground below. "I don' know how I knows this, but I think i's true."

"Fair enough," Seth replied. "Shall we try to fly out of this hidden ledge and through the waterfall so that we can begin our trek to the cavern?"

Billy bobbed his head up and down. "Yep, I's ready." He climbed upon Shadow and settled himself on the warmth of her back. She lifted her head and turned to make certain that Billy was holding on tight. He grinned up at her and demonstrated his grip on her scale. She shifted her feet so that she was able to turn around in a semi-circle and face the waterfall straight on, then she glanced over to Seth and Una.

Una still had her tail turned towards Shadow and Billy. She had not changed position since before Seth climbed upon her neck and shared his faerie dust. He was uncertain as to how he would get Una to fly, although his first priority was to get her facing the waterfall and standing beside Shadow.

"We need to all go together, at the same time. If I can't get Una out of here successfully, you and Shadow need to come back for me, okay Billy?" Seth felt trepidation. "I don't know what we'll do if this doesn't work," he added.

"I won' leave ya, Seth. I promise," Billy assured the faerie. Shadow swished her tail in agreement. "See? We's in this together, all o' us."

Seth took a deep breath. He leaned forward and wrapped a chunk of Una's mane around his fingers. "Are you ready, Una? Without you, we can't save magick and heal

Mother Crystal. If we aren't successful with leaving here, then I 'm not sure as to how else we can save you, Shadow, Billy, myself, and all those who've been taken from our realm." He took another deep breath and said, "Fly, Una, fly."

The unicorn lifted her front legs and arched her back. Seth beat his wings in time to their hearts. Slowly, they lifted off the rock ledge and hovered in the air. Seth let out his breath and glanced over at Billy. The troll was smiling widely. Shadow spread her wings and flew into the waterfall.

Seth leaned forward as though he were steering the unicorn. He focused on the waterfall and they floated towards it in slow motion. It took ages before they reached the water, but once they entered its spray their speed increased. Seth kept his eyes open and glued forward. The water drops stung on his eyes, yet he did not relent and close them. As they passed through the waterfall, their connected rainbow brightened.

When they had cleared the waterfall and were floating above the pond, Seth breathed a sigh of relief. His lungs expanded and he was able to take deep breaths. Shadow and Billy were not far ahead; they had remained in one spot above the pond, waiting in case they needed to re-enter the waterfall to rescue Seth.

"Ya made i'!" screamed Billy. "Woo hoo! We's got th' unicorn and we's all safe an' ou' a th' water." Shadow circled around and came up beside Seth and Una. She touched her nose to that of the unicorn and licked at Una's horn.

"Let's get over to the safety of the shoreline," directed Seth. He kept Una moving forward over the pond until they were safely above the soil. He flapped his wings for a slow descent to the ground. When Una's hooves made contact with the shoreline, she lifted them one at time and stomped them into the soil.

Shadow landed smoothly beside the two of them. Billy patted her gently on her scale in appreciation of their success. "Amazin' how well tha' all worked. We have th' source of pure magick and now we jus' needs ta get ta Mother Crystal an' heal her." Billy slid off Shadow's back and landed on his bum, struggled to his feet, and rubbed at his leg. Slowly, he limped over to Una. "Ya still have th' glitter on ya, Una. Can ya fly withou' Seth on ya?"

Una shook her mane, which caused Seth to swing about as he continued to hold onto her. He let go and allowed his wings to take over in up righting himself in the air. "I don't think she can fly without me. I steered her to the soil. It was like we were floating rather than actually flying. Besides, I think that the walk will do us all good. We can feel the ground beneath our feet, which should also let us know if something changes that we wouldn't be able to notice from the air."

Billy hobbled over to one of the packs and rummaged through it. "I needs a hat. Don' feel good withou' a hat." He pulled out a pair of boots and a slicker. "Huh, coulda used this in tha' storm." Finally, Billy was able to locate a blue hat, which he promptly placed upon his wet head. He quickly retrieved the thrown items and cinched the pack closed.

Seth placed his feet on the ground and walked around Una and Shadow. "Without light, it'll take us longer to reach the cavern than it would've if this were daytime. Well, maybe it is daytime, but anyway, without the light of the sun we'll have to take our time, so that we don't come across any surprises with the terrain. We need to keep close together, but not so much so that we are tripping upon each other. I think, also, that we should stop every one hundred feet to check in on each other and make certain that we aren't harmed in any way." Seth looked pointedly at Billy, who was now bent over looking at one of Una's back hooves.

"I think that Shadow should be in the lead and I'll take up the rear. If we have Una behind Shadow, her horn can display some light for you to follow, Billy." Seth touched Una and led her directly behind Shadow. "I'm trusting that you know the way east, Shadow, although I don't think that you've been to the cavern before. What's important is that we travel east from here. We can't miss our destination, as long as we keep going east."

"Will i' look diff'ren', Seth? There's no vegetation anywhere, so's ya gonna notice i' withou' vegetation?" Billy positioned himself behind Una, keeping close to her tail.

"The landscape won't have changed," said Seth. "I'll be able to identify the area based on the lay of the land. I've been there on more than one occasion. As you may recall," he paused, "I was there when Mother Crystal was demolished."

Billy moved his lips, yet no sound came out. His eyes drooped with sadness and he glanced away from Seth at the memory of finding Seth at his doorstep shortly after the destruction that occurred within the cavern walls. Billy straightened up his back and faced forward, which was right at the tip of Una's tale. "I's ready ta go."

Seth smiled at Billy's back. His heart felt strong and he longed to hug the troll in front of him, yet he resisted. Instead, he said, "Shadow, can you take us east?" As the dragon moved forward, the others followed close behind. Una was the only one who was able to adjust quickly to the pace at which Shadow chose to lead the group. Billy hurried forward, only to find himself bumping into the back legs of the unicorn. Then he would take a slower pace until it became difficult to see in front of his own feet. It was a constant battle of finding the right foot pace to keep up with the movements of a dragon who could see everything in front of her.

As they wound their way from the pond to the deserted grasslands above, no one spoke. Seth focused on his feet and allowed the green glow of his wings to cast shadows. Every now and then, Seth made animals with his fingers and watch them dance upon Billy. The troll did not have time to entertain himself as he was too focused on keeping upright and on his feet. Una was quiet, which Seth began to think as normal for the unicorn. If he listened carefully, Seth could identify which foot was being lifted and which foot was being placed on the ground as Shadow led them towards the cavern.

If he were honest with himself, Seth knew that the knot forming in his stomach had more to do with actually reaching the cavern than with not being successful on this journey. When he had awoken to find himself alone in that demolished cavern, he had never felt so alone and so lost in all of his life. He feared that stepping back into that space might devastate his soul or impede his progress in saving Mother Crystal. The more he thought about it, the more Seth wondered if Mother Crystal was as damaged as he remembered or if she was more damaged than he had noticed. He brushed aside the pain in his abdomen and focused on the creatures in front of him. It was his job as Crystal Guardian to make certain that they all arrived safely to the cavern. Whatever happened within its walls would have to be dealt with once they were inside its depths.

A cool breeze blew as they trotted across the bare landscape, where no rock formations protected them from the elements. Because there was no longer any vegetation to keep the soil rooted to the ground, bits of dirt blew in their eyes and covered their skin and clothing. Billy adjusted his hat, so that the front of it hung down in front of his eyes and kept out some of the soil particles. He trudged forward, tripping on his two feet, until he nearly fell upon Una. Seth held out his arm to assist Billy in keeping on his feet.

The silence of the world was deafening. Where there would usually be the songs of birds and crickets, there was nothing but a whistle from the wind. No leaves rustled in the breeze. Since they had left the vicinity of the waterfall and pool, there was no indication of water rushing or moving. The rocks that were scattered about the ground would now and then grind under their feet, but not enough to create the feeling of life. As each of them inhaled and exhaled, the sound touched Seth's ears and kept his heart close to the three creatures with whom he was travelling.

After a while Seth stopped making shadow puppets and just put one foot in front of the other. It definitely took longer to walk to the cavern from here than it would have taken to fly. He rubbed at his eyes more the further along they went. He was not tired, but his eyes found the darkness a strain. It was becoming more and more difficult to see in front of his feet. He twitched his wings to create more faerie dust to help them see their way. When this did not help his vision, Seth squinted at Billy's back.

"Is anyone else having trouble seeing our way?" asked Seth.

"I's findin' i' darker too," confessed Billy. "I kep' thinkin' tha' I was tired. Bu' then I was thinkin' how we haven' been up from sleep long enough for me ta be tired." He turned around to glance at Seth. "Oh!" he gasped. Billy covered his mouth with his hand.

Seth stopped walking. "What is it, Billy?"

"Ah, you's no' glowin' so much anymore, Seth. Yer wings is pale an' they don' glitter no more," he mumbled. Billy reached out to touch one of Seth's wings. When he pulled back his hand, there were no faerie dust remnants on his fingers. "Tha's no' good," he added.

Seth peered at Billy's hand and felt his insides tighten into more knots. "I have no faerie dust left? How can I not have faerie dust?" He beat his wings in an attempt to create dust, to no avail. Seth hurried over to Una and flew up to her back. He searched her fur for the bits of faerie dust he had used on her earlier. Her coat was pristine white, as though she had never come in contact with his magick. "This can't be!" he cried. "There should still be bits of my green dust embedded in your fur!"

"Loo' a' her horn," Billy called up to him. "I' don' glow no more, either."

Seth stepped along her back and climbed upon Una's neck. When he reached the top of her head, he focused his vision upon her twisted horn. The rainbow colours were gone. A white glow emanated from her horn, yet it did not span very far into the space beyond her body. Seth touched the tip of her horn and noted that it was no longer warm. Suddenly, he reached behind his back and touched his own wings. Dread seeped into his soul as he realised that his wings were cooler than their usual temperature. His heart skipped a beat, which caused Una to shift her hooves.

"We are dying," Seth whispered in horror.

"Wha's 'at?" came Billy's voice from down below. "Wha' ya say, Seth?"

Seth dropped to his knees and began to weep. His head rested in his hands and he sobbed from the depths of his heart. He did not hear Billy make his way up onto Una. It was not until Billy had placed an arm around his shoulders that Seth realised his friend was sitting beside him. "I's gonna be 'kay. Ya jus' cry i' ou' and then we's be on our way," he murmured into Seth's ear.

Seth shook his head in protest. "No, it's not going to be okay, Billy." He cried and leaned his head into the crook of Billy's arm. "The magick is truly dying. Una and I are dying with it."

Billy stiffened. He looked from Seth to Una and back again to Seth. "No, you's no' dyin'. Ya can' die on me." His face contorted and two tears fell from his eyes. "No, Seth. We gonna save magick and then ev'ryone is gonna come back ta Faerie and i'll all be good 'gain."

Seth shook his head. "No, Billy. Things are never going to be as they once were. There've been too many changes in our realm for everything to be as wonderful as it has always been. I no longer have faerie dust and Una has lost her rainbow. Our magick is fading. If we don't reach Mother Crystal soon, then I'm afraid that the pure magick in Una's horn will no longer exist. If that happens before we get to Mother Crystal, then we won't be able to heal her. At that point, our realm will die, and so will we."

Billy pulled back from Seth and slid off of Una. "Then we's needs ta hurry. We can' stay here an' cry 'bout i'. We gotta get ta th' cavern now. Le's go!" He stumbled forward, tripping over his feet as he rushed past Seth and Una. Billy climbed upon Shadow and said loudly, "Move! We all's gotta go quickly. Seth, stay on Una, so's we can travel faster. No more stoppin' for nothin' 'til we in th' cavern."

Shadow and Una were able to walk much faster without having to wait for Billy and Seth to catch up with them. Within an hour, the four of them were at the mouth of the cavern, where Mother Crystal had been defiled. Seth used his wings, which were slower than usual, to fly over to where the purple bush had once been used to hide the stairwell entrance to the cavern. He pushed at the ground, which shifted and opened up to reveal the stairwell hidden within the land.

"Billy, can you lead us down into the cavern and help Una down the stairs? Shadow and I can fly down behind you," instructed Seth.

"Yep, I can do tha' fer ya." Billy descended into the cavern. He held onto Una as the two of them took one stair at a time, being careful not to trip or miss a step on their way down.

Seth climbed upon Shadow and held tight to one of her scales. "Follow them, Shadow."

CHAPTER 29

The cavern was dark. It no longer glowed from the beauty, life, and magick of Mother Crystal. The vegetation that had once grown in these depths without sunlight had vanished during the fight with Lillian. Scars from the fireballs filled the cavern walls and the dirt floor. The smell of burning flames remained in the air. Seth averted his eyes from where Mother Crystal had pulsed with life. The silence from above echoed within the walls of rock.

"She don' look so good," commented Billy. He let go of Una and tentatively walked over to what was left of Mother Crystal. She had become a small shard of alexandrite crystal, destroyed when Lillian had attacked her. Drops of murky liquid surrounded her. There was no indication that the water had once been a beautiful pool full of light and colours. "Can I touch her?"

"I don't see why not," replied Seth. "We once touched her. She'd welcomed us and even sang a soothing song that touched our hearts. Maybe you'll feel a remnant of her."

Billy crouched down in front of the crystal shard. He reached out with one hand and placed his palm face down upon what was left of her. "She's cold. Why's she so pale? I though' she'd be bright and clear."

Seth climbed down from Shadow, afraid to test his wings in flight now that his faerie dust was gone. He made his way over to Billy and forced himself to look at what remained of Mother Crystal. The knot in his stomach grew and spread throughout his body, making him feel hot and cold all at once. There was no indication that she had once been a magnificent part of the world. Seth placed a hand on Billy's knee. "She pulsed with life before," he sobbed.

"She'll pulse 'gain, Seth. We's jus' gotta give her some o' Una's magick." Billy patted his friend's head in reassurance.

"Una no longer has rainbow colours and I no longer have faerie dust. I think that we might be too late to save magick and heal Mother Crystal here." Seth gasped for air between his sobs.

Billy raised himself onto his feet and stood tall before Seth. He frowned at the faerie before glancing over to Una and Shadow, who were waiting silently for further instruction. "I's surprised a' ya, Seth. I ne'er though' you'd quit on me. We didn' come this far ta give up 'fore we tried. So wha' if ya no longer have faerie dus' and Una don' make a rainbow? I's got no magick an' I's still here. Shadow has los' Sabrina an' she ain' complainin'. We can' leave ev'ryone in tha' vortex forever. Our realm is dyin' 'cause there ain' no ligh' no more. If we don' do this, we's nex' ta die. Once we run outta food in our packs, tha's i'. There's no food ou' there or righ' here. So tell me, Seth, wha' ya gotta lose fer tryin' even withou' th' pretty glitter?"

Seth felt shame at having let Billy down. "I'm sorry, Billy. I think that I let the darkness enter my soul and take away my hope. You believed in me and left everyone else to come with me, knowing this would not be simple. I didn't think that we'd lose more magick on our journey here. I'm not used to doing everything without the other Guardians. We were trained to use each others' strengths so that we could

298 | VAN MOL

increase our own. When we started our trek in search of Una, I knew what we had with us and how I could use it to our advantage. Then, when we found Una and were able to take her out of the waterfall, I foolishly thought that the remainder of our journey would be simple. It never occurred to me that our magick would fade so quickly and so substantially in such a short amount of time." He raised his chin and searched Billy's face. "You are a better Guardian than I have ever been, Billy. It is you who is the true Crystal Guardian, not I."

"Oh gosh," Billy breathed. "Bein' a Guardian's th' mos' prestigious rank in all o' Faerie. Only ya faeries born special get th' chance to become one. I ain' even a faerie."

"You may not have been born a faerie, Billy, but you are the bravest troll I know. In fact, you are more special than anyone has ever given you credit for." Seth beamed with pride for his friend. "If it weren't for you, Billy, we wouldn't be here right now. It was you who discovered where Una was located. It was you who knew to come with me rather than to stay with everyone else. I wasn't even sure that I was doing the right thing by leaving everyone, even though my gut told me to come back here. You are the most loyal friend I have." Seth threw his arms around Billy's stomach and hugged him with more strength than he thought was left inside his soul.

A tear fell from Billy's eye and fell upon Seth's wing. The tear sparkled, glittered, then made a trail around the edge of his wing. Billy gasped in surprise. Seth's wing started to glow deep green. Slowly, the green began to glitter and the faerie dust reappeared before it spread to his other wing. "I's not lost, Seth. You's gettin' th' magick back. Yer wings is glowin' 'gain."

Seth wrapped his wings around his body so that he was able to view them. He jumped at the change. "How is this possible? I didn't do anything different!"

"No, ya didn', bu' I did," admitted Billy. "I gave ya yer magick back, I think. Ya made me feel pride an' i' came outta my tear, so when i' fell on yer wing, th' magick grew."

Seth's eyes grew large and he watched Billy closely. The troll looked as he always did, a little bit out of sorts and dishevelled, yet there was a new brightness to his aura, as though he were channelling something truly amazing and magickal. Seth opened his wings wide and silently walked over to Una on his bare feet. He raised his hand up and touched her front leg. "It's time to introduce you to Mother Crystal, Una." Seth led the unicorn to what was left of the crystal. "This is where magick and all life, as we have known it, was born. It is time for us to heal her and make her whole again, or as whole as is possible now."

Seth bent one knee and beat his glittery wings in a slow rhythm, until he reached Una's twisted horn. He hovered in front of her eyes before he reached out to touch her source of pure magick. She was cold, just as he had expected, yet Seth wrapped his fingers around her tightly. He closed his eyes and sent white light into her horn, pulling it from above where it was not visible to the naked eye. When he opened his eyes, Seth could see the white light moving through the two of them and back into the ground. The cavern was bright. Rainbows littered the space between the rock walls.

Una bowed her head. Seth kept his fingers wrapped around her horn, yet he managed to turn his own head to examine the cavern. Apollo was tinkering with his chariot, while Archangel Michael stood silently in front of the desecrated crystal. Billy and Shadow were near the stairwell watching the magickal connection between Seth and Una. Three balls of light bounced off the walls and laughed. Seth whispered to Una, "Let's go to Mother Crystal now." The unicorn lifted one hoof in front of the other until they stood in front of Archangel Michael.

Seth let go of Una's horn. He turned on his feet, which were now safely planted on Una's nose. "Billy," he called down. "Can I use one of your kitchen utensils that I know you have hidden in one of the packs we brought with us?"

"'Course, Seth," he replied. Billy shifted from beside Shadow. He climbed upon her and began rummaging in one of the packs still attached to her back. He pulled out a grater, which he tossed to the ground. His arm disappeared into the pack. With a bit more rummaging he was able to retrieve a small whisk from the bottom of the pack. He held the whisk in his left hand and slid off Shadow. Billy stumbled over to Una and Seth. "This'll work fer ya." He held the utensil up high. Seth opened his wings and flew down to Billy. He reached out and took the whisk from the troll and hurried back up to Una's nose.

"This shouldn't hurt at all, Una. I'm simply going to scrape some of the pure magick off your horn and sprinkle it upon Mother Crystal," Seth told her soothingly. "Can you bend further forward so that we're right above her?"

Una moved her hooves forward another two spaces. She bowed her head so that her neck touched against her chest. Seth settled himself behind her horn, so that he did not have to balance upon her forehead. He held onto her horn with his right hand and stroked the whisk up and down her horn. The pure magickal dust sparkled snow white, silver, red, green, blue, violet, indigo, yellow, orange, and gold. It fell away from her horn and floated to the ground, leaving rainbows in its wake. The pure magickal unicorn dust glistened upon Mother Crystal, forming a swirling dome around her, protecting her from anything non-magickal.

Seth stopped stroking Una's horn. He watched the magickal dust and the rainbows it created. The bouncing balls of light hovered near the wall. Billy stood under Una's belly, where he had found himself once Seth had taken the whisk from him. Shadow had her tail wrapped around herself and her wings pinned against her back. Apollo stood on his chariot, watching the white light grow in the cavern. Archangel Michael stood with pride on his face as he examined Seth.

The dome ceased swirling. The rainbow colours parted. Mother Crystal was still pale in appearance, but she took shape into what she had once been. Her transformation was slow, yet steady. She went from a shard of alexandrite crystal to the formation of a small quartz. Her edges became sharp and distinct. Within the depths of her form, bits of triangles and octagons sparkled. She widened before she began to gain height.

The droplets of water that had once been a pool scurried together across the ground. As they came together, the drops expanded around the growing crystal. The liquid was clear and colourless. Mother Crystal continued to increase in size. Seth could not take his eyes off of the transformation. He continued to watch from his perch upon Una, who had not stirred since Seth ceased scraping her horn. He felt a warmth at his heart chakra. He placed his left hand upon his chest, just to be certain the feeling was really there and not part of his hope.

When she was one-fourth of her original size, Mother Crystal stopped growing. The pool covered two feet in all directions around her. It stayed clear, without the colours that had pulsed through the pool prior to the damage that had occurred in this sacred cavern. Mother Crystal pulsed pink once and became clear just as she was meant to be. Seth's eyes widened at the sight. Billy crooned in pleasure. Shadow thumped her tail. Una lifted her head. The three balls of light bounced off the walls again. Archangel Michael sighed in relief. Apollo reached for the straps of his chariot.

"I thank you, Seth," called out Apollo, breaking the silence that came with witnessing such a miracle. "Now, I can return to the sky and chase away the night." He lifted the straps of his chariot and gave them a tug. Upwards and through the rock wall he disappeared.

"You have done well," acknowledged Archangel Michael. He moved his gaze from Seth to Una to Billy and to Shadow. "Together, the four of you have saved Mother

Crystal, this realm, and magick. The life that was taken from this realm was devastating. The darkness that descended upon this world will slowly recede, yet it will never truly be gone. Fear now has a place in the hearts of many. It is the light that you bring to all that you do which will help to keep that fear from taking over again." He walked across the cavern and reached up to the balls of light.

"In honour of your bravery and persistence, I am giving to you the precious gift of three lives who were lost in the black vortex." Archangel Michael held out the palms of his hands. Two balls of light landed on his right palm while one ball of light landed on his left palm. They slowly turned into three faeries with glittering wings.

Billy hollered, "They's alive!" He clapped his hands and rushed forward.

Seth's heart skipped a beat as he recognized Georgia, Javier, and Jayne. Shadow let out a flame from her mouth and settled herself on the ground. Her eyes drooped and she curled herself into her tail and wings. The three faeries were pale and dirty. Although their wings glittered with magick and dust, they appeared tired and worn.

"Ye's alive! How'd ya get here?" asked Billy excitedly. He bounced on the balls of his feet, barely containing himself from pulling at Archangel Michael's arms.

"Where's everyone else?" Seth asked quietly. He glanced over at Shadow, who had turned into herself.

"For now, these are the survivors of this realm," Archangel Michael stated matter of fact. "I cannot save everyone today. It is now up to those of you within this cavern to go forth and bring about growth and change in Faerie and the rest of this realm. Things will be difficult, but I am certain you will all prevail in your attempt at healing this land."

Seth flew off of Una and landed beside Jayne. He took her cold hand in his and squeezed gently. "Will anyone else come out of the vortex as time passes and as we heal our land,

Archangel Michael?" Jayne gazed at the angel, pleading him to say yes.

"Perhaps others will come in time, dear Seth. I am not in charge of the future. I can only help you in this moment. For now, you must be strong and grateful for all that you have saved. Without the four of you, these three faeries would still be lost in the darkness. Enough will be provided from the land for your survival, until you are able to create more life and growth throughout the land. I can tell you though, of some things that will occur, if you would like," he said.

"Oh please do," trembled Jayne. Her voice was hoarse and scratchy, as though she had not used it for a long time.

"We'd like to know that the others won't be in that darkness forever," added Georgia.

Archangel Michael began, "Those of you in this cavern will survive long lives. You will be able to bring back the vegetation and the insects in this world. Magick was saved; therefore, you will continue to have access to it. Find ways to harvest the magick, so that your realm grows faster than those worlds that are not blessed with such magick. In time, at least a few of each magickal creature who were lost to the vortex will return. The balance of nature must be kept, as that is your daily responsibility. A piece of the darkness will always remain here, but do not fear it, as there is also the light. Hope reigns within all of you. Hold onto that when the despair seems greatest."

Javier twitched his wings with effort. "Will we be strong again? We lost our powers when we were taken from here. Will they come back as they'd been when we were superheroes?"

Archangel Michael smiled down at Javier. "Your powers were never truly gone, Javier. They were just suspended in time, as it were. The more you use them, the stronger they will become. Just like anything else, you can only get better when you practice a skill and condition your body."

The angel bent over and placed the faeries on the ground beside Billy. Billy instantly pulled Georgia into a hug, and then he did the same with Javier and Jayne. "Oh, I's so glad you's here and alrigh'."

"I will leave you all now," said Archangel Michael. "Do not be afraid, for I am always around. I suggest that you leave here and make your way home." He opened his blue wings and faded from their vision.

"Let's go home," Seth said simply. He held out his hands for his friends. The five of them linked hands and made their way over to the stairwell. They took each step one at a time, until the troll, the dragon, the unicorn, and the four faeries exited the cavern and entered the dawn awaiting them with renewed freshness and hope.

Melanie Van Mol lives in Kamloops, British Columbia, Canada with her two cats, Fred and George. When she is not writing or teaching, Melanie spends time with her writer's group: Some Good Karma, Some Bad Writing. This is her second novel, her first for all ages.

Twitter:
@MelanieVanMol

Facebook:
www.Facebook.com/VanMolAuthor

20305859R00179

Made in the USA
Charleston, SC
05 July 2013